IRIS HOUSE

Legacy

IRIS HOUSE

Legacy

BOOK 1

BARBARA GODFREY

Ordering Information:

For orders and inquiries, please contact:
1-888-404-1388
www.goldtouchpress.com
book.orders@goldtouchpress.com

Printed in the United States of America

Chapter 1

B RENDA WAS WONDERING IF she had done the right thing!
It was cold and she was trudging through unfamiliar streets. She was lost, and running out of time. *'What, was she doing, suffering a mid- life crisis or something?'* These thoughts and more went through her head. Some of the memories were good, and some not so good. She thought back to the memories of past summer days that seemed to never end; longingly thinking of heat and sunshine, where had the sun gone?

The memory of warm sun jolted her back to the here and now. She had to get to her appointment, although she wondered what was the point for yet another rejection.

Her reflections in a shop window stopped her on the thought. I don't look too bad, she mused, trying to buoy her spirits. Looking at her salt and pepper hair still with more pepper than salt, at that moment up in a loose bun to match the suit for the interview, she still had a firm trim figure and she still had some colour in her skin. I know I will never be a Kate Moss, too many years and Chardonnay's, but I feel only twenty-six if at times I look and feel as old as Methuselah!'

The ringing of Big Ben brought her out of her revelry.

'Oh Christ, I am going to be late, I have thirty minutes to find this place. I thought I knew where it was after Dennis gave me directions, but perhaps I should not have asked him while the soccer, sorry football was on the TV.' She walked on, being jostled by crowds filing out of an underground station she was pushed aside and found herself stumbling through an ornate gate.

Peace descended on her. The air was suddenly warm, quiet and still, the smell of new mown grass and promises wafted over her. Slowly she followed the path that was in front of her, moving through the green break in the concrete jungle outside. She walked through this wonderful place, and marvelled at the distraction it gave to her jumbled thoughts. She was loath the leave the peace.

'A few minutes surely would not hurt,' she assured herself, 'I can still make the interview?' She hoped so, as she did not want to leave, but she also had to make it to the interview, it was a feeling she could not shake.

She did not know why she had let Dennis persuade her to ring, but once she had been given the phone number, the compulsion to ring and book an interview had taken over. Dennis had told her that his friend Lulu, had been contacted in regards the job, and she had sworn it was tailor made for Brenda, so Dennis had passed it on. A job that she didn't have a description for, apart from PA, for a firm that didn't advertise it service, even Lulu didn't know exactly what they did. Oh, why was she even bothering, it had been two months already, she would have to make a decision soon, to either stay and tough it out or leave. It was quite a simple choice really, but one meant success and the other defeat, going back to a life she did not want.

A noise up ahead told her that she was not alone, a cry, oh that did not sound good. No, it was more than a sob, it was a deep mournful sound. Oh, she knew that sound, one of despair, of defeat, of no hope left. She knew what that sound meant, as she herself had uttered the same despairing tone many times. Her feet moved towards that sound, someone was hurting. Round the bend in the path a flat green swatch of grass, with benches placed around appeared, some benches hidden by bushes in one space she found the source of the despair and stopped in her tracks.

A man was sitting on a bench just around the corner, a miss-mash of papers and newspapers on the bench and around his feet. He had a newspaper open and crumpled in his fist another moan of denial escaped his lips. Brenda moved he stopped looked directly at her, taking a breath furtively looking around to see if anyone else was there and had heard him.

'Sorry, I am so sorry, I don't mean to intrude, but I could not help it,' hesitating as he had not moved or said a word, Brenda looked around, copying what he had done, wondering if she had missed something. 'I mean sorry, it really cannot be that bad, can it?'

Brenda looked again, an awful thought intruded in her brain, as she recognised the man sitting on the bench. Adam Bennett, the US film and television star, what was he doing in London, could it be had she; 'Oh I am sorry have I stumbled on a film set, I didn't mean to!'

Then she realised there were no cameras, crew or lights, this was no film set. This was just a man who had received some bad news, and was in trouble.

'How did you get in here?' Came the gruff request from Mr. Bennett, as he straightened up and glared at her.

'The gate was not locked and I was pushed through it. I apologise again I did not mean to intrude; I am trying to get to an interview and am a little lost. I was hoping a walk through these beautiful gardens would be a shortcut, when I heard a noise, I thought someone was hurt, I was just trying to see if I could help?'

Brenda stuttered to a stop, looked squarely at the man who now rose to his full height and moved towards her.

'No one can help me, this is a private garden, it only has one gate, so please use it and leave immediately!'

Brenda straightened up, her full height of 5ft 2in, no match for the 6ft 4in of towering rage coming towards her.

Still she hesitated, he was still in pain, 'I will go, I have no wish to stay where I am not wanted, but, please think on this. What is causing you pain today, will be a memory tomorrow, whether happy or sad, just a memory. We all can live with our memories, it is how we continue to live, grow and survive, but we can never let people or memories overwhelm us. I am sorry if I have intruded.'

As she watched the expression on his face change to one of incredulity, wondering if she had gone too far, concluded quickly that discretion was the better part of valour she beat a hasty retreat. Before he could fling more than spiteful words at her, moving quickly retracing her steps, she closed the gate firmly behind her.

Taking a deep breath and shaking her head, looking up and down the now nearly empty street, realised she was just around the corner from the office she needed.

Forty-five minutes later, she was back on the street. *'What a waste of time that was'* she thought. Mind you I would have loved the job, looking after people had always been her speciality, and this was the ultimate job in looking after people. This had been clear from the outset, it was so tantalising, but so out of reach.

A coffee shop, on the corner "Mamas Kitchen", offered all kinds of coffee and delicacies, was an inviting interlude. With nothing else to do for the day might as well go in for coffee, it would while away some time, and she could daydream some more about the job she would love but was not to be. It seemed that Mama herself was real, as she moved to assist Brenda when she walked through the door.

'Table for one?' she inquired, showing Brenda into a corner table when she nodded, asking what she would like. Taking her order and moving back to the kitchen to fulfil it, leaving Brenda to her thoughts of the recent interview and of Adam Bennett.

I want that job; she thought looking out of the window at the people traffic flowing past. People with a purpose; people idling the morning away, happy people, sad people, people of all walks of life. People of all different shapes and sizes, she tried to envisage the types of lives they lived by the speed they walked past the window.

The mothers out for a stroll, you could see were paced by the ages of the infants and toddlers in the prams and strollers.

The workers scurried past some quicker than others, probably determined by how late they were going to be at the other end, and who would be noticing that lateness.

'I want that job!' She could not move away from the fact that Lulu was right, the job was just up her ally, the PA of all PA jobs. She knew she could do it, but her resume she was sure would let her down; she did not think the interviewers would read between the lines. Her hospitality and secretarial background was not going to sell her to them. They would not see what she was capable of, by the bits of paper she had filled out, although she had tried to fill in the blanks she knew were there during the interview. Trying to

make them see what she was capable of after nearly thirty years of working, organising a husband, that was a distant memory, bringing up two children, a better ongoing memory. The various rolls she had worked in, organised was her second name, and that when it was broken down into it basics, was what the job was that she desperately wanted.

Adam Bennett his face seemed to be reflected in the window, as her thought moved away from the dream job that was not going to be. How could she feel so sorry for someone after such a strange, short meeting? She could still see the anger in his face, but strangely could also see the sadness and pain in his green eyes. She laughed at herself, remembering her words to him, probably thought I was a nutter, being sanctimonious and preaching. Remembering the look on his face, the sadness in his eyes, that changed to the anger when he realised he was not alone.

Mama came up interrupting her flow of thoughts, asking if she wanted a refill, Brenda nodded it was great coffee. She knew she would have to make some decisions in regards to her future, right now it was pleasant sitting in the warmth, spinning day dreams of what might have been.

Dennis was all questions when she got back to the apartment. It was great of him to put her up, but she really could not stay too much longer. They had been friends for a long time, he was her brother from another mother really, but she knew she was stretching the friendship. It was why he kept on giving her all these telephone numbers for job interviews. He was working harder than any employment agency! Brenda could not make him see that the leads he kept giving her were right job, wrong decade.

She had faced the facts that she was no longer a dolly bird, if she had ever been one, but she was the wrong side of thirty, in fact she was the wrong side of forty just. At many of the interviews she'd had, the first thing they did was a double take when she walked in the room. In fact, she had walked away from places after seeing the number of 20-25 year olds sitting in the waiting room, all with their college degrees and killer suits (on both male and female applicants).

But bless his little cotton socks; Dennis would not see that her age, as well as her looks being the main problem at many of the interviews she had been to. She could not turn back time, however, she was trying to keep a positive outlook, bolstered her flagging spirits by listing all her attributes, but on days like this one, it was difficult.

'Well what did they say?' Dennis asked again as they sat on his miniscule balcony, even in the chilly air, drinking a glass of wine to finish the day with.

'They thanked me for my time, asked me to leave my phone number, as they had more people to interview, and they would get in touch. Dennis, it is what the last five places I went to said. I am not getting my hopes up, but you can thank Lulu for me, she was right, I did like what I heard about the job. I saw the next people in the waiting room, the leggy blonde was stunning, if she has the right qualifications, I think the job was hers'.

Brenda relaxed back into the chair, a feeling of hope was there, she knew something was happening, but she just could not put her finger on it, sipping her drink, pulling her shawl around her shoulders, trying to ward off not only the chill of the evening, but a shiver of sadness. Not seeing the sad expression on Dennis' face, as he looked at her in the gathering gloom.

'I will see what happens tomorrow, but if nothing happens by the end of the week I will go back to my Uncles, he can always use a hand behind the bar in the pub. In any case I cannot stay any longer here, you need your life back!'

'Brenda don't even think about it, you know you are welcome to stay as long as you like. I have a good feeling about this one, I know, I know I have said it about a couple of the others, hey you did get second interviews on those, so come on let's be positive. Tomorrow is another day!'

Brenda looked at him, wondering if he could know about her encounter with Mr. Adam Bennett, but of course it was impossible, she had not told him of it, it just didn't seem right somehow. It would be a trust misused, even though what happened was not much, it was the look in his eyes Brenda remembered, not the angry words.

Chapter 2

'*ANOTHER DAY*,' BRENDA THOUGHT, light filtered through the curtains, she had heard Dennis leave for work, wondered what was in store for her, she was tempted to stay in bed, not wanting to face reality. *Come on Brenda, get up, a cup of coffee, perusal of the job adds,' she* admonished herself,' *it was Wednesday, half way through the week.* It was also two days before decision time, to stay or to go. Getting up and putting on the kettle as she stood watching the city wake up around her, the kettle whistled, coffee made as she was about to sit at the table her mobile rang, realising she had left it in the bedroom, hoped to catch it before it went to voice mail.

'Good morning Brenda, this is Linda McGill from Pickworths. I hope I didn't catch you at an inconvenient time?'

Stunned Brenda stammered something that must have sounded ok as Linda continued.

'We would like you to come back for a further interview, if you are free this afternoon say at one o'clock?'

Hoping to sound more gracious and in control, Brenda replied in the affirmative, confirming the time of one o'clock. Hanging up wondering if her dreams may be coming true, trying to not be too optimistic, as her dreams had been shattered before. Tried to be level headed and practical, heading back to her coffee and the job ads in the paper.

One o'clock seemed to take ages to arrive, but arrive it did. Brenda walked up the steps ringing the bell with five minutes to spare. Trying to settle her nerves as she walked into the waiting room, she was not alone.

An elderly gentlemen very distinguished looking, white/grey hair neatly trimmed dressed in a grey pin striped suit, with waistcoat that had a chain and she was sure at the end of which would be an elegant fob watch in the pocket. Twinkling grey eyes over a very extravagant handle bar moustache, rose as she walked into the room, Brenda thought that was the epitome of a lost age, was sad for the loss as it did make her feel special.

'I am sorry, I was told by the receptionist to wait here?'

'I am waiting too dear lady, please don't mind me. I assure you it is a pleasant change to have company, and such pleasant company at that!'

Brenda realised that he was a flatterer of the first order, but he seemed a very kind one. He had some papers in a folder, which started to slide to the floor as they spoke. Brenda was the first to retrieve them for him, realising they were travel brochures, kept up the conversation, more to relax her nerves than anything else, asking where he was going. Ten minutes or so later, Linda made an appearance, apologising asking Brenda to step into her office. This interview was better than the first one, asking her more practical questions, and how she would approach different scenarios. Linda also explained a little more of what they expected of her, and what they were offering in return. She tried not to show her reaction to the salary and expense account figures, especially when an apartment was included in the deal. As she walked back to Dennis's apartment, she found herself with a smile on her face that even a London drizzle could not wipe off, oh how she wanted this job!

She was preparing dinner, which she rather enjoyed, it was the least she could do for Dennis, he would not take any money for board, so she bought and cooked the evening meal.

Her phone rang, 'Brenda, Linda McGill here, again I hope I am not ringing at a bad time?'

'No Linda,' hoping her shock did not come through in her voice, 'I am just preparing dinner, how can I help?'

'Well I was hoping you could spare me half an hour, can you come around. My partners and I would like to offer you the job! I would have left it till tomorrow, but James is heading off to Italy in the morning, and would like to have everything organised this evening, can you come around?'

The room seemed to spin a little, Brenda took the phone away from her ear, and took a settling breath, 'of course I can, I can be with you in about fifteen, twenty minutes will that be ok?

'Perfect, see you soon.'

'Oh Linda, by the way, thank you.'

'Don't thank me yet Brenda, I am going to work you like you have never worked before, but I think you are up to it. Thank me in six months then I will accept it, see you in about fifteen minutes.'

Brenda sat stunned, looking at the phone in her hand after disconnecting the call. I got the job, I got the job she whooped around the flat, then stopped as her brain began working again, moved into overdrive. Leaving a note for Dennis, gathering the paper work she thought she would need, leaving the apartment wondering if she was doing the right thing, with Linda's warning ringing in her ears.

Chapter 3

THE AFTERNOON RUSH HOUR was just beginning Brenda decided to walk to the office, arriving a little short of breath but just on the twenty minutes Brenda had said. Linda herself opened the door, ushering Her through the door and into the building.

'You made good time, I was not expecting you for another ten minutes at least, this time of the afternoon.'

'Ah well you didn't take into account the fact that I haven't walked I floated. I still cannot believe you are actually offering me this job!'

'Come with me so I can really explain this job in more detail. I need to get some more details from you as well, so we can get organised, and the paper work filled out, come through.'

Brenda was taken along a corridor to a rear office, this was the most magnificent of rooms, she had ever seen. It was a dark mahogany and leather refuge, from the furniture to the very full bookshelves that lined most of the walls. The tasteful landscape paintings, and the many framed certificates and honours, with the smell of leather and fine cigars came together in a heady mixture of calm and peace. This was an office of importance, Brenda thought, and the elderly gentleman of the waiting room.

'Brenda, may I make formal introductions, Sir James Pickworth – Ms Brenda Chalmers, I think you may have met?'

Recovering quickly from the shock, and with more aplomb than she felt, Brenda moved forward her hand outstretched, 'Sir James, it is a pleasure to see you again!', her hand was taken into a firm grasp, there came from the gentleman in question a smile and a dark chuckle.

'My Dear, I have final say on all of Pickworth employees. They do not continue if they fail me, I must tell you I have passed on your insightful comments to my own dear secretary. Emma was most impressed and asked me to say thank you, now welcome aboard, I hope you are going to say yes?'

'Well I would like to hear a little more, from what I gathered from yesterday and this afternoon, the job sounds similar to an upmarket, live in Personal Assistant role, is that correct?'

Linda broke in, 'yes, but with a twist. We are a firm that handles VIP clients, which at present is small, but very elite. We handle anything and everything they may need when they visit. Accommodation, travel, events, day to day details that entail almost round the clock service, without being obtrusive or inflexible. We offer these personages the equivalent of a five-star hotel, but with the added twist of them being in their own space, their own home away from home, so that they do not need all their usual entourage to make it work, in a space the general public know nothing about.'

James must have seen the confused expression on Brenda's face, 'the client arrives, then to the paparazzi that may be following him or her, they check into a hotel. Staying only long enough to advertise that is where they are staying, then they move through the building and into one of our apartments!'

'I understand,' Brenda answered, 'a VIP would then be able to be anonymous, be able to have a 'normal' life. Our role, I take it is to take care of the mundane, daily tasks, that their usual retinue would handle, shopping, driving if required, and similar, is, that right?'

James turned to Linda and smiled, 'I told you she would be quick.'

Linda smiled and turned to a folder on his desk, as he continued, 'to a certain stage yes, we are in the business of assisting these visitors to have as much as we can, a normal semblance of life. Being able to make their own choices, but still have someone assist in the order of their busy days. A local person, there to help if they do come on their own, or with just one assistant. To give them a space of peace and calm after dealing with the hoopla of facing the paparazzi or stares of the general public, when they are at work, giving a peaceful secure space when relaxing, at least as much as we can. With all the doubles cropping up it is usually relatively easy for the recognised to pass themselves off as their doubles. It is our business to try and help them avoid any confrontation in the first place!'

Brenda nodded trying to take in all he was saying, as well as implying, as he continued, 'we have a very high standard, our client list is not very large, but growing. We vet them to the same high standard, even higher sometimes than our staff. We are not a brothel agency, we do not procure illegal drugs or drugs of any kind, or allow any kind of prostitution. We are in the business of decency and normalcy, we have never and never will felicitate any kind of illegal activity. We even retain, in writing, the right to remove them from our premises and black list them if they even have a whiff of scandal or wrong doing!'

James was quite adamant in his attitude as he spoke, it made Brenda sit up a little straighter, again concentrating on what was not said, even more than what he was saying.

'We usually operate by word of mouth. A celebrity comes to shoot a film, or a diplomat has a tour of duty, they stay for anywhere from a week to three or six months, have the Pickworths treatment, enjoying the lifestyle, tell their friends about it and so on. We do not advertise but we have a waiting list for our services, so we have decided to expand. We are in the process of refurbishing a building for Pickworths use; it is actually not far from here. A Georgian building, each of the four levels is an apartment, almost ready for guests to occupy. Now as you have been advised, Pickworths organises dinner parties etc., for the guests if so required, so the ground floor flat is for the use of our employee. Then that person is accessible and has easy and ready access to the occupants of the apartments above, with of course subtle control of access to the building itself. I like to think of the person's role as similar to that of an old-fashioned Chatelaine, except you don't have to carry all of your accoutrements on a belt around your waist!'

Brenda laughed with them both, relaxing a little in their company, there was that feeling again, one of belonging, she shook her head. Seeing the job roll out before her, but knowing that it was going to be hard work, she was excited and wanted to know more.

'It sounds as though I will be more of a dorm master to unruly children, when do I start?'

James and Linda looked at each other, chuckling at her enthusiasm.

'Well we would like you to start as soon as possible, but we have a complication.' James continued, 'and that is the building itself! The apartments, we have been told are finished, we have been told they are, by the contractor we hired to refurbish them, except the one that will be occupied by yourself. That one was not accessible until recently, we could not gain entrance to complete the work. So, if you are accepting the job, as it will be your apartment, would you like the overseeing of completing the work?'

Brenda gasped, again that waft of something came over her a scent she knew but could not name, a happiness with a touch of something, she was not sure of. They were going to trust her with the completion of the upgrade to the building, another test perhaps. Well she knew she could do it, but it was a great boost for her moral that they were willing to trust her.

'I would be honoured to do so, thank you. I take it I would be refurbishing with the view of dinner parties, soirees etc.,' they both nodded affirmatives, 'so it would need to be finished to a high standard, but be functional, easy care. OK I know I can do it, of course it depends on the budget?'

'I just knew it, just like a woman, mention decorating and how much can I spend is the first question!'

James turned to Linda laughing, 'I think this lady is going to do just fine. I would like to inspect before we invite any clients to stay, if you don't mind Brenda. So, our time frame, well I am heading off to Italy, as you know, I will be away about ten days. As it is a long weekend this weekend, there are a few things you will need to complete before we can let you have free reign with the prospective clients, I think two weeks from today for an inspection. I will leave you in Linda's capable hands, to finish the paper work we need, Brenda, my dear welcome to the firm!'

He bowed, taking one of Brenda's hands kissed it lightly, leaving the room. Brenda suddenly felt insecure, wondering what she had let herself in for. Linda smiled, motioned for her to move to the table and chairs set in the corner. The folder now spread over it, the paper work was about to be done.

'Are you all right Brenda, you seem a little hesitant?'

'Sorry Linda, but I suppose I need a little more confidence in myself, hopefully I can use a little of the confidence Sir James and yourself are showing in me, I only hope I don't let you down!'

'Nonsense, usually each operation is run independently by our, what did James call them 'Chatelaines' I like that term, but we don't hang you out to dry, we are always here to help, all you have to do is ask, we will be right here for you. Now I need to finish up this paper work, we have already completed the security check!'

Linda handed over two pages with the full terms of employment, to which Brenda scanned, realising most of the details were logical, even the police check, at one of them she stopped and gave Linda a quick glance as she was getting the information from her folder; a raised eyebrow was all she was given.

'Driving qualifications, well I have been driving since I was a teenager, my son of course always doubts that I even did receive my license!' Linda smiled, 'I always meant to do a defensive driving course but I never seemed to have the money or the time for it. I can also drive a mini-bus and a one ton truck!' Linda raised an eyebrow at that comment, 'moving house, which I did a lot, it was just one of those things, I found it quite easy really.'

'At least you have a manual licence, which it will make it easier to fit in if we need to. We find the guests we cater for usually request we organise a car and driver for them, and we have a very good firm we use.'

Linda looked at Brenda taking in all this information was amazed at how calm she seemed. She wondered how she was going to react to the state of the apartment, then the life she was about to begin. Watching as she assessed the requirements on the pages she had been given, she realised this 'Lady' as James had called her would do just fine. She not only had the level headedness but also that certain quality they were looking for, and Linda also realised she was ready for the challenge this role was going to give her.

'Now that we have all that done, we not only have an account open for your salary, but also a separate one to use for the final fit out of the house, the main contractor bills come back directly to the office. You will have to keep all receipts and a record of all the spending, but you know all of that. We have an amount in estimates given by the builders and interior designers, already on site, feel free to query what they are doing with them, but they have advised us the job is nearly finished? For the next few weeks till you settle in, and finish the building, James has advised that we are not to limit you too much, although he was quite sure that you would never overspend but do a very good job. If we can help please just call, in this folder are phone numbers, email addresses, the current builder and interior designer being used at the moment, also some useful trade people we have used in the past. I have to admit to you Brenda, this place and especially apartment one, have not been touched in a very long time. I didn't want to do this, but James seemed to think you needed your own space sooner than later, was he right?'

Brenda looked at this woman who had just offered her the world, amazed that Sir James had picked up so much in their conversation in the waiting room that afternoon. Nodding, she told Linda a little more of the situation she was in it seemed the right thing to do.

'Yes, he was right I have been staying with a very good friend for nearly two months now. Dennis, that is Dennis Brookes, is great but he only has a one bed roomed flat, he has been sleeping on a sofa bed. I have to tell you I was two days away from leaving London, I was going to head back up to my Uncles place for a while, to see what I did next. I am so glad I rang for an interview, I promise to do everything I can to justify your faith in me.'

'Brenda for the next two weeks, you will wonder whether you are on your head or your heels. There is an incredible amount of work to do, especially in your apartment, a lot of facts to learn, and more paper work to get through. When you get to the end of that and open, then you will have my and Sir James's respect, you will have earned it!' Linda leant over and gripped Brenda's shoulder to empathise her support.

'OK, here it is,' she passed over a concertina plastic document folder, with duplicates of all the paper work they had just done for Brenda. 'The address of the building is inside with two sets of keys. Instructions on the security arrangements are there, you have already been listed as the building manager. Power and water are connected, but I suggest you visit the place and see what you think. Please do not think too badly of us when you do see it, hopefully it gives you a clean sheet to work with so to speak, enjoy!'

Brenda stood and took the folder, slipping it into her case decided it was time to go and tell someone, the world maybe, of her good fortune.

'Thanks Linda, are you going away as well, or are you the main office Chatelaine?'

Linda laughed, advising she would be there till the following week, when she would be away Tuesday to Friday but always accessible on her mobile.

Laughing with her, Brenda took her hand, trying to gain strength from this confident woman, leaving the building floating back to Dennis's unsure of what she had let herself in for.

Chapter 4

D ENNIS WAS JUST OPENING a bottle of wine when Brenda walked back into his apartment.

'Where did you go? Brenda, are you all right? What has happened?'

Euphoria total and complete, a whiff of flowers something pleasant, engulfed Brenda, all she could do was laugh. She laughed until she cried, because she could not make up her mind whether she had just landed the best job in the world, or if she was going to regret being a nursemaid to a lot of uncaring high flyers. Dennis had to prise the case from her hand and put a glass of wine in its place.

'Now, tell me because I cannot make up my mind, are you happy or sad?'

'I am happy love, happy, happy, happy I got the job!'

Dennis looked at her as though she had hit him in the stomach, stunned with a look on his face to match. Then it hit him, she had the job that Lulu had suggested, incredulous he looked at her again.

'You mean the one Lulu said to try for?' Brenda nodded, 'the one you had the interview for yesterday?' Again, she nodded, 'they rang you up again today.' Brenda held up two fingers, 'they rang you twice,' she nodded, 'and that is where you have been at the third interview where they offered you the job?'

Brenda nodded; taking a sip of wine she filled him in on the details, with the added bonus that she now had somewhere to live apart from his place.

'It comes with living accommodation, that is fantastic, you are made my friend, made for life, it sounds like a job that was tailor made for you. I cannot think of anything that you would not be able to handle. Congrats, Brenda love, see I told you something was going to happen for the good, didn't I?'

Brenda laughed again, grabbing her case pulled out the details of the building, asking if he knew of the address, and what she could expect. Dennis's eyebrows went up and he whistled appreciatively, looking at her with such an expression on his face, she wondered what was wrong.

'Dear heart you have landed in clover, think Mayfair meets Toorak, and you have an idea of where your new apartment is, Barrister belt no less. What did they say they have done them all up?'

'The apartments for the clients have apparently been completed, I don't think Linda or Sir James have inspected them yet. The one for me had a tenant till just recently, I didn't like to ask but I think he/she may have been elderly. Linda told me the power was on, we could go and have a look tonight if you like?'

'If I like, you ask me to visit the Holy Grail of London postcodes and leave the question open, of course I bloody like, before or after dinner?'

After a hasty meal, they set off, with the security instructions, a tape measure, note book and flashlights, just in case. Linda and James were right; the place was very close to the office, just one street and around the corner. The four-storey high Georgian house was dark, in the middle of the row, between restored and lighted houses.

Construction boards covered the ground floor windows; a large half empty industrial skip was positioned over what was the small front garden it also was blocking part of the footpath. Brenda held the key to Apartment One, which had a separate entrance, moving into the front lobby, unlocked the security system as instructed. They were greeted with a dark and dingy entrance hall, not what either of them were expecting. The smell that wafted over them was overpowering, she left the front door open in the hope of moving some fresh air into the apartment.

'Elderly definitely, and recently deceased, judging by the smell!' Dennis muttered as he looked around the entrance hall in wonder.

Brenda could not move, the hall was wonderfully proportioned, it stretched before her with a couple of doors to the left, at the end was a flight of stairs going down.

'Dennis, do you think I have the basement as well, is it possible?'

Dennis shrugged an answer, moving into the room through the first door in the hall. There were mounds covered in dust sheets hiding what looked like stacked furniture in the room, after they carefully lifted a corner to check. There was a very ugly gas fire in the centre of the wall opposite the door. It struck Brenda as odd that the whole area, hallway and room was clad in very cheap timber panelling. A single cable with a bare light bulb on the end hung in the centre of the room, through a clearly false ceiling, giving a watery very inadequate light. Everywhere you looked, there were more timber batons keeping the reams of black plastic in place that covered every wall and even the floor.

It gave a very claustrophobic feel to what should have been a beautifully proportioned room. She turned to look at where a bay window should have been, but she could only see more stretches of black plastic, blocking any view. Her feet made crunching noises through the layer of dust that was everywhere.

'Must have been an attempt to modernise perhaps, has been here a while judging by the dirt?' Brenda said to Dennis, he nodded. 'All I can say it was one ugly attempt, and I would sack the interior designer, all of it definitely has to go. They must have cornered the market in black plastic and timber sheets!' Dennis laughed moving back into the hallway.

'I am going to need one hell of a cleaning team. I am also going to have the electrics and plumbing checked, I don't care what Linda and Sir James said this place is not nearly finished to allow guests!'

Dennis had heard her muttering, 'I can help you there, and with just the people you need, hold on!'

He pulled out his mobile dialling a number, moving out to the front door for fresh air, talking animatedly to someone who clearly knew him very well. Brenda moved out into the hallway, walked down and through the second door in the hallway, flicking light switches as she passed, but only one in five lights worked, it gave a very dark dingy feel to the place. Walking through into the room at the back of the house, found herself in a dining room, again another low and false ceiling, with more black plastic and wood panelling. The kitchen was off to the right of the main section, it seemed under the grime to be in fairly good nick, although trying to see around the black plastic and shrouded furniture stacked in the space she wasn't too sure what was in there. Moving back into the hall, Dennis was striding towards her with a big grin on his face.

'Ok, all arranged; Stan and his cleaning company will be here at ten tomorrow, Ben and Matt, they are brothers, one is an Electrician the other a Plumber, very handy in families, especially building families. They are coming around about eleven if that is ok with you, of course?'

Brenda didn't know what to say, so she just hugged him. 'That is very OK, how do you know these people? Don't tell me met them in the pub of course!' Laughing at the expression on his face as she guessed the truth of the relationships.

'How did you know, well I did, as a matter of fact, but I have also been using these guys for the last four years. They all do a damned fine job; most of all they love a challenge. Believe me Brenda this will be a challenge; how long did they give you to get this place habitable?'

'Two weeks, hopefully it is not as bad as I think it is in the other units. As long as we can clean out the stench, we can work in it, perhaps all the plastic will be a godsend?' A shiver ran down her back, she almost thought she heard laughter, shaking her head. 'Let's keep looking, the dining room is huge, what you can see of the kitchen is ok as well; I don't think anyone has made a meal in it for a very long time. Someone took great care of the furniture, there are covered pieces stacked all over the place. I will wait till daylight to uncover those with a dust mask on my face!'

Dennis agreed, after a quick look in the room, opened the door directly opposite the dining room, giving a view and another putrid smell, saying as he quickly closed the door, 'Powder Room!'

'I think the drains are blocked, definitely need Ben, he will need to check every tap and sink in the entire building, as if it is blocked here, it will be blocked in the entire building! Come on let's look at what is downstairs; Brenda love, you sure hit the jackpot, you do have the downstairs as there are no bedrooms up here!'

Seeing sense in his words Brenda flicked on the switch at the top of the stairs, jumping back sharply after an electric shock. 'I only hope Matt is as good as Ben then, as he will have to check every switch and power point. Linda said the electrics had been done in here, I am now more certain than I was the need to check all the apartments, if this is the standard!'

Dennis nodded and moved down the stairs, torch ready if the light decided to die, the smell of mouldy carpet and cabbage added to the original smell from entering the building, rose in nastiness as they moved down the stairs. '*Why is it in a place with elderly people you smell cabbage?*' Brenda thought. Coming to the bottom of the steps into a corridor mirroring the one upstairs, even down to the now familiar panelling and black plastic. Three doors were in the long wall opposite to the stairs, with two doors in the wall space under the stairs. Stains on the carpet gave an indication of the functions in one of the rooms, the ancient laundry was complete with clothes and putrid water in the washing machine, clothes strung on a line in the room. Brenda closed the door, trying not to think about the length of time it had taken for the room to get into that state. The second door opened onto a broom closet complete with various brooms and brushes, which made her laugh as the cobwebs and dust on the cleaning tools told a story of their own. Dennis called from down the corridor' he was standing in the doorway of the bedroom at the front of the house.

The walls were again covered in black plastic and timber panelling, but in the centre of the room was a very modern hospital bed. Small tables were everywhere, each surface crammed with either ornaments or ornate boxes. Nearer the bed the remains of meals could be seen, mouldy mounds that did not sweeten the putrid air. Dennis carefully moved through the room to a slightly open door to one side of the bed.

'Hey it's a bathroom of sorts, that has also been used as a kitchen. Not very sanitary, but we now know why the rest of the house is so dirty, it hasn't been fully used as a home in a very long time. Check the door on the other side Bren, what do you bet it is a wardrobe come pantry?'

Brenda moved very carefully through the room, wondering how anybody, especially some one elderly could have managed it. Sure enough, the walk-in wardrobe was complete with clothes and sealed boxes, there were also cans of food on the shelves and other food stuffs now very out of date. They moved out of the room, without saying too much, what could be said? Brenda thought it sad that someone could die, with no one to care, to have no one come and sort through their possessions, to give closure. She would be back first thing in the morning with boxes, clearing them away to check on ownership at a later time.

The next room had no window, but more panelling and black plastic. There were broken bits of furniture in the middle of the room, no clue as to what it had been before the destruction. They moved out, Dennis suggesting the big skip outside would be useful to dispose of the rubbish. The last room, at the back of the house had the same wall treatments; there was a broken window or something in here, Brenda thought, as a slight breeze wafted by her face. This room had a wonderful king sized bed frame right in the middle of the room, a mattress, that had seen better days, half on half off the slatted base. Dennis checked the back wall it only had one door, and led to a storage area, inside he found bedside tables, two chests of drawers and more boxes and crates.

'Must be the extras from the front room, the bedside tables would not be high enough for the hospital bed, why keep the accessories and not keep the bed? Guess we will never know, wonder where the other beds are, more than likely they are what is chopped up in the middle room? Well Brenda you have the makings of a wonderful place. I only hope you know what you are doing, it is going to take a lot of hard work to make this place habitable in two weeks. I just wonder in what state the other apartments are in?'

It was a thought Brenda had been wondering herself, 'I intend to find out tomorrow. I am going over every inch of this building, as I am not putting my or Pickworths reputation on any shoulders but my own. If I have guests expecting five-star accommodation, they are going to get six!'

Brenda moved back into the hallway, trying the door opposite the last bed room, but could not budge it. 'Do you know of any locksmiths at all Dennis?' she asked as they climbed the stairs, she carefully flicked off the light switch, moving out of the house with her measurements and notes. Switching on the security alarm they left, pausing for a moment to look back at the darkened house, waiting to show its true potential as a wonderful piece of architecture. Walking back to Dennis's place making plans, throwing ideas into the melting pot, only to realise until all the cleaning was done, the electrics and plumbing checked, nothing at all could be organised. Brenda went to bed knowing her time at Dennis's was numbered, what a glorious time she was going to have refurbishing and updating her new home.

Chapter 5

T HE SUN ROSE AND so did Brenda, her brain ticking over with ideas and plans for the building. Moving quietly through the flat, she left a note for Dennis. Picking up the supplies she had packed the night before moved her way through the quiet (at least for London) streets. Standing for a moment, taking before pictures of what was to be her home. Quietly she moved through the apartment, taking more photos, chronicling the tired rooms for posterity, and to make sure she didn't miss anything, thinking she would put them into an album to show her children, still unsure of what it looked like as the black plastic and panelling blocked the light completely.

Removing it was too big a job for her on her own, so she moved down into the cluttered bedroom. Slowly she wrapped and packed all the nick knacks and ornaments that were on the tables in the room, filling the boxes she had brought, and some she had found in the wardrobe. The tables themselves were all shapes and sizes, beautiful timber dulled by dust, and others covered in cloths, again with a layer of dust she stacked as best she could in the corners out of the way.

As she pulled the cover off one of the tables next to the hospital bed, after clearing the bottles of pills into a separate bag to dispose of properly, a book appeared on the floor. Picking it up, a sheet of paper fell out of it, she realised the book in her hand was a journal, as on the first page was the name Iris Fitzgibbon Boerchermeir, presumably the now deceased tenant, a beautifully engraved rosewood box that was underneath the bed held, on quick inspection at least three more journals. That feeling of suspense, that more was to come held her for a moment, again that elusive scent, she was about to unfold the paper when a hello came from upstairs. She yelled a hello back, picked up the book, paper and box moving up the stairs into the hallway. She had been in the room for hours, not noticing the smell; she had been so engrossed in the task she had set herself.

A lean and compact dark haired man was standing in the open doorway.

'Hi, you must be Brenda, I am Stan – The Cleaning Man!' he said with a smile. 'I rang Dennis he told me you were already here, I know I am early but I had a thought the job may be bigger than Dennis was saying?'

'I think you are right Stan, thank you for coming,' she took the outstretched hand and shook it, 'come in and take a look around, I would value your opinion of what you think can be done!'

Stan shook her hand, walking with a smile into the house, turning to show a grimace as he took a deep breath. 'Someone died in this place, right?' Brenda nodded, 'thought so, there is a distinctive smell, but easily cleared once you can open up the doors and windows to let fresh air into the place.'

Brenda relaxed; here was someone she felt she could trust. They walked into the front room, Stan tutting and muttering to himself, 'no one been in here in a long time. Put up the plastic and panelling to cut out the light and stop fading, but what were they protecting, stranger and stranger!' Brenda could hear Stan muttering as they moved around the ground floor; he also had a raft of facial expressions that she hoped she could read properly. They moved down into the basement, Stan really tutted in disgust at the state of the carpet. 'No way to save that, it has to be tossed.' He bent down and very easily pulled up the rotting carpet that ran in front of the steps. Revealing an equally filthy underlay, then the original tiled floor! Brenda didn't know who was more surprised, Stan looked up at her a smile on his face, 'now wouldn't it be nice if they were ok all the way down the hall? I want to see, don't you?'

Brenda nodded and bent to help Stan pull up more of the putrid carpet. Rolling it up to the end of the hall, stopping at the front bedroom doorway, looking back with a great big smile on both of their faces.

'I hope I find some more good surprises; you are my lucky charm Stan, keep on with the magic please. It is going to take quite a bit to get me in here in two weeks!'

'No sweat Brenda, let's check the rest of the place, this is a great start, shall we see what other surprises this grand old place has?'

Stan moved into the front bedroom that had taken all of Brenda's time that morning, telling Brenda he had a contact that would remove the hospital bed, he was surprised it had not been cleared away before. He turned as a watery shaft of coloured sunlight fell across the bed. Both of them turning to see where it came from, the beams came through a stained-glass window that was above the doorway, directly opposite the bed. The gap in the panels now apparent with the small amount of daylight filtering down through the stairwell, showed a magnificent stained glass window of a bunch of blue Iris's.

Stan looked at Brenda, a dawning expression on his face, matching the one on hers, 'you don't suppose the timber sheeting in the house is hiding a lot of beautiful stained glass do you Brenda? I mean the rooms would be very dark without windows, and in a terrace house how do you get light into a room?'

Brenda grinned, 'I hope so Stan, but how do we find out, and should we pull it all down before I see what work needs to be done? I need advice and was hoping a complete check first then see?'

Stan nodded, 'hmm, yes inventory first then plan of action. No good going off without one, but, let's just see what's in this room, shall we?' Brenda was still stunned from the carpet and window, but could not resist the look of expectancy on Stan's face; she nodded in agreement for him to proceed.

Stan pulled a screwdriver from the pocket in his overalls, stretched up and carefully, slipped it to the side of the uncovered window, prised the sheet next to it from the wall, it came away surprisingly easy. Brenda helping where she could, he continued taking down panels on the door wall, revealing three very beautiful stained glass windows, the middle one a bunch of flowers, the ones either side with a single blue Iris flower in the centre of each one. They filled the space above the door, between the picture rail and cornice, bracketed within steel frames, at least that was what they looked like to Brenda's untrained eye.

Stan could not stop, he was pulling the panelling down around the room, revealing two more windows evenly spaced on the internal wall between the bedrooms. To Brenda's surprise they found a couple of paintings that were just boarded over, another one over what would have been an elegant fireplace, but was boarded over and an ugly twin gas fire to the one in the sitting room was in its place. She was thinking who would do such a thing and why, a flash of the front room and the ugly gas fire, the walls with all the panelling, just what was being hidden.

Stan was in wonder as well, this place was amazing, what could be going on here, he broke into her thoughts, 'did you say the house has been empty for a long-time Brenda?'

'No Stan,' Brenda finally found her voice, there were too many shocks arriving at once, 'the house has only been vacant for a short time, I think less than a week. I believe the elderly tenant a lady had lived on her own for a very long time, she was a recluse I believe. Perhaps this panelling was an attempt to keep heat in and cool the place in summer, but the old lady refused any massive destruction. I am eager to see what is hidden behind all this timber in the whole place!'

Stan nodded motioned for her to move out of the room, they were going up the steps when a knock on the door heralded the arrival of the rest of Stan's cleaning crew. Stan introduce his spritely elderly parents, as Nona and Poppa, his niece Bella and nephew Pico, laughing with her when she commented about keeping business in the family.

'Do you mind Brenda, I need to know if we can use the skip outside, as we have to remove all this panelling and timber sheeting before we can clean. That is if you want to strip it all out, you don't want to keep the timber panelling, do you?'

'No Stan, I hate the timber, I think this house has been in the dark for too long. Let's see what is hidden, but I need to check first what needs to be done. I don't want to pull down the protection of the panels if I am having major building work done. It would be nice to get some natural light in here, and fresh air by opening some doors and windows if possible. First things first, let me see if we can use the skip outside, I will call my boss and see what she says, you marshal your troops and give instructions!'

Before she could do that, another knock on the door heralded two very handsome men on the doorstep. Ben and Matt were twins, something that Dennis had not informed her of, they were apologising for being early, but as Stan had said before them, did not believe Dennis's time frame would be accurate. Six foot odd tall, muscled in all the right places, blue eye blonds, with broad grins on their faces and hands outstretched to say hello. Greeting them and welcoming them to the madness, asking them to take a look around, checking the usability of every tap, sink, toilet, shower, appliance, light switch, electrical socket and plugs they could find, and tell her what needed to be done. They moved off with Stan, who of course they knew, he rapidly filling them in on what he and Brenda had found. Brenda for the first time, but it would not be the last, she was sure, called Linda.

'Linda good morning, are you busy, I need to clear a few things up with you?'

'No Brenda, I was wondering if I would get a call, but this is earlier than I expected, its barely ten o'clock, what's up?'

'Well I am at the house; firstly, can we use the skip for the rubbish I need to toss? I promise it will be stacked properly and not just tossed in. Secondly, there is a hospital bed, in what must have been the recent tenant's bedroom, do you by any chance know when it is to be collected, if not then the cleaning crew I have can deal with it?'

'The bed I have no idea about, do what you think is best. The skip, I will make a call to the contractors and call you back. I don't think it will be a problem, are you having fun yet?'

'Of course, I love dirty smelly apartments. Ask me again after the weekend though; I am only just getting stuck into it. You did say I had complete autonomy in what I can do?'

'Yes Brenda, it is your home. We know you will do what is right, will call you straight back.'

Brenda looked around, she wanted the ugly panelling and plastic to be gone, she could see the elegant rooms sparkling and being used as they should be, but to do it properly she realised would take a little time. She heard Stan talking with the brothers, moving through the rooms, Nona and Poppa trailing behind muttering in Italian in very disparaging tone. Patience she said to herself, all good things come to those who wait. The platitudes going through her head were beginning to annoy her when her phone rang.

'Brenda no problems the contractors didn't want to take the skip away too soon. They advised you could add to it whatever you want. They will be there on Tuesday to take down the scaffolding and boards over the windows, anything else?'

'Yes, can you ask them to hold back on everything. I am going to check all the apartments before the building is signed off. If the standard of work in them is not far superior to what I have encountered on the outside of the building and also this apartment then I am very worried!'

'Now you have me worried. Do you want me to bring anything around to you?'

'Thanks for the offer Linda, but no, are you going to be in the office this afternoon, I may need a break, and can come around to give you an update?'

Linda agreed, ending the call with a smile on her face.

Ben, Matt and Stan were waiting for her, as she walked back into the front room. Stan's crew busy bringing in cleaning supplies around them.

'OK guys, give me a report. I need to know where I stand before we start ripping the ceilings down and the panels off the walls!'

The report was what she expected. Ben advised he had unblocked the toilet on this level, a simple thing, as he shrugged his shoulders, although he advised the downstairs one could not be salvaged and would need replacing. He couldn't check water or gas lines in the kitchen or the apartment until the furniture was removed for access.

The rest of the flat seemed ok, but he had never seen uglier gas fires in his entire life.

Matt had checked the wiring, finding and fixing the faulty switch at the top of the stairs. He also advised a fully comprehensive report would have to wait till he could inspect the walls without the furniture and panelling.

'See the main walls Matt, you mean the switches we see are temporary?' Brenda asked, everyone looked at him eagerly.

'I believe the panelling is supposed to be temporary. Once it has been removed we can check the wiring properly. I don't think it has been touched in a long time, Dennis said when he called yesterday, that it had been redone, but I can't see where; if the switch at the top of the stairs is any gauge we may have to rewire!'

Everyone was looking at her, Brenda took a deep breath and plunged, again that feeling of rightness and anticipation came over her.

'Ok, the main priority is light and air, so I don't know whether it is in your job descriptions, but I cannot take the panelling down on my own. Do you guys want to give me a hand, I would really appreciate the help?'

'Appreciate what?' came from the front door. Dennis was standing with a box in his hands, kettle, mugs, tea, coffee and a box of biscuits nestled inside. Over the tea break that was immediately called, it was decided that sheets of timber panelling from the front bedroom would be put over the tiled downstairs hallway, to protect the floor until the heavy work, if any, was done, the smell of the carpet was just too much to leave. The panelling taken out in full in the front and dining rooms, the black plastic off the windows too, to allow light and fresh air into the dingy rooms, but left on the floor till the last minute.

Brenda had never seen such enthusiasm, Ben and Matt brought in their ladders and tools, to do the job properly. Stan handed out facemasks, saying better to be safe than sorry; no one knew what was going to happen once the false ceiling was removed.

Ben and Matt started in one corner of the room, after Matt had removed the bulb, carefully with everyone watching from the hallway, taking down the timber batons that seemed to be holding up the false panels once these were removed the ceiling came down very easily and with only a minimum amount of dust. With roughly two hours of hard work, not only was the false ceiling down, revealing the original ceiling with its picture rails, and ornate ceiling centre rose and cornices. The pristine walls revealed original wallpaper, still looking as fresh as the day it was hung, but very dusty.

The biggest surprise was revealed between the two rooms, not a wall, but glass panelled folding doors from wall to wall. Above them in the space between the picture rail and cornice the now familiar stained glass panel insert. The black plastic and boards were carefully removed from across the window area in the sitting room revealing the wonderful deep bay window, complete with drapes. Stan tut tutted at the filthy state they were in but he thought were cleanable, he would take them to someone he trusted, at least they did not disintegrate when taken down.

The shutters were closed and as the scaffolding and boards were still on the outside covering the window the decision was made to leave them closed. The timber panels on either side of the fireplace were removed, the ugly gas fire removed by Ben and happily thrown in the skip. Revealed half bookcases either side, with spaces for what would be two very large paintings in the niches. The original fireplace was missing, a gaping hole in the wall all that was left, but that did not stop the smiles that were appearing on everyone's face at the treasures being revealed.

Dennis moved into the dining room with Poppa and Pico to take the panelling off the other side of the folding doors, to prepare for the removal of the false ceiling and panelling. Again, with the removal of the batons around the walls the ceiling came down very easily, revealing an even more ornately decorated cornice and centre rose, both of the ceiling roses called out for very large chandeliers to hang down from them.

The folding doors creaked as they were opened as far as they could with the plastic sheeting on the floor, telling everyone that they had not opened in a very long time. They did not open fully, but Brenda could see them in her mind's eye opening to allow the rooms to work as one when needed. The timber panelling as it was removed was being stacked neatly in a corner, growing higher with every passing minute, the smiles and happy sounds around the room growing in proportion to the stack. Dennis, Stan and Poppa had moved to the back wall, and were rolling the plastic up from the bottom, waiting Ben and Matthew to arrive with the ladders. Suddenly there was light in the dingy space, beautiful sunlight, fractured and spliced with colour, dulled by the dirt on the glass, but brightening the darkness, flooded the room, and bounced around. A sigh seemed to echo through the halls, the smell of Gardenia wafted through the room.

'Did you all get a whiff of that?' Dennis called, 'much prefer that scent to the stench we had, hey who has a key?'

Brenda stunned as she had smelt that fragrance before, but it held a promise, she just knew; moved over to the French doors that had appeared from under the black plastic, marvelling at the intricate design that appeared in the doors and window surrounds on either side. Suddenly she had a vision of a young woman, it had to be Iris, standing in the conservatory that she could see on the other side of the door, a sad smile on her face, and nod of her head, another waft of gardenia and Brenda knew she had been given her blessing to continue.

'Ah keys, well I have nothing on my keys from Pickworths, any of you know of a locksmith that comes out on short notice? I want to open these doors to allow more fresh air than what is coming through the broken panes, to air the place, I think I may also need a glazier, anyone?'

Stan was talking to the shy Bella; she with Nona and Pico had been moving the furniture out of the kitchen area while the rest of them had been taking down the plastic and timber.

She moved over to Brenda, 'sorry my English not good. Are this you need, we found in kitchen drawer?'

A set of keys on an old fashioned hinged key ring were in her hand, 'Bless you Bella I think so!' she said out loud, and *Thank You Iris*, she said in her head, looking out the French doors, but the vision had gone.

Setting the large key in the centre lock of the doors, pushed them outward with difficulty, accumulated leaves, dirt and bird droppings made it heavy work, but with the help of Ben, Matt and Dennis pushing, then Stan once an opening had been achieved slipped through with a broom and spade to sweep the mess away, they did not open fully, but sufficient to allow fresh air to flow through the space after being stagnant for so long.

Four steps down and they were in a jungle, everyone stepped down into a conservatory that had been some one's pride and joy in the past. Now the plants were overgrown and going everywhere, Brenda knew she would need expert help to catalogue and tame them, dirt and debris from broken windows littered the floor.

As she looked to the right along the back of the building, she caught a glimpse through the dirt and grime covered roof and walls of the conservatory, at yet another ugly monstrosity she had seen that day, this one a lot larger than the gas fires! Another thing to add to the list she thought; there was a box structure covered in corrugated iron sheets that ran from the bottom of the house to the top of the building. One of the panels was slightly askew, whether by natures hand or shoddy workmanship, Brenda swore to find out, standing on tip toes she struggled to see what the structure was covering, she could just make out the bottom level of an old fashioned large circular staircase. Brenda could only see a small part of it, she called Ben over with his height hopefully he could see more, of course everyone came.

'I think I see a door through the gap, it definitely goes up and down the building Brenda!'

'That must access the door opposite the back bedroom, there must also be access from this kitchen,' she waved her arm at the space that without all the furniture was a kitchen. 'was there a door their guys, I didn't see one, of course it must be behind some panelling!' she could see the wonder in every one's face. This building was a treasure in this day and age. People destroyed and then rebuilt more than saved buildings like this.

Dennis and the crew hurried back in to move the last bits of furniture from the kitchen to take the last of the panels off the back wall, revealing a glass topped door and window, both with broken panes. The French doors on inspection also had cracked panes, but only the plain ones the stained-glass ones were intact.

Brenda's camera was working overtime she just had to get a complete history of what they were doing, really to prove that they had done it. Everyone had smiles on their faces as the light started to come flooding into the once dingy rooms.

'Hey Brenda,' Matt was coming back into the room, 'hope you don't mind but I have just called our brother in law, Charlie', at Brenda's nod and quizzical look he continued, 'well he is a damned good glazier, also dabbles in electrics, but he is good at what he does. He said he would be round tomorrow, but otherwise don't touch anything! You don't mind do you I know you will need not just anyone, Charlies speciality is old houses!'

'No, I have no objections, I don't mind keeping the work in the family, so to speak. I think we have done more than enough for one day guys. I thank you from the bottom of my heart for your help. I will need your services in your correct capacities, not just in demolition, in the next couple of weeks, you know what I need!'

Brenda was interrupted by a yell of help, coming up the stairs, carrying between them, what looked like a very heavy old tea chest was Dennis and Stan.

'We went to explore the door downstairs; the same key for the conservatory opened it! It's filthy in the stair well, but sound, all the area needs is a good clean.' Dennis had a grin on his face like a Cheshire Cat, 'when we pulled the panel off beside the door we found a cupboard, stacked inside was this,' looking at Ben and Matt he said, 'there are at least two more down there, want to bring them up?"

Once the tea chests had all been retrieved, the tops were gently taken off, to reveal the original light switches and face plates. Three chandeliers stacked very carefully two in one chest, with a very large third one in another. Matt beamed, 'that's better one less headache, I was wondering where the main chandeliers had gone and it looks as though you have a spare?'

'OK people, on that note although it is still early, I will definitely call it a day. I will be back tomorrow, I hope to see you at least Stan, so we can really get stuck into the cleaning. I thank you for your help today, I would not have been able to do this on my own. It was nice to share the experience with people who appreciate what I am trying to do. I also intend to keep your services as I believe I will need them, so who is back tomorrow?'

The affirmatives rang around, everyone left after some of the black plastic was taped over the broken glass in windows and doors. Dennis left with everyone, going to the pub for a well-earned pint, with all the troops, it was Brenda's idea, she was going to report to Linda, told them she would catch up with them all in a while.

Before she left the house, Brenda gathered the journals together, as she was straightening the papers to put into her briefcase, the letter from the journal she had found that morning, which seemed a lifetime ago, again fell to the floor. Picking it up, she opened it finally reading what was on the very expensive parchment paper, she stood stock still in shock. The colour drained from her face when she realised what it said. Laughing she shook her head, denying the words written in beautiful copperplate hand writing on the pages. She definitely needed to see Linda, pronto.

Chapter 6

Linda looked up and took in Benda's dishevelled appearance, then looked at her radiant face. She simply reeked of satisfaction and anticipation. If she were this happy after twenty-four hours of hard work, what would she be like when the construction phase was finished?

'Sorry to come looking like this Linda, but I thought I had better come around pronto. I have a few things to ask you about, have you time?'

'All the time in the world, especially as you have had me intrigued since your phone call this morning. Before you go through the other apartments, I suggest you ring the security people and let them know you are in the building.'

'Thanks, before I forget do you know of any gardeners, especially anyone who knows how to handle conservatory plants?'

Linda looked a little startled at the request, but picked up the phone.

'Emma, what was the name of the chap Sir James knows at Kew Gardens? Ah yes thank you.'

Turning after finishing the call and handing Brenda the slip of paper she had written on, the name Norman Greenwell and a phone number. 'I think he can help, when you ring just tell him Sir James told you to call!'

'Thank you, I won't explain why just yet, trust me I don't believe it. The work on the apartment is going to take a little longer than two weeks. I was hoping to stretch it to four? I also thought that while I am doing the work, it would be a good idea for me to stay in one of the apartments. In fact, I am hoping to spend a couple of nights in each of them to check them out fully. The wiring you said had been completed did go into my apartment, the electrician Dennis put me onto was not impressed with the way they left the bare wires hanging from the ceiling!'

Linda looked shocked, 'we were told that all electrical work had been completed. Still Mrs Boerchermeir could be a cantankerous lady, they may not have got in the door!'

'Have you ever inspected any of the apartments Linda?'

'I got to the hallway of number one, once and was severely yelled at. I did venture into the doorways of two and three, but could not actually go into them for the workmen.' Linda stopped on the thought, Brenda watching her thought process cross her face. 'I think it's a great idea Brenda; you can make sure the current contractors complete the work properly. I am sure we have missed things, we had organised for furniture, well the interior designer has sent a bill for furniture, and it was going to be delivered this week. Yes, the more I think about it the better I like the idea. I will get you the plans, architect and interior designer's drawings, all the details sorted out for you, when were you thinking of moving in?'

'Tomorrow, into apartment two, I know there is nothing in any of them, but I can borrow a mattress, won't be the first time I have slept on the floor. I also have a few things at Dennis's, I was planning on buying a Kettle, Toaster and mug on my way back to his place. I will be fine as long as the water, gas and electricity stay switched on!'

Linda laughed, 'you mean it don't you!' Brenda nodded, 'I can't change your mind,' she laughed again as Brenda shook her head in a negative. 'Well then I won't, you know what you are doing, I will ring the furniture company later and see if they can at least deliver a bed and comfortable chair for you, but hold them off on the rest.'

Brenda laughed relieved that her idea to oversee the last of the construction to be on site when she really started the update on her own space was going to be ok.

'Whew, that's good, now to something completely different. I found something when I was packing up the effects in the bedroom.' She handed over the journal she had found on the floor. 'I found this under the hospital bed, when I picked it up this fell out!' She handed Linda the letter, 'I think it may be her will, I will tell you I was just a little surprised when I read it.'

Linda took the letter, sat back and stared into space when she finished.

'James said they could not find a current will, although they knew one had been drafted, no one knew where it was. Congratulations Brenda, looks like you have an inheritance, I cannot think of any one more deserving!'

Brenda gasped, 'Me!'

'You found the will, it states quite firmly that the person inherits "all goods and chattels entailed to the writer of the will, within the building, exterior to the apartment (whatever that means) but not the building itself etc." Mrs. Boerchermeir died without any children or family to leave anything to, she was the last in the family. I will get the legal eagles to check on everything, but I do believe congratulations are in order.' Linda smiled happily, moving over to a cabinet in the corner, returning with a bottle of champagne and two glasses.

Handing Brenda a filled glass, 'I would have done this last night, in congratulations for joining our little group, but Sir James is a stickler for alcohol and the workplace. In light of that letter I cannot think of a better reason to celebrate, don't you agree?'

Brenda was numb; she took the glass and sipped it to steady herself, again that feeling of rightness and anticipation came over her, and there was that wisp of something fragrant. Watched as Linda photocopied the letter, handing the original back to her.

'Thank you, Linda, well today has been one of surprises. No I am not telling you what and when, but let us say I am going to enjoy the next four weeks. It will be ok to delay till then, I don't want to let Sir James down?'

'It is fine, I told him four weeks would be the bare minimum, he argued two at the most without seeing the place. I have of course not scheduled anything for six, but have not told him. I think he knows any way, but let's me get away with it. I mean what are grand-daughters for if they cannot twist grandparents around their little fingers!'

Yet another shock, Brenda started to laugh at the ingenious expression on Linda's face, the two women only a few years between them, realising they were on the brink of friendship,

Brenda left the office with a little more paper work than she wanted, made a detour back to the house to leave it for the following day, as that would be where she home was going to be. The feel of the whole building had changed in just one day. A sense of hope, a sense of awareness seemed to be there, Brenda walking the rooms of apartment one, saying thank you to the unseen occupant of the place, the smell of gardenias wafted around, Brenda smiled, saying to the presence she felt, she hoped she would like what she was about to do.

As she stood at the French doors, it was still early, took the chance to ring the number Linda had given her. She was in luck, she asked to speak to Mr. Greenwell, saying she was ringing on behalf of Sir James Pickworth. Silence for about thirty seconds, then a deep resonant voice came on the line.

'Mr. Greenwell, thank you for taking the call, my name is Brenda Chalmers, I am the new building manager for Pickworths. I have a problem and Sir James advised me to contact you, may I ask for your assistance?'

'Depends on the assistance, my dear,' came back down the line, 'my time is quite at a premium, but for James I am willing to listen.'

Brenda asked if he had free time the following day, as she would prefer to show him, as she could not explain the assistance she needed properly over the phone. He finally agreed to give her an hour of his time, asked the address, then gruffly put the phone down. Brenda smiled, it was all fitting into place, Iris love not long now she thought.

Dennis arrived back to find Brenda in the midst of packing.

'Did I miss something, we missed you at the pub, why are you packing?'

'Well my dear friend, I got fed up of sleeping on your lumpy bed, besides I have got a better deal!'

'What pray tell would that be, as I sure as hell cannot see you sleeping in the apartment, you don't even know if everything is good to use. Talk about lumpy beds; try the sofa bed for a change, hmmm. Seriously Brenda what is going on?'

Brenda explained to him her idea that she had passed by Linda that afternoon, of living for a couple of nights in each of the apartments before the VIP's did, it also made sense for her to be close when she put her ideas into operation for her place, she did not want to see any damage done, she wanted the job done right.

'But there is no furniture in any of them, where are you going to sleep? How are you going to eat? You haven't even inspected any of them yet!'

'Dennis love, thank you, I know you care, but it is time I gave you your life back. Besides I know you will love being able to say, "*I am just popping round to Brenda's*" to everyone. Don't deny it, and you will be welcome anytime day or night, but I have to go. Now can you be a dear and organise for my boxes to be brought around tomorrow. Linda said she was going to see if the furniture company they are using will be able to deliver me a bed, but just in case can you organise a mattress for me?'

Dennis laughed and hugged her. Realizing this was part of the dream that was becoming a reality for her. He could not deny her the happiness she could see for herself, even if it was going to be bloody hard work for the next few weeks.

Chapter 7

THEY DROVE TO THE house, all her belongings including a folding bed, table and chair fitted into the small van Dennis had procured for the move. Throwing her suitcases and boxes, the newly bought kettle and toaster on the top of it all, made their way through the light traffic, daylight was just breaking when they arrived at the house. They were just getting out of the van when another pulled up behind them, it was Stan and the team.

'I knew I was an early bird, but Stan this is ridiculous! How did you know I would be here?'

Stan smiled, nodded in Dennis directions, 'I know Brenda, but when Dennis rang me last night and told me what you were going to do, Nona was insistent we be here. She wants to see this place spotless more than you do, she did not like leaving yesterday without even cleaning a room! What can I do, I have to listen to my mother, so here I am!' He nodded at the boxes and furniture in the van, 'you don't really mean to stay, here do you?'

'Yes, Stan I do! I mean to oversee this job, I want it done properly.'

'Err, Brenda, no offence meant, but moving in where?' he turned to his mother who was chattering excitedly to him, shrugging his shoulders turned back to Brenda, 'Nona wants to know if you need the place you are moving into cleaned, before you move in?'

Brenda shook her head and chuckled, 'Stan supposedly all the other apartments are finished and just waiting for furniture,' at his look she continued, 'I know, I doubt they are as well, so could Nona please give apartment two a once over for me, then I can move these pieces in, to be here and oversee exactly what is going on!'

Stan turned and asked Nona, who beamed and gathered up her things, along with Bella, ushering her into the house and up the stairs. The groans and mutters in fluent Italian flowing back down the stairs gave a very good idea to everyone what she thought of the state of the apartment put a smile on everyone's faces.

Brenda then gave Dennis, Stan, Poppa and Pico a hand to clear everything out of the van, plus the cleaning equipment that Stan had brought taking it all into the front room of apartment one, while they could still hear Nona in apartment two, the tone of her voice saying a lot even if you could not understand the words spoken. Dennis promising morning tea again, left with a cheery wave. Brenda then asked if Stan could go through all the apartments and see if his opinion of the state of them matched her own.

'We should probably ask Nona and Poppa, Brenda. They have more experience than I do with old houses. They were the ones who said I had to do this favour for Dennis, coming over yesterday. All they could talk about last night was what they could see for this place. They were also impressed with the way you were going to bring it back to life!'

There was a knock on the door before Brenda could reply, followed by a deep cough and "anyone there?" Standing on the doorstep was a rotund little man, neat as a pin in an immaculate suit stood Mr. Norman Greenwell.

'Mr. Greenwell?' Brenda said going to greet him, at his nod continued, 'thank you for coming this early, can you please come this way. Excuse the mess, I have just started to move in and renovate the apartment, still taking stock so to speak.'

He took the proffered hand, thinking to himself what a waste of time this was. The place was a mess, wondered how he was going to pay James back for this.

Brenda had a good idea of what he was thinking, by the expression on his face, glad they had removed the plastic the day before. She was going to enjoy herself when he actually got into the conservatory.

Norman was looking around as they walked through the hallway door into the dining room, giving a gasp at his first glimpse of the beautiful French Doors.

'My dear, my dear oh what have we here, oh my dear a treasure, a rare and complete treasure!'

This was just the door, Brenda wondered what was going to happen next, thank fully Stan appeared to assist in opening the doors. Norman nodded in acceptance of the assistance as he moved to stand framed in the doorway, happily humming to himself as he inspected the now open doors.

'Oh, yes never been touched since being installed, oh you beauties, original paint work too, I have no doubt.' He was muttering to himself, Brenda could almost see him wanting to do a hop skip and jump in excitement, then he turned and really focused on the conservatory, taking a deep breath to steady himself.

'Mr. Greenwell, have I something here to be proud of, once it is tamed of course?' Brenda could not help asking.

'Oh, yes my dear, the doors are only a part of the prize you have here. Original structure still has most of its glass, and judging by the growth original plants as well. Although a great many of them have gone to seed, you can still see the Orchids and Gardenia are flourishing still.' He then launched into a description of the plants he could see from the steps. Stopping suddenly turned to look at Brenda, 'I would be happy to strip all this out for you, so you could use the structure, or even take the whole thing away if you are rebuilding?' He left the question hanging, looking at the woman next to him, trying to assess her reaction to his request.

Brenda was stunned for a moment, could not accept that anyone could or would contemplate the wholesale destruction of her beautiful conservatory, it was unthinkable.

'Mr. Greenwell how could you say that, no and no again, that is not happening. You may for Kew Gardens record, take samples and seeds from all the plants in the building, but it is staying put, I need to know how it can be restored, in situ, as a working and functional conservatory!'

The expression on his face was for a moment unreadable, and then he smiled, wondering if this lady would be the one who would not disappoint him. Would be one of the few who valued the old buildings for what they were, not what they could be vandalised into being.

Brenda continued, as the smile spread to his eyes, 'what I need to know so I do not ruin this wonderful room is specifics, how do I restore it, and can you help me to restore it?'

He looked at her earnest face and decided he would take the gamble.

'Interesting, yes of course we can at Kew Gardens, and my department specialise in assisting in the rebuilding, or refurbishing of outside areas, including conservatories. This is an extension of the house my dear, and I would have left you standing if you had agreed to my removing of it. The ladies of the house on summer nights, after dinner, would have promenaded in here, while the men smoked their cigar's, and drank port. It was also a place in winter the sun would warm, heady with oxygen given from the plants, a most beneficial place to be. We will probably find it attached to the central boiler system of the house, for the really cold periods.'

He stopped and looked at Brenda, watching the look of wonder on her face. He had not miscalculated, he was sure here was a person who was intent on restoration of the place, which was an interest dear to his heart. Here he was sure, was someone that would go through the restoration process to the bitter end, and not give in to modernisation half way through. He allowed the hope to blossom and thawed a little more, 'what time frame do we have?'

'Actually Mr. Greenwell.'

'Please my dear call me Norman, we will be working closely together.'

'Norman', with a nod of her head in acknowledgement that she had passed a test of some sort. 'what I would like to do initially is clear a path to the other side, as I am sure there is another set of doors there. There has to be access to the small garden you can glimpse and the commons beyond.'

Brenda suddenly realised that the commons she could access from the back gate was the same commons she had stumbled into a week ago. Shaking her head continued, 'that makes this place so secure. I plan to see this wonderful place restored to its original purpose, but I also have to access the gardens, as this is the escape route for the fire exits, when restored to use.'

Brenda turned and pointed out the corrugated iron box, and was gratified to see the shudder run through her companion.

'Once the building has been turned into the four apartments, the building approval will need clear access into the gardens as a fire escape. I will hopefully be able to take some time but I need information!'

Norman beamed, yes this was the one, the one who will restore my faith in mankind, he thought, oh the possibilities. His mind ran with what he would need, how many assistants and what equipment.

'All right my dear, for James I will do this. May I have your number again, I need to see whom I can get to help, it has to be the right people, the ones who know how to handle your rare and exotic blooms, as well as the rest of the plants. I need to get to work, can I start on Monday, no it's a public holiday isn't it, right then, first thing on Tuesday I will return.

At a nod he shook hands, took the number, and was moving out of the building, with a longing backward look and touch of the French doors on his way out. Another of Stan's shrugs seemed to sum up the whole experience. Brenda knew she had the right person, knew she would have to thank Sir James and was itching to find out how they knew each other.

Chapter 8

BRENDA SPENT THE NEXT couple of hours taking Stan, Nona and Poppa through the entire house. She was glad she had taken her Dictaphone, so she did not miss any of the damning conclusions they gave her, vowing she would do the same with Ben and Matt when they arrived. One of the main things she had to ask and check that was glaringly missing on the walk through, was the access to the fire escape, as Stan said building regulations would require an alternative escape route.

Apartment two was vetted as so, so by Nona once cleaned. She made it quite clear, speaking through Stan that it should be a temporary arrangement only, apartment one was Brenda's apartment, as it was waiting for her! To which Brenda agreed, as the décor in all the other apartments was definitely not to her taste.

Matt was waiting with Charlie when they got back to the ground floor, Ben hovering, Brenda asked him to go through the apartments, Stan said he would fill him in, both of them left heads bent together. Brenda then turned to be introduced to Charlie, he was a dark contrast to his brother in law, but with equally broad and muscled shoulders from hard work. He was eager to see what Dennis had roped Ben and Matt into, what they had unearthed not only in apartment one but the whole house. He was overwhelmed with the quality of the untouched workmanship he had seen as they waited for Brenda to arrive. Brenda could only agree with his comments, especially when he saw the chandeliers in the boxes, echoing Matt's comments of relief that the originals had been found.

He looked over the conservatory, all the windows, stained and plain, the French Doors, and back door from the kitchen, moving everyone into the front room and the bay window still tightly shuttered.

The men very heroically managed to open the protesting shutters, even with the liberal quantities of lubricant they had attacked the hinges with the day before, they squealed in protest. Once open, they to Brenda's sorrow had many broken panes, some of the stained-glass ones as well, she looked over to Charlie, who was taking photos on his phone and jotting down notes on a pad humming to himself, a smile on his face.

'I cannot see what you are smiling at Charlie? These windows are a mess, what do you see to smile about?'

'I get to fix them Brenda, that is what I am smiling about. I get to use techniques that have not been used for decades, to bring these beautiful windows back to life. The pieces are all here, Stan told me that he and his crew have picked up every piece of glass as they found them and put them in this bucket.' He held up a plastic bucket that was almost half full of glass pieces, plain and also coloured, 'I have one great big jigsaw puzzle to do, oh I do love a challenge!'

Understanding dawned on Brenda, 'oh I see you are looking forward to the challenge of repairing the windows, while I am looking at the challenge of repairing the whole building, we have similar tastes then Charlie.' A mutual smile of understanding passed between the two, 'well while you are into challenges how about I throw a curve ball at you, and ask for you to see how we can make the windows more energy and noise efficient, while not destroying them or replacing them? By the way can you and Matt please check out all the apartments, they are supposed to be completely finished? Stan has already given me Nona and Poppas opinion Ben is now as you know, going through them, and he hasn't even heard what I want from him in here. I am expecting a visit from the original contractor/builder, architect and interior designer this afternoon; I want to have all my ducks in a row so to speak. Can I ask for your assistance, and you don't know a builder by any chance?'

'To be included in this job, you can have my first-born Brenda. I don't have much on at the moment, same as Matt and Ben, so we are all at your disposal. As a matter of fact, you have two builders already, he nodded in Matt's direction. Both Ben and Matt joined their dad Glen in the family business. He had them building houses at fifteen, but they drifted into plumbing and electrics, keeping it all in the family so to speak. They can give you an opinion and probably will, but Glen is the one you want for a definitive opinion, and a trustworthy one at that. I would deem it a great honour to help rebirth this wonderful building, let me take a few more measurement and another look around. Noise and energy, that could be interesting, without replacing, oh listed building, hmm that will be a challenge?'

As Charlie moved away a thoughtful expression on his face Ben came and stood next to his brother, a look of disgust on his face. She looked at Matt, who was trying not to chuckle at Charlie's introspection, acknowledged Bens presence, and looked back at Brenda seeing the question in her expression.

'Yes, it is true,' Matt answered the questioning look, 'but dad would skin Ben and me alive if we usurped him in this Brenda. Although he is 'officially' retired, he was all ears and comments when we told the family of this place last night. We have a favour to ask?'

'Ask away, Matt I am open to any suggestions or help you may offer.'

'Well it is about Dad and our sister Rebecca?'

'Don't tell me Master Carpenters both of them.' Brenda said with a smile.

Both of them laughed, looking at each other, twin speak in full gear. Brenda thought she knew what was coming, again that feeling of rightness, and a waft of gardenia floated around, she could feel Iris's presence, comforting, calming she was helping direct her to the right people.

'Well Dad offered his services if you needed them, told us to tell you he was available. Rebecca could be of assistance, she is in the last year of her architecture degree, she is specialising in the interior design and structure of Georgian, Edwardian and Victorian houses!'

At the expression on Brenda's face he stopped and looked at his brother, wondering if they had pushed too far. Brenda was incredulous, even with the forewarning that Iris had given, that this was meant to be, she was meant to do this, to meet this incredible and talented family, to accept the help from wonderful people that rallied around her. *Thank you, thank you Iris,'* she thought, knowing without a doubt that she was indeed guiding people to her, friends she had yet to meet. *'I hope you are having a grand time,'* she thought, *'please don't stop whatever it is you are doing.'*

'Matt, you are a godsend, you and your family. As I told Charlie I am meeting with all the people who have supposedly nearly completed this 'restoration', she smiled at the grunt of disgust that came from both of them. 'What I need is a list of things not done, or not done right, what is missing etc., starting with the fire escape. Do you think Glen would come and bring Rebecca, if she is free, with him, to check over the place before the so-called experts arrive?'

Matt nodded and was leaving to call them, turning when Brenda said, 'hey you know the rewiring if we need to do it, can we re-use the copper tubing we uncovered when we took off the panelling, I would rather use something already in situ than destroying the walls to bury them. I am sure I remember seeing it done in a history book once, perhaps check with Rebecca please?' He nodded again, as he resumed his dialling saying he would check with Charlie as well.

The morning moved on, Stan with his team had worked wonders on the main floor. The walls gleamed; the original paper once the dust of ages had been cleaned off, looked as though it had just been hung. Powder room was cleaned and ready for use again, windows sparkled, light and air flooded the rooms, all the furniture that had been found in the kitchen and the rooms downstairs, apart from the king bed frame, was now in the front room, cleaned and lovingly put back under dust covers until needed. They had by mutual consent not lifted any of the black plastic on the floors, that was definitely going to be the last thing done. She was checking the uncluttered but very old kitchen, making notes and rough sketches of what she would like when Dennis arrived, with lunch and a delivery.

Chapter 9

Dennis had arrived to find a very handsome woman surveying the outside of the building. A willowy blonde, the look in her green eyes a million miles away when he walked up to her. '*I bet I know who this is!*' he thought.

'Mrs. McGill from Pickworths by any chance?'

Linda turned surprised at being addressed, 'Yes, and I would take bets that you are Brenda's Dennis, pleased to meet you.' At his puzzled expression of how he was known, she nodded at the box in his hands, 'Brenda told me you bring morning tea and lunches!'

Dennis smiled, laughing with her, 'are you coming in to have a look, not much to see at the moment, but it will be fantastic!'

'No, I don't think I will. I don't want to intrude, Brenda has enough on her plate. Do you think she will complete the job on time?'

'Don't you worry about Brenda, once she sets her mind on a job it is done on time and with all attention to details firmly in place. I have known her a long time, only once did she have a problem, she solved that by divorcing him. It was tough on her and the children but she bounced back. Your firm have got one hell of an organiser on your hands, you won't regret it, why don't you come in for a look?'

'Again, no thank you Dennis not today. I think Brenda wants me to see it finished, not the beginning stage. Could you please give her this, it is all the building information, oh, and could you get her to sign this for me, I need it back today. Tell her I look forward to her dropping by this evening.'

'Not a problem, I will drop this round after the break, would that be ok?'

'Fine Dennis, I look forward to future meetings. I know there are going to be many of them!'

Linda turned and with a last look at the still boarded house moved back up the street, wondering how it was going to be turned into what they wanted in such a short space of time. Dennis turned the opposite way juggling the paper work Linda had given him and the box, he was just going up the steps when a delivery van pulled up, the driver asking if he was in the right place. Linda had kept her word, furniture for apartment two had arrived. Calling Brenda, she was signing for the bed, dining table with four chairs a sofa and squishy chair when Nona appeared taking charge. Tut tutting the deliverymen all the way into the apartment, when she saw the modern all white furniture that was delivered, made known her dislike all the way up the stairs.

'Does she know I have my own linen?' Brenda asked Stan quietly as they watched her disappear.

'We took the boxes up after the apartment was deemed cleaned Brenda. I think you can be assured the bed will be made, whatever else was in those boxes will be cleaned and put out ready for use, before she comes back down. Don't worry that's Nona, it is what she does, just worry if you have any food in the fridge, she is likely to cook dinner for you!'

Brenda must have looked startled, as Stan and the others around her started to laugh.

After the lunch break, she asked Stan to check through the whole house, and move any boxes or furniture found into the front room, so she could see what was in her inheritance, although not believing it herself, and not telling anyone until she could see the substance to what she had read the day before.

He nodded understanding, moved off to the kitchen area motioning for her to follow him. Beside the newly found back door, was a cupboard, but as Brenda looked at it, something just didn't seem right. Stan pressed a knot in the wood, a front panel swung open. Brenda gasped and the room spun, *Iris what have you given me*, she thought. Neatly stacked in the space were a lot of heavily padded oblong shapes, with more tea chests, trunks, boxes of every size, and on top of the lot four very tarnished, dust covered candelabras, with other mysteriously wrapped objects.

'I reckon this runs behind the powder room, someone went to an awful lot of trouble to make sure these were not found easily. I only found them because I was holding my hand over the knot to remove the panelling. Shall I move these out as well? Brenda, are you ok?'

'I am fine Stan, fine.' Brenda smiled at him, still recovering from the shock, 'this just gets better and better, it is though Iris knew one day someone would come along to restore her and her family's life. I firmly believe what we are looking at is a legacy; the only way the dear old lady could give it. She had no family, no children of her own, she was an only child, there were no uncles or aunts, so when she died alone in this place last week she was the last in the line of a great family. Did you know her great, great (could be a couple more in there, but you get the idea) grandfather was Lord Norman Lucas. He built this row of houses, and called it Steel Street, because that is what he made them out of. I saw the original plans there were in a journal I found when I cleaned up Iris's room. He was a visionary of his time, everything he did he built to last. Iris was named for the flowers in the stained-glass windows, I found out she was 104 when she died in this house alone!'

Stan was shocked and it took a lot to do that. He thought he had seen it all, but this gentle woman before him made him rethink. There was kindness, good in this world, and just a few people like Brenda, that did not live in a completely disposable one, who valued life and the good parts of what had gone before. He knew he and his family had found someone they wanted to get to know even better, and help them what ever happened.

'No, I didn't know, but now I do. Just makes me determined to do the best job I can, and help in any way we can. Why don't you go upstairs, settle into the apartment,' pointing to all the paper work that had been left on the bench in the kitchen, 'check on all the information the boys, and Dennis has just given you. I can handle this, Pico will help, Poppa will direct, I will make a list of how many items and what they are, if we can easily unpack them to check, will that be ok?'

Giving him a hug, Brenda thanked him, saying yes to the list, gathered up her papers, and moved out of the way.

Chapter 10

B RENDA WAS REVIEWING THE information her 'Team' had given her.

Glen with Rebecca had arrived quickly, Brenda had a suspicion they had come up to town just on the off chance she would call. Glen's comments on the place were colourful to say the least. Rebecca as blonde and tall as her brothers, had almost as much to say as her father about the décor of the apartments, in the same tone of derision as her brothers.

Brenda put her to work checking the architects plans against the detailed drawings and information that she had found while skimming the journals the night before. Asking her to liaise with her father and brothers, to check each apartment and come up with a list of defects or still to do's in each apartment. Then asking if they all could wait, until she had spoken to the 'experts' about to arrive.

When they did, Brenda kept them out on the pavement, while introducing herself, giving them a business card, a bundle of which she had found in the file, with a note from Linda, *'Brenda, sorry rushed job could only get 25, I think you will need them. More to come, have fun Linda!'* The business card was very simple:

PICKWORTHS
Brenda Chalmers
Building Manager
Phone: 44 0202655656
POBox E44, London Exchange EC1
Email:- calm@pickworths.com

Brenda laughed at the email address, which was at that time so not her state of mind, but was very pleased with the very stiff expensive card to hand out.

She requested them to walk through apartments three and four, then to meet in apartment two, checking each one and making a list of their own of things to finish or redo. They looked at each other, back at Brenda as though she had asked for the moon, going into the house by the apartment door entrance, passed the firmly closed and blacked out front door of apartment one.

Half an hour later, they were seated in front of the glass table that had been delivered that morning, with Brenda behind it. All of them spoke in turn, stating they could see nothing wrong with the apartments, even the one they were in, they were all ready to be signed off as finished, the builder even stated that final inspections had been organised for the following Tuesday. Brenda looked at each of them in turn, the Interior Designer, a young woman who could not look Brenda in the eye, Mia Farrington-Smythe, was in fact looking very uncomfortable, looking around the apartment, anywhere except at her colleagues and Brenda. Mr. John Hemsworth, Architect and Mr. William (Bill) Gardiner the Builder/Contractor were watching her with supercilious sneers on their faces.

'Well I am so pleased you think you have done a wonderful job. You really do not think there is anything wrong with what you have done. You do not think you have done a criminal act in the way you have handled this beautiful building. You have stripped out nearly everything you could and turned it into a building of mediocrity!'

'Now see here,' John jumped to his feet, 'how dare you,' and the sneer was profound, 'say that our work is a criminal act, our brief was to refurnish three apartments, possibly four, to bring them into the twenty first century, and that is what we have done!'

'You stripped out the soul of them you mean. Did you actually read the brief from Pickworths? Let me remind you of what it says, she pulled the contract towards her, that she had found in the papers Linda had given Dennis, *"bring modern function to the existing building without destroying the integrity of the original property."* I would take that to mean you do not remove everything and paint it all in gloss white.

She was pleased to see a flush of embarrassment from Mia as she hid her face behind a curtain of dark blonde hair. Bill jumped to his feet yelling above John, as to whom the hell was she to tell them off. What right did she have to claim they had not done a good job, Sir James was going to hear about this shoddy treatment they were all receiving.

Brenda put up her hand to halt any further comments from the angry men in front of her. Very grateful that she had used the phone, installed that morning, to call Sir James and forewarn him of her discoveries in the build. She hit redial, putting it on speaker, it rang three times 'Hello, Brenda are they all there?'

'Yes, Sir James indeed they are!'

'Gentleman and Lady, I think you should know of my reputation by now. I would like to introduce to you the newest member of our team at Pickworths, Ms. Brenda Chalmers. She has been installed as the Building Manager for the building you are in at the moment, and I am very annoyed at the information she has passed to me this morning. She is to see that any work is completed in my time frame, and not you're never ending one. She has our full authority to get the job done, and done to her specifications; she has our complete faith and trust to bring this job to her high standard of completion. I suggest you listen to her and do as she bids! Are you all listening to me, John, Bill and Mia?'

A very desultory yes came from the three people that had sat stunned when the call had been answered, subdued that they had been out manoeuvred.

'Now I am off to golf, anything else you need Brenda, call me anytime!'

She put the phone back on the cradle, taking a moment to look at the stunned faces in front of her.

'I do not want to destroy Sir James faith in your skills and talents, but I will not let you get away with the shoddy and downright dangerous things that have gone on in this building. Before you get up to argue with me, that I do not know what I am talking about, I want to introduce to you 'My Building Team', who have compiled a list of problems they have seen on checking the building over, they do have the qualifications you require!'

Ben, Matt, Charlie and Rebecca walked in followed by Glen, serious expressions on all of their faces, coming to stand behind Brenda.

'Bill, you old fool, what the hell have you done to this grand old building?' Glen looked directly at Bill Gardiner, who's mouth had dropped open as they walked into the room, then he turned to look anywhere except at Glen.

'I take it you know each other,' at Glen's nod she continued, 'good then perhaps you can take Mr. Gardiner, and point out the very obvious flaws in this building. By the way Mr. Gardiner you will not be taking the scaffolding down on Tuesday, in fact you had better order more,' at his quizzical look Brenda continued, 'for the rear of the building, but I will let Glen explain why!'

She turned then to the architect, who seemed surprised that she would turn on him.

'Mr. Hemsworth, I take it you did not attempt to remove, what I hope is the exterior circular staircase at the rear of the building?'

'Where were we going to get the money to do that! We would have had to rebuild the place if we tried. I think the staircase is actually part of the structure of the building!' he replied sullenly.

'In that case, whatever possessed you to enclose that beautiful staircase in that grossly ugly edifice?'

Turning to the men in the room, as beseeching them to back him in his work, 'Well I thought the corrugated steel sheeting was echoing the industrial theme of the building!'

Clearly waiting for the nods of agreement from everyone.

'It looks like a very poor outback outhouse, it is an eye sore and it is coming down!' He started to complain, Brenda looked at him, he then realised that the only person he was getting any support from was Bill Gardiner, Mia had turned fully from them both. Brenda continued, 'it is coming down, you are going to give Sir James a triumph of design in glass and steel!'

'How am I supposed to do that, can you give me a lead, as you clearly know more than I do!' was the sarcastic response from him, as he realised he was on very shaky ground.

Charlie was the quickest, he winked at Brenda giving her the briefest of cheeky grins. Brenda had whilst taking them around put her ideas to all of them to rejuvenate the spaces, and to give their versions of her ideas if possible.

Charlie paused to look at this man with pity on his face, passed over a plan clearly showing the existing staircase (they all hoped was there), that incorporated a lift large enough for two people into the whole structure. Brenda hid her shock that Charlie had time not only to nut out what she had suggested, but had the skill to produce such detailed drawings in so short a time. *Oh, Iris have I got the right people with me or what, hold on this is going to be one hell of a ride!'*

'We build in steel, what I could see through the gaps in the enclosure, same as the original stairs,' Charlie was explaining his drawing to the stunned man, Mia looking over their shoulders, Rebecca watching with interest. 'Of course, you will have to rethink the plans for the apartments, as you now have to have clear access to the fire escape, they will also have to be level, as this then gives you wheelchair access, which is a missing component in your design. The landings are still there, just the doors have been blocked, is, that right?' He nodded as Charlie continued, 'not a good idea to block off an emergency exit. How were you going to get the building certificate and regulations signed off?'

The now deflated architect just looked at Charlie, not saying a word, looking over to where Bill was standing with Glen, a very heated discussion was happening between the two builders, Matt and Ben beside their father with bemused expressions on their faces. John looked more closely at the drawings on the table in front of him, 'this is brilliant. You are actually using the original steel to anchor the lift well. Enclosing the entire thing in sheets of glass, the frame is steel, how do you know the glass will fit?'

Charlie just threw a look at Brenda, she could almost hear him thinking, *'you use a tape measure and ring the glass people to see if it does!'* The smile on his face and look in his eyes was everything, he sighed showing he had no time for people who think their own importance was prominent. The tension was broken, John and Charlie were joined by Bill, Glen with Ben and Matt trailing behind. Rebecca had taken Mia aside, she was showing her some of the designs she had also come up with that morning. Brenda moved towards them to give Rebecca support, but she need not have worried, the benefit of growing up with two older brothers gave her the authority she needed. She was pointing out that modern did not mean ripping everything out. Rebecca knew of Mia Farrington-Smythe from one of her lecturers, him sighting Mia's work as an example of what not to do. Rebecca had told Brenda that she repeated the one design over and over, white and chrome, in different textures, but always white and chrome. The fact that Mia was only a year older than Rebecca was the bonus, Brenda realised they could get on well, given half a chance after this initial shock.

'Ladies and Gentlemen, I think we can work out the problems. I also think we can bring this building back to life in the way it was meant to be. The only real problem we have is time. You!', and she looked at the original team, 'have been at work on this project for nearly six months. We will be taking it back at least two, and then I need it fully completed in four weeks!'

Before John or Bill got to their feet to complain, Glen spoke, he would have been a Viking in a previous life, Brenda thought. He was built big like his sons, but he had that quiet competent air that nothing was beyond him. She liked what she saw immediately, so did Iris to judge by the gardenia that was around, when she was introduced to him and Rebecca earlier. Liked him even more when he confirmed, in a quiet forceful manner, that all would be completed in four weeks; Bill, John and Mia all looked at him with shock.

'Four weeks,' Glen continued, 'or no one will get paid his or her final payments!'

That made everyone sit up and take notice, the fact that it had come from Glen and not Brenda enforced it even more.

'I suggest you all get cracking,' Brenda stated in the silence that followed, 'this building is waiting to be reborn the right way. I also suggest to get it done, your team of workers Bill, now work with my team, you report and work with them, they report to me!'

'Where will you be Brenda, how do we contact you?' Mia spoke for the first time since she initiall said everything was as it should be in the apartments, in the same very subdued voice.

'Mia, I will be right here, I am going to base myself in apartment two, then will spend time in three and four to see they are completed to Pickworths, and my standards. I have already notified the neighbours, and have requested permits to work over the weekends, which we will need. I suggest you all get a move on, now!'

They moved; Ben, Matt, Glen went out with Bill for another check over the apartments, to see how much they were going to have to remove from the rooms to open up all the back doors, hopefully without doing too much damage to the existing work if at all possible. Charlie with John moved over to the kitchen bench to compare notes, also for Charlie to explain who he had contacted in regards to the steel, glass and lift companies, who could also come up with the goods required at short notice.

Brenda moved over to Charlie and John, asking if she could interrupt them but she needed an architect's perspective on a job for herself. She moved them down into apartment one, very grateful that Stan, Nona and Poppa had stayed behind after Pico and Bella had gone to another job, following in their wake. Not giving John a chance to really see what a treasure she had, she did not like him, and from the chilly atmosphere in the apartment Iris agreed with her.

'I am going to need a kitchen, capable of feeding two or twenty. I realise this area is not in your original brief, but wondered if you could come up with something for me?'

Charlie and Stan waited in the background as Brenda steered John into the kitchen area.

'I require something in the style of the original but very modern, easy to use.' She moved over to the panel Stan had shown her before, opening it up for him and Charlie to see the space behind the existing wall. Charlie gave a gasp, John did a double take.

'I don't think I will need this anymore, so it gives us more space. What I need from you John is an architectural perspective, as we will need a hallway through the house out to the back to access the new lift. Can you please check for me, load bearing walls, what permits would be required etc., but let me remind you of what beauty is and was in this building, that I do not want destroyed any further!'

Brenda moved as she spoke, over to the butlers sink and bench, in the space that the ugly gas cooker had been removed from, stood and motioned for Stan to help her pull the piece of panel off the wall, Charlie coming quickly to assist.

In the dark space a stained-glass window was revealed, because of the very limited amount of light, you could not see it fully, but could just make out that the Iris had multiplied, in the centre of the window, the bouquet was framed with gardenia flowers, buds and vine leaves, the whole thing went from bench top to picture rail and was about two feet wide, framed in black steel. Brenda was still stunned by the find, wondering at the time what else was hidden?'

'My oh my,' John gasped, 'yes I see, well I will work with Mia and come up with a design. I take it you want this yesterday?'

'Yes, that is right, but you will not be working solely with Mia, you will be working with her and Rebecca!' He turned and looked at Charlie and Stan, who both shrugged as though to say, *there are new rules in place now'* the matching grins on both of their faces priceless. Brenda continued, 'Rebecca is the only person I will trust who will give a Twenty-first Century functional kitchen, for efficiency but put it in the era this building requires!'

He knew better than to argue, after asking Charlie to come by his office later to discuss, took his leave, muttering to himself as he left.

Charlie gave Brenda a hug, 'thank you, I enjoyed that so much. This is just spectacular, and very rare,' he was pointing to the window, 'we will handle it with the respect it deserves, when we get to that stage, I promise. I had better go, got to contact the steel works, then ring the glass and lift people before he does!'

'Don't tell me 'Family'?'

'No, but very good friends, when I rang them to check details they were so excited. I have a feeling that they have already started getting everything needed together, just need to tweak a bit. Oh,

I am so excited, will ring you later.' He went off whistling a happy tune, Stan chuckled to himself as he watched him walk out the door.

'Do you want to put the boards back on the window Brenda?'

'No leave them off for the time being Stan, but make sure they are not thrown out please. I believe they will be needed when they come to fix the kitchen, better safe than sorry. Rebecca and Mia have already gone I think, Rebecca had enough notes to make another book, so I think they have gone shopping. Are you off as well?'

'Yes Brenda, both the girls left about ten minutes ago, we are going as well. Nona wanted to ask you something before we left she is in the front room.

Chapter 11

BRENDA WALKED INTO A room that had shrunk again. Furniture under dust covers, boxes, paintings, statues, suitcases and trunks, were stacked neatly in front of the fireplace and in corners out of the way. Nona walked up to her and took her over to a tea chest, pulling off the dust cover, turned and spoke to Stan. He nodded in understanding, but before he could translate what was said, Nona to the surprise of all said in halting English.

'I will clean, for you, promise!'

Confused, Brenda looked into the tea chest, it was full with silver ware, candlesticks, platters and one of the large candelabra inside the box, the others on the floor beside it. Nona put a hand on the tea chest and one over her heart, speaking all the while as though making a pledge.

Stan touched her arm, and started to translate for her, 'Nona wants to take this chest and the silver ware home, if you will let her Brenda. When she was a young girl, back in the old country, she used to help at the big house. She was shown how to clean the silver, and this reminds her of then. She understands if you don't want to let it out of your sight, but she is pledging that it will come back almost the same as the day it was first polished!'

What could Brenda say but yes, of course. She trusted these people, they were the salt of the earth, and trust was what they survived on. Brenda nodded her head yes, Nona beamed pulling her into a hug, kissing her soundly on both cheeks, talking all the time. Stan chuckled, 'she wants you to know that she does not like the other apartments, and would prefer if you could change them;

the house does not like them either,' the whiff of gardenia endorsed her statement. 'But she realises you can only do what you can, this she knows!'

'Now,' Stan continued, 'we are going and will be back next week!'

What could Brenda say, as she could feel Iris's presence urging her to trust in her instinct. Brenda nodded her head in agreement to what the wise old woman had said, as Stan continued as he misunderstood Brenda's hesitation.

'That is what Nona said Brenda,' bringing her out of her reverie, 'if you need us before next week just call us. Dennis has the number, but there is not much we can do until the builders are finished. I will bring this back, 'pointing to the silverware, going over to help Poppa pick up the chest settling another candelabra on top handing the last one to Nona, 'on Monday to check, but call me if you need me.'

'I certainly will,' Brenda answered, 'by the way I need your bill for the last two days of hard work. I meant it when I said you were going to be an ongoing part of my team, I am going to need an ace cleaning crew, every time one of the apartments is empty. I am even going to recommend you to Pickworths CEO, so watch out you may get more work than you bargained for. Could you please list what is in the chest Stan, I am going to have to catalogue everything we have found!'

Stan smiled and handed her two sheets of paper, one was his bill, the other an inventory of the opened boxes. It was pitifully small compared to how many boxes there were still to be opened and checked. Brenda looked at the sheet, noticed a number on each box, one was asterisked it was the one Nona was taking. He was gone before she could thank him for his efficiency, but she waved goodbye from the steps.

Brenda moved up to apartment two as Ben, Matt and Glen came down from the upstairs apartments, nodding to her and going straight through to the laundry room where hopefully the back door out to the landing was still in place. Trailing them into the room was Bill, who had a very thoughtful expression on his face, he was making copious notes on the notepad in his hand. He left quickly after a good look at what had been done, telling Glen he would be back in the morning with his men.

'What was all that about?' Brenda asked as the three of them, once he had gone out the front door, burst into laughter.

'Sorry Brenda, but I have been waiting a very long time to see that man taken down a peg or two. He thought he was so superior to anyone else, but he has been sitting on his backside, for the last few years, and not taken a controlling interest in the projects he had. He farmed them out to project managers, and not checked them, well it is coming back to bite him, at last!'

Ben and Matt had calmed down a bit as well, 'What Dad is not telling you Brenda,' Matt interjected, 'is that he was nearly put out of business by that man. Well Dad survived, just, he built well, but always seemed to miss out of the prestige jobs, they went to our 'friend' who just left. I wonder how many other jobs he has bodged?'

'He is certainly not happy now Matt, but will he fix what is bodged and fix it properly?'

'Oh yes, Brenda, he will fix it by god, and no further payment is required of your company either.' Glen turned to her, after watching out the window, 'I made it quite clear that all payments made, cover any work that has to be redone. As it happens they have made laundries in the apartments, covering the fire escape doors with cupboards, possibly making it an easy job to fix.'

'Perfect Glen, I need you and your boys to do other things for me, although they will also have to the supervisors of their particular fields. Could you all spare me a moment, before you leave, I have to ask your opinions on something?'

Leading the three men into apartment one, they all commented on the number of boxes and furniture stored in the front room. Brenda nodded but continued on into the dining room come kitchen space, and waited as they took in the space behind the false pantry, and the newly revealed dark but still beautiful window.

'Wow when did that all appear?'

'It's beautiful!'

'What a piece of workmanship that is!'

Were the comments from all once the shock had worn off a little, Brenda asked the three men to give their opinion of the possible layout of the new kitchen.

'We may have to use some of the space for a hallway for the upstairs apartments to have access to the lift, also we may need a ramp or two. This area does give us some leeway though doesn't it Glen?' Brenda turned and looked at them asking questions with a quirk of a raised eyebrow.

'You have been thinking this through haven't you!' Glen said, looking first at Brenda then at the pantry and window wall. 'Your wall here at the pantry is false, they would have had to have access to the back of the house originally, not just through that back door. Hm, yes, it is wider, could be, could be. I know the front two doors are a later addition, I would just love to have a look at the flooring, hmm!'

Ben and Matt just followed their father around, making notes of what he said, Brenda realised they had done this before. They all moved back into the dining area, surveying at a distance, the kitchen area.

'Whatever we do we will have to check with the interior designer, to check authenticity'

Ben turned to Matt and mouthed "Mia", pulling a very disgruntled face to empathise his dislike.

Brenda laughed, turned to Glen, 'actually it will be Rebecca, Mia is now working with her, I hired Rebecca early this afternoon. She knows more about this type of architecture than that so-called specialist John Hemsworth! Besides I trust her, I don't trust that man, or Mia at the moment, neither does Iris!' She ignored the startled looks from the men in front of her wondering who this Iris was. Glen was beaming, Ben and Matt bursting with pride for their sister.

'Thank you, Brenda, you don't know what this means to my family. We will not let you down, will we boys?' Glen was looking at the two young men, with a look that said, you had better not. Brenda took the proffered hand and shook it firmly to seal the bargain just made.

Chapter 12

'WELL MR. HADDON, LET us get one thing straight, I am employing your whole company,' and she pointed at all three men standing in front of her, 'to work not only for me but for Pickworths. I would like your budget and cost estimates on how you would finish this build. I would also like your friendship, as I like your family, but I realise that is early days yet. You deal fair by me and Pickworths, then Mr. Haddon we shall get on very well indeed!'

As Glen nodded in understanding, looking at both Ben and Matt, Brenda continued, 'I not only have the headache of trying to finish my apartment, but also fix the whole of the bungled original work. We both need to know if the structure is sound enough to be able to utilise the new-found space. Hopefully, we will find it was the house's original hallway, or a couple of rooms unused since the split of the house into apartments. Is it possible to come up with something for me, checking with Rebecca of course, I have given her the journals I found, which I believe will be a vital source of information! I do not trust John to do anything in a hurry, but I do have to let him try for Sir James' sake'.

Glen was again looking around, pulling out a tape measure giving instructions to the boys, who were already checking the walls and floors.

'I also have another project to add to the list, downstairs? You have been downstairs Glen, or did the boys just give you a whistle stop tour before our meeting?'

'Well I didn't see much Brenda, but I really like what I am seeing now, this is just amazing. The boys said no one has touched the place in over fifty years!'

'I think it will be closer to one hundred, let me show you around, and you two finish off what your dad needs, meet us downstairs when you are ready.'

Ben and Matt, both nodded in agreement, engrossed in trying to see every detail. As Brenda and Glen disappeared down the stairs to the basement, they decided to get accurate measurements the pantry wall just had to go. The timber, they found, was not very securely attached, to the half brick wall the window was in, or the wall at the other end, it was an easy job to push it over. By the time, they finished they found Brenda and Glen in the front bedroom examining the window above them. The hospital bed had been removed earlier in the day, Stan's contact coming through. The boxes and tables were now upstairs in the front room; only the plastic on the floor and the shuttered window remained giving the room a very hollow, empty feel.

'What I want to know has the dumping of that large skip and putting up of the scaffolding done any damage to the basement area and the window. I know that the upstairs bay window was damaged, Charlie has the bits in a bucket. I am apprehensive in removing this plastic in case it is worse for down here? I also do not know what awaits us when we open the basement door that was rediscovered on removing of the panelling, what do you recommend?' she asked Glen.

'There is only one way to see,' Glen said, turning to her a broad smile on his face, 'Ben, Matt go on up and see what is happening behind that skip, see if you can see any damage, I bet there has been, I think they were a little late in covering the windows, as they were with the bay up above! Charlie told me the shuttering was an afterthought once they had broken a few panes. There will be damage, Brenda, it is what I expect of this lot of builders, but nothing that Charlie and the rest of the team won't enjoy fixing!'

He said with another smile, he turned hearing Ben and Matt above him, but not being able to make out exactly what they said, he thought he knew from the tone of voice the boys were muttering in.

As they came back into the bedroom, after their inspections, 'A right mess in the garden dad,' Ben started to say,

Matt interrupting him, 'No care taken at all, to the walls, garden or windows. One of the panels is half off, and we could see at least one broken pane of glass!'

Ben continued glaring at his twin, 'You cannot even get down to the door, rubbish and refuse hide the bottom two steps, good job you didn't open it Brenda!'

Both of the young men were obviously disgusted, their father was a very tidy careful builder, Brenda was more and more impressed with this family.

'What I thought boys, well nothing we cannot fix tomorrow. We will get rid of that monstrosity of a skip, after we have added to it, get a smaller one that will fit better on the pavement. We can see about a permit; did you say you have already spoken to the council about some permits? I need to check what you have requested, if you don't mind Brenda?'

'Fine with me Glen, I actually found documents saying that Bill Gardner had applied for extension permits but as far as I know never used them. I am so glad you came along, I am sure you are more qualified to check them out, and know what to ask for, I am very happy to pass that onto your shoulders!'

Moving over to the side wall, where the bathroom/kitchen, and closet had been revealed, Brenda turned to the three men, with a smile on her face.

'Can I please ask if it would be possible to have a proper functioning bathroom and walk in closet, I would like the same done in all three bedrooms if possible?'

'You want a full bathroom in each bedroom?' Ben asked.

'No not full, but a little more elegant than this,' pointing to the one in place, 'perhaps a shower room, or wet room. I don't know I am not a designer, speak to Rebecca please, and don't forget the walk-in wardrobe as well!'

The three men looked at her, Glen chuckled muttering 'just like my wife!' Ben and Matt were taking notes and measurements of the space, they moved into each room, with the furniture removed, and the false walls demolished they were all very well proportioned rooms, adding bathrooms and walk-in wardrobes would not reduce the size by too much.

'Hey Brenda, you know your idea of reusing the tubing we found,' Matt asked as they were measuring up the middle room, 'well I talked to Rebecca, and you were right, they did use the tubing for the electrics, well at least they were supposed to, I only found it used in the front bedroom! It was only in recent time they buried the cables in the walls, so it will work. Charlie and I checked the tubes we found in this apartment are ready to be reused with modern cabling, neat eh!'

Brenda laughed at his boyish expression, moving them all into the back bedroom, telling them she wanted to use this room as her bedroom, it felt better. The ladders were brought in, the black plastic was removed, this time sunlight filtered in through the grimy windows, the shutters firmly back in their place. Some of the windows were broken, dirt and droppings were piled on the window seat in the alcove formed by the shape of the window, a mirror to the one in the front bedroom. Both windows going up from the picture rail, the back window with the conservatory steps from the dining room above going over the top.

'Well you never know what wonders you will uncover in this game, we will use some of the plastic to cover the broken ones Brenda. Ben, you take the measurement so Charlie can come and replace these in the morning, got to keep the wildlife out.' She caught a glimpse of the bones in amongst the droppings on the seat. 'Brenda, can you go and get Stan's dustpan we will take care of this mess for you. Matt, you go and get a rubbish bag and tape out of the van please!'

Brenda left with Matt, as requested, handing the brush and dustpan to him on his way back down the stairs.

Glen and the boys left not long after the clean-up, with measurements and smiling faces, promising results as soon as possible. Brenda sighed as she was alone in the house for the first time. Quietly she moved through the building silently telling it to wait, everything will be all right, making sure all was locked for the night. She rang the security company to advise them she was living in the building, staying in each of the apartments to vet them, asking them to please not panic.

She picked up a cup from the top of one of the tea chests that Stan had managed to open, going out to give an update to Linda.

'Do you ever move, you were in the same position when I left last night?'

Brenda said as she walked into Linda's office. This time she had the bottle of champagne, Linda took one look, smiled moved to the cabinet for two glasses.

'OK what is the celebration tonight? Or is the fact that you have actually got through your second day a celebration in itself?'

'It's only been two days, my god it seems as though half my life has gone!' she laughed with Linda, 'ah but I have achieved so much in two days, I am amazed at myself. You had better warn Sir James that I have just increased the budget, added to the build in fact, but it will look spectacular and will be so much safer!' Brenda took a sip of the champagne and relaxed in the chair.

'Well as it happens celebrations are in order, congratulation on your inheritance Brenda, everything is correct in the will, it is all yours! The legal eagles checked, double and triple checked, the goods and chattels left by one Iris Fitzgibbon Boerchermeir are all yours. They are still digging of course, can't stop them, but they were adamant everything in that apartment, at least, belongs to you!'

Stunned Brenda took another sip of wine, hoping to settle the butterflies in her stomach. 'Don't I have to sign anything or swear on a bible or something?'

Linda laughed, 'no my friend, you signed what you had to this morning, Dennis brought it round this afternoon.'

'Oh, I had no idea; perhaps I had better start reading things before I sign them. Well that is a first; I land the job and an inheritance in one hit. I hope the bubble or dream I am in does not burst, it would be very hard coming back to earth!'

Brenda lifted her glass in a salute to the universe, Linda echoing it.

She then gave Linda an edited version of her day. The meeting with the original so called renovators, telling her about the more competent people who had become her crew. Her meeting with Norman Greenwell from Kew, her telling of his emotions on seeing the structure and conservatory his enrapture on finding his treasure, had tears of laughter running down Linda's face. Linda was fascinated as Brenda outlined the bare bones of what she wanted to do, amazed at the energy and enthusiasm that flowed from her, her call to Sir James that night was going to be interesting.

Finally, Brenda stood and put the cup on the coffee table between them, Linda lifted an eyebrow in query.

'I have never seen that pattern before, I would have bought at least a teacup and saucer if I had, as the Iris and Gardenias are two of my favourite flowers. I think it is Royal Albert? I wonder if you know of anyone who might be able to value it for me, I have a few more bits and pieces in the inheritance that I will need to have checked to see if any of it is valuable, any ideas?'

The cup Linda had in her hand was delicate porcelain; the deep blue Iris was intertwined quite simply with a vine, leaves, small gardenia flowers and buds, with a gold rim. Very simple design, but to Linda it screamed expensive. Brenda's inheritance was more than she thought, and she deserved every piece.

'I am sure Grandfather will know someone, I will check with him when I ring, do you want this back?'

'No not immediately, I cannot use them in the house anyway, not the state it is in. I haven't finished cataloguing everything, keep it till you come to dinner!'

Linda laughed and walked Brenda to the door, watching as she walked away with a definite skip in her step.

Chapter 13

BRENDA WOKE IN A strange room, but it was light and airy. *Ah, that's right no curtains, must get onto Rebecca about that in this room at least.* Five am, as she got ready for the day she ran over the conversations she had the previous night with the residents in the buildings on either side of hers.

It wasn't really too bad, only one flat was occupied on one side, two on the other. The couple were very happy to hear the renovations had an end date, as they thought they were never going to end. Brenda did not sugar coat the amount of work still to do, warning everyone about the very large cranes that would be arriving, there would still be noise aplenty but it would end. The other two flats were occupied singly by businessmen, who quite bluntly told her they were fed up with everything, almost to the point of legal action. Brenda managed to calm them down, as they realised that there would finally be someone there to oversee the work, and make sure it was finished. She did not say she was the building manager, they just assumed she was the project manager hired to move the build along.

Brenda smiled as she made coffee and contemplated the day to come, jumping as the intercom beeped, who could be here at this time? She should have known, the Haddon's on-masse. Brenda buzzed them in and put out more coffee cups, this apartment she would have to tell them was the official tearoom for the build.

They arrived with boxes, Ben opened the one he was carrying, it had what looked like some very delicious cakes and buns, Charlie right behind him with a box of pies and sausage rolls.

73

'Have to feed the troops today, Brenda! There are going to be a lot of people around, so thought we had better have a powwow to see exactly what we are going to be doing!' Glen smiled he seemed to have dropped ten years of care and worry from his face overnight, there was a vitality to him that she found infectious. 'By the way my wife Julie and daughter Gabby baked yesterday, they wanted to help in some small part as well!'

'Thank them so much for this Glen, add it to the bill, the catering company will not miss out if this is the standard of fare,' laughter rang around the room.

'Well don't just stand there everyone, let's get Brenda up to speed!'

Rebecca came breathless up the stairs. 'Thanks for the help you lot, cared about the food but not me with my load!' Red-faced Ben and Matt hurried to relieve her of cloth samples and books. She turned after a withering glare in their direction.

'Sorry about not organising any curtains in your room Brenda. Mia mentioned at the end of our meeting yesterday that no curtains or blinds had been installed. It was too late to do anything last night, but I will rectify it today, I promise.'

'No worries Rebecca, I needed to be awake early,' gesturing at the men spreading a lot of plans on the table. 'I cannot believe what I see, did you lot get any sleep last night?'

Glen laughed, 'We got a little, well when we left I could not get over the space in the hallway, and thought it was odd. Rebecca with help from a couple of Iris's journals is where we found the solution!'

'Tell me, I have only glanced at them I realised they could be useful, I am hoping to read them fully, at my leisure, when I get some, go on what did you find?'

Rebecca continued at a glance from her father, 'well in the oldest of the journals Brenda, is a set of drawings, you told me you had seen them, they outline exactly what the house looked like originally.' Brenda nodded as she had seen the drawings but not realised the true significance of the them till now. 'The stairs and powder room are not original, in fact the apartment stairs and front doors are what was originally rooms blocked off to give the two separate entrances and the stairs to the apartments above. The internal stairs in apartment one were from the drawings a circular stair to the basement!'

Brenda was stunned, again the building was throwing up answers to what she thought would be major problems.

Glen continued, 'in fact it could be quite easy to make a hallway to the rear of the building, for access to the lift and fire escape. It does mean we have to reposition the stained-glass window you found, and remove the powder room!'

'I cannot lose the powder room Glen it will be needed. My job, when I begin it, and hope that what I am about to say does not leave this room please, is not only to manage the building, but organising functions for the people in the building! The apartments are going to be leased, long and short terms, like a holiday letting. The guests will be VIP's that much I can tell you, here for anywhere from a week to six months at a time. So, I will need a powder room somewhere on this floor for use on occasions?'

Glen nodded looking at his children, who nodded in his direction, 'we thought as much Brenda; you would not be so concerned with the state of all the apartments if you were going to sell them off. So, this place will be like a boutique apartment hotel, five or six star?'

Brenda laughed relieved that they understood, it made it so simple that they did, and wanted to help her achieve her goals.

'Well I am aiming for six of course, but will be happy with five and not the two it is at the moment!'

Ben had been conferring with Matt and Charlie, 'hey Brenda, what do you think of moving the powder room into the conservatory? There is this dead space to the left of the stairs as you go down into the area. As we are going to have to put new plumbing and wiring in place for the new basement bathrooms, we could easily have connections there, putting at least one, possibly two powder rooms in the space?'

'That sounds great boys, we will have to get Norman Greenwell the man from Kew, who is going to rejuvenate the Conservatory for us to agree, but I like the idea!'

'They will also be useful out there, when the conservatory is in use not only by you Brenda, but also the other tenants.' Rebecca put in, 'well they will have to be able to access the conservatory, from the lift and fire escape, but won't have to keep running back upstairs to use the loo!'

Everyone laughed, Brenda going and giving her a hug, telling her it was a brilliant idea, but how did they find out that everything they had talked about was feasible?'

'We will find out in a couple of hours,' Glen put in, 'I rang a colleague of mine, Dan Jones.'

'Who just happens to be the owner of the steel works I rang Brenda. He has been waiting as long as Glen to see Bill Gardiner get his just desserts!'

'As I was saying,' Glen glared at Charlie for interrupting, he just laughed and helped himself to a bun. 'Dan was most interested in the project, he is also a structural engineer, so when he gets here we will not only check on the hallway, but the replacing of the original circular stairs to the basement, and the repositioning of the powder room and making it two!'

'I have another request: yes, I know I keep adding to the list. I would like to deaden noise wherever possible. I mean when people are using the powder rooms in the conservatory, I do not want the whole building to know, especially me, if I am in bed, I definitely do not want to hear anything. The new hallway, as sound proof as possible in point of fact I need the whole house to be insulated, not only for soundproofing but for heat and cooling. I also do not want to hear the lift being used, nor should the other tenants be aware of people coming and going. As I have told you VIP's will be using those apartments, I hate to bring the twenty-first century problems into this wonderful place, but any glass will need to be extremely tough, bullet proof in fact Charlie if it exists. I would also like to be as ecologically friendly as possible that goes for everyone. I have already asked Charlie to help with making the windows in this building as energy efficient as possible, I am asking the rest of you to help as well, where possible. I know it is a lot to ask, but I have to try and think of any guest's security and comfort. You can make a guess of the security protocols this building will need, which have not been addressed by the previous 'restoration' work, well they will need to be even better once we actually get up and running!'

A thinking silence descended over everyone, Brenda could see that they had understood her needs, and would try very hard to fulfil all her requests.

'OK Brenda,' Glen broke the silence, 'I think we can do what you ask, but it depends on the engineer's findings, also John the architect was supposed to be furnishing me with details, he said he would be over today didn't he Charlie?'

Charlie nodded his mouth full of bun.

'Well we will get him together with Dan, I had better give Marcus a call,' at Brenda's raised eyebrow at the new name, 'Marcus Cammington, he is the Glass Man, any shape, size or thickness. It might be a good idea to have it slightly tinted, as it would cut down heat and glare, especially round the new lift structure, or can I leave that to you Charlie?' Charlie nodded again, a grin on his face.

'Ok everyone, I want to see how much of the rubbish we can put into the monster skip before it is taken away, might as well use it right to the end. The rest of the lads will be down stairs, so come on you three, Charlie you have glass to replace, stop stuffing your face and get to work!'

Chapter 14

THE MEN LEFT TOGETHER, leaving Brenda going over with Rebecca exactly what she had gleaned from Mia, which was not a lot. Rebecca showing her the fabric and paper swatches they had come up with during their discussions. Rebecca advising that she was trying to match the paper that was in apartment one, not the colour but the design to give some heritage back in the other apartments, but not go too overboard. She would have to wait and see what damage was done as the back doors were reinstated, Mia would be around later, she was scouring warehouses to find the right fabrics and wallpapers to fit with the updated design they had agreed upon.

They both went out and watched as the big skip was removed, after Glen's team had added to it, seeing the smaller skip replace it on the pavement, now allowing pedestrians space to walk through.

Brenda was introduced to Dan Jones, as she expected he would have been an ideal model for an old fashioned black smith. A big man, he towered over her, a big grin on his face seemed to be a permanent fixture. Nothing she believed would trouble this man, he and Glen matched in temperament, and she had no doubt in knowledge of their crafts as well. He was relishing the job as Glen had told him, finding no significant problem with the time frame given. He was waiting for the lift people to arrive, to see what they needed, from his works, to provide the frame for the actual lift, working on the problem of how they were going to camouflage the lift mechanism in the roof area.

'You realise Brenda, that your basement staircase has probably been used in someone's barn conversion, a long time ago. Don't worry though as I am taking photos back to the works, we will have a brand new one, looking the part very quickly!'

'Ah, Mr. Jones about that, I really would like to improve the design if I can, not only of the staircase, but of the building itself. Would it be possible for you to check if we can insulate between the floors, and also the walls of the building, I would also like to put wooden treads or treads we can carpet, into the staircase frame? It would be a lot quieter in the entire house. Especially, as the carpet in the basement has gone and I am not replacing it, the original tiles are still in place have you seen them?'

As he said he had not looked around, and told her to call him Dan, offered to give him a guided tour. Inside was a haven of peace compared to the number of people working in the front yard. As they moved down the internal stairs a shout rang out, they had found the bottom of the basement steps. Brenda moved to the other side of the door, but Ben told her not to open it, they still had a lot of clearing out to do. She moved back to the other end of the hallway to help Dan pull up the timber panelling that was over the floor. He produced a small torch from one of his copious pockets, to check the tiles, moving over to the spot the staircase would have originally rested, found the collar set in the floor for the central pole, and where the bottom tread would have hit the floor a slim steel plate could be seen.

'Marvellous, oh that is going to make my job so much easier. It proves what Rebecca has found Brenda. That originally you had a spiral staircase from basement to first floor, all we need to do is replace it. If you don't want the full metal treads, but something we can add timber too, makes my job a little easier. I can liaise with Glen, do I give estimates to him, or should I send them straight to you?'

'If you can co-ordinate with him, but please send to me,' she handed him one of her business cards, 'I want the new staircase done right Dan, cost is not so much a consideration but quality is.' He nodded in understanding.

They were just replacing the timber sheeting when Glen called down that the lift people were there asking Brenda if all the apartments were open. She told Dan to say everything was unlocked, ready to be checked. Dan gave her a big grin and left with promises of good things to come.

Charlie was coming down the stairs as she stood in her daydream of imagining the people who would have used and cursed a spiral staircase.

'Penny for them Brenda,' she jumped at Charlies voice, then immediately went to give him a hand. She was enlisted to assist in the grand opening of the basement window. The liberal quantities of oil that had been worked into every hinge, lock and bracket in the entire apartment had worked brilliantly. The shutters moved, still taking a little persuasion, back into the niches made for them so long ago. Brenda was a little horrified at the damage to the actual window frames and panes of glass, but Charlie reassured her that it was nothing that he Ben or Matt even, could not fix. Reassured Brenda left him to his work, after he told her he could manage on his own, for now.

She moved upstairs, out the front doors amazed at the difference the removing of the skip had made. The scaffolding of course was still there, but without the large skip it looked so much neater, the house seemed to breathe a sigh of relief. She turned to find a group of men huddled over the bonnet of a car, looking at sketches and diagrams.

'Gentlemen, you can use apartment two as a base to go over things, better than the bonnet of a car!'

'Thank you, Brenda, I didn't want to impose, but it would be good if we can use it as our field office, so to speak?'

'Of course, you can Glen, you know it is just a room to me at the moment, off you go!'

As the men passed her, Glen introduced the new faces to her, John Sark was his foreman and right hand man, the firm handshake and direct look, gave her the right feeling, here was another competent, careful builder. Bill Knowles, was Bill Gardiners foreman, she only got a nod from him, then he turned back to the plans being rolled up. Her hand was taken and vigorously shaken by a slender, scholarly man, Glen introduced him as Marcus Cammington, the glass man, his grey eyes had a twinkle in them, as he kept hold of her hand, thanking her for the opportunity to show off his, and his companies skills. Smiling at his effervescent behaviour, she received a brief salute from both Bill Gardiner and John Hemsworth, as they followed Glen up the stairs. Stopping on the top step wondering where Dan was, to find him inspecting where the original railings had been roughly removed and tossed aside lying in the small garden, sadly shaking his head at such an act of destruction.

Everyone moved into apartment two, Glen quietly asking her to stay, for her input into the proceedings, which drew raised eyebrows from Bill Gardiner and John Hemsworth.

She noticed another new face talking to Matt, when he noticed her gaze, motioned to Matt who moved them over to her.

'Brenda,' Matt started, 'please can I introduce Brent Winegood, from the firm of Winegood and Tate, who are supplying the lift for us.'

Brent started to say something, when Charlie bounced into the room, breathless from his run up the stairs.

'Cannot wait till we get the lift in Brent, it will make it easier to get from the bottom to the top, without straining!'

Glen harrumphed, asking everyone to look at the plans John had come up with overnight, a smug expression on his face at his achievement. After Brent, Dan, Marcus and Charlie had dissected them pointing out the faults and problems with the very over the top fanciful design, his expression was not so smug.

The original drawings by Charlie were retrieved, with an additional set that Dan produced out of a folder; everyone agreed the simple structure that Charlie had drawn the day before, had been transposed into proper structural and building plans; the contrast between the two architects styles was amazing, and Brenda knew which one she preferred, so did Iris, judging by the gardenia floating around.

Brenda wondered how Dan had produced such detailed plans without seeing the structure itself, then realised that Rebecca had been taking photographs of as much as she could, tramping around in the Conservatory, those with Charlie's drawing, were all Dan needed it seemed.

Dan explained that it was possible with the standard lengths of steel he had in stock, vertically and horizontally, to make the frame, that was not a problem, he turned to Brent with a query on his face.

Brent smiled at them all, 'I have never seen such an old building that could so easily be altered to add a lift, and with very little damage. We will have to make alterations to the roof line, but that is only minor, the main mechanism is housed directly over the lift well, therefore needing its own separate roof space, but we will need to extend the existing roof to join this new area to make it seamless, also to get power cables from the house to the lift itself. We do actually have a lift that would be a perfect fit for the build, it was ordered for a building down at Canary Wharf, but never used. There would have to be power on its own, and Matt,' he turned to Matt who was listening with everyone else, 'we will need that on a separate grid, also a small generator for times when power is out, might be a good idea?'

'We will start working on the uprights for the lift.' Dan put into the silence around him, 'my guys at the works eager to get started on Tuesday, we also will be able to have any extra steel for the landings and back doors if needed, we have to see what is there first of course!'

Marcus added in a quiet voice, 'The larger pieces of glass may take a little longer to organise, although we just finished an order that has just been cancelled that might fit the bill, we can just cut them to the measurements, but I don't think the time line is too tight, again like Dan, my guys are eager to begin what is a very unusual request!'

'I believe that structurally, everything is fine, still have to check a couple of things with Dan here as the structural engineer. So, once we are able to check out the outside staircase and the landings with the sheeting removed, then correct measurements can be given to both Marcus and Dan. We can also put in the extra supports for the new lift area, which need to go in very soon, to allow signing off by the building examiners!' Glen finished with a look around the table.

'Gentlemen, can I have a bottom line here?' Brenda asked into the thoughtful silence that followed Glen's statement.

'Well if you want to have a look out the back-window Brenda, you will see that scaffolding is already being raised, over the safely covered conservatory,' a side-glance at Bill Gardiner was all that was needed. 'I rang the council and advised them of what we're doing; they allowed us to take the trucks through the service road onto the commons, as there was no way we could park out the front. A pylon machine will be here on Monday, sorry to the neighbours on a bank holiday. As you know there is a gap on the right-hand side of the conservatory, where the staircase is, so we don't even have to clear much to get a level base. It is all in hand, you will get your fire stairs and lift, and we will be completed in four weeks!'

Brenda was relieved' she had heard only the negatives, not the positives of the conversations. Nodding at Glen, then at the men around her, left and went to do some checking of her inheritance, trying to be around for questions and advice, but not in anyone's way.

Chapter 15

REBECCA AND MIA FOUND her in the midst of a tea chest, still in a daze at what she had been given, still with no idea if valuable or not, although the wafts of gardenia that floated around made her think she had been given something wonderful.

'Brenda, are you busy? Oh, what a lovely pattern, is that a dinner set?'

'Actually, Mia, I am not sure, there are a few boxes that have this decorated crockery, and it may be more than just a dinner set, possibly a tea set as well. I am very confused, but very happy to see you both!'

'I have an Aunt that works with Sotheby's, she could probably recommend someone to come around and check the pieces over for you, if you want?'

'Mia that would be wonderful, I am trying to make an inventory, but I really do not know what I am making an inventory of, apart from this very beautiful dinner set, there are crystal pieces as well. I definitely do not have a clue about the paintings we found, or the ornaments and statues that were hidden away. Would you please contact your Aunt and see if she could help, I would appreciate it? Now what can I do for you young ladies?'

Mia turned to Rebecca asking her to show Brenda what they had set up, while she went to phone her Aunt straight away. Rebecca moved to the folding doors, easily opening just one side, directing Brenda into the dining room. Two trestle tables had been set up, fabric, wallpaper, cushions, blinds and curtain material spread across the two tables, spilling to the floor in a riot of colour. Her dining room had been turned into an Aladdin's Cave, she said to Rebecca, as Mia came back into the room.

'All set Aunt Maud will check with her boss, and see if someone can come around next week. I told her that would probably be all right, judging by the people around at the moment, it is better to wait!'

'Quite right Mia, thank you. Now what have you two girls been up too? I am fascinated by the colours and different design on the wallpaper samples. Definitely love the blue that will suit this place very well, but the maroon is quite stunning!'

Both of them launched into what they had come up with for the updated, old style interiors they had compromised on. Rebecca had mooted a reduced Victorian theme, with accent walls of wallpaper complimenting the original one found in apartment one, and accessories that gave some colour, as they would keep the walls not wallpapered white as it would save some time.

'I like the idea, how about you just do one accent colour per apartment, say the maroon in four, blue in three and green in two? We can keep the silver in this apartment!'

'Why the silver in here Brenda, I thought you might like the blue in here,' Rebecca said as she was moving the samples around the floor to make four distinct places.

'I think I have inherited a lot of blue, but I was thinking of the silver for reflection purposes. To mirror the original paper that still is fantastic, and add to the light factor in the dark hallways, especially the basement hallway!'

'Ah yes, that would make sense, it is quite dark down there, and will be more so when we take out the oblong steps. We could also see about mirrors on one wall to help with reflecting some light?'

Mia was making notes on a pad, sketching in ideas as they came to her. 'This will work, I can almost see it, what about the fireplaces, they were boarded up in all the apartments as well as here, I took the original hearths from two, three and four, wonder if they are still in place in here? John wanted me to throw them into the skip, but I have them safe and sound at my warehouse, I can bring them back at any time to reinstate them?'

Brenda nodded very pleased with the change of attitude in Mia, she was looking at the world through different eyes, some encouragement, and contact with Rebecca helping her see a new path. Brenda motioned to them both to follow her back into the front room, going to a corner of the room, removed the covering from a lumpy pile, to reveal one of the original marble mantles, with its firebox complete with tile surround. Rebecca happily counting up to eleven covered pieces in the corner, 'looks like you have them all one for each room here, and two per apartment!'

'Oh, how wonderful,' Mia gasped, 'I was wondering how we were going to replace all of the fireplaces. I see Iris or her family were thinking two steps ahead again!'

Nodding her head in acknowledgement of the truth in Mia's statement, Brenda moved them back into the dining room.

'Thank you, Mia, please do not take offence, but I do not like the modern soulless decoration that are in the apartments at the moment. I do understand, that at the time you were redesigning this space that was what 'bringing the apartments up to date' brief was thought all you had to do, and you were encouraged to do that!' Brenda put up a hand to forestall the explanation she was sure was about to be given. Mia smiled at her realizing Brenda would understand the limitation she had been working with, mainly in her own mind.

'I have been looking through catalogues,' Brenda continued with a nod, 'as I need to purchase at least five gas fires for apartment one, then I think we can just put back one in the main rooms of the others, or should we put main rooms and main bedroom that will be replacing them all; I will leave that decision to you both. What do you think of this range of gas fire inserts we can put them into the original fire surrounds, now that we have found them. What other pieces have you in your warehouse Mia?'

Mia started to say something when her phone buzzed, 'oops Rebecca we are supposed to be at Mannocks in thirty minutes! Sorry Brenda that's the specialised fabric and wallpaper warehouse, you have to make an appointment to get in and we got a cancellation, if we don't go now it will be another two weeks for the next one. I will check what is at my warehouse in regards to pieces saved, although I don't think there is much apart from the hearths!'

'Go, go leave all this, you can use this room for your storage if you like, only keep it away from the conservatory, there will be a lot of traffic going in and out of those French Doors next week!'

Mia caught her arm as they were walking to the door, she had to make Brenda understand what she now realised.

'Brenda, I want to thank you for giving me a second chance. Rebecca and you have opened my eyes to a new concept, and demolished my previous blinkered view. She has made me doubt the parameters that I was told I should be working with, opening my eyes. Thank you and I am so sorry for the damage I have done to this wonderful house.'

'That's fine Mia; just do a great job from now on. I want a professional job that gives a quality finish these apartments deserve. A five-star luxury hotel feel if that is possible, listen to Rebecca she knows what she is talking about!'

Both of them laughing as they left, Brenda felt a soft breeze and whiff of gardenia, knowing Iris approved.

She wandered up to apartment two, talking into the Dictaphone she used to record her jumbled thoughts, when she heard raised voices as she walked through the door. She was still recording when she found the source of the voices in the laundry.

'It's criminal, that is what it is, and you should know better Bill. How were you and that architect going to get the building certificate, how many bribes where you prepared to make?'

'Now see here Glen, you can't say that there is anything wrong with this work, just because we cut a few corners, Pickworth was never going to see anything wrong. Don't tell me you; and you Dan have never cut a few corners in a build here and there?'

'Cut corners, I can't say that I have, you give a quality product to people prepared to pay for it, and I know they have, but this, man you cannot be serious, this is not a small matter!'

Brenda could hear Dan adding a few words decided to step in.

'Gentlemen, it is nearly lunchtime, do you think we need to take a break? What are you doing in here?'

Glen, Dan, Bill and his foreman Bill Knowles turned as she spoke.

'Ah Brenda,' Glen turned towards her, 'we are checking where the back door should be. With the scaffolding up to this level, we sent a workman up the stairs, he declared them very safe and solid, he put a drill through the wall below the lintel, which is still in place. We thought we would find out what state the wall was in so we can organise a new back door, and see how we are going to fix the new and improved landing to the building again, if need be!'

Brenda nodded and then looked over Glen's shoulder to what seemed to be a bit of timber sheeting and some insulation hanging out of it.

'Well when we put the drill through, and found where the door was in here, went to pull down what should be the double brick wall, all we found was a bit of plywood and insulation to make it sound solid, with only the outside brick in place, not the solid double brick wall the safety code requires!'

Brenda could see why Glen was angry, but she could also see that Bill's lax manner and his workmen's lack of respect for the building code; and she noted Bill Knowles very guilty look; was yet another gift from Iris and the house, helping to restore it within her time frame.

'Why thank you Mr. Gardiner, you have surely done all of us a big favour!'

Glen's jaw dropped at the unexpected praise, he started to round on Brenda, but Dan held him back; he had seen the Dictaphone in Brenda's hand, that was now hidden in a fold of her jumper, still recording.

'Yes, well thank you Ms Chalmers, it was an expedient use of time and materials, that I realise now was the wrong thing to do, but of course it helps us to complete the renovations within your new time frame!'

'Did you happen to do this with all the doors, and just how did you fix the attic apartment, with all the building regulations that you need to complete?' Brenda asked quietly. He started to explain the how's and whys, while behind him, Glen's face registered understanding, Dan was trying not to laugh at this man slowly hanging his company's reputation and himself.

Bill Gardiner began to get into his role of astute builder and read from his notes, ignoring the frantic motions that Bill Knowles, neatly blocked by Dan, was making. Blindly Bill told of how they had shored up the ceiling in the attic, and how with a minimum of work for maximum payment they had altered the apartments for their coats of gloss white paint.

'Well,' Brenda said in a pause, not wanting this farce to go on any longer, 'I think that is all we needed to hear. Please take yourself and workmen, along with Mr. Hemsworth. Please ask him to leave all drawings and plans would you, and leave the job site immediately. I think Pickworths has had quite enough of your slipshod and dangerous business practices. We can continue from now on without you, your company and associates assistance!'

Bill Gardiner could not believe his ears, he; he was being fired. Too late he looked at Bill Knowles red face, and realised his pride and arrogance had made him brag, as he thought being a female she would be impressed. He looked at the woman who seemed so pleasant and weak, realising she was in fact a very strong willed lady.

'What about my final bills, Sir James will be hearing from me, we attend the same clubs you know!'

Glen snorted, 'after the substandard job you have managed to do on the over the top quote you submitted, and yes I have seen it. I think you have been paid over and above what the job was worth. If I could I would be telling Sir James to stop the cheques, but I bet you both have already cashed them. The bill for the extra scaffolding and what is here already will be sent to your company Bill, I suggest you leave now and pay that bill when it comes in!'

'You will be hearing from my solicitors, we had a contract with Sir James, he is the only one who can cancel it. You have not heard the last of this, I promise you!'

Brenda did not wait to hear any more, knowing Glen and Dan would see the three men, minus anything to do with the build off the premises. Humming a happy tune, she switched off the useful Dictaphone, and went up the stairs to apartment four. Ben, Matt,

Glen's foreman John Sark and Brent were trying to work out how they could raise the roof, get a lift mechanism in place and covered, without seeing the outside, the scaffolding had not reached the attic yet. Brenda advised them not to worry, as she just knew that the staircase would reach the attic area, Lord Lucas would have made sure it did.

'By the way gentlemen, I will reiterate what I have said before, this lift housing must be in soundproof surroundings!'

Brent turned first, the others following 'Why?'

'Well just think on this; you have paid over two million pounds, which I am told an apartment in this part of the city would be worth, for your five-star luxury pied-a-terre, right in the heart of London. You move in and all you hear all day and night is the sound of gears and cogs working when the lift goes up and down! I think you would be seriously pissed off, rightly so, don't you think?'

Ben and Matt both knew what Brenda wanted, but were having a hard time convincing Brent of this, as he was sure that being out from the building would be sufficient noise protection. Having Brenda being so explicit in her requirements, made him rethink this as he realised it would not be.

'It is lunchtime fellas; come on a break is needed. It is one o'clock, and I have been going since five, you lot earlier than that. You boys,' she pointed to Ben and Matt, 'need to go and see your father and Dan, oh yes, the Haddon's are going to be busy people!'

As Brenda and the boys made their way down from the attic, Dennis with enough sandwiches and rolls to feed an army was coming into the house. Passing on the way three very disgruntled and angry men on the way out.

'What has gotten into those three?' he asked as he walked into apartment two, he nodded at the stairs.

'Long story and will be better told at leisure, over a long relaxing dinner. Dennis, can you please make sure everyone has a break for lunch, I have to go and see someone very quickly!'

Dennis nodded, Brenda was gone with a quick detour to the table, checking on her phone that the person she had to see was at the office, almost as quickly as the three men, whose cars could be heard revving, tyres screaming away from the building.

Linda was in the office as Brenda hoped she would be. Looking up in surprise as she walked in, 'what four o'clock already?'

'No, but I thought I had better give you a heads up, before all hell breaks loose!' Linda just raised an eyebrow for her to continue. 'I have just fired the original building team, oh with the exception of Mia, she has been led to a better path!'

'I hope you had just cause, they had contracts!'

'Oh, yes all photographed and documented, they had a choice, walk or I charged them with gross negligence and fraud. We also have verbal confirmation from one of them about how they had ripped Pickworths off, and the dodgy building practices they had that were commonplace. Yes, all witnessed and caught on tape, I think you had better warn Sir James that he is going to be receiving a couple of angry phone calls!'

Relief washed over Linda, finally they had the proof to dismiss them, as they had wanted to for months. 'Well you have done a great job, and you definitely have sufficient reason for dismissal. Perhaps Sir James should just casually mention to some of his associates that he had to let that particular firm go!' Brenda nodded a smile forming on her lips, 'ah, who did he get to step in at short notice to complete such a specialised renovation?'

Brenda smiled a little more, handed over a "Haddon & Son's" business card.

'I will not be around later, I am going home via the bottle shop, and buy at least a dozen bottles of wine to begin my wine cellar, a meal I can heat up, if my designers have kitted out the kitchen with a microwave, put on some relaxing music and be in bed by eight!'

'Music how can you put on some music, those items have not been added yet, I know!'

'Ah, well you see, I told you about my boxes, it is amazing what you can put into a standard shipping box!'

WITH THAT PARTING COMMENT, Brenda turned and walked out the door, feeling much better and very sure she had made the right decision. She was even more certain as she walked into Steel Street from her shopping. There was a change to the feel of the place, the huge ugly skip had gone, even with the new smaller one, and the scaffolding still up there was a subtle change to the to feel of the whole street.

The garbage that is usually associated and scattered around a building site was gone, the area was clean and neat again. You could see the walls and tiny garden, which someone had even cleared of weeds, with the steel staircase leading to the basement door. Everything had been swept clean, then hosed down, Brenda realised that the building would need to be painted, something that the original builders had not started, or even thought about, she mused. She could see the main doors painted a deep rich red, making a mental note to ask Rebecca and Mia about it, she was smiling as she walked up the clean steps and into apartment two.

Looking around the kitchen, wondering what she was going to put the flowers she had bought on impulse, Iris's being prominent into, when she saw the vase that had been in one of her boxes was washed and on the shelf in the kitchen, '*Thank you Nona,*' she thought. She moved to get it and felt a breeze on her cheek, following the fresh air into the laundry found a timber panel in place, sealed with duct tape, stuck on it was a note: -

Brenda,

DO NOT THINK OF GOING OUT OF THIS
SPACE, UNTIL YOU HAVE A HARD HAT,
TOMORROW! Glen.

'Brenda, are you back?' was yelled down the stairs.

'In apartment two Glen,' she yelled back.

'Come up to four, if you are free will you please?'

'Charlie, went back to the workshop, said he would be back tomorrow, with more pies, (Gabby my daughter is his wife, takes after her mum) not early as he had some final details to attend to for a project he was working on, do you know anything about a project?' Glen asked her as she walked into the Laundry room in apartment four.

'Glen there are so many things happening around here, I cannot think of which of the fifty or more that are on the go he would mean!'

Ben, Matt and Dan all laughed at that, but it was true. How they were going to get everything finished in four weeks Brenda did not know. Then she looked at the determined faces in front of her, *these men just loved a challenge*, she thought, *and by god I think they will do it, after all we have Iris on our side.*

Glen motioned for her to move over to the where the original fire escape door space had been revealed, the scaffolding was complete, but Glen held her back when she went to move out the doorway, 'oh no, not without that hard hat madam, tomorrow. You can just lean out and look at the space quickly. It is amazing, that man may have saved our bacon, by not doing what his architect told him too. That fool wanted to pull down the staircase, how they were going to get the building certificate without a fire escape I do not know. But all Bill's team did was to enclose it, John apparently came up with the corrugated iron sheets as a stop gap, never touched the crown of the stairs, or damaged how it was attached to the roof, or the building. It looks as though we can adapt what is there to suit our needs with very little damage. Anyway, we don't have to worry about them for a while at least, see what the men have been doing next to the conservatory Brenda?'

'We have marked the position of the six-new foundation supports; very nice area in that basement that I doubt anyone knew about, we drill and pour concrete tomorrow, for the two in the garden, then leave for forty-eight hours to cure. We can then crane in the steel to make the frame for the lift, with a bit of luck we should have a working lift by the end of next week. Once we have the outside work done, the scaffolding can be removed and we can then concentrate on finishing the apartments, and really getting stuck into yours. Four weeks Brenda, I promise you we will be finished in four weeks!'

'I know Glen, I do not have a doubt that you and your incredible team will have this all done for me in four weeks. But, why six supports, and why two in the garden, you should only need four according to the plans? Hey, Glen do you think you could possibly put a ramp from my apartment landing into the garden, possibly even one leading into the conservatory as well?'

Brenda turned as Glen also turned to the rest of the men in the room, 'and that gentlemen all, is why we have marked six holes not four, pay up please!'

She laughed with them as they all pulled out wallets and passed a five pound note over to a very happy smiling Glen.

Raising an eyebrow in question, Ben jumped in, 'Dad said when he saw the amended plans, and could see just what space there was out the back of the building, as soon as you saw the space, you would ask for a ramp into the garden next to the conservatory, and also would be asking if access into the conservatory could happen. Brent then asked how could you envisage that as you Brenda had no idea as to exactly what the 'garden' entailed apart from the conservatory. Dad then bet us all that within five minutes of being able to see out of one of the higher laundry doors, what you would ask, and you did, my father a sheer genius!'

Everyone laughed again, Brenda going up and giving him a hug, just happy in the atmosphere that surrounded them, with the gardenia floating around, Iris was also happy. There was purpose, purpose with a clear and defined reason and goal, to bring the house into the Twenty-first Century for sure, but not destroy the heart and soul of the beautiful building. It was clear now that everyone concerned was in the same mind.

'Well time to pack up, we cannot do much more today. Please do not go out on to any of the landings, they are quite solid, but some of the sheets used to encase it are very loose, I don't think much of the footings they used either!'

'I promise to restrain myself Glen, I am about bushed anyway, its paper work a glass of red and hopefully a decent night's sleep for me!'

They all left after seeing to a temporary cover for the door, Brenda followed them, securely checking and locking all the internal apartment doors on the way down. Dan and Glen were waiting outside apartment two for her, the others said good night and left.

'We just wanted to show you the proposed layout of the new hallway! We really won't know how exactly it will work until we demolish the walls in place at the moment. The doors into the building will remain in the same position, but we will rebuild them both with wider openings to allow for easy wheelchair access. With windows in the doors and possibly a window in-between them to allow for more light. There is a good-sized floor space before the steps begin, so tomorrow we check the supports for the stairs, then perhaps take the wall down!'

They moved into apartment one, Brenda seeing the masking tape on the plastic covering the floor, about two-thirds the way across the existing stairs, we are actually just halving the space from the edge of the apartment stairs and the sitting /dining room wall, putting a hall down the middle. When we remove the existing powder room, we will see how much space we have to work with. I am waiting for Dan here to give us the first of our miracles,' as her questioning look Glen continued, 'your new stairs. At the moment, we will need to have those in place before we can remove the existing one, and then replace the wall between your apartment and the hallway to the back of the house. Although Dan here found the post and plate for the original staircase, we may have to move it towards your new wall, just to utilise the space better. Well we will see, don't want to use the newly cleaned basement door until the scaffolding is down, it is just too dangerous. We won't be in too early tomorrow, it is Sunday, there also will not be as many workmen for the next couple of days, we will increase the number towards the end of next week to assist in the construction of the lift well!'

'I wondered why you just didn't move the scaffolding from the front to the back Glen, although it is great that you did not, as I now want to have the place painted, but why didn't you?'

'Charlie, he didn't want us to take it down, so if you want to have the place painted, which will be the icing on the cake, let's just leave it. Bill Gardiner then cannot use it anywhere else and make a mess. You don't need a painter, do you?'

'I do, so please get whoever you recommend to come around, or talk to Rebecca please, she knows him too?' at Glen's nod and smile, 'probably need him from the middle or end of next week?'

Dan was smiling, 'Well for my part you will just have to wait and see. We also need to check the floor for how they repaired it when they removed the first circular stairs, but I don't see it as a problem. You have not been tempted to take up the plastic on the floor and look Brenda?'

'No, until we have too, I don't want to remove any protection for whatever is under there, and I don't think we will be disappointed, there is time yet. When we take it up to check for the staircase we can check a little of what is down then, if need be I have Mia and Rebecca on standby with carpet!'

'So, we can check when we get the wall and powder room down, Ben and the boys doing that tomorrow aren't they Glen?'

'Yes, I need to ask if we can utilise the bathrooms in the other apartments, thank you,' as Brenda nodded, 'it means we don't have to bring in porta-loo's, the council and neighbours will be pleased.'

'So, we get organised, we will get the revised plans into the council, get the inspectors out to see what we are doing on Tuesday, I don't see any problems with that!'

'No, you don't,' Dan turned to him, 'because you do not have to bribe anyone, you just do good work from the beginning!'

Both men laughed and left, wishing her a peaceful night. Brenda left apartment one after a last look around, taking her camera, she took pictures to record the monumental changes being worked on the once lonely and abused building. She lovingly handled the silk fabrics on the trestle tables and watched as evening settled over the conservatory. Not long before you sparkle again, she promised. A knock at the door broke into her day dreaming, it was Dennis, on the doorstep, take away dinner in hand.

'Not sure if you had plates, but we can eat out of the boxes, I want a full description of what went on today! Now where is your corkscrew?'

She laughed, closing the front door and securing apartment one, took the proffered bottle and pushed him up the stairs.

Chapter 17

BRENDA WOULD HAVE TO do something special for those two girls, she thought as she stretched. After she and Dennis had demolished the food, heated in the microwave that had appeared in the kitchen, finished a full bottle of red between them, she had kicked Dennis out and gratefully crawled into her bed. Remade with new linen, in a room that was homely with new accessories completed by curtains that completely blocked out the light. The morning sun did not wake her, but Glen and the team leaning on the doorbell!

'Come on lazy bones,' Ben yelled into the intercom, 'it's 9am time to do some demolition, my favourite part of building!'

Brenda laughed, coming down in her robe, let them into apartment one, then went to get dressed and put on the urn, another new addition to the kitchen, clearly Rebecca knew what her father's crew required to make them happy, everyone would be wanting a hot morning cuppa.

She was amazed when she went down the stairs to find all the pieces of the powder room, cleaned and wrapped placed on plastic in the front room.

'No need to waste them Brenda,' Ben said at her comment, 'if you don't want to use them, we can always give them to one of the groups that build homes and shelters for charity. Failing that we can put them on eBay?'

'I have heard about those groups Ben, let us just wait and see how the plans come out, but if they do not fit with Rebecca or Mia's design to charity they go, not eBay!'

He grinned, it was infectious, 'it's ok Brenda, I wouldn't do it, just wanted to see your face,' laughing he turned back toward the rear of the house and where everyone had congregated.

Matt appeared, 'I have cut the power in here, it is so neat that all the apartments have their own power source, much easier to work with!' Both men had that wonderful expression of a puppy waiting for a stick to be thrown, Brenda could not help but laugh with them. Glen appeared cup in hand, he obviously needed his morning cup of tea, urging his sons to get on with it, he wanted to see what he was working with. Smiling broadly, Matt took his father's cup took a swig, moving out of reach as he gave him playful swipe, pulling Ben and a couple of workmen with him.

'I promise you all a full and hot cuppa very soon!' Brenda called after them, 'that must be stone cold if you made it here Glen, as I know the urn is not hot yet!'

'Ah Brenda lass I bring my own, well Julie made it for me in a flask, and he pointed to the trestle table out of the way, where he had put his flask for safe keeping. 'Did the boys bring up the baking?'

'Yes, thank you, I saw the boxes in the kitchen. When this is all over, I hope to be able to have Julie, yourself and everyone here for dinner, to enjoy the treasures I have been finding.' He turned to answer when a hammer blow drowned him out.

The powder room took very little effort and time to take down. Once done the wall with the window was revealed and looked very unsafe indeed.

Glen took one look at the bottom of the wall, then at Brenda's worried face.

'Ok, I will call it morning tea break, that wall doesn't look too good, and I don't want to take any chances with the window. We will wait for Charlie and Dan, they will not be too far away. So, quick cuppa to wake everyone up, the water is hot in apartment two!'

Brenda was pleased with Glen's caution; she had put the boards back over the window but was still worried about its safety. She found herself in a queue to get her coffee, noting the three new faces lining up with them.

'Did they work for Bill, Glen?' she quietly asked.

'Aye lass, they did, but before Bill they worked for me. Damned fine workers, near broke my heart to let them go, but I wasn't getting the jobs. They approached me the other day, and told me a few things, asking if I was hiring again, as they no longer wanted to work for our friend, ashamed of what they had done because they needed the wages. I took them on, as they know what they have done here, and will make the job go that much quicker, hope I can keep them, after this?'

'Don't worry Glen,' Brenda put her arm around his shoulder, as gardenia floated around, 'I think Haddon's & Sons is going to have a little upsurge in jobs very soon!' Glen was startled, but nodded his head.

'Right then, you lot, tea break over! Jock (to one of the new men) you go with Matt, he has to check the electrics are safe and bring in the generator from the van, with the lights, we are going to need to see what we are doing. Fred, George will be ready to cut the new stud work for the wall once we have the figures.!'

Teacups were all put in the sink, with a nod to Brenda from the happy crew as they left the apartment. The place was quiet, until Ben started whistling off key.

Brenda was struck again by the difference in attitude from the days before. No sullen looks or shouted instructions, even to the subdued use of swear words. The men knew what they had to do, clear and precise instructions were given, all needed equipment and materials were ready. Glen and his team were damned good, old fashioned builders that took pride in their work, and importantly their people.

She had finally found time to sit at her laptop, hoping to be able to transfer all the information she had been given, into the accounts she had set up. Spreadsheets had never been her forte but she was persevering, at least she understood what she was doing. The sound of quiet industry was soothing, she kept going to the top of the stairs to listen to some of the conversations that floated up to her from the ground floor. Enjoying the feel of people in the space, the smell of gardenia wafted around her as she listened.

A cheer went up, and a few minutes later Charlie came running up the stairs.

'The powers that be have decided to redo the shape of your kitchen Brenda. So that wonderful window has to be moved for safety. I have also been working on that curve ball you gave me, come on give us a hand!'

Glen and the team were standing by, the lights had been set up in the hallway, gave the brightest light that had been in the area since the building was split up. Charlie had removed the original covers over the window, handed Brenda a sheet of plywood, with sponge and quilted padding on one side, he had another they both fitted the internal dimensions of the window perfectly. The wall up to the window had been removed; showing one side of the steel frame the glass was set in. Charlie went into the apartment, putting his plywood in place, motioning for Brenda to do the same. Ben then slotted a flat plastic tie through a gap between brick and frame, winding it across the plywood tightening it slowly, he did three around and two top to bottom. Charlie told Ben to stay where he was, with Matt and Glen coming up to help as Charlie cut the metal pieces anchoring the window to wall, slowly tilting it towards Brenda and the guys. More hands appeared, including Dan's making sure the window was supported while the bottom pieces were cut free. Once it was out, and placed in the second box that Charlie had made, everyone breathed a sigh of relief, moving the whole thing into the front room for safety.

'Dan glad you could make it!' Glen yelled through the window space, 'what do you think? Will we have any problems structural wise, I got the boys to take down part of the wall, I didn't think it was load bearing?'

'It probably isn't Glen; I have been studying the plans. Rebecca gave them to me so I could check a few things, you don't mind do you Brenda?'

'Dan if it helps I don't mind at all, I am now more determined than ever to read those journals, everyone is finding useful information in them but me!'

'I know, if it helps I am not reading the actual journals, just checking the plans and drawings in there. Glen did you ever wonder how they could just close a couple of rooms, put in a staircase and convert the building into apartments? Well they could because this house, possibly the whole street is built on steel grids, alternating steel grids, along with the steel uprights to the roof, so in fact all the internal walls are not load bearing, you can make any configuration you want!'

'You are kidding me!' Glen's face had lit up with a beaming smile, 'you are not, are you. Oh boy, does that make me feel so much better. I was wondering how we were going to support the upper floors staircase, give Brenda her wall and still be safe. Oh, boy thank you original architect, thank you. Brenda, you do not know how lucky you are!'

'Don't I Glen, I have watched my fair share of renovation programmes on the TV, don't think I did not have concerns about removing walls and supporting staircases. But I knew we would figure something out, I have seen this place done in my dreams. With that piece of good news, I ask you to check if we can insulate between the floors as well, I would like if we could insulate everywhere, internal and external walls, not only for heating and cooling purposes, but for noise cancelling between the apartments, can I leave you both to sort that out please, perhaps blown in insulation will work? So, what do we do now?'

Dan just laughed with them all at her enthusiasm, 'I get to check that the journals were correct, in fact I am going over every inch of this place, and I will check on your request for insulation. Where we put the new doors out to the landings, in the apartments. We mark out your new kitchen and dividing wall then wait for the inspectors to come on Tuesday, to give the all clear for our new building. We hope to have the plans all printed by then, my architect is working on them for us!'

Glen nodded at each item Dan said, confirming the order of work over the next few days.

'What size doors are you putting in the back here, and the access to the fire escape in all the apartments Glen, as they cannot be a bog standard one, they will all have to be a little wider to accommodate wheelchairs. I was thinking down here if you put glass in the door surrounds, a glass panel above and in the door, itself, that should also help the light situation. If we can have glass topped doors, possibly barn doors, that match the one out of the kitchen in apartment one it will add to the continuity in the house, that will also help with light in the laundries as well!'

Brenda had motioned to both of the men down the now opened space that was her secret room. She pointed out in the brightness from the arc lights the space there was in the back wall. 'This was probably a set of double doors, when you get full access to the outside staircase, I bet you five pounds that landing is wide and stretches from the edge of the house to just past the back door in my apartment, and I also bet the original lintel for a double door is still there as well!'

Glen was looking at the wall, 'I was going to order a slightly wider door, as I wanted to give you most of the room back for your kitchen!'

'I will get quite a bit back Glen, I think a wider door and glass around it will be a better idea, with a new window at the front, glass panels in the doors and frame, surely that will give enough light during the day. We will just have to wait on Matt and Charlie to come up with something wonderful for the night!'

'Well lass, if you are sure that is what we will do. Now as to the new kitchen wall, I want to put a slight kink in it, going straight from this door once replaced, to just under where the top of the staircase is on the first floor, angle it slightly, then straight to the front wall. This eliminates blind corners, and it is easier for wheelchairs, it is an elegant solution without losing too much, what do you think?'

'That sounds fine Glen, I don't think it will take too much away from my kitchen, as long as you have measurements for Rebecca, Mia and the architect to work with!'

'I had better get cracking on taking some of those measurements so we can get them to your architect Dan. It is his son-in-law Brenda, damned good one too,' he said in an aside. 'Come up with those drawings you produced didn't he Dan?' Dan smiled and nodded he was engrossed in the measurement he was taking.

He was flabbergasted by the feat of engineering that he was seeing before him, and it took a lot to stun him. He thought he had seen it all, but this house kept throwing things at him, kept him unbalanced in a way. He did not know if he liked it or not, all he knew was that he was having the time of his life, with people who were along for the ride, the smile just kept appearing on his face.

Chapter 18

BRENDA LEFT THE MEN to the job of tidying up all the debris from the destruction, moved upstairs to tidy the tea cups from the morning cuppa, they would be needed again. She also needed a respite from the shocks she was getting from this house. It had only been four days; four days and already you could see what was to be. They had done so much she kept waiting for the bubble to burst, thinking the inspectors on Tuesday would find something to stop her. She just had to get this job completed in four weeks, although she knew she had six, wanted to enjoy the house for two weeks before her first guest was to arrive. Then her real job would begin. For the first time, she wondered who they would be, couples, singles, celebrities or mega moguls. They would all get the same treatment at 'Iris House'; she stopped in her tracks, wondering how she could register the name.

A tapping noise interrupted her thoughts, looking around saw Charlie on the scaffolding outside the window, motioning her to come over. Puzzled she wondered what he was doing, as he shouted for her to help open the window. It was a little reluctant and took both their efforts, but it moved eventually.

'Yet another example of the standards of Mr. Bill Gardiner's Building Company,' Charlie said as he checked the window, 'probably didn't bother to take out the sashes and check them, yet another thing on my list, check all of the windows!' Brenda was watching for Charlie to give her the answer as to why on a Sunday he was on the scaffolding two floors up!

'As I said downstairs, when we took the window out in the kitchen wall, I have been working on the curve ball, you gave me when we first met!' At Brenda's questioning look, 'remember, to make the windows energy efficient,' at her dawning look of comprehension, 'well I thought about the design, then thought if I was going to make it energy efficient might as well make it bullet proof too. Marcus and I discussed the idea, don't worry he thinks you want the protection for possible bomb attacks, by the way he thinks you are a little paranoid, to stop him being suspicious I agreed!' He ducked as Brenda tried to swipe him on the arm, he moved out of the way and signalled for Jack to help him hoist up what appeared to be another window.

'Yes, it is another window, identical in dimensions to the original, but with the modern steel techniques we have today a whole lot thinner, I have been plaguing Dan and his team, but they came up with this yesterday, I just added the glass, we situate it no more than 5cms away from the original frame. You can still open the inside window, as you normally would, you can also slide this window up, but only 10cms, enough for air but not much else to get through!'

As Charlie was speaking the black frame and glass appeared, so did Jack who nodded a hello. Then they both set the new window in front of the original, immediately the difference was apparent, the light quality had a slightly smoked appearance, but it was the lack of noise from in front of her that impressed Brenda. It took a few moments to jiggle and secure the new window in place. Charlie jumped down the scaffolding and ran into the apartment.

'What do you think? That is not bad at all for a first attempt: here let's just pull the inside window down again and check!'

Together they carefully pulled the inside window down in place and stepped back to take a look.

'That is wonderful Charlie, you don't notice the outside window, it is a mirror image, you came up with that in three days, you ought to get a bonus!'

Brenda could not help it she turned and gave Charlie a hug, and kiss on the cheek.

'You are a wonder Charlie Waines and your blood is worth bottling!'

Charlie, slightly embarrassed as Jack was still watching from the outside of the window blushed brightly. 'Thanks Brenda, you don't know how much this job means to all of us, we just want to do well. Now I have the second windows for the front, Dan was not impressed with the speed the powder coating was done, but I was persuasive. Minus apartment one, I am still working on that, it's the bay shape it is a killer! The works have promised the rear windows very soon as well. So, Jack and I had better get on with it, we have to wash all of them first, now have to check the sashes. I will see if I can get Ben or Matt to give me a hand, they can at least help us haul them up the scaffold!'

Laughing at his obvious discomfort at her praise, she watched him leave, blew a kiss to Jack on the scaffolding, he quickly moved down to meet Charlie at the bottom.

Brenda went back to the computer and worked steadily, listening to the sounds of the workmen downstairs, chatting to them when they came for a break, and occasionally glimpsing Charlie or Jack as they worked on another window. Slowly the noise decreased, Dan and Glen appeared at the door.

'All the workmen have gone Brenda. Calling an early day probably won't be much we can do tomorrow either, apart from digging the supports for the ramps. We will see, what do you think of the windows, can we see them from the inside?'

They both moved over to the window looking out onto the street. With all of them in place the noise level had been greatly reduced, it was a very peaceful area.

'Love the smoky colour the glass gives the room, he is a clever lad that Charlie. Knew right away that he had ideas in his head, what do you think Brenda?'

'I think he is worth his weight in gold, but won't tell him. I also think someone should tell him to take a patent out on this solution.' They looked a question at her, 'have you seen how many houses there are in this street alone, you all could make a fortune!'

They both laughed realising she was right, 'did you get done what you wanted today, both of you? I didn't know if you wanted my help so just kept out of the way, you knew where I was if you needed me.'

'There was not much to do Brenda,' Dan said, 'we really have to wait the Inspectors before we can go much further. Get the foundations in and set so they can give us the go ahead inside and out on Tuesday. That is when they are coming right Glen?'

'Yes, Dan all arranged, they cannot wait to see what we are doing, as they had no reports from the last lot, I have an idea they did not know building work was going on! Ah well we will see on Tuesday, but we will see you tomorrow Brenda, be here about ten, it is a holiday, I think the neighbours have been disturbed enough!'

Brenda walked them out and down to the ground floor, shocked as when she started to walk down the stairs she could see both the front doors. The whole ground floor could be seen from front to back. She could see the internal folding doors wrapped and propped carefully against the far wall, with the stairs down to the basement, in the centre of the floor, looking a little out of place, but had been given a temporary balustrade around the opening for safety. Everything was swept clean, temporary sheeting placed on the floor, it was the neatest building site Brenda had ever seen.

'I have to hand it to you both, when you work, you work very well indeed. This is just amazing.' They both looked a bit flustered at the praise, but saw Brenda meant what she said. They went out, with her following to say goodbye to the rest of the men. Cheerfully waving and calling see you tomorrow, Brenda went back inside closing both the doors, wondering what Dennis, Linda and Sir James would say if they could see the place at the moment.

Chapter 19

ONDAY, IT WAS MONDAY! Brenda had to keep reminding herself of how long she had been on this job. No, she thought, it wasn't really a job at the moment, it was a labour of love. The job part would come in about three weeks, if all went well. She laughed as she remembered Dennis comments when he came around for his inspection the previous evening. Flabbergasted, shocked and wondrous of the space, would cover the main points. He had invited her out to his favourite noodle bar for dinner, as he could see she needed a break. She had agreed but insisted on paying, as she now had money to do so. He argued a bit, but eventually she won, and they had a great night. She went to bed happy and content that all would be well. Iris and the house itself were helping, how could they fail.

Monday, it was Monday, she had showered put the coffee and urn onto heat. Was pottering around checking details on the plans that had been left, wondering how the new plans Peter, Dan's son in law would come up with. Dan had also said Peter was working with Rebecca on the new kitchen design, as well as the lift housing at apartment four. She was at the intercom before it had stopped beeping.

'Did not think we would catch you twice Brenda, good morning.' Glen said as he walked into the apartment, carrying the morning tea box. 'Julie sends her regards, and accepts the invitation to dinner whenever it occurs. She put a special treat in there for you, hope you like chocolate!'

Glen handed over a smaller box today, there were going to be less workers, but on top was the most delicious looking chocolate éclair, Brenda had seen. 'It looks delicious and very fattening Glen, thank Julie for me. If you give me a home number I will call her directly to arrange a date, as she is I assume the Social Director for the Haddon Family, she is the one I ring to organise with?'

'You assume right Brenda, here let me write the number down before I forget.' He found a notepad on the table and wrote his number and address, adding Dan's families as well. 'Might as well give you Dan's, they live just down the road on the next farm over, his wife is fit to burst over this place. In fact, I think you have the whole village interested, you may have a best seller on your hands if you ever make that 'Renovation Photo Album' public. I know of at least ten people who would buy one!'

'Buy one of what,' Dan's voice came from the doorway, he came through slightly ducking his head, introducing Peter to Brenda.

'The Renovation Photo Album Dan. Hello Peter nice to see you again, has this man had you working the midnight oil, you look a bit peaky?'

'No Mr. Haddon, I just had the flu, that was why I was at home. Beverly and the kids didn't need to get it Dan suggested I stay in the barn to get over it. I just happened to be in the right place at the right time, would not have missed this for the world. Ms. Chalmers, thank you for letting me help, Dan has been telling me what a remarkable place you have here. You don't mind my being here do you, I am not contagious any more, just don't seem to have much energy!'

Peter would have been called a tall, very athletic man, if he had not been standing amongst Dan, Ben and Glen! He looked a little scrawny next to the three large individuals they were, yes, he did still look a little peaky. Brenda took the proffered hand and welcomed him to the fold, hoped he would come and visit anytime, his plans had been invaluable.

'Just don't bring those two mischief makers, don't think we can look after them at present!' Dan put in gruffly, but the twinkle in his eyes belied the gruff voice.

'Dan means my boys, his two grandsons, Mark and Adam. They are four years old, twin's boys and into everything, especially things they are not meant to be in!' Peter rolled his eyes and made grabbing motions, 'I think that was the reason Beverly, my wife, suggested I go and stay with her parents. I do not have any family, so it was kind of them to offer and take me in!'

'Yes, well don't go on,' Dan said gruffly, everyone could see he was trying to hide his discomfort in being seen in so kindly terms, 'come on Peter show the lady the plans you have come up with!'

'Oh, that reminds me Ben did you bring that box up from the car, the one for Benda, because you know we won't be able to restrain her for long!' Ben nodded and pulled a box out from behind his back, and presented it to Brenda, everyone eagerly watching for her reaction.

Inside the box was a silver hard hat, painted on the front was "Lady B", her very own hard hat. She laughed and hugged everyone, putting it on to show it was a fit. Telling Glen that he should not have done it, as they really did have no way of stopping her climbing the outside stairs, she wanted to see the view from the top!

Peter had been unrolling plans, much different to the ones John Hemsworth had submitted. These were clearer, no fussy side and cross diagrams, at least not on the main page. It showed the lift at the side of the landings, the enclosure being incorporated into the existing steel fire escape, with a plan underneath showing the glass outer shell enclosing the whole; landings, stairs and lift it was beautiful in its simplicity. The main outer shell, ran from the side of the house, around the original staircase, encompassing the landings, down into the garden and across to the conservatory, it was a modern-day vertical conservatory for the staircase.

'Is there any way we can divert any rain into tanks?' Brenda mused, as she looked at the plans, 'it would be a shame for it all to go into the storm water drains?'

The men around the table gave a collective groan. 'Brenda please, don't come up with anymore ideas, we are going to have enough of a problem as it is!' Glen said.

'But Dad, we have to see what is really at the bottom of that staircase, haven't really explored down there, while we have the crane, there may be a space for a rainwater tank?'

Glen turned and looked at Ben, then at Matt who was nodding his head, as though seeing his sons for the first time, he then just sat down at the table with his head in his hands, he was shaking. No one knew whether it was laughter, tears or anger. He finally looked up tears of laughter running down his face.

'I knew it, I just knew it, you yes you Brenda Chalmers, what have you done to my sons! Oh, it's Brenda won't like that, oh Brenda won't like the pink hat dad, or Brenda likes these buns mum, what are you doing to my sons"

Brenda took a step back, wondering if she had done something wrong. Then saw the laughter in Dan's face, the look of amusement on Peter's, the utter look of stricken embarrassment on Ben and Matt's, then Glen laughed a rich deep belly laugh that was infectious. 'Whatever it is you and this house are doing to them, keep on doing it. What my boys have been doing for you is the best work they have done in years, and it's nice to see them thinking of someone else for a change, please do not stop!'

'Now then, we have had our fun; let's just see what is going on out the back? You', to Brenda, 'have a look over these drawings with the architect and see if there is anything you don't like, while I get this lot to work. Peter don't come out in the cold, Lady B here will show you around so you can see what you are working with!' Brenda was still laughing at the look on Ben and Matt's faces, but pushed them all out of the apartment to check if the extra workmen and equipment had arrived. Peter was still wiping happy tears from his face as she returned with a cup of herbal tea.

'You probably won't like the taste of this at the beginning, but I use this all the time. It is no good while you have the flu, but it really helps the immune system fight back after. The slight amount of tea tree helps to clear the head and sinuses. Try it, I will not be offended if you leave half of it, but it might just help!'

Peter gratefully took a sip, grimacing at the aftertaste but gamely took another. He then showed her on the plans what he thought for the inside of the house. Moving down to apartment one to really have a look around. Peter suggested under the stairs three lockers, for the use as letterboxes for the upstairs apartments. It would be better than having a row of letter boxes marring the front of the house. Brenda could not see that much mail would be coming in, but realised it would be good storage for winter coats and boots. She realised that the letter slot was in her front door, all mail that did arrive would be safe and secure, so could see the value of a locker arrangement on the ground floor in any regard for deliveries.

She queried him on the conservation requirement of the build, wondering if they should have someone to come and look at the house before they tore it apart.

'I checked for you Brenda, apparently, you are now restoring it to what it was, with a slight change,' Peter said quietly, 'you are putting back what was closed up, and giving the main apartment, yours, back its soul. I don't think anyone dare say a word against you, you have not destroyed the top apartments, but are giving back in yours, and helping in the others by giving them some soul. We will see what the inspectors say tomorrow, they are due early in the morning, Dan and Glen will be camped out at your doorstep at five!'

'I will be up waiting with them. I am so nervous, but your plans are great, I love the way you have put the original window back looking down my hallway over the circular stairs. I only hope we can move the staircase to the basement, as it will awkward with the door to the dining room so close.'

'That will be a very small problem, we will have to wait and see tomorrow. Not that Dan and Glen will see a problem, just something that needs a solution, I do not think 'cannot do' is in their vocabulary.'

They both laughed and moved into the dining room, where they could see through the still grimy glass the workmen in the garden next to the conservatory, putting in the final stages of the footings for the ramp from her landing to the garden. Brenda could not help it, but went over to the back door, unlocking it, putting her hard hat on, opened it slightly to see if anyone was there working above her, seeing no one around, walked out onto the extensive landing.

Yes, Brenda thought, seeing the large landing wrap around the staircase, going from the sidewall to past her back door. Seeing for the first time the ornate panels in the railings, and then noticing the floor she stood on, was also not solid steel plates, but had the same pattern punched into it. Peter, also wearing a hard hat, followed her out, joining in her excitement of seeing and touching the staircase for the first time.

'Ho, Brenda, knew it wold not be long before you ventured out!'

Glen yelled from the midst of the workmen helping the digger prepare the footings, Brenda realised that the landing was almost at the same height as the garden, looking over the edge down into the basement patio, quite a distance below her.

'Don't get too comfortable there, as soon as we have finished, with the two posts here we intend to get rid of this monstrosity,' and he waved at the cladding, 'so we can see what we are working with for the rest!'

'Cannot be soon enough for me Glen, just had to touch it. I can wait until the cladding is down before I climb the stairs to the top!'

Brenda turned back to Peter, 'I do believe that what we are standing on is strong enough to hold anything we do, but I see the need to have a secondary structure to make sure, I only hope the inspectors agree! I don't think I am looking at this through rose coloured glasses am I Peter?'

'No Brenda if you are we all are. Glen and Dan are very practical men, they don't often see things through rose coloured glasses as you say. If they say it can be done, it will be done, rest assured of that. Now I need to go back upstairs to jot down the changes I need to do, and it's a bit chilly here, so I will leave you to your watching.'

Brenda watched him go back into the house; she stood watching through the gaps in the corrugated iron as the workmen finished the posts. Then moved back into the house, to watch the demolition of the box around the staircase, mentally cheering, with gardenia around her as each panel was removed, allowing light to shine again on the true beauty and strength of design that was hidden.

Chapter 20

As the workmen finished taking away the monstrosity, Brenda came out onto the landing, torch in hand, and went down the stairs not up. It was another new place to explore, and now could with some daylight flooding the once gloomy area.

She was struck by the space there was, most of the muck and refuse was of the organic nature. The staircase she realised was not a full circle, it did not stick too far out from the back wall, it was really an oval kissing the outside wall on its way up, touching at each floor, the upper landings being quite a bit smaller than the one outside her apartment she realised exactly where the doors should have been, and she vowed would be again. It was a sculptural element integrated into the building, showing off the elegant design of the original steelwork. The large landing at her backdoor, did cut out a bit of the light underneath it, but that did not matter, it was the shape the patio took from the basement door that caught her eye.

There was a retaining wall, which ran from the conservatory to the other side of the garden, it reinforced the garden where Glen and the team had been working putting in the posts for the ramp. The top was level with the conservatory floor, it followed the contour of the landing, but was about two feet from the side wall, was about seven or eight feet at its widest point, and almost eight feet in height at the tallest part. There were overgrown plants flowing in profusion out of the inbuilt garden boxes that made up the wall, to a point on the conservatory side, that was suspiciously flat, well it was slightly curved to fit in with the rest of the wall, but no planter boxes. Brenda moved some of the hanging foliage aside so she could see some of the ceramic tile that made up the wall, in hues of blue and green, even in the dirty and grimed state they were in, Brenda could see they were top quality. Turning to look back at the house, noticed the tiles also on the floor of what was a spacious and tranquil patio, so glad that the previous builders had not damaged the floor by digging holes for the monstrosity. Making a mental note to remind Glen to be careful, and remove the tiles carefully, but knowing he would be, when he did dig for the footings.

Thinking of the plants reminded her that Norman Greenwell from Kew would be arriving in the morning. He had rung on Saturday advising he would be arriving with ten workers, and reminded her that no one, and he meant absolutely no one was to touch anything. Not even sweep the floor, she laughed at his authoritarian manner, but he had promised the conservatory would shine again. Brenda chuckled thinking she should get him to check this area also, it could have been a kitchen garden, it was in the right place for a kitchen in Victorian times, a fleeting realisation was there but she could not grasp it. As she thought of Norman, kept looking around, and returning to the flat area in the terrace, beside the staircase, she also remembered him say the conservatory would have been heated in some way in winter. She, Glen and Ben had tried to find how that might have been accomplished with no success.

Her gaze kept looking at the flat area, moving over to it, gardenia floated around her, pulled aside the creeper growing in profusion in the area, finding herself holding onto an orchid, a delicate spider orchid in the most beautiful shades of blue. As she moved it aside, she could just make out the vertical and horizontal lines marking a door! Not a flat door, this one was delicately curved to fit into the wall, as she ran her hand over the door, moved a tile that was hiding a key hole and ring pull. She had the keys found in the kitchen with her, a small one that fit exactly, twisting it with effort heard a click, hooking her finger into the ring pull, gave a mighty tug, kicking away some of the debris, opening it enough to slip through.

There was a short hallway, with hooks and benches just inside, showing in the light of her torch, it led right under the conservatory. Tears were running down her face, *'thank you Iris, oh thank you love.*

How hard it must have been for you to seal this up how can I repay you? The only way I know how, by restoring this wonderful building,' she thought. As she moved into the dark space mirroring the floor span of the conservatory, but in the darkness, it seemed to go on forever. She realised as she recognised some of the piping and tubing running around that there was one person at least that had to see this immediately.

'Ben, Ben, where are you?'

Brenda ran up the stairs two at a time, until she got to the second floor, stunned workmen looking at her, wondering what was going on.

'Ben, BEN!'

'Brenda, hey whoa, hold on what's gotten into you, slow down you will hurt yourself!' It was Dan, with Glen closed behind him, 'Ben is down in apartment one being useful!'

'Brenda, I am here, what is the problem now?'

Catching her breath, she turned a smile on her face, 'you had all better come; Iris has been at it again!'

They looked at her, and followed down the stairs, picking up a confused Ben as they went down. When they got to the bottom, the door because of the plants had closed, so no one could see anything.

'We will need a generator and a light or two, Jack would you be good enough to go and get it please, we will wait, it is worth waiting for!'

Glen nodded at Jack to go, 'and a broom please!' she yelled at his retreating figure up the stairs.

'Lass what are you upset about, you know this space is bigger than I thought it would be. It is quite pleasant, be even better once we have it cleaned up. How have the flowers grown down here?' Dan was looking around, checking out the wall with the overgrown terraces. Jack arrived back, Peter and Matt helping carry the lights and broom, curious at all the noise.

Brenda took a deep breath, and the broom Jack was juggling, as gardenia floated around she swept and explained.

'Well I knew you would not let me go up the stairs, so decided to come down. I haven't been down here either, I was curious, the retaining wall goes up to the level of the floor in the conservatory, if you look at the back wall it is built in steel. By the way please be careful and remove the tiles in the floor before you drill the support holes for the new framing!' At Glen's marked look, 'I know you will be but I just have to say it. The flowers got me thinking about Norman Greenwell from Kew, he will be here tomorrow,' the men gathered around nodded, still wondering what she was getting at.

'This space here just looked decidedly odd, so I moved the flowers, look at them, they are Spider Orchids, how they are here I do not know, but look at the colour!' Both Glen and Dan looked and then looked at each other, Iris Blue, wonder dawning on their faces. 'You won't have to worry about the rain water tanks Ben, because they are already here!'

Brenda swept aside the debris from the door, held aside the flowers, pulled the door open, eagerly assisted by Dan and Ben once they got over the shock, the door came fully open under protest, and fitted neatly around the contour of the landing. Carrying the generator in through the doorway Ben followed Brenda into the space, followed by everyone else, waiting till Matt and Ben had the generator working, powering the lights dispelling some of the gloom in what could be seen as a workroom under the conservatory.

Matt and Charlie were wandering around looking at the ceiling, which seemed to be a lattice work of steel grids, muttering to themselves moving over to the side of the room and looking up.

'There seems to be glass panels up there, is the floor in the conservatory covered, looks like they are set in the floor, that would send some light down in daylight, once clean of course, but what did they do at night, gas light perhaps?' They looked the question at each other.

Everyone was moving as in a dream, not touching anything at all leaving the layers of dust over everything, they all knew that this find would have to be carefully treated. There came a shout from Ben who had wandered further into the gloom, had everyone following to find out what the shout was about.

'I knew it, I just knew it, with everything else, why would they not have wanted the gardens to survive?'

Brenda had caught up first, standing in awe as a massive water tank to one side of the underground cavern loomed in the dark, opposite to a boiler system. Ben was lovingly inspecting every inch, tut tutting at the neglect but whooping in delight when he found a working part.

'We must be at the edge of the garden Brenda, what a space,' Glen said into the hushed silence around them all, 'they excavated the whole garden, put in the tanks and boiler, then put a roof over this place, put the garden back and built the conservatory, amazing!'

Peter and Charlie appeared out of the gloom to one side, 'You have got to see what is over here!' Peter pointed his torch to a gap between the workshop benches, it was not another workshop but a wine cellar. From the top shelf to the bottom, it was a sommeliers dream, under the butler's bench in the middle of the small room all around the space, in perfect conditions for storing wine, on shelves and in boxes covered in dust of ages there were bottles.

'Oh oh, my god do you think it is drinkable?' Jack asked in wonder.

Brenda could not speak, could not move, Matt was the quickest and caught her before she hit the ground. She felt dirty, dusty, could feel the grime under her fingers, wondering where she was she came too, feeling the tiles under her, the strong arm around her. Suddenly a feeling of frustrations flowed through her, wanting this to be clean now, it was affront that something so wondrous, so beautiful had been ignored so long.

'Oh lass, thank goodness. Are you all right now, gave us all a shock, no don't try and sit up, Ben went to get some water. Although I think something a little stronger would be welcome for all of us. Jack, stop poking around there, we have to leave this for the moment. We are going to lock all this up, we are not going to tell anyone, and I mean anyone about this. We have to get the plans for our work through the inspection. Thank goodness none of the new foundations have touched the retaining wall of this wonderful place. We will deal with this after, I mean after we have the lift in place, and have the time to restore this wonder to its full glory, do you agree lass?'

Glen was looking at her concern in his face, 'Oh yes Glen I agree, I agree wholeheartedly. I think we concentrate on what has to be built to be able to live in the house, before we concentrate on what has to be restored. Ben, I know love, but please I don't think I could take it knowing strangers were down here, she sipped the water that Ben handed to her, gaining strength from the arm Matt still had around her, looking at the concerned faces in front of her. 'I won't mention this to Norman and no one else will please, I will call him back later, once the construction of the lift is finished. I promise you Ben you can fix this up, just not at this moment understand?'

The smile that broke out on Ben's face was infectious, everyone was smiling he nodded at Brenda in acceptance of the truth in her statement. Charlie came over slowly helping Matt to help Brenda stand, 'I am sorry gentlemen, I do not know what came over me, I never faint! This house is just giving me one shock after another. Now I think we deserve a celebration, Peter if you would like to come with me, I put something in the fridge yesterday to celebrate the demise of the monstrosity. I think a double celebration is due, and flu or no flu you are having a glass with us!'

Chapter 21

EVERYONE MOVED OUT OF the work shop, taking one last glance at the treasures so recently discovered, shaking their heads as the door closed, hiding it all from view again.

Brenda began sweeping debris back to the door from view turning to Glen who with the others was standing bemused at her antics.

'Don't be in too much of a hurry to clean this place up, please Glen. Once we have the posts in place, oh, did I ask you to be careful removing the tiles where the new posts will be?' at his nod she continued, 'it can be one of the last jobs on our list, because we will have Norman back for the plants, I think some of them escaped the conservatory, in fact,' she looked around the space and back at the men in front of her, 'we will make it the very last, and we can discover the door again. Now how much have you to do?'

'I was nearly finished, if Matt, John and Jack give me a hand we will be all done in about twenty minutes.' Ben advised, at her nod they all left; after Matt was sure Brenda could stand on her own two feet. Charlie said he was on his way to find her to ask if he could take the window with him, he wanted to check it over and clean it up. Leaving quickly to put it in his van when she said of course, grabbing Dan to give him a hand promising to be back quickly. They left in high spirits, Brenda told Glen to go and finish what he was doing, taking the rest of the men with him, saying she would see them all in apartment two in half an hour.

Peter walked slowly beside her, deep in thought. There was something magical happening here, he wished he could talk to Beverly, she would understand. There was something about this

121

project, and this lady slowly walking in front of him, he knew he could not say anything, but would be able to soon, then he would enjoy seeing Beverley's face shine, as he showed her over this remarkable building.

As though reading his mind, Brenda turned as they got to apartment two, 'by the way Peter, I am planning on a dinner party to help celebrate the re-awakening of this place. I hope you and Beverly, is it?' Peter nodded stunned, 'will be able to make it. You can also bring your two young hellions, I am sure there will be enough people around to look after them. Please don't forget to put your name and address on the notepad by the phone, so I can co-ordinate with her!' Peter shook his head as he walked over and dutifully put his home number and address on the pad under Dan and Glen's, there is definitely magic happening here, he thought.

The popping of a champagne cork brought him out of his reverie, moving into the kitchen to help Brenda assemble some plastic cups, the champagne and beer on the tray, she had also put on fresh coffee and the urn was bubbling merrily. Seeming from nowhere Brenda assembled not only the drinks, but some cheese and biscuits with nibbles in bowls, putting them on the table, that he hastily cleared of his plans and notes, he would finish them and make copies at Dan's place this evening, going over them to make sure he had crossed all the "T's" and dotted all the "I's", he did not want to be the one that held up this incredible transformation.

The men slowly arrived all of them asking if Brenda was feeling all right, Brenda thankful that they would think of her first. Dan, Glen and the boys arrived last of all; by this time, she and Peter had given out the drinks as wanted.

'Well Glen, can I entice you into a champagne or beer, I offer both as I realise that real men are a bit finicky?' Glen laughed, asking for a small glass of champagne, the boys opted for a beer, and Dan asked for a cup of tea. Brenda saying, she had made a pot, quickly going and bringing his tea, seeing everyone was served turned to the group in the room.

'Gentlemen, I thank you, Iris Fitzgibbon-Boerchermeir, the gentle lady who was the last in her family, and died in this house;

oh my, it was two weeks ago today, is thanking you by making her gifts open and available to us all. The house thanks you, as it needs to be used and useful, helping us seemingly over coming massive obstacles. So, I ask you to raise your glasses to continuing good luck, may you help us to completion – "Iris House!"

A chorus of male voices rang out 'Iris House', drinks taken everyone resumed a conversation, happy chatter surrounded her, a whiff of gardenia meandered its way through the workmen in their dusty work clothes. Brenda turned again, 'Gentlemen I am sorry, Iris is reminding me, can you please all of you, write down your names and addresses. I am planning a little gathering at the completion of this makeover; I would like it if you and your families would attend. Don't forget to add your partner's names, as it will be them, I will be ringing to organise with, please remember your Social Directors all deserve to be acknowledged.

A laugh rang out; the men moved over to the table to put their names on the list, the house had touched them all. The building itself was unique, and although it was in a row of houses, probably built in the same way, this being the middle house, seemed to be the best and was the biggest. It's uniqueness in being in the same state almost as it was built, gave it a certain something, all of them wanted to see it sparkle. Gradually they all left, Glen Dan, Charlie, Ben, Peter and Matt dawdling making sure that they took care of the tidying up, Brenda felt special. She could not understand what had happened in the workshop, but she now felt rejuvenated, she knew that they were going to succeed. Eventually she shooed out the dawdlers, telling them she needed her beauty sleep especially if they were going to be back at the crack of dawn the next morning. Glen laughed at that saying probably would, they needed to make sure they had not forgotten anything with the discoveries of the afternoon.

Brenda once quiet had descended after everyone had gone, took her phone, put her hard hat on, moving down to the back door of apartment one, fresh glass of champagne in hand, she slowly climbed to the top of the staircase. The sun was just in that hazy moment when the day starts to become evening, then the magic of the night turns the yellow bright of the day into the cool blue of the night.

As she stood drinking in the view across the commons seeing London on its best behaviour, and sipping her champagne she rang Linda.

'Hi there, yes I am at the house. It has been another eventful one. No, I will tell you about it when you get back, what time is your flight?'

'I leave at ten, Brenda, you have me curious now. How are things going if it has been an eventful day?'

'I will tell you better after about eight am tomorrow, have the building inspectors coming and I think, an awful lot of quick talking to do. I think the previous builders had a pet building inspector, so they did not file any of the usual paperwork required. Hopefully the dodgy structures that were there, which should not have been, and we have removed will be ok. We need their tick of approval before we start putting things back again. I know I am sounding a little crazy; I will put it down to lack of sleep. So, when do you get back?'

'Saturday at four pm, you now have me very curious, so will look forward to next Monday. Don't worry Brenda, everything will work out. By the way Sir James sends his regards. A few of his associates were very interested in Haddon & Sons, they have all cancelled contracts with Gardiners!'

Brenda laughed and wished her Bon Voyage, hanging up the phone. The last bit of information in regards to the Haddon's from Linda being the icing on a very large cake. Toasting the sunset and pouring the last few drops of champagne over the staircase in benediction, thanked the house and resident unseen spirit again, a waft of gardenia, acknowledgment of her action.

Going down the staircase, out to the front doors to make sure they were securely locked, ringing Dennis to say she was going to have an early night, she would see him tomorrow. Did a last few jobs, getting the apartment straight for the very early morning she was sure to have. Gratefully crawled into bed, with a very contented sigh and smile on her face, putting worry aside, enjoyed the peace of her own space.

Chapter 22

THE SMILE WAS STILL on her face as she woke before the alarm the following morning. The sun had just turned the night sky a peachy hew, so it was a little before sunrise. She showered, getting dressed for what was likely a busy day, organising herself, making sure that if she was needed, although apart from making cups of tea or coffee, she did not quite know in what capacity, she would be there.

The coffee was brewed, urn boiling merrily when the Haddon's, Charlie along with Dan and Peter arrived at six thirty. Ben was carrying the usual morning tea boxes, everyone very eager to get on with the build. Glen and the boys, after a quick cuppa, went down to check on what else they could do before the 'Inspectors' arrived. Dan was going over some plans Peter had laid out on the table. Brenda listening in and wondering how she could broach the possibility of replacing the old and tired internal wooden staircase with a steel one matching it if possible with the steel work on the outside stairs. When Dan turned to her after Peter had said loud enough to break into her introspection, 'Just ask her!'

'Yes gentlemen, can I help, have I missed something?'

'No Brenda, well it is a flight of fancy really. I was thinking on my way home last night, you know the steel mill,' she nodded, 'well it has been in my family for a very long time, in fact my forebears have always worked in steel, whether as old fashioned blacksmiths, way in the past, to wheel and cartwrights, in the not too distant one. You get the picture?'

Brenda nodded again, wondering where this curious conversation was going.

'Well, the short story is that my men have been ferreting around in the oldest part of the works, and have come up with some steel moulds they match the pattern on the outside stairs and in the landings, they have been working with them for a few days now, we will have your replacement internal circular stairs ready to go very shortly, using those ancient moulds to give exactly the same pattern, is speeding up the process nicely!'

Brenda went to give him a hug, thanking him and his men profusely.

'Now hang on a minute!' he moved her to arm's length, 'what I say next might upset you, but I was hoping if it is in the budget, I want to replace the first old wooden internal stairs with a new one made in steel, the others are in good shape so can be left as timber. We can put carpet on the treads so it won't be noisy, but the frame would then match all the other staircases in the house, what do you think?'

He stopped looking embarrassed, but hopeful. Brenda could not help it and took a turn around the room as though thinking over the proposal, before turning to him giving him a very large smile, 'Dan how do you do it?'

He looked at her, seeing the smile, smiled as well, 'Do what?' he asked.

'Read my mind, I was just wondering, and hesitant to bring it up with the injunction from yesterday to not bring any new projects into the mix, if I could change the staircase. You come up and ask me! Mate I would kiss you if I could reach you, yes please tell your workmen to go ahead and play!'

Dan smiled broadly, bent down so Brenda could plant a kiss on his cheek. He left to tell Glen of the new addition to the front of the building whistling a happy tune. Peter meanwhile was removing one sheet of plans from the pile in front of him, adding another that showed the steel straight staircase in place of the timber one, with the addition from the street of a rather nifty wheelchair ramp.

'I had to do a plan with the change in place, as Dan said you would be sure to go for it, as it was meant to be, especially when they found the moulds. He already has the guys back at the steel works working on it, should be ready by the end of the week or early next!'

Brenda laughed making a cup of tea for her, and a special brew for Peter, who admitted to feeling better. They chatted about houses, children and what twists fate can bring while waiting the inspectors.

It was not the inspectors that arrived first but Norman and his team.

'Good Morning, Ms Chalmers, Mr. Haddon I believe he said his name was sent us up, hope you don't mind?'

'Norman, good morning you are early, and please call me Brenda we are going to be working closely together now and in the future, I hope.'

She introduced Peter saying that the apartment was the official tearoom of the site, and her temporary abode while the work went on downstairs. 'Please let me show you and your team where everything is, welcome all to Iris House!'

Norman beamed in the welcome, thawing from his first visit. Having had a glimpse of what this lady had done since his last visit was truly amazing. Hopefully he could help her a little more with the conservatory. Peter was showing him the plans for the house, and the situation of the new powder rooms in the conservatory area. He was impressed by the way they were to be blended into the surroundings, making use of the same style and pattern of steel that was throughout the house.

'You don't mind us putting the new amenities in the empty space do you Norman, we could not see that it was interfering with too much of the conservatory?'

'Peter, I think it is an extremely good use for what would have been filled in with some ferns. In fact, once they are built we can landscape with plants to help them blend in!'

Brenda smiled at the two men, 'thank you from me as well Norman, I appreciate that you might have wanted to use the space yourself, I apologise for not asking you before the plans were drawn up!'

'Please, don't think on it Brenda, you have to use the space as you need it now. You are not taking away from the wonderful conservatory, only adding modern amenities to it. I approve, now as everyone has had a break, we must get to it!'

'I will come with you, to see what you have planned for today, you have already met Mr. Haddon the builder, I will introduce you to Mr. Dan Jones if he is still here, he is the owner of the steel works "Jones Foundry", that is providing the steel pieces we need. I believe that once the madness of the work here is finished, we will have leisure to find that they were the original suppliers of steel to this street. I also want to introduce you to Charlie Waines he is our Master Glassman!'

They had all been working hard in apartment one; Glen had not only built the new stud wall from the new found back wall to the front as far as he could with the stairs in the way. He had marked out the new position for the spiral stairs. Brenda moved Norman over to him, Charlie and Dan, introducing him properly to the men.

Norman had sent out his team to bring in some of the equipment they needed while he stood chatting to the group. Glen advised him of the permission they had to move equipment on the access road to the commons. He was very interested but advised that they would have to find the outside door in the conservatory, then the path to the gate first, before it could be used. He was a bit upset that the workmen had trampled the garden to install the first of the posts, but realised they had tried to keep to a single path.

Brenda walked with him into the apartment, pushing open the conservatory doors, as wide as they would open.

'Don't worry Brenda, they will fit back properly very soon! I have an absolute wiz whose speciality is French Doors, and he is really looking forward to getting his hands on these beauties!'

Brenda laughed, walked with him into the conservatory, going over to the space that the powder rooms would be in, a string outline through the ferns showing where the base would be, and on the wall chalk notations for plumbing and electrical.

'These men of yours are very neat, I admire that. Could use their skills on a couple of jobs I have on hold at the moment. Would they be interested do you think? Of course, once they have finished here, this build is definitely the main priority.' He turned then as some of the team members came through the partly opened doors, 'ok Tristan, Mary I need to know what is here,' he pointed to the marked out area, 'and the remnants of what was here, if anything remains. Then we photograph and remove, marking on the grid where the plants came from so we can put everything back correctly, once we have cleaned up, you both know the drill!'

He pointed to the plants in the conservatory as he directed his team members, now moving into the space, setting up tables and laptops. Matt appeared with a small generator, explaining that until the inspectors arrived and passed the work, there was no electricity in the apartment, in any way using the generator would be easier than having cords everywhere if they needed power for the laptops. Norman thanked him for his consideration, turning back to admonished his people to work and stop marvelling at the proportions and size of the conservatory, it wouldn't clean up itself'

Brenda made her escape, telling Norman she would see him at morning tea, advising the rest of his workers they would be welcome. Leaving to smiles all around, excited chatter amongst them as to what reassures lay in wait in the jungle depths, followed her back into the house.

Chapter 23

'HOW ARE YOU THIS morning Brenda? I didn't get a chance to ask at morning cuppa?' Matt asked as they moved back into the strangely quiet apartment.

'I am fine, thank you Matt, thanks for your support yesterday, I would surely have had a nasty concussion if I had hit the deck. It wasn't a very soft place, I am just itching to find out what I landed on, but I will be patient. This house has waited too long; I am trying to not ruin it by rushing into things, where I can. At least I hope I am not rushing into this project. But I have guests coming in five weeks, three weeks now to the completion, two to test-drive everything so to speak, then the first guests arrive. I am putting a lot of faith in you, Ben, Charlie, Dan and your father. This is not too much for him, is it?' at his look, she continued, 'I heard some chatter bits and pieces from the workmen, they are worried about him, has he not been well? Sorry, I was not eavesdropping but sound does travel up that stairwell! You will tell me if it does get too much for him, as Sir James be damned I will slow everything down so he can rest and then complete everything!'

'Thanks Brenda, I appreciate that, if Dad heard it though he would call it a damned cheek. He wasn't well we had him in hospital a few months ago. To tell you the truth I think it was despair, he had, so many disappointments, and had to let to many men go. Then winter was bad, he sort of went into a decline, Mum, we couldn't do anything to get him out of it. A few jobs came up, and he perked up, but this, your house Brenda this place has given him life again. We are watching him, but I don't think a relapse is on the cards.

Just look at him, he is in charge doing what he loves, either building new things, or seeing the best of the old buildings coming back to life under his hands. It should be us thanking you!'

'No, not me, thanks should be given to Dennis he was the one who called you, and for that he has earned my undying gratitude for bringing your family into my life. As well as Dan and Stan of course, oh I hope Nona approves of what I am doing, she will just love cleaning out the basement patio, can you just imagine the noise when she sees it for the first time!'

They both laughed, that brought Glen over to see them. Matt asked about the electrics in the apartment, especially in the kitchen, once the go ahead was given. They moved over to the trestle tables that had been set up to put out the plans, Brenda also placed an album of photos on the table. Between them they roughed out the various areas and how they might be used. Brenda also asked for some twenty first century technology from Matt, but with a Victorian twist.

'I know you will like this, but I would like you to work with Rebecca and Mia,' at Matt's raised eyebrow, so much like his father, Brenda continued. 'This place is going to be six star so the inclusions, the lighting, computer links, Wi-Fi, entertainment centres, internet, oh Matt use your imagination as to what I will need. I want you to fit out every apartment with the top of the line everything, but it must be easy to use and unseen when not. I will leave it to you and your sisters good taste, just put yourself into my future client's shoes, think what you would expect to find if you were paying a thousand pounds a night for accommodation. Then magnify that by four, I will need the same to be able to help if problems occur, although I hope I would be able to call on my expert team at all times, can you do this for me?'

Matt was shocked and took a step back to look at this wonderful person, taking a breath realised she was waiting for an answer, 'you have just told me I can do what I want with anything that uses electricity in this building, and then ask me can I do it! Step back lady, just watch me work, excuse me I have a few phone calls to make. Dad, call me when the inspectors arrive, I will be taking measurements upstairs!'

Glen laughed as he left, 'Now lass, Julie has just been on the phone. You wouldn't have any idea about prospective jobs arriving in my patch, would you?'

Brenda was saved from answering by Dan, escorting five men into the apartment. From the expressions and very bright shiny coats they were wearing realised these were "The Inspectors!'

Chapter 24

GLEN MOVED OVER TO the men, taking a very reluctant Brenda with him. After introductions, one of them with a very superior attitude and expression turned to her.

'I believe that there have been some irregularities in this build Ms. Chalmers, would you care to explain?'

Glen and Dan bristled, both of them not missing the open hostility that oozed from this man in their midst. Brenda just nodded at them, sensing they were ready to defend her, turned her shoulder on this individual, turning to the group as a whole, she was not about to play this person's one on one game, from this day forward everything would be open and above board, the way Glen and his team worked.

'Gentlemen, my team who very recently took over the refurbishment of this property were not aware of any problems until after the contracts went through, and my building contractor Mr. Glen Haddon contacted your office. I was only employed as the site Building Manager recently, and I had to wait until all the documents from the previous builders were handed over, before my team could take immediate action. I have no idea how the system works for your departments, but on checking all the documents, and records handed over by the original reconstruction team, I could not find either requests for and no inspection reports to or from your office at all. As you can see, the original builders and architect are no longer on site, we are endeavouring to repair the damage done, and organised this visit to appraise you of the situation immediately, I promise we will not be backward in our reporting. Therefore Mr.

Haddon my builder and project manager, Mr Mason the architect and Mr. Jones who is our Engineer, will be quite happy to answer any questions on our works. I point out the updated plans from my team, which we have submitted to council, also a photo album showing exactly what state I found this building, when I moved into apartment two. Incidentally, it stated that all the apartments had apparently passed a building inspection, according to a certificate found in the files we received? I shall leave you in Mr. Haddon's and the team's hands to show you around. Morning tea will be available in apartment two when you are finished.'

She turned, nodded at Glen and Dan, going back to apartment two, leaving the inspectors with varying expressions on their faces.

Rebecca arrived and was a welcome distraction she came bearing another load of fabrics, these in silver, blues and greens. With the most delicious maroon red she had seen, it prompted Brenda to advise her she had organised with Glen for a painter to come and give a quote for all the painting, inside and out.

'Oh, that will be Mr. Greenhill, dad always uses him.' She looked out through the window thinking hard, 'yes that will be good he has a great team of blokes and they know their stuff. I am glad you are going to be painting the house, it could do with it!'

Brenda laughed showing her some of the colour charts she had picked up.

'The main building colour has to be white, to fit in with the street, and heritage council. I wanted to paint all the outside doors front and back a deep Victorian Red, if there is such a thing, what do you think?'

'Hm, yes that will look startling, especially if you plant the little front garden with red and white roses. We will need him to help on the inside as well, he has two people that are brilliant at hanging wallpaper!'

'I think it will be a fantastic idea, when we get to that point. Now I don't know if Matt has had a chance to tell you, but I gave him almost carte blanche on putting the most up to date technology in all the apartments, including mine. I warned him though they had to be blended into the surroundings. I will say to you what I said to him, put yourself in the place of my prospective tenant, for however long they are here. What would you expect if you were staying in a six star, thousand pound per night hotel. Now add to that it will have to be extremely simple to use, especially for me, I am too old to be trying to learn anything too technical, I have problems sending a text message!'

Rebecca laughed, giving Brenda a hug, said she had better go and see Matt before he got too carried away.

As she moved out of the door, the inspectors with Glen, Dan, Charlie, Peter and to her surprise, Norman came through. Teas and coffees were dispensed; Brenda could not gauge the temper of the room, judging by the gardenia, neither could Iris. Wishing she had not spoken so boldly to the first inspector, but he had just raised her hackles so, looking in his direction, he noticed made his way over to her, still wearing the same supercilious smile.

Norman had also moved to her side, as soon as he had a cup in hand, talking animatedly about what they had found so far in the conservatory, he turned and looked slightly irritated at the smarmy inspector when he joined them loudly clearing his throat to announce his presence.

'Ms. Chalmers, thank you for your hospitality. We have made a thorough inspection and while there are irregularities we realise none of them have been made by yourself or your team. My Colleagues agree, and we will be discussing the new works when we get back to the office, we will let you know in due course!'

Brenda was crest-fallen, she had opened her big mouth. The supercilious smile was back on the inspector's face, he knew he had them in lockdown, with the words "in due course" meaning he would take his own sweet time, this is going to take months, she thought.

'May we continue?' Norman turned and introduced himself with his full name and to Brenda's surprise his title, 'it is most inconvenient, we have to move on from here you know. We are being held up by the building works, to which approval has apparently already been given to the previous builders and architects. Surely you can see the benefit of allowing Ms. Chalmers and her excellent group to complete, in better style and taste the restoration of the building. It has taken too long as it is!'

The supercilious gentleman had faltered when Norman introduced himself, again he looked at him, as though seeing him for the first time. Norman just smiled back as he sipped his tea, turning to Brenda, waiting for the penny to drop. A look crossed the inspectors face, trying to interpret the tone of voice, the meaning behind the words just quietly spoken by Norman. There was no doubt that Norman looked different in his overalls and work boots, it took a while but suddenly the expression on the inspector's face changed, he recognised who he was talking too, astonishment crossed his face, his Adams-apple in his throat bobbing up and down as he swallowed down what appeared to be hasty words.

'No, of course we cannot hold up the works,' he backtracked magnificently, 'we will be ratifying the new plans, with the original confirmation still standing. If Ms. Chalmers or her representative would call into the office later this morning, we can have all the documents stamped and approved!'

'Thank you, I appreciate your assistance in this matter.' Brenda wondered if she had heard right, but just kept talking while her mind was racing. 'If you will excuse me I will go and tell my team that they can go ahead.' Brenda still did not know what had happened, but when the inspectors left she was certainly going to find out. Norman had done or said something, but she did not know what. She thought she would burst but she hoped she looked outwardly calm as she moved over to where Glen, Peter and Dan were standing, Jack was a little way back, she fleetingly wondered where Matt and Ben were, all of them had a very glum expression on their faces.

'I am sorry Brenda, I do not know what to do. I, we did everything right; they were not impressed from the get go, picked every little thing to pieces, even stuff that had been passed done by the previous builders, was our fault, they were completely negative, it was as though they had all been told this was a no go from the outset!'

'I think they had Glen, don't worry though. We have a green light, don't ask me how, but Norman, yes Norman just got us the go ahead. We are to send our representative down to the council later on to get the stamped and approved plans!'

Glen looked at Brenda, then over to Norman he noticed the look and raised his teacup in salute, he just broadened his smile as he continued to talk to the inspector in a hushed and what seemed a forceful voice,

Dan smiled as well, nodded muttering under his breath, Brenda didn't hear what he was muttering, and it was probably a good thing that she could not. You could see that her team were willing the whole party of condescending inspectors worlds away and quickly.

Chapter 25

THERE WAS A FURTHER fifteen minutes of stilting small talk before they left. Everyone waited until the front door had firmly closed before a whoop of relief rang around the room. They descended on Norman, Glen beating Dan by a handshake.

Brenda gave him a hug, 'how' she asked, 'do I want to know how you just pulled our chestnuts out of the fire; yes, I think I do, how did you just save our bacon Norman. Thank you so much for doing that by the way, but I was standing right beside you he had just said go jump, and you asked one question, then he gave us carte blanch, come on give?'

'No need to worry, my dear. That particular personage is known to myself, and Sir James. I had a phone call from Sir James last night, somehow, he knew that particular inspector was going to be in the mix, and he asked me to make sure I was in earshot when they arrived, and just happen to be around when they gave their decision. It was an easy thing to remind that particular individual that I knew he was a very good friend of Mr. William Gardiner. Seemed that he did need to have his memory jogged, he remembered just in time I think!'

Relief flowed through the group, gardenia floated on the air, thanks were expressed by everyone, Norman turned a little pink smiled his appreciation, finished his tea and left.

Into the silence that followed Glen said he would go himself to the office that afternoon.

'I am the only one not able to swing a hammer Brenda,' he said, 'I can also check that the full approval for everything we have done, and perhaps things we have not thought of yet,' and he smiled at her, 'are on the authority I collect.'

Dan had been off in a corner on his phone, he came up saying he would be back later, he was heading off to the foundry to do some checks on all the firings and to see that nothing was missed.

Sounds of industry and happy voices could be heard all over the house. A smile had appeared on everyone's faces the atmosphere was electrifying. The feeling of triumph was euphoric, the house seemed to realise it was finally going to be a home again, contentment, rainbows and the beautiful scent of gardenia followed people into very room.

Brenda had been working on her cost sheets, as Glen and Dan had finally given her an estimate of the works. Spread sheets had never been her forte but she was trying, the quotes to her seemed very reasonable, compared to the ones from William Gardiner, she would just have to wait and see what Sir James thought when he returned.

She had a call from Dennis, wanting to know what had happened with the inspectors, telling him they had the go ahead, but to get the full unabridged story he was to come over for dinner and bring noodles.

The work had been going on around her, as she sat at the table in apartment two, hearing the odd burst of sound, the voices of the workmen floating up the stairwell. She was shocked later that afternoon as she descended the stairs.

The original internal basement stairs were a thing of memory, the hole for the circular stairs, carefully covered was now in place. The large space it had been was very quickly being filled in, in fact if Jack and Fred didn't take a break on the table saw it would melt. Telling them to chill for a while, they did have time, sent them up for a cup of tea, she would square it with the boss she told them.

Going in search of Glen, when she found him pouring over the plans in the dining room, she asked for a dance. He laughed explaining that as they could bring the bits of the staircase in the front door, they could use the new found, waiting to be replaced back door and not have to keep going through her apartment with building materials. Besides they had to clear the areas to reposition everything, also needing to check what the flooring was to be able to replace it, he was very surprised, but was not going to tell her what it was.

'You have been itching to remove those stairs since you saw them, don't give me that guff. I approve though, wish I could keep the space but I will have quite a bit!' Brenda said, making him laugh nodding his head in agreement.

'I have also checked on the sound proofing insulation you wanted throughout the house Brenda. I have a firm that specialises in retrofitting old houses coming tomorrow morning, to give advice and to help if they can. I am also removing the front doors tomorrow, as they also need repositioning, and to make space for the new window that was going to be in-between the doors. I removed the internal folding doors to be able to clean them without damaging them and to clean the tracks easily, they will be put back shortly as well. Dan was going to pick up the new door and frame for the back wall, and he is finding out if the front one will be ready tomorrow as they promised, to fit as well.'

They walked the floor ending up at the kitchen space, looking at where the new framing was going in.

'I have organised for deliveries of doors and timber to be made tomorrow or Thursday,' Glen continued, 'I tell you I got an awful shock this morning when that twit nearly didn't give us that permit. Glad, I went and checked the details, as they had the wrong date on it, would you believe they had dated it for next month. I could just see it, we going ahead, they come for their visit next week, check the certificate, "oh, dear this doesn't authorise any building till next month, tear it down!" They very quickly changed it, want to know how I did it?' Brenda nodded sure the punch line would be good. 'I just mentioned I would have to speak to my friend Mr. Norman Greenwell, did they move!' Brenda and Glen laughed together.

'I hope you are not laughing at me, I heard my name?' Norman walked into the room, looking around at the changes this team had wrought in so short a time. 'My you do work quickly, efficiently and well. I must have a talk to you Glen I have some projects, works put off because I could not find a competent sympathetic builder, I need to know when you would be free?'

Glen sobered immediately, 'Norman thank you, no we were not laughing at you, I was telling Brenda how I got the council to keep to their agreement,' at Norman's raised eyebrow, 'I threatened them with telling you of their mistake!' Norman looked at him and chuckled, realising the implication of what Glen said.

'Well that is fine, it was what I was asked to do after all. Now please both of you come and see what we have accomplished in the greenhouse!'

His team had gone, taking with them all the specimens and seeds collected during the day. They had made some progress, clearing along the wall where the new powder rooms were going to be placed, putting down some boards in the space they would be installed. They had swept as well but only showed the timber floor; Brenda did wonder if he knew that this floor was false, but he continued before she could find the words to ask him.

'I thought my team should start in this area, as Ben and you Glen will be wanting access to start on the powder rooms. Besides we need to get through to the outside doors; so, we go down one side of the large centre planter, and up the other, it will take a few days, I really do not see us getting to them till Friday.'

He turned to her, taking her arm to go back into the house, 'Brenda you have a wonderful collection here, gone very wild, if you do not mind I have a suggestion to make. Can I put your conservatory and grounds as an annex to Kew, under my control? We can then come and be your gardeners, keeping everything in check and healthy?

Brenda was taken aback by Norman's request, she hadn't thought that far ahead, but realised the merit in having the eminent people at Kew Gardens look after the small collection she had unearthed.

'Thank you, Norman, I am flattered, and would certainly like to accept your proposal. I am only the building manager here, so will have to check with Sir James,' a waft of gardenia swept around them all, Brenda realised Iris was approving, she smiled to herself knowing Sir James would have very little to say about it, but had to stall Norman for an answer. 'I will most certainly be urging him to accept. I promise to keep the plants watered hopefully I will be allowed to pick flowers for the house, but anything else I am a brown thumb to my elbow!'

Norman laughed and said of course, he was going now, and would see them all tomorrow, he was determined to get to the doors and out into the garden, to check everything out.

'I think he is going to be disappointed,' Brenda said after he had gone. Charlie had joined Glen and herself, Ben and Matt trailing in his wake.

Charlie with ever present cup of tea, and sweet bun, motioned to Norman's figure skipping down the stairs to the street. 'Why is Norman going to be disappointed Brenda, he is as happy as a clam. I was talking to a few of the team, apparently, they do this often, get a call to help with a conservatory, get their give advice, help tidy up. When they go back for a follow up visit more often than not, the plants have gone and a dining table is in the room! Or worse Jeremy said at one house on a return visit, they found the new owners had ripped out the most incredible hot house orchid collection left by previous owner, tossed them outside no less, and put his gym equipment in the place, can you believe it!'

'Yes, I can, I now understand why he was a little bitter and cynical when he first came. I promise you gentlemen I will never remove this inside miracle garden. You, Ben had better be a miracle worker and get the watering and plumbing systems up and running, when you can!' Ben nodded and said it was not going to be a problem, once he had proper access to the workshop to work on the boiler and pipes.

'The reason I said that Norman will be disappointed when he gets to the outside garden, there will be no big trees. Never will be!'

'Oh of course, how can you have big trees, nowhere for the roots to go. Ben, did you get to the end of the workshop, did you see what it was made of?' Matt asked.

'No I was too interested in the plumbing. We will find out, but Brenda I am sure there are a couple of big trees towards the end of the garden, you can see the tops. Perhaps because they are by the gate to the commons they have grown, or perhaps the workshop does not go as far as we think? We will find out eventually I can have patience!'

Glen looked at Brenda mirth bubbling up inside him, sparkling the once tired eyes. Matt and Charlie laughing at the ingenious expression on Ben's face.

A clamour and cry for help came from the front door. Everyone rushing to assist Dan and his foundry men in with their gear, including what Brenda thought was a very large door and frame.

'Glad you fellows were still here. Sorry I am late Brenda, but I had to pick up that door,' turning to Glen, 'front one will be ready and hopefully delivered tomorrow late.' Glen nodded, 'both have been made with the side panels for glass inserts, neatest thing I have seen, hey what happened to the stairs?' Dan was looking around wondering what was going on, then his face cleared as it dawned on him what Glen had done

'You sneaky thing, could have waited for me I wanted to help pull them down. We use the outside stairs?' Glen nodded.

Brenda picked up a steel cylinder, which could only be for the new circular internal stairs, that Dan's men were bringing in in pieces around them. 'No Brenda this one stays here, gravity will help us position it we just slide on the risers, position and lock!'

'So, what do you want to us to do Dan, how can we help?' Brenda asked eagerly, she wanted the stairs in place almost as much as he did, and no more than Iris, as she sniffed the now familiar fragrance around them all.

'Well to tell you the truth Brenda, the only thing that has to go down is the new pilot post, that we have to put in the floor to set overnight.' Dan introduced her then to his foreman and right hand man Greg Baines, who took her hand gently in his massive paw. Dan was big but this man was huge, stood at well over six feet six and was built like a brick outhouse, all muscle. Brenda felt dwarfed by so many large bodies, but had never felt so safe, she could see the gentle twinkle in this man's eye he liked a laugh like everyone else.

'OK Greg, so what do you suggest we do? I take it we have to make a hole for the pilot post, and of course that has to set, therefore it has to go in tonight, right?'

Greg laughed and said of course, the voice that came out of the massive frame was deep, resonant and unusually soft for the size of the man and the profession he worked in, he was as she found out a blacksmith, in this day and age, as well as an exceptional steel man.

While Brenda took Greg down the outside stairs and through the basement door to place the pilot hole, the rest of them manhandled the big door down to the back of the house, to a great deal of grunting and groaning she should add.

The floor in the basement was still covered in the timber sheeting, so Brenda helped Greg to remove it showing him the almost pristine tiles, that she and Stan had discovered just a week ago. Shaking her head as she realised it was only Tuesday, helped Greg remove the remainder of the coverings that had been left up to the door.

Surprised, and yet not really surprised when they found the tiles went to the wall. It hit her then that this was a brick wall, a very substantial brick wall that was part of the original house. With a sudden insight, she realised she was missing something, something niggling at the back of her mind, a thought she had fleetingly before, she realised. A whiff of gardenia surrounded her, soft laughter could just be heard, the pieces fell into place. The terraced wall, the tiles underneath where the stairs had been; where was the door, there had to be a door, as there was enough space for at least two more rooms in this area.

Brenda pushed the thoughts aside, to concentrate on helping Greg he was very carefully lifting the tiles from the floor. Explaining in that soft quiet voice, he would need them, as when he took out the old post hole, he would fill it in, and use the tiles he was lifting to cover the spot, no one would then know the position had been moved. He chuckled as Brenda asked if he needed any more help, said he could manage, but could she get Dan to uncover the opening, so they could put the post down to make sure the position was correct?

Leaving him carefully lifting tiles, she went out the back door and looked at where the spiral staircase was, looking closely at the wall behind it. Really looking at it this time, not just glancing and assuming what it was. She then noticed the stairs stopped off centre, way off centre to the wall, her jaw dropped as she realised that the brick work just didn't fit, and that she could see an oversized lintel mirroring the one above her that was being fitted with the new door.

Her brain reeling, she slowly made her way up the stairs, watching as the men shimmied the new door and frame into place. Finding Dan, who with Glen was standing back admiring their handiwork.

'What do you think?' Glen asked her, 'Does this fit in with what is in our head?'

'I am flabbergasted I did not think you would be so quick. It looks amazing, and the light that it allows into the hall is fantastic, I can't wait till the glass is in place and it is finished. Oh, Dan, before I forget, Greg wants the cover taken off the staircase hole, so he can position the pilot piece in the right spot!'

Dan left taking Jack with him, Brenda walked closer to the door in its frame. Touching it making sure it was real, feeling the ghosts of owners past smiling at her as something original to the house was restored.

'I wanted to have this door fitted first Brenda, so we can stop going through your place all the time. Dan will be back in the morning with the crane, he wants to get the two ramps in place, we only needed the two post in the garden to fit them both, we have taken up the tiles, where the four for the lift enclosure will be, we have drilled two of them, we will get the other two done tomorrow, then they will be fine by the end of the week. Norman will be back in the morning, won't he?'

'Oh yes, he plans on discovering the outside doors tomorrow, if he can. Why do you want to speak to him, oh of course,' she answered her own question, 'we need to take out that panel in the conservatory to add the ramp? Do we need to worry about a replacement door for the space, it would be nice if it was just open? I mean I will be locking all the doors to my place on a night-time so will be secure enough. Did we find a solution to the door problem out of the main ramp to the garden, I can't remember if we did?'

'Yes, we did, please don't worry, Dan is dealing with it.'

Laughing with her they walked back into the house leaving Ben and Matt to cover the unglazed frame and door with plastic, 'We can finish that in the morning, Charlie has the glass already to go, I think he is keen to show you he can put in a pane of glass!'

Brenda laughed again saying she never doubted it. They all moved back into the front area to give Dan a hand with the holding of the staircase pole. Ben chastising Dan for doing all the heavy work by himself, 'worse than Dad you are, not a spring chicken any more why didn't you call for help?'

Dan muttered under his breath, while Glen just chuckled in the background. He and Matt were checking where the finishing of the stud wall would be going in the morning, to finally give Brenda her apartment back with it privacy. They were just finishing off putting the cover back over the hole when Dennis arrived.

'Is it that late already, Julie will kill me. Come on boys it has been a long day, can't stay Dennis, will catch up with you later in the week.' Glen and the boys taking Charlie with them left as Greg walked from the back door standing beside Dan and dwarfing Dennis.

'Just as well,' he said to the retreating backs of the workmen, 'I didn't bring enough to fill Ben's bottomless pit anyway!' Laughter could be heard from the street.

Chapter 26

S UDDENLY THE HOUSE WAS quiet. Brenda told Dennis to put the food upstairs, to comeback bringing two of the large flashlights from the kitchen down with him, curious Dennis quickly did as he was asked, knowing Brenda would have a very good reason for the strange request.

'What's up Brenda, why do we need flashlights? My god those blokes work like demons. You did say you only got permission to do the work at ten this morning?'

Brenda nodded her head as she led Dennis out onto the outside staircase for the first time. Dennis stopped and looked around at the structure, enjoying as they all had the beauty and feel of the pattern in the steel. 'Wow!' was all he said, as he followed Brenda downstairs.

Looking around the patio in wonder as she moved through the basement door, 'what are we doing down here Brenda. You have something on your mind, come on give?'

'I, we found something yesterday Dennis, I would show you but as we have so much on our plate at the moment we, Glen and the boys, decided to just shelf it for the present, but when I can I will ok?'

'That's ok love; I just want to be part of this. I was in at the beginning, I will be there for you through it and right to the bitter end! Now, what are we doing down here?'

'Well something came to me when I was helping Greg this evening. I hope I am not going mad, but I just thought it incongruous. Think about where we are standing, then the house for a second Dennis take a look around what do you come up with?'

'Apart from my groaning stomach,' at her look he turned back to contemplating the surroundings, 'ok I will be serious.'

Brenda nodded and stood to one side as Dennis walked the hallway, went back outside to look at the patio and the house, came back muttering to himself.

'We are standing in the basement of your apartment, no stairs internally up, being put in, tomorrow right?' Brenda nodded letting him talk out loud, 'so at the moment we have a wall,' he went over to it and smacked it with the palm of his hand, 'a solid brick wall,' he said shaking his hand because it smarted. Then his face lit up, he ran out of the basement door again, back in very quickly, 'a solid brick wall almost in the middle of the basement of a house that goes further on so where is the door!'

'YES!' Brenda shouted, it echoed around the house, Dennis jumped at the noise, 'where is the door Dennis, there has to be at least two more rooms down here!'

Dennis was excited, at her look he picked up a hammer from the tools laid neatly beside the door, walking up the hallway to the front of the house, gently tapping as he came back to Brenda a smile on his face. He got to the area the old laundry was placed, the appliances had been removed, even sink and cupboards had been tossed into the big skip on the first day. There was a decided 'donk' sound, not a solid wall, eagerly Dennis motioned Brenda into the space to tap with a screwdriver he handed her, while he moved out and stood on the other side of the flimsy wall, as they tapped they realised that something was not right. With nothing in the space, she could see where the old sink had been as there was water damage on the wall behind it, the pipes still in place on the wall.

'Dennis come in here, I think we can pull away the panelling, it is rotten!'

It was a tight fit, but together they removed the water rotten wall, revealing another painted surface, looking closely they could see the heads of nails and a large crack running vertically up the wall. The Stanley knife borrowed again from the tools Greg had left, helped score the gap wider, prising the hammer and screwdriver into the gap pulled the timber from the wall, after a lot of pulling cursing and grunt they shortly revealed part of a glass topped door! The pipes for the laundry sink blocked the door somewhat and the wall cut the door in to thirds, but it was a beautiful solid door with clear glass on the top, and gentle carving on the bottom. Brenda was making mental notes of who to show this to then laughed, they all would have to see.

'Iris I hope this is the last of the shocks, you can't have anywhere else to go, I hope!'

'Dennis, I haven't told anyone this, but I have to tell you. You know when I was clearing out Iris's room, I found her journals?' Dennis nodded, trying to get his breath back, trying to understand what was going on; this house had more rooms than the Tardis!

'Well I found Iris's will; in it she left all her worldly goods and chattels to the finder of the letter. I had Linda check the details, whatever we find in this house, but not the house itself, it seems, is mine – I am her Heir!'

He turned to her, stunned 'What, say that again, Brenda you are not making sense, are you saying all the boxes, furniture everything that is not bolted to the floor in this place is yours?' she nodded.

'I have no idea of what I have been given, or if any of it is valuable. It may be just a lot of old junk, but the fact is, I who have never even won a two-dollar lottery ticket, in the space of a week, have landed the job of my dreams, and received an inheritance of my dreams. I have no idea of its value, just the fact that I am on the receiving end gives me goose bumps. Dennis when we go through that door,' at this look, 'yes, we are going through that door, it will be another shock to my already overloaded system. The rooms may be empty, but I am not betting on it. Iris, or her relatives did not close up or have closed up places without something in them, to preserve a slice of their lives, our history, so people could see and believe they had lived a good and full life!'

Dennis stood looking at this friend of many years, dear to his heart, the sister he never had, his only thought was joy for her. She deserved this change of fortune, goodness knows she had worked hard all her life for it.

They both stood looking at the door now revealed in all its glory, still with the wall splitting it and pipes in the way, but looking magnificent. Brenda was nervous should they open it? Silly really as they could not put the concealment back, it was in pieces all around them. She took a leaf out of Glen's book, with Dennis's help took the debris out of the hall and stacked it neatly in the patio area. Back at the door, fitted the big key on the found set of keys into the lock, perfect fit, a waft of Gardenia just slipped by, sure now that she was meant to find this place the key turned with a satisfying 'clunk'.

Dennis pushed down on the brass handle, put his shoulder to the door pushed it inwards, it moved with surprising ease. They stepped into a dark interior, the flashlights scattered the darkness as they passed the light around the room.

'Ben is going to be really ticked off,' Brenda said in awe as they moved into the original kitchen!

'Why is Ben going to be ticked off?' Dennis repeated not willing to move into a room that was just waiting for the butler to appear through the side door.

'He is going to have to move the laundry!' She said quietly as she moved slowly into the room shining her torch into the gloom. Dennis chuckled the spell broken following her in, moving towards the rear of the room, there was a massive AGA stove along the back wall, he moved to the door on the left-hand side.

The room was surprisingly clean just very dusty, it was the details under the dust that were scary. In the centre of the room was a big kitchen table, used not only to eat at but also to prepare the meals for the family upstairs. In the centre of the table, was a large crystal oil lamp, beautifully proportioned, large enough to shed light over the whole of the table. Along the walls the original gaslights, with their crystal toppers, etched with the same design as on the oil lamps, just waiting for the match to light them. A dresser was on the wall beside the door, it was functional with glass topped cupboards, it stretched along the wall to the back of the room. There were plates, cups, glasses lined up neatly in them just showing through the dust that had settled over everything. Copper pots hung from a wooden frame suspended by chains from the ceiling. The larger ones, their copper sides had a patina of age on them, but the colour showed in the torch light, were on the AGA waiting for the cook to make dinner.

'Brenda come in here!' Dennis had moved into the room on the left out towards the patio area, 'I think this might have been the Butler's Pantry!'

Both torches illuminated the room; floor to ceiling cupboards lined two of the walls. Boxes were stacked on either side and in front of what could be a window out to the patio, the boxes were hiding timber shutters similar to the others in the apartment. Beside the door, they had come through two sinks could be seen, a beautiful deep porcelain butlers sink, and the remains of a wooden sink that had rotted but you could still see the outline.

'Why a wooden sink, I have never seen anything like this before Brenda have you?'

'Amazing, just amazing, I remember watching one of those restoration programmes on the telly. If I remember rightly a wooden sink was put in the butler's pantry to wash the fine china and delicate crystal glassware, the wood being softer on them than a normal sink. This is fascinating Dennis, just fascinating.'

Dennis nodded, moving slowly round the room, pulling open cupboards where he could, besides one of the sinks, he pulled out a silver tray that needed a good clean, admiring the design he could just make out etched into it, after he had swept his hand over it to clear away some of the dust, to see it through the grime. He shone his torch around the room, the crystal oil lamp in the centre of the smaller table in this room, a twin to the one on the main table, tried vainly to sparkle under its cover of dust. Dennis sighed in awe of the history they were discovering, turned to put the platter back, swinging his torch fully into the cupboard realised that it held an old fashioned safe, Brenda heard Dennis gasp moved over to him, by this stage resigned to anything this house and Iris threw at her. Gripped Dennis shoulder, gently moved him to one side, tried one of the keys on the key ring, it fitted perfectly, with a sigh from herself and Iris she opened the safe.

Inside was very neat and dust free. There were bundles of papers, a small strong box, which she lifted out and put on the table. Some bags of coins, and on the top shelf some velvet covered boxes. Her hands were shaking as she moved these and a bundle of the papers, putting them on top of the strong box.

Dennis noted her shaking hands and the pale colour in her face, decided that was enough for both of them. Taking the keys from her, closed and locked the safe, handed her the velvet boxes, picked up the strongbox and papers, ushered her out of the rooms. Another stronger waft of gardenia passed over them, causing Dennis to sniff out loud, a smile crossed his face, '*I think Iris approves,*' Brenda muttered.

Dennis nodded, 'I don't know about you, but a stiff drink and dinner will be very welcome now. Come on Brenda, we cannot do anything tonight! Nona and Poppa are going to be very pleased, they will have a wonderful time cleaning this place.' He gently nudged her out of the kitchen door, closing and locking it again, 'come on now let's go!'

'Stan said he would be here yesterday, I wonder what happened?' Brenda muttered her mind a sea of fog, just too much to deal with at once.

'Oh sorry, I forgot to tell you he rang, Poppa wasn't well, nothing serious, but Stan had to do two peoples' work, he said he would be here tomorrow. So, you can show him this place and see if Nona and Poppa will come and help again?'

They had slowly made it up into apartment two, Dennis depositing the strong box and papers on the table moved into the kitchen to get both of them a drink. Brenda slowly followed him into the room still in a state of shock.

'Ben is not only going to be annoyed but Glen is going to be furious with me!'

Brenda stated as Dennis took the boxes out of her hands and put a drink in their place. 'Why?' he asked as he put the boxes on the table. 'Because not only are we going to move the laundry, we are going to move the kitchen as well!'

Dennis looked at her, taking a sip of his drink, slowly understanding what she had said.

Brenda suddenly knew what she had to do, all sense of confusion disappeared.

'Can you call Stan to get here with Nona and Poppa tomorrow please, and organise the food, I am starving. I need to call Glen, I am going to need him and the gang here early tomorrow, we have some redesigning to do!'

Chapter 27

'JULIE HADDON!'

'Mrs. Haddon, good evening, I am sorry to disturb you, I am Brenda Chalmers, we haven't met yet, but I believe I am responsible for all of your men and women folk being away very long hours!'

'Brenda, Ms. Chalmers, yes but I think I should be thanking you for doing that, and giving them purpose, please call me Julie, is there anything wrong?'

'No Julie, and please call me Brenda, your men folk do. Thank you for those delicious cakes and pastries you send, I hope you will be sending me a bill?'

'What bill Brenda, I have to feed my troops, I just add a few extra in case. Do you want to speak to Glen, he is hovering?'

'Yes, thank you Julie, I am sorry but you are in for another early morning tomorrow.'

'I am used to them, thank you for the call, we will meet soon I am sure, I will pass you over to Glen.'

'What's up lass, the door didn't fall out, did it?

'No Glen, but another one opened. Let me just say Iris has struck again. No please don't interrupt, can you get over here very early in the morning, I don't mind how early with Rebecca, Dan and Peter?' He muttered of course, but why?

'You did say that you would be getting the plans stamped for what we had and the unexpected, didn't you Glen. Well the unexpected has happened. I don't want to say any more, but we are not doing what is on the beautiful plans Peter has drawn, we will hopefully be doing better. Tell Ben, he Matt and Charlie will be needed, with another generator and more lights!'

'Ok lass, we will be there, that house is a conundrum for sure you think you have it pegged and it throws another one at you. Ok I won't press you we will be there around five, better driving at that time anyway. Sleep well, see you in the morning!'

Dennis left just after eating, promising he was going to be there in the morning taking a day off, he wanted to be there when Glen and the boys arrived. He wanted to see first-hand the expressions on their faces, not have it told second hand.

After clearing the food off the table, Brenda pulled the velvet boxes to her, opening one found herself looking at what seemed a wonderful pale blue sapphire and diamond necklace with matching earrings and bracelet. The next, exactly the same pattern but emeralds and diamonds, in the last box rubies and diamonds, find a nice pattern and stick to it she thought; she was beyond shocks now. Another smaller box held two sets of very fine freshwater pearls, with earrings. Then the last of the five boxes was in two parts, earrings in the top, necklaces in the bottom. A pair of earrings in the shape of an Iris flower caught her eye, in the bottom she found the matching necklace, Brenda sighed, knowing these had to have been favourite pieces and worn frequently. Tears were rolling down her cheeks, but she had not realised she was crying until the drops fell onto her hands, holding the precious jewellery.

'Iris how can I thank you?' she said out loud to the unseen spirit, the scent of gardenia wafting strongly around her. 'Why me, I do not deserve all of this, how can I repay you and the family for this bounty? I have already promised to restore laughter and happiness to this house. What else do you want me to do, I will follow my heart and hope that is enough!'

She picked up the box with the two sets of pearls with the matching diamond teardrop earrings, sparkling in the overhead lights, she did know the value and quality of this type of precious work. Mother and daughters, she thought immediately she knew she was right. *I shall pass a strand on to my daughter, she will appreciate the beauty of a matched pair.* She had a vision of the years she and her daughter had worked in Broome, saving every penny to purchase the single pearl pendants they both cherished. Ghostly laughter brought her out of her reverie, wiping the tears of remembrance from her face, she picked up the Iris pendant thought it was made out of sapphire and emeralds bound in gold, the clasp was quite worn so she knew it was a very loved piece, she heard a sigh and wondered if she had made it or Iris?

Slowly she closed and put the boxes aside, determined to put them back in the safe until she could find out if they were real or just pretty pieces of glass, the ghostly laughter made her doubt the latter. With trepidation, she started to pull the strongbox and papers towards her, but a strange reluctance came over her, and she thought that she should not look in the box, but find someone else. Instead she pulled her expanding file over, she had bought it to keep track of all the papers she had and was receiving, from everyone. Finding the sheet Linda had given her with 'useful' telephone numbers on, found the lawyers name and phone number, in small writing under the printed details was written *very helpful and contact at any time*. Brenda also realised the name was the same as on the inheritance letter so Mr. Lawrence Morecombe QC, you will be getting a phone call from me in the morning and you can look through that, putting the papers and bundles on top of the strong box, with a pat, she picked up the velvet boxes taking them into the bedroom, for a little better security, and went to bed.

Chapter 28

S HE WAS AWAKE BEFORE the alarm went off. Showered, dressed, coffee brewing and urn bubbling checking on her hand drawn plans on the table, next to the strong box, when the Haddon's, Dan and Peter buzzed her.

Going down she opened the door, leaving it unlocked for Dennis, ushering them through apartment one to the back door. Glen asking 'Ok lass, what is going on, what have you and Iris been up to?' Brenda didn't answer just checked to see if Ben, Matt and Charlie had the small portable generator and a couple of lights with them, Rebecca was armed with her camera.

'I am not the only one who likes pulling things apart,' Ben said as they passed the stack of timber in the patio area, then he saw the laundry. 'Brenda what have you done to the laundry?', then he saw the door, 'and what have you discovered here?'

They had all trooped into the hallway and seen the door in its darkness. Matt and Charlie looked at Brenda with a grin on their faces, and began to start up the generator for light. Rebecca ran her hand over the door, the handle and fixings, wondering at the age under her hand.

'Original Brenda, definitely original, what have you found?' she was taking pictures as she spoke, to which Brenda was thankful as she was still shaking. A shout from upstairs heralded Dennis's arrival, Glen and Dan laughed at his 'Wait for me!' as he ran through the house and down the stairs.

Brenda laughing with everyone as he explained, breathlessly, his part in finding yet another of Iris's secrets. Watching as Brenda opened the door, as they moved in Matt and Charlie put the lights just inside the door in the corners of the room and started up the generator, everyone gasped.

'Oh Wow,' came from Matt and Charlie as they moved over to the table to take a closer look at the oil lamp. Rebecca was trying to take photographs of everything at once she kept going 'Wow' at every shot.

'Well lass, this was definitely worth getting up early for. She kept her best to last didn't she,' Glen commented as they wandered around the room. Comments came from everyone as they explored the space, finding not only the butler's pantry but also the laundry to the front of the building. The old copper tub was still in place, washing on the pull-down line falling apart at the touch, a window high up still with glass in place, that you could see the bricks that had been used to seal it from the outside.

Peter came over to Brenda, with Dan and Glen, followed by everyone else.

'So,' Peter said, 'you want to relocate the laundry and kitchen I take it?"

Glen and Dan looked at Peter, then at Brenda to see what she said, but they both knew what was coming and smiled.

'Yes, I do. I would like to use the space as it was originally intended. I am going to use the space upstairs as a proper dining room, if you put the table I think is up there across the room and not down it will make more sense. If possible I would like to keep the carcass of the AGA, I doubt we could remove it anyway, but update it to gas?' A questioning eyebrow was raised at Ben, who smiled. 'Perhaps we could incorporate a dumb waiter beside the new stairs to help in getting the plates and food up and down the spiral stairs. Please my friends,' they had all gathered around, 'I know I am asking a lot on top of the supreme efforts you are already giving, but I am asking a little bit more!'

They all looked at her for a heartbeat, then smiles broke out, Glen and Dan's just getting bigger.

'What the heck Brenda, I speak for my side of this caper let's give it a go!' Dan said, 'but don't get your hopes to high, we have to get the ok from the builder, but I cannot see that there will be a problem structurally. Well Glen, what do you say, your lot will have to check the build, Rebecca you have to buy the bits and pieces to bring the area into this century. Peter, you have to get the plans sorted, what do you all think?'

Brenda was suddenly overwhelmed by the commitment this group of people, who were strangers only a week ago were giving her. Feeling very grateful they were willing to go along with her ideas and madcap schemes.

'I will take whatever you can give me. I do not mind eating noodles with Dennis until it is completed. This is my project of course, the lift well and stairs, the other apartments take priority, I don't mind waiting.' Brenda added quietly.

Everyone looked at Glen, his smile broadening even more, 'well everyone, I think this lady has been in the dark too long, how about we bring her back to life!' He looked pointedly at Brenda, but addressed his remarks to the room in general. He held up his hands to quiet the cheers and whistles that broke out. Brenda giving him a hug saying quietly thank you.

'So, what do we do first?' she asked to the room in general, 'I think we will need boxes to pack all of this up,' she pointed around the room, 'then clean I suppose. I need to check if Stan is still coming today, maybe he can bring some boxes, then we can move everything upstairs to be catalogued and this place can have a serious clean, what do you think?'

'I will call Stan,' Dennis said, 'I need to check with him from my call last night, he will definitely need the full team with him!' Dennis had the broadest grin on his face he was enjoying himself immensely.

'Thanks Dennis, ok cleaning taken care of, what do we do till then Dan, Glen?'

'That is up to Peter to plan and Rebecca to give us a time frame for the fixings. Ben, you need to check the plumbing, Matt you and Charlie need to see about getting electricity in here. So, until the 'experts', and Glen chuckled to himself, 'have done the checking I think a good clean in her is first priority, don't you?'

'Just a moment, before we go off half cock!' Rebecca piped up stopping everyone from moving to touch anything, 'I need to take more detailed photographs of this place in situ, so nobody can move or touch anything for at least an hour or more!'

'That is all right sis,' Matt put in, 'Ben needs to close off and cut down those pipes, downright dangerous they are. Then we have to look at taking down the wall that is also obstructing the door. So, while you are in the kitchen taking the photos we will do that. Why don't the rest of you go and brainstorm upstairs with a cup of tea, I will have mine white with two sugars please. By the time, we have fixed up the entrance, Stan and his lot will be here to help us pack and move things, then they can clean and we can see what we have to work with!'

Glen laughed, clapped him on the back, saying good idea son. Rebecca had a grin like a Cheshire Cat on her face, shooed everyone out, closing the door. Brenda realised that Matt and Rebecca were right, so she moved upstairs with Peter, Dennis and Glen, Dan going to answer a question Charlie had asked.

Chapter 29

Peter and Glen saw her drawings on the table when they walked in, then the strongbox.

'Crockery and pots were not the only things you found were they Brenda, what's inside?' Glen said pointing to the strongbox.

'I have no idea Glen, I was going to open it last night but found I couldn't. So, I am going to ring the lawyer Pickworths uses, hopefully he will take it away and check it out, and not come back with bad news. I found a couple of other things, let me show you this,' she passed Dennis who smiled at her, offering tea's or coffees to all. Coming back into the room with the sapphire and diamond box of jewellery, showing them to the men, who whistled in appreciation.

Glen just shaking his head, 'oh lass, that is just beautiful, did you find that last night too? You know I have seen that pattern somewhere?'

Dan stomped up the stairs grumbling all the while, 'they told me to go and get a cup of tea, told me to relax and chill, me relax and chill, humph. They were just having too much fun and didn't want to share!' Everyone laughed, Dan came over to them seeing the strong box and then the necklace snuggled in its box. 'Oh oh, Iris did keep the best till last, that is the same pattern that is in the steel work, is it yours?'

'That's where I have seen it before,' Glen said slapping his forehead, 'you are right Dan see Brenda?'

'Of course, it is, knew I had seen it somewhere. I am going to confide in you all before the kids come up for their cups of tea, Dennis knows I told him last night; I am Iris's heir!'

The stunned faces looked at her, slowly comprehension dawned on them all, and they smiled at her.

'When I was cleaning the mess before you gentlemen became my friends,' they nodded lifting tea cups in acknowledgement of the fact, 'I found Iris's Journals, you know that they have been extremely useful. What you don't know was that they could not find her last will. Well I did, it fell out of the last journal that had been somehow kicked under one of the tables that were dotted around the room. No one cared enough to clean up after her when she died, so it was there when I came in. It stated that the person who found the letter was to inherit all her goods and chattels in her dwelling. So, to answer the question Dan, yes, I suppose these are mine. Silly isn't it, I don't have a lot of jewellery, now I have some pieces that cost a house to buy, if of course they are real?'

The silence that followed her statement was absolute, Glen broke it by going and putting a sustaining arm around her shoulders, as he could see the tears flowing down her cheeks.

'Lass, no wonder you reacted the way you did in the workshop, and I have no doubt these are the real deal,' he pointed to the necklace. 'I wonder you had the courage to go into the kitchen, so many shocks. Well you deserve all that is coming to you. You are spreading it around as well,' Dan and Peter nodded in agreement, 'I think Iris could not have hand picked a better person to be her heiress, and that is a fact!'

Dan, Peter and Dennis all seconded Glen's statement, lifting their tea cups in salute. She went to make a cup for herself, she also needed a break to blow her nose and wipe the tears of happiness away. Coming back to have a discussion amongst them of what they could actually do. As long as they could get new plumbing and electrics into the new rooms easily, there was no problem in just reusing them as they were intended. The laundry could be reused with new appliances, Brenda stated she didn't think she could use a laundry copper anymore it took too much time. The men raised their eyebrows at the comment, wondering how she knew it took too much time. The main kitchen was basically ok in its layout, reorganising it to add modern appliances like a cooking range, large double door fridge and a pantry.

Brenda then asked if they could possibly remove all or part of the wall into the Butler's pantry area, to make the actual kitchen larger, moving the sinks and adding at least one dishwasher if possible. She would not be having the services of a butler, but if she was going to do the entertaining that was expected she would need the space for caterers when she did. Peter thought it made sense, but until they could thoroughly explore the what's and how's could not say a yes or no.

Rebecca was the next to arrive, begging for a cuppa before the boys arrived, which would be soon. Brenda laughed and gave her a hug, moving with her into the kitchen to make teas and coffees for everyone. Soon the room was full of happy people seen and unseen. The smell of gardenia wafting around while they all gave advice and suggestions for how to complete this amazing transformation. Brenda reiterated that her apartment was the last in consideration, the lift and the other apartments were the top priority, they all smiled and nodded in acceptance of this. Stan appeared in the doorway to a chorus of cheers, a smile broke out on his face.

'Dennis said you had something urgent for us Brenda? From what I have seen down stairs, there is still a lot of building to do, what's up. I brought back the box, Nona and Poppa are waiting downstairs!'

Immediately Dennis with Rebecca went down to bring them up for a cup of tea. Ignoring their complaints, they arrived to be seated and given not only the drink but offered a biscuit or cake as well. Poppa did not look too well, using Dennis to translate she advised him she had a special job for him today. No lifting, or strenuous work, he was to ask if he wanted anything moved or lifted, she would be very cross if he tried himself. There would be plenty of people around to help him, they would be told to stop and help if he asked!

Nona just looked at Brenda, while Stan was bemused at what she said, smiling and nodding their heads. Brenda realised that both

Stan and Nona had been trying to get him to slow down, and he not taking any notice of either of them, but he would of her.

Once tea was finished, Glen and Dan realised it was seven thirty already they had things to do, men would be arriving if they hadn't already.

Brenda, Dennis and Rebecca took Stan, Nona and Poppa down through the house, stopping when Norman and his team arrived.

Norman beaming at everyone, marvelling at the space in the apartment, where had the stairs gone?' He urged his team through the house into the conservatory at top speed, he had a mission, and no one was going to stop him. Brenda telling him to remember tea breaks, she smiled at the crew going past, then took her group out the back door.

Stan stood stock-still, Nona smiled even broader, running a hand over the staircase as in benediction. Poppa went over and checked the edge, coming back telling everyone it was very good.

'You have done very well, very well indeed Brenda, a treasure you have found!'

'You have not seen even half of it, come on,' Dennis said, 'lead on Brenda!'

When they got down to the patio area, Brenda heard Nona gasp, but ushered them all into the hallway, where Brenda stopped short. Not only was the laundry gone there was nothing on the new-found kitchen wall, apart from the door!'

Rebecca turned at her gasp, 'the panelling was all rotten Brenda all of it, so Ben, Matt and Charlie decided to remove the lot to the brick, it made sense.'

By this time everyone was down the stairs, Brenda opened the door into the kitchen, immediately Nona and Poppa were exclaiming, moving around the room, talking and gesticulating so rapidly that Stan and Dennis could hardly keep up in the translation, Rebecca standing next to Brenda nodding her head understanding some of the Italian, a smile on her face.

Suddenly Nona and Poppa both turned and pointed to Brenda; Stan shrugged and turned with a look on his face, saying what more can this place throw at you, asking a question with his eyes.

Brenda laughed and hugged him going over to Nona and Poppa doing the same, 'Stan please ask if Nona could clean this place up. I will need Poppa to then catalogue everything in this and the next room. We will need to box everything, and move it upstairs, set up a trestle table in the front room, put Poppa behind it to check everything being brought up. Dennis has volunteered to help him, he has taken the day off today. This will keep Poppa useful but still.'

Dennis nodded in agreement, 'wouldn't miss this for the world,' he said with the broadest of grins on his face.

'Nona please, I would like her to call in as many people as she needs to be able to clean this place. We need it clean to see what we can do, I intend to remove first with a view to reusing everything, but unless we can see we may miss something?'

Stan nodded his understanding, and also why Dennis had asked him to bring boxes, lots of them, turned to translate to both his parents. Poppa beamed, aware he was being kept quiet, but as he was going to be useful to this lovely lady, he was very happy. Nona was bopping up and down on the spot talking nineteen to the dozen, she started to push everyone out the door and up the steps telling Stan to get the people together to help do what Brenda had asked, 'The Family' had to be summoned.

A very hectic couple of hours later the house was humming with workers.

The Kew Gardiners were in the only serene place. There were workers out the back of the house preparing the structure for the lift. The old kitchen had 'The Family' happily packing and moving boxes upstairs, where Poppa and Dennis were trying to catalogue onto Brenda's laptop the riches they were finding in the cupboards and butler's pantry.

Dan was happily going from putting in the new basement stairs, to checking the outside work with Glen, then helping, when requested, moving boxes and pieces of furniture found, out of the kitchen and upstairs.

Deliveries kept coming, apartment three was being used as a warehouse with Peter, Rebecca and Mia, once she got over the shock of seeing the kitchen, going around helping wherever they could. Brenda moved around the groups, getting yelled at by Nona, but happy to assist where she could. Nona had insisted she was the only one who could clean the oil lamps, they were delivered once deemed clean, in sections by Bella, to the spare wardrobe in apartment two, the only safe place in the madhouse!

Chapter 30

IT WAS ABOUT ELEVEN o'clock and for once peaceful in the front room of her apartment, when Brenda heard a loud 'Hello, anybody hear me?' coming from the front of the house. There could be no knock as true to his word Glen had removed the original doors and was in the process of reframing for the new improved ones. A man about Peter's size was standing looking a little out of place amongst the workmen. The fact he was wearing a beautifully fitted charcoal suit and highly polished brogues, might have been the giveaway that this had to be Lawrence Morecombe QC, the lawyer she had rung earlier to see if he could spare her some time to come and check out the strongbox. He had not hesitated, stating yes, he knew who she was, and it would be a pleasure to call around.

Brenda accepted the firm handshake, looking into the clear blue eyes of, what she had to admit was a handsome man, and he matched his phone voice perfectly. Well built, not too muscle bound, certainly filled the non-padded shoulders of the suit well. He stood a shade over five feet eight inches tall, with a distinguishing hint of grey at the temples of his dark brown hair. The twinkling blue eyes were smiling at her, and she felt a little perplexed, wondering at the feeling that she knew him, a waft of gardenia floated around and she smiled.

'Mr. Morecombe, I presume? Well you wanted to see the house. I am sorry that it is more in pieces than whole, but let me show you around if you have the time?'

'I certainly have enough time to view this work in progress, please call me Lawrence. What have we here?'

Shaking off his own feeling of knowing this woman who had just come into his life, but he did like the frank look and strong handshake. Wondered fleetingly why he had asked her to call him Lawrence, but was too late to say anything else. Disconcerted by that pull of attraction; to cover himself he motioned to the boxes and moved at Brenda's wave into the front room, where Dennis and Poppa were struggling to check and catalogue the items from the kitchen.

Introducing him to Dennis and Poppa, telling him that the boxes were part of her inheritance. He looked at Brenda, at the boxes and around the room looking at the first quality antique furniture he could see carefully stacked and the numerous boxes in the corners. Making a mental note, he picked up a knife from a box of cutlery that was being checked and written up.

'I think I had better make sure you have sufficient insurance not only on the house but the contents as well Ms. Chalmers!'

'Please if I am to call you Lawrence you can call me Brenda!'

'Do you know what you have here?' he continued after a nod to acknowledge her request, he looked at the knife he had perfectly balanced on his finger, noting the delicate engraving on the very sharp looking blade, as in pristine conditions as the day it was made. 'I do not know either, but I can tell quality, and this,' he pointed to the cutlery box he had lifted the knife from, 'is top notch!'

'I certainly realise more and more that I have acquired the best. Mia Farrington-Smyth, one of my interior designers, has an aunt at Sotheby's she is coming over with some others on Friday I believe, to check the pieces over, so hopefully I can give you an estimate after then for the insurance?'

A cheer went up from the hallway, everyone went to see what was going on, they arrived just as Dan's head appeared in the stairwell, the circular stairs were almost finished! Dan stretched to shake Lawrence's hand, welcoming him to the mad house. He laughed at the introduction, Brenda motioned him into the relative quiet of the dining room, going out into the conservatory. Suddenly another shout was heard from the far side, still hidden by a lot of overgrown shrubbery.

'I think you are bringing some good luck with you Lawrence, seems they have found the outside conservatory doors. They did not think to find them till Friday at least.' As they turned to continue the tour a voice came out of the plants ahead of them.

'Well look what the weather has brought in, Larry Morecombe as I live and breathe, how is the Polo going?'

'No good the horses keep drowning!' came the very quick reply from the gentleman beside her, Norman came out from the shrubbery. Brenda laughing as the two men, who clearly knew each other well said hello. Norman again asking what he was doing at the house. Lawrence explained that he was Pickworths lawyer, surely, he remembered that James had taken on his firm a few years back? Norman thought a moment, said something vaguely remembered, he was very happy to see him again, but he must get back.

'Take good care of this Lady,' he said as he disappeared into the shrubbery again. Shouting that they had found the doors, but there was still a great deal of work to do to get them open.

'Well Brenda, you have your champions, Norman is one of the best judges of character around, if he states I have to take care of you, then I most certainly will!'

'I should hope so,' came a voice from behind them. Glen had returned from the works, with some of the new soundproof panels to insert for the hall wall, 'we definitely do not want to fail at this stage!'

Brenda laughed at Glen's very stern voice, introduced the two men, who shook hands and sized each other up. Glen wondering if Lawrence would be a good man to have on your side, Lawrence realising that Brenda did indeed have her champions, here was another one. He wondered again at the strange feeling, the pull that he needed to help her in any way. Giving a mental shake to pull his thoughts back to what Glen was saying, as he was explaining how the apartment was going to look once the panels and walls were in position

They left Glen to continue the tour, out the back door onto the landing, Lawrence becoming another of the 'Wow' advocates, on seeing the outside fire stairs and landings for the first time. As they started to go down to the basement, Nona, Stan and 'The Family', were coming out to climb up.

Stan was in the lead, 'Brenda that is very good timing. We have finished in the rooms, I was just coming to get you. Should I go and find Peter and Rebecca to let them know as well?'

'Thanks Stan, yes could you please!' Brenda asked after she had introduced Stan to Lawrence. She turned to Nona, 'Thank you and the Family for all your hard work today.'

Nona beamed, took Brenda's hands pulled her down and kissed both cheeks. Looking at Lawrence smiled saying something in an aside to the rest of the Ladies huddled around. Which made Lawrence flush slightly and cough, all the ladies were nodding at Nona's words. Stan ushered them all up the stairs and out, saying he was going to ferry them to the next job, but he would leave Poppa to keep him out of mischief, if that was all right, he would be back to pick him up later. Brenda called after him to remember to tell Peter and Rebecca they were finished.

'This way Lawrence, you might as well know that since I have been here, the last tenant of the house, did you know her at all?' at his negative shake of his head she continued, 'well Iris has had fun pulling surprises on us, this is just the latest!'

Brenda then described the downstairs hallway to him of a week ago. *I made it to a week,* that made her stop in her tracks.

Lawrence prompted her to continue, 'A week really?'

'Sorry,' Brenda said, coming out of her revelry, 'I just worked out that I was employed a week ago today, what a week it has been!'

'Congratulations, it seems to have been quite a week for you, here's to many more,' Lawrence was smiling and had taken her hand to shake it, but he was loath to let it go it felt so good in his. He shook his head at his fanciful notions.

Brenda laughed, saying not like the last one or the three to come, she hoped, reluctantly taking her hand out of his, it had felt so good being held. Taking the lead, she took note of the very clean hallway, the boards back over the floor but she just knew they had been cleaned. Opening the door into the completely changed kitchen from the morning, she stopped so suddenly Lawrence walked right into her, putting his arms around her to stop them both from falling.

'Sorry, I am so sorry,' Brenda whispered her apology, but what she saw had left her so stunned. 'Those Ladies are fiends. How could they do this spectacular job in so short a time, I will let them loose on any house I own, if I ever own one!'

Lawrence wondered what Brenda was so surprised at it was a supremely clean, tidy and inviting room. All he could do was think *'she belongs in my arms',* he also realised in that moment she had leaned back into him, she fitted just right, a waft of fragrance he did not recognise passed him, before he reluctantly let her go.

The timber gleamed in the light sent out by the lamps on the stands in the corners of the room. The table was scrubbed clean waiting for vegetables to be chopped and dinner prepared. The floor was spotless, although tiles were broken and missing in places. They moved into the old laundry, the copper so dusty and green just a scarce two hours ago, gleamed. Into the butler's pantry, with all the boxes removed, revealed full length shutters, which were tightly closed, this room even with only the lights in the corner, shone dully, smelling of a mixture of lavender and gardenia, Nona's special blend and Iris.

'A very nice room,' Lawrence said as they walked back into the main kitchen area. Brenda was standing at the AGA caressing the now clean and sparking enamel.

'I think you should know I found this room at eight pm last night Lawrence. No one knew of its existence before then, Iris had sealed it, or I think now, more likely her father a long time ago. When Glen and his men arrived at five am this morning, the dust of ages and quite a lot of the boxes that Dennis and Poppa are trying to catalogue were displayed or stored in these rooms. What you are seeing is a miracle, and I am asking those people for more of them. By god I think they will give them to me!'

Lawrence did not understand how this beautiful room could have been boxed up until this morning, but then the whole apartment was a surprise. Brenda turned as Peter and Rebecca walked into the room and gasped.

'Holy Cow, how did they do this! If I hadn't seen the before, I would not believe this!' Peter moved into the room, stretching out his hand to Lawrence. 'Peter Mason, Architect and friend of Iris House, welcome to the club Mr?'

'Oh, sorry Peter, where are my manners. Mr. Lawrence Morecombe QC may I introduce Peter Mason Architect, and Rebecca Haddon (Glen's daughter) one of my interior designers.'

Brenda pulled her mind back to the matter at hand, this room would be used again, it had to be, it felt so good to be in here. Even though it was not on, could not ever be in its present coal fired state, the AGA seemed to radiate warmth and comfort. Peter was telling Lawrence about the plans for the house. He had brought his rough layout to begin measuring in earnest. Rebecca was asking him what he thought about the house in general.

'This building site has promise. I wish I could have seen it before, everyone is so shocked by the loveliness of the place now it is clean!' He said moving around, he also liked the feel of the room, wondering at why the place felt so familiar, and he felt so at home.

'I took photos of it all, Brenda has the before photos of the whole house, and a few of down here, prior to the destruction then the reconstruction. Here, let me show you the first shot I took coming into the hallway!'

Rebecca pulled her digital camera across the table, found the one she wanted, turned it to show Lawrence, then she ran it through the sequence. He did not believe his eyes, now he understood why Brenda had faltered. Looking from image in the camera to the image his eyes were seeing, he also took his hat off to the cleaners, wondering if he could employ them himself?'

'I am sorry Lawrence,' Brenda stopped at the look on his face, he was looking at the wall behind her, she thought someone else was coming through the door until she caught a glimpse of light. Above the doorway and along the wall, the same treatment with glass panels in the space between picture rail and cornice, mirroring the ones between the bedroom side of the basement. Brenda was sure that had been a solid wall to the ceiling when she checked it bringing Nona and the Family into the room. Then she realised Nona had seen them from inside the room, probably side-tracked either Glen or Dan to take the bricks down, restoring the hall to its original design, and letting a little more natural light into the room. They were as beautiful as the others, sparkling gamely from the light both artificial and natural.

'Please Brenda call me Larry,' he said absently, trying again to place the feeling growing in him. Watching the light play on her face as it was turned up to view the windows, she just recently realised were there, he knew this woman, but how, where?

'My mother was the only person who called me Lawrence, and usually only when I had done something to displease her!'

Brenda laughed, 'Larry!' she said bowing slightly in acknowledgement, 'I don't mean to keep you!'

'Oh, you are not, I assure you, and the work you have done in so short a time, makes me want to come back and visit this remarkable venture again and again, that is if I am allowed?'

'Well we will have to see, can you hammer a nail?' a negative shake of his head,' hum,' are you any good with a paintbrush?' another negative shake of his head, and a very forlorn expression, 'fix a leaky tap, or change a plug?' yet another shake.

'I do love to cook a little. I make a mean Steak Diane, complete with Duchess potatoes I may add, and my Gnocchi is not bad either. I also make a mean cup of tea with all the trimmings, and better coffee!'

'Good then Larry you are welcome any time. We have more than enough of the others around here!'

They laughed, Brenda remembering what the time was, 'as I was saying, I am sorry the time has run away, can I show you what I rang about?'

'It is fine Brenda, I am really not needed until later, but yes let us go and see what you have discovered!'

He called a goodbye, 'I will return!' through the door at Rebecca and Peter, both of whom had been very interested in the exchange between Brenda and Larry, and the wafts of gardenia they could smell, suddenly engrossed in going over the plans spread across the kitchen table, shouting a belated farewell back.

Dan called them from the top of the now fully installed circular staircase, so they could be the first official users of the same. Brenda felt a great sense of achievement on reaching the top, the first project done. Dan told her he was not putting the oak treads in till the job was finished, the steel base was ok for work boots. Larry was congratulating him on a fine job. Brenda turned as they walked towards the hall way telling him to go down and check the kitchen, angels had been in there. Dan looked at her, nodded understanding, watching with interest as Larry and Brenda walked out through the space for the pocket doors to the hallway would be, the wall now almost complete.

Brenda could not stop smiling.

Chapter 31

Larry followed up the stairs, his mind racing with the feelings of belonging he had, just walking around the house. He could almost picture the house as it was, but that was silly, he had only been here once before. He could not hide his disappointment at the décor as he walked into apartment two, it was not what he was expecting at all.

'Yes, this is not to my taste either, I am afraid,' Brenda had not missed his look of distaste, 'I was a little too late to stop the destruction of these apartments. But I am going to try in my own way to bring them back a little. Over here Larry, I have some other things to show you, would you like a tea or coffee?'

He opted for coffee and offered to make them both a cup, as she went to get the jewellery boxes from the bedroom.

She had to put some space between them; she had caught the whiff of gardenia down in the kitchen, she had also experienced the feeling of belonging when his arms had stopped them from falling, wondering what Iris was up to but making a fair guess of it as well. Yes, she was attracted to him that she could not deny, he seemed kind, but she had been badly hurt and would not willingly be hurt again by a handsome face, there had to be more, but she could not deny the feeling that somehow, she knew him?

As she put the boxes on the table, Larry came out of the kitchen with the coffee and stopped. Brenda was standing in front of the window the sunlight that was streaming through had a bronze tint making her glow with a golden hue. She was intent upon something in her hands that sparkled brightly in the light. She turned and smiled at him, thanking him for the coffee. He gave himself a mental shake, wondering just what it was he had just seen, then he looked at what she was holding in her hands.

'Whew Brenda, where did you find these? Just incredible, can I put this one on you, you really cannot see necklaces like this to the best unless they are being worn?'

Brenda nodded and tilted her head to one side as he put the shimmering necklace around her neck fastening it with a little pat. She turned, Larry gasped, she looked stunning! Even with a dirty smudge on her nose, hair falling down from the knot on the top of her head. She was wearing and old school sweatshirt, dirty torn jeans and old paint splattered sneakers. He could not take his eyes off her she was as beautiful as the necklace that was sitting sparkling around her neck.

'Well how does it look? I could not bring myself to put it on last night, all I wanted to do was look at it to convince myself that it and the others were real!'

He nodded, couldn't think of any words to say, as she went into the bedroom to have a look in a mirror. Confusion ran through his brain, he was acting like a love-struck schoolboy not a grown man, definitely not a twice-divorced man with grown children. What was going on here, get a grip Larry, he thought. He was falling fast and he didn't know why, but he actually thought he liked the feeling, hoping secretly that it may be mutual.

Brenda came back with the necklace in her hand, Larry was bending over the other boxes. Shaking his head in wonder, as he looked at the other two necklaces, he turned at her footsteps, holding up the pendant.

'That so far is my favourite, as I can see a person wearing that on a daily basis, I did try that on, and liked what I saw. How do I get these valued Larry? Who do I trust? I have shown you as I know I can trust you, *also Iris believes I can, she thought*, 'I wish Sir James was here he would know who I could contact?'

'It is fine Brenda, I know someone who will come around and see you. I don't think it is a good idea to take these out in public, even in the boxes! Right now, please put them in a safe place, probably where you found them would be good. Now as I realise there is a great deal more to your inheritance than was thought, let me have a look at this strongbox, I take it this is really what you wanted me to look at?'

Brenda opened it with yet another key on the keyring that Bella had found in the kitchen, a waft of gardenia floating round the room. Larry opened the top, had a quick look at the letter on the top of all the papers and stopped. The letter gave a clue, but he just knew he could not discuss them with Brenda at this time and definitely not in the house, with workmen everywhere. They would need careful checking and handling to find out exactly what they were about, and would definitely not be saying anything to Brenda until he was sure of his initial thoughts. That and the wonderful fragrance he could not name seemed to make him very cautious. This lady he unconsciously knew had been given more shocks in this one week, than most people could cope with, better he took the box and papers away, then it would also give him an excuse to come back. Which he really wanted to do, this was a fun bunch of people on first impressions, people who he would like to get to know better, even begin again with Norman Greenwell, which had been a friendship that had lapsed.

'Well there is a lot of paper work in there, do you mind if I take it back to the office? I promise not to lose anything. If you want I can leave my watch here as a surety, but if I leave it then I won't be in time anywhere, especially if I get an invite back for another delicious cup of coffee?'

'Silly, you know the coffee is awful, I bought the best instant I could find as brewing takes time, and only a morning cup at that, but it never tastes as good as, 'and they said together' real Spanish coffee!'

Laughing at the whimsy of both liking Spanish coffee, Brenda took the key off the key ring handing it to Larry.

'No, I don't mind you taking the box or the paper work, I know it will be in safe hands, and the watch will not be necessary, I will put the jewellery boxes away safely. I had better get back and see if the troops need me. Please come back as often as you wish, you will always be a welcome visitor, to see how we are going, if indeed you are just around the corner as you said you were?'

Larry pulled out a card handing it to her so she could verify the address of the office, pointing out his private mobile number for her to ring at any time if she had questions. After adding the loose papers to the box, then closing and locking it, picked it up with ease, putting the key in his pocket reluctantly took his leave. Easily moving down, the stairs and out the space for the front doors.

Not really wanting to go, but now not having an excuse to stay. He easily carried the box, although Brenda knew it was not light, skipping out of the way of Glen and his master carpenter Nigel Hawthorn, Brenda had been introduced to the new face that morning, as they were trying to finish the frame work for the new front doors.

Brenda watched as he moved easily down the street, carrying the strong box as though it weighed nothing at all. *Never hit a nail or used a paintbrush huh, my left foot*, she thought. Still he was very pleasant to watch, *did she want to see him again, yes, she thought, yes, she would like that.* One thing she did realise as she turned back into the house with gardenia floating around, and under the watchful eyes of Glen and Nigel, that a relationship, friendship or otherwise, between her and Larry, was not going to be entirely her decision, Iris was definitely up to something.

Chapter 32

COMING OUT OF HER reverie, she could be of no use to Glen or Nigel, although they had been very interested in her watching Larry as he walked away. She wandered down the rebuilt hallway to the new back door.

Charlie and Rob were busy putting the glass into the doorframe and side panels, there was the same wonderful bronze tint to the plain glass, as Brenda reached them she was surprised and gratified to see the window above the door was not plain. A modern impression of the Iris flower was in the centre of the lead light window, a modern but still beautiful update on the windows in the rest of the house.

'Charlie, that is quite beautiful,' pointing to the window, 'you have out done yourself, where did you find something so beautiful so quickly?'

'Thanks Brenda, the artistry comes from my wife Gabby, Glen's daughter. She has been making mosaics and lead light windows, as well as being a damn fine pastry cook, for years. I saw this in her work shop and thought of this house, as it was the right size for above the door and similar in design to the rest of them, thought you would appreciate it, you don't mind, do you?'

'Mind, Charlie, how could I mind, it is beautiful and it belongs here. Thank Gabby for me and I insist on buying that separately, as it is her work, she deserves to be paid for it not lumped in with your bill, understand?' He nodded grinning, knowing Gabby would be thrilled.

'Does she have any others at all?'

'She has a few smaller ones, some of them about half the size of that one. Why, what is going on in that mind of yours?'

'Well, when the dust has settled down, so to speak,' he chuckled, 'I thought it might be nice to see if we can get more natural light, as much as we can in a basement, into the hall and kitchen. If we could make some windows in the wall, possibly a window next to the back door, I would also like to renovate the basement door from the street with a glass insert in the top part, to help with the light? Perhaps you can talk to Marcus, or better still put some of Gabby's work in the spaces, it would help with the light and tie in nicely with the theme of the building, what do you think?'

'You would have to check with Glen, Peter and Rebecca before they really start on the kitchen, Brenda,' at her quizzical look, he went on. 'Cupboards, once in a kitchen design very difficult to move around,' understanding what he was saying she nodded. 'I know Gabby has at least three windows completed, with various flower motifs, and she was going to start on a tall one, I am sure she could adapt it to be used next to the basement back door, no two panels are ever the same, that is probably why I like them so much, all of them are arrangements on a theme, so to speak. Three plus the back and front basement doors, would that be enough do you think?'

'To be quite honest Charlie I really do not know. I will go and check with Glen, Peter and message Rebecca to check. Have you been in the kitchen recently?' he shook his head no, 'you have to see what Nona and 'The Family' have done, they have wrought a miracle, it is so beautiful, ready and waiting for the kitchen staff to move right back in!'

A noise from the back garden made both of them jump. Charlie looking, turning back to tell Brenda they were going to swing the first of the ramps in place. He had already removed the glass from the panel they had selected to be the new doorway into the conservatory. Yelling down the hallway to Glen, telling him what was about to happen. They made their way over to where everyone was congregated, Brenda making sure she had her hard hat on, she did not want to miss this. Rob yelled at their retreating backs, that it was ok he didn't mind finishing up the work at hand on his own, you both enjoy yourselves!

Charlie and Brenda laughed, thanking him very much indeed.

Norman when approached by Brenda, Glen, Dan and Charlie that morning had at first resisted the idea of cutting into the conservatory. Then Charlie pointed out that they could use the glass from the removed section to replace some of the broken ones. He could also take the steel piece back to Kew for their archives. Charlie had then explained what they planned to do to make the conservatory more energy efficient, giving it an extra skin going over the top of the original with the energy conserving new glass, this would also help to preserve the original structure for years to come.

Norman had been very impressed by the new updated windows at the front, and with the man who had designed and engineered them. He also saw the benefit, after his initial reluctance to the way it would indeed preserve the conservatory. So, he thawed a little, after listening to the ideas coming from this very talented team. He realised the section was ideal to be removed, making the conservatory more useable to everyone in the building, not just the people in apartment one. Immediately taking a couple of his workers to photograph and catalogue the plants growing where the section would be removed and the ramp added, tamping down the earth to show where the new path would be into the area.

Brenda watched with Charlie and the crowd on the landing as the crane that had arrived earlier that morning onto the commons, lifted the smaller of the two ramps up and into place, slowly bringing it down to the correct angle. It fitted to the original landing from apartment one, with a very slight downwards tilt before it kissed the bottom edge of the conservatory, looking as though for all the world, it had been there from the beginning.

Dan motioned for the foundry men to make sure it was correctly placed at both edges, the original section of the landing railing was removed, so they could weld it in place, they made sure it was going nowhere in a hurry.

Within an hour the ramp was positioned, the piece of conservatory wall had been removed, and all pieces were in a Kew van to be moved and kept safe, secure in their archives. Brenda was invited to be the first to use the new ramp into the conservatory; she could not help it but shout a "Yahoo" and do a little jig in celebration, yet another success in the rejuvenation of Iris House was complete.

The longer ramp from the landing into the garden was in two sections, with a cross beam being put in place on the two posts they had recently added, then the first ramp from landing to beam was lowered into place, looking to Brenda like a bridge from landing to garden, the slope downwards to give a gentle incline from landing to garden when both pieces were put into place, slightly more than the conservatory ramp just enough to drain water away from the house, welded into place at landing and beam by the foundry men. Then moving into the garden to position the second ramp from beam to ground, and making sure both of them were not going to move any time soon.

While the second ramp was being positioned, more of Dan's steel workers removed the original railings from the landing giving easy access to allow the side railings to be Fitted into the garden and conservatory, making the ramps safe and secure. Then the crane was used to move all the pieces of the new powder rooms on trolleys, onto the landing to then be moved into the conservatory for positioning.

Many hands helped move the base into place at its designated spot, which could be found by the six posts that had been positioned to raise it slightly off the ground to allow easy access for plumbing and electrical pipes in their sound proof conduits to be attached. Dan had been very pleased with the base of the frame, which he had designed and made to mirror the conservatory floor, as seen from underneath, with the tile inserts. Once the base was in place, the crane then placed all the pieces, the soundproof panels that made up the walls both internal and external, the steel uprights to support them, and the roof panels with their own double glazed skylights that could be opened slightly for ventilation were stacked onto the landing to be moved into place when needed.

All in all, it was a very busy day, there were smiles and rainbows aplenty filling the house. By the time, Stan had come back to pick up Poppa, they had catalogued a few of the boxes. Brenda told Stan to advise Poppa he would be needed again the following day if he were free? Poppa asked if Dennis would be there as well?

Dennis piped up saying unfortunately he had to work, but he had a couple of students he would ask if they would come and help, they both needed some extra cash, and they spoke fluent Italian. They could help Poppa and also, they could use the Laptop better than he could, so would be more efficient. Brenda gratefully, telling Dennis to send them along assuring him they would not be idling their time away. Stan advised Poppa what was going on, he nodded his head in agreement, telling Stan he liked this lady!

Stan also declared that they were all work fiends for what they had achieved. He thanked Brenda for keeping Poppa in a sedentary job, active but quiet, as the doctors had warned him his blood pressure was too high. He thought he could still do the work Stan did, and no amount of telling him would convince him otherwise.

'That is perfectly fine Stan, I will need him again tomorrow and possibly the day after, at least he understands what he is handling, better than I do at this time. Then when we get into next week, and I need the 'Dream Cleaning Team' again, I will find something else for him to do, to feel needed but not strenuous, I promise!'

Stan laughed asking how she liked the kitchen, he had been part of it and even he doubted his eyes.

'Stan those women are miracle workers, you know that, I am going to let them loose in the entire house before we open, so warn them please!'

'They cannot wait, I will see you in the morning when I drop Poppa off.'

He left with Poppa, who chattered to him, clearly telling him about the day just passed, he smiled back at Brenda nodding his head as Stan told him about returning the following day to continue in his work. Stan smiled as he looked around at a house that was being transformed into something beautiful in such a short time.

As Brenda and Dennis went to view the transformation the steel men were working out the back of the house, Dennis gave her a couple of computer disks. Telling her they were the back up for what they had managed to catalogue that day, he had a smile on his face as he knew in part what she had inherited, and it was not the junk she thought it was, as least to his untrained eye and Poppa's knowledge, she was going to be in for a big surprise, he thought to himself.

The uprights from basement to the landing had been put in place beginning the framework of the lift. With them in place Brenda was puzzled as where they were positioned seemed to put the garden ramp out of place, with a frown on her face she moved over to Glen, Dan and Brent standing watching as the men tidied up, saying hello and asking about the placement of the ramp, and uprights.

'Well with our discovery the other night Brenda, it put a whole new twist on things,' Dan answered after a look at Glen and Brent. 'We called Brent, who talked to Peter, to see if what Glen and I asked was feasible?'

'That was, come on fella's, don't keep me hanging here?'

'Well we asked Brent if it would be possible to position the lift so it could run from the basement patio all the way to the top?'

'The only thing stopping it is about two feet of steel landing!' Brent put in, enjoying with the others the look of sheer incredulity spreading on Brenda's face.

She turned to ask the question of how it could be fixed, before the words could be said, Dan turned her to see two of his men with oxyacetylene torches walk out on the landing. He moved everyone back into the house until the cut was done to remove the oblong of steel, then the workman removed the piece of railing at the same spot. Taking both pieces away with them, Brenda said the position of the ramp then made sense.

'Well it would be a pain having to lug the shopping down the spiral staircase all the time, now wouldn't it? Although I think the glass enclosure of the lift should stop at your landing Brenda, as the landing itself gives enough protection from the elements in the basement.'

Brent was saying with a laugh in his voice, everyone was smiling broadly, going to see what had been achieved. An oblong had been cut into the edge of the landing, the exact dimensions of the lift, the foundry men returning with a sheet of timber to block the hole until the lift could be put in place.

Norman came up as they moved back into the conservatory, watching as Jack and Fred came up with another piece of timber to seal the conservatory against the unpredictable British weather.

'Well I think I can safely say what is happening here is a triumph. A triumph of mixing the best of the Victorian and Georgian eras with the twenty first century for sure. Thanks to your leadership and imagination Brenda, we might even make it in your four-week deadline!'

'No doubt about it Norman,' Glen said, 'I reckon we will finish in three weeks if the weather holds fine!'

'Do not even think about weather Glen, we are going great in the conservatory, you can now clearly see the path on both sides of the centre planter, which we didn't even know was there before. Come up with quite a few specimens we thought were gone long ago, also enjoyed tidying up your glorious collection of orchids my dear. So, we plant back the ferns and the plants we know should be in the area, we can supply you with those from Kew. Check the watering system, which reminds me I have to chat with that son of yours Glen, so Ben and my man can sort things out. See the building water tight, clean up the path to the garden gate, all simple really!'

Everyone laughed at his basic no nonsense account of what was an incredible amount of work. No one doubted even for a moment, he would achieve what he said, with the help of his very talented crew.

'By the way my dear, Justin noticed that there was a terraced wall down in the basement, did you want us to check that for you as well?'

Ben tensed at Brenda's side, Glen, Dan and Charlie looked at each other. Brenda was ready for the question, had been waiting for it all day, because they could hardly miss the terrace as they crawled and pulled weeds from the garden above it.

'Actually Norman, I was going to get you and some of your team to come back and fix up the terrace. You cannot work down there at the moment because of the steel work going on for the lift. So, would you please come back and not only do the terrace, but I was going to ask your opinion of putting a show of red and white roses, with possibly some lavender in the little garden at the front, once we can get to that as well?'

'Perfect my dear,' he said nodding, 'I was going to ask about the front. I will have Tristan and Mary look at a range of plants for both areas, so we are ready when we can access the areas safely. I have always been a big fan of Lavender, so will add it to the list. Did you want to make the terrace, at least the reachable area a kitchen herb garden, that would have been its original purpose?'

'I think so, but will leave the choice in your very capable hands. We have time to do that properly, once the mad rush to finish the construction has been completed.'

He nodded saying farewell to everyone, left with the remainder of his team, Brenda realised it was five pm already.

'Well I don't know about you lot, but I am bushed, what are we doing tomorrow?'

They all laughed, Peter had left with Rebecca she to liaise with Mia, to check on the details of adding Gabby's windows in the walls and beside the doors downstairs. Brent advised they would be continuing the steel framework for the lift, as this was Thursday, he would be back on Monday to check when they were ready to install the actual lift.

Charlie said Marcus had the glass in hand even for the new sloping roof to cover the ramp into the conservatory. The temporary front doors were in place the window a board at the moment. Charlie advising there was going to be a slight hiccup with the completion of that one and the ones downstairs, but nothing they could not overcome. Glen chipped in to advise his men were ready to install the new back doors starting with apartment four, as if they did that one first they could then work out how to install the lift correctly.

Dennis laughed, 'You lot have just dismissed what to anyone else would be six-month's worth of work, as if nothing at all!'

Startled they all looked at each other and laughed again, as they realised that Dennis had the right to it, but Brenda never had a doubt. She had the right people to do the job, she had no doubts that the original team would have still been in the middle of their shoddy work, milking the job for all it was worth. Not this team, this team would accomplish the miracle, she and Pickworths would have the house that haunted her in her dreams.

Deciding a night at home with their families was a good idea they started to say goodbye, Brenda realising that the following day was Friday, with a shudder she anticipated the visit from the Sotheby people, finally she might have some idea of the worth, if any, of her inheritance, still not accepting what she had been given.

'Hey do you realise tomorrow is Friday? It is truly amazing what you can achieve when you have the right mix of people, and I have the best. Now go home everyone, I am taking Dennis out for something other than noodles tonight'. She ignored Dennis groan and mutter of I like noodles. 'Then I am coming back to sleep, no exploring, no discoveries, just eight hours of blessed oblivion, see you all in the morning!'

Chapter 33

THE RESTFUL SLEEP BRENDA had promised herself was full of nightmare scenes, where the lift crashed, water poured over, into and through the house, loud explosions, and bright flashes. Strange people walked the halls and rooms, not unfriendly just she realised curious. She woke before the alarm, feeling strangely disconnected. Unsure of herself, her abilities, again the self-doubts that had plagued her for years reared their ugly head. Trying to dismiss them she spoke the mantra that had calmed her at times like this, when her life was going well and the demons of the past always came back to haunt her. She tried not to listen to the negative voices in her head, moving into the shower she repeated,

'I am protected by Divine Love, I am always Safe and Secure, I will Achieve!'

As she repeated this mantra, washed away the nightmares and doubts, again came a waft of Gardenia, Iris (she realised) was helping to calm her down and dispel her fears.

The Haddon's with Charlie and Peter found her in the front room, she gasped at the enormous boxes of baked goodies they were carrying.

'Julie and Gabby have outdone themselves, Glen. Surely they would make a fortune in the catering business?'

'Tried that they did Brenda!' Glen answered as they walked up to apartment two to deposit the boxes and of course for a morning cuppa. 'They got hit with the Foot and Mouth outbreak we had a while back, so could not travel to cater for functions. Then the strike by the EEC stopped the building work, that dried up another source of income for them. So, they put everything on hold until you came along. They are having a grand old time at the moment everyone is so appreciative of their fare!'

'They think a small army will be here today then, judging by the amount of food you brought!'

'Indeed, there will be, we are just the beginning,' Peter said and Brenda realised that his words were prophetic.

Norman was the next to arrive, his team raring to go. Ben had added two more plumbers to his team, he was ready not only to continue with the conservatory additions, but also amenities in the new bathrooms, kitchen and laundry. Peter had solved the problem of how to run new pipes in to the old kitchen by simply putting in a false floor.

'You have to step over the lip in the doorway, so I just made it a step, there is plenty of head room. The wide oak flooring Rebecca has picked fits in with the rest of the house, so it was an easy fix!'

Dan with his foundry men arrived next with the crane, some of Brent's team to help make sure all angles were checked.

Stan and Poppa arrived with Dennis, and the two students Philippe and Maurice. Poppa sized them up, spoke to them briefly and then beamed. Stan translating that Philippe came from the next village back in the old country, and Poppa knew his grandfather, everyone laughed as Philippe reddened and looked mortified, but just gave a Gaelic shrug. Watching as they moved to get set up for the day's inventory, Brenda asked if they could make two copies of everything, as she thought it would be good to give a copy to the Sotheby people for their records.

Dennis waived a cheery goodbye, telling Poppa to remember the tea breaks, and not to work too hard; Poppa just nodded his head as he directed the two boys into the front room to start the cataloguing.

As Brenda walked him out to the front door, Dennis advised he would not be around at the weekend, he had a phone call from his folks, so he was heading down to visit them, leaving later that afternoon, hoping she understood.

'Dennis, of course it is alright, you don't need my permission. I am feeling guilty that I have been taking up all your time. Go and give them both a hug from me, apologise that I have monopolised your company all this time!' He laughed checked on his students one more time, then left with a waive and smile, taking Stan with him.

The house settled down into industry. Everyone knew what they had to do, and just did it. There was the usual banter back and forth, but very little swearing or shouting out of line.

Quiet Italian could be heard from the front rooms, as Poppa guided his team. One student bringing the boxes to the tables, Poppa then unpacked them, to be photographed labelled and then described into the laptop, the box then numbered with the laptop reference, then carefully repacked again.

Glen, Jack and the rest of the builders were split into teams, some on the installation of the back doors in all the apartments, rebuilding of the front doors, the new floors in the kitchen and the making of wardrobes and bathrooms in the bedrooms.

Rebecca and Peter decided that the old laundry found in the kitchen, could be reused as a laundry and powder room with new appliances, and fixings that would only take a small amount of space. Brenda was gratified to see her suggestion of using Gabby's stained glass windows in the kitchen wall had been heard and worked on, as holes appeared in the walls, waiting to be framed and fitted with the windows.

Matt was next to appear, with a group of people in zip up suits of startling blue.

'Hi Brenda, meet my Tech Team!'

Brenda nodded and greeted each of the mixed group of men and women who were smiling and looking around eagerly.

'They are here to prep the building for the new wiring scheme over the weekend, to do what you want we have to work from scratch, and begin from the top down. We are going to use your idea of piping as in your apartment to run the wires and cables. Brent wants us to have the lift on a separate system, so we measure and check everything first, then it should be smooth running. I have put temporary lights in the kitchen, but we have plans to reuse the old gaslights we found, just you wait and see!'

She laughed at his enthusiasm, sending him on his way with a reminder to have his team and himself take tea breaks, they had brought more than enough cakes and goodies

Moving through the house she enjoyed the atmosphere of anticipation that was flowing through the whole place, it was a lovely feeling. As she entered the Conservatory she found Rebecca next to the steps from the dining room, on her hands and knees with a bucket of hot soapy water and a mop, a section of the timber covering that was over the entire floor propped up on the side of the steps, on seeing Brenda she stood up quickly.

'Ahh Brenda, glad you are here want to give me a hand? Mia sends her love and will see you later she was chasing up a couple of cabinets she heard of.'

'Love to help Rebecca, what are you doing?'

'I am trying to see what the tiles are like out here, so I can match them in the powder rooms. I also know what is underneath this place as well, my brothers cannot keep secrets from me, I cannot wait to see it! The way my big brother is going, he will have the place finished before I can get the tile for the floor!'

Gladly Brenda picked up the mop with a smile, truth to say, she had been itching to see what the tiles were like from the top, and how they worked with the workshop underneath. Also, the Kew Team had been working magic in the area, and it was looking like a garden you wanted to visit not the jungle it once was. When they had thoroughly mopped the area just beside the steps from the dining room, it showed a large middle square tile, boarded by oblong opaque glass tiles.

'Hmmmmmm,' Rebecca said, on her knees her nose a scant inch from the surface of the clean tiles. Taking photos on her phone, and making notes in her ever-present notebook. Brenda wondered if she should warn her about the trickle of dirty water heading her way from the unclean section of the floor.

'This could be tricky!' Rebecca muttered, ignoring the trickle of water seeping into the knees of her jeans. 'I don't think we can get the same. I will try of course, but I think we might have to resort to good old ceramic or porcelain, but I think we can match the colour!' She was writing in her notebook taking photos from different angles, a smile of satisfaction on her face. Brenda could not help herself, she had the mop and the soapy water, quickly she lifted a few more panels, washing the whole area clean a wave of gardenia swept over them, Rebecca looked up at Brenda and smiled, 'I think Iris approves?'

'I think she does luv, I truly think she does.' Brenda answered with a matching grin.

Norman coughed coming down the path from the front of the conservatory, 'Brenda, Rebecca, ah so you couldn't wait I see!'

'Norman,' Rebecca said jumping up, 'I am sorry but Ben is moving so quickly, I needed to check on the tiles. I knew they were here, I helped Tristan lift the first timber panel back in the beginning. Am I right in saying the larger square is Italian marble, and the framing tiles are Venetian Glass?'

'Quite correct, my dear, quite correct. I was leaving the panelling in place until Ben is finished, and as you so correctly pointed out he is working like a demon. I do like this outfit, they do things right the first time and efficiently.' Rebecca blushed at the praise for her family, he went over to her taking her hand. 'It is refreshing in this day and age to find people who take pride in their work, and want to complete tasks to the best or better than their ability. Please do not think I say this lightly my dear, but I have been searching for your father for years. I have too many projects that I need his expertise and attention to detail on, he can be working for the next century and still need time. I will be needing all of you after we complete this madness called 'Iris House', although I hope I don't lose the friendship of the lady who is running the ship, so to speak?'

'Never Norman,' Brenda said to cover Rebecca's shock at what Norman had said, 'you will be tending all of the gardens at Iris House for as long as I can see, and then Kew will have the handling of them after we have both gone to dust! I intend to leave them to be used as they should be, not to be left neglected again.'

'Thank you, for that Brenda, are you free at the moment, I came to ask you to take a promenade with me, the first in this place for many a year, we have found and opened the outside doors!'

'I am waiting for the Sotheby people to arrive, unless Rebecca needs me?'

Rebecca shook her head, still trying to assimilate what Norman had said to her, she had to speak to Dad, Mum is going to go into shock, she thought. That was what all the phone calls were about, Norman had been networking for them!

Norman nodded at Rebecca, took Brenda's hand and pulled it through his arm, putting her palm and fingertips gently on his forearm, giving a feeling of security and gentle support. As they wandered through the now delightfully light and airy space, Brenda realised the glass had been cleaned and also replaced where needed, no more murky view out of the windows. He pointed out the orchids, some in bloom, some just the wonderful dark green and dappled foliage, the scent of gardenia wafted around them as they walked.

'That's strange,' Norman interrupted himself as he sniffed, 'you have an extensive collection of Gardenia's my dear, but none are in flower at the moment!'

'I think Iris approves of your work Norman,' he looked at her a little startled, 'we are all smelling that fragrance when we discover, uncover or do something right. Iris has been my constant companion since I walked into this house, you and your team have done a wonderful job here, in such a short time. I know it is not finished, and will take a few months, if not years before you are happy with it,' he smiled again, 'but I think it is beautiful as it is, it can only get better!'

Norman was delighted, this lady, although stating she had a brown thumb, clearly knew a little about gardens. She had even named a couple of the orchids, and plants as they walked through what he had to agree was a delightful place. Yes, he knew she would look after the conservatory as it was supposed to be, making sure Kew could look after it in years to come. This place would again become a place of rest and solace it was supposed to be once more. Norman pointed out the alcoves halfway down both sides of the conservatory, into which tables and chairs could be situated. Then they arrived at the outer doors these were massive, the whole height of the conservatory, they opened outward, folding back into the niches similar to the French doors from the dining room, making a portico, that some sweet-smelling Jasmine was going mad over. Norman stopped her stepping out on the still unclear, but marked path to the garden gate and the commons she could see beyond.

'We can't go any further without hard hats Brenda, as they are still working with the crane and steel beams above us, what do you think?'

Brenda turned on the spot and looked back into the conservatory with wonder and gratitude in her eyes. Wonder that they had turned the jungle into such a welcoming space again after so long neglected, gratitude that the miracle had been achieved in such a short space of time. Dan came over to them, seeing them at the doors.

'Don't come any further at the moment Brenda, where is your hard hat?'

'I won't Dan, Norman has already stopped me, isn't this wonderful! I just walked through the Conservatory, what a miracle!'

Dan nodded, although he had not been inside, he had been watching the progress to stop any of the Kew people from wandering out. 'Not yet, have been too busy with our own project, you can step out and see, nothing happening at the moment!'

Brenda and Norman ventured just a little way out to view the back of the house for the first time in a very long time. Already you could see the framework for the lift, and how this new enclosure worked in harmony with the existing spiral staircase and platforms. They could see where the spans of existing steel, tied back into the black frame work of the conservatory, against the white walls of the building, it was a modern-day sculpture from Victorian days.

'It is brilliant Dan, you and your workers have done wonders, as have Norman and his team. I hope you will all join me in the conservatory at the end of the day, it is Friday after all?'

'Of Course,' Norman and Dan said at the same time, 'a good time to catch up on what everyone is doing, and organise a plan of attack for the days to come. It will be good to chat to everyone, there is so much going on around here!' Norman said, Dan agreeing with him.

Brenda walked back through the conservatory with Norman, asking him about the plants as they moved through. Rebecca had carefully replaced the timber over the tiles, to save them from Ben and his workers boots, Norman chuckled, very efficient indeed he muttered.

Chapter 34

BRENDA WALKED INTO THE dining room, looking at it with an eye to placing the table and chairs that had been found. Hoping her dumb waiter could be incorporated into the design, a large buffet would be needed for laying out plates and serving dishes, they would need to know where the dumb waiter was going to go so they knew how much space was left. Mia walked into the room, advising that she had met the team from Sotheby's outside, and brought them in, hoping she didn't mind, bringing her out of her reverie.

'Mind, no of course I don't Mia,' she went over and gave the young woman a hug in reassurance, 'is your Aunt with them?' at Mia's nod yes, 'well come on, introduce me, can you stay, it would be nice to have a friend around?'

Mia looked a little startled, but moved with Brenda back into the front of the house. Pondering what she had said, and the hug, it was nice from a very nice person; but it made Mia a little uncomfortable, with what she had been asked to do.

Before she met these wonderful people, she had never even thought of a building having a 'soul'. She was in interior designer because that was what her mother and uncles had told her she would be, no questions, no asking what Mia wanted, this is what you will be and this is how you will do it, was what she would do, even if she had any other ideas, they were not to be worked on.

She had in this company, realised that the ideas she had did matter, her feel for fabrics and her intuitive style with furniture, were an asset. Rebecca had helped, more than any teacher, or her family, she had believed in her, helped her to understand she was more than the strict confines her past had put her in. The heady possibility of working on a more permanent basis with Rebecca had crossed her mind, as she liked her forthright and down to earth style. Brenda had given her a second chance, she meant to take it with both hands, but she had some damage control to do.

First to the building she had helped almost ruin, then to the rumours she was asked to spread in the days after her 'team' were fired. The fact she had only been working with them because her mother had asked a favour of John Hemsworth, and he had quiet bluntly told her to do the most minimalist décor she could do, then she had spread the rumours in the twenty-four hours before Brenda had asked her to stay on, so short a period, but what damage had been done, she hoped by doing the very best she could would help redeem her in Brenda's eyes when she found out.

There were four people in the front room; one lady and three varying in age gentlemen. Mia went up to the lady took the outstretched hands, accepted the false air kiss on each cheek that went with the false greeting.

'My dear Mia, after the stories you have told my sister, I had to come,' she looked pointedly at Brenda, the dishevelled appearance, torn jeans, well-worn sneakers, was well on the way to dismissing her as just one of the workers. The telephone call she had received from her sister a few days ago, had her expecting just what she was seeing, and the rumours, well she was also on the way to believing them seeing the mess around her. The phone call she had received from Mia the previous day, only made her wonder about this person, that had arrived on the scene, and she decided to reserve her judgement.

'Introduce us dear, don't forget your manners!'

Mia blushed, the set down again what she expected, understanding that her phone call had not helped the situation, the damage of her spiteful words to her mother what seemed a lifetime ago, was still there.

'Ms Brenda Chalmers, may I introduce my aunt Mrs. Maud Prendergast, head of Ceramic section at Sotheby's, I am sorry I will have to have my aunt introduce the others.'

'That is alright Mia, I think your aunt may like to do that. How do you do, welcome to Iris House, I hope you can help me out of a quandary I am in?'

Brenda moved forward, shaking everyone's hand as Maud introduced them, they in turn handed out their business cards as well.

George Fredrickson, Art section; Michael Jarret, Silver / Gold ware; Frederick Austin-Healy, Furniture. They all had the disdainful look that she had seen so often, looking at Poppa who did not have anything on the table at the time, feeling the atmosphere, clearly Iris didn't like these people either. Poppa had told both Philippe and Maurice not to show anything to the strangers until Brenda gave him permission, he did not like the haughty lady who looked down her nose at them all.

'Thank you for coming at such short notice, I don't know what Mia may have told you Mrs Prendergast, but I need your assistance. I have recently come into this inheritance; I need to get a professional viewpoint, especially for insurance purposes. I have also been in contact with the National Gallery and the Victorian and Albert Museum, both were impressed I was having your firm to do a basic check of all my found pieces, as I would love to reuse all of them if possible, but I need to know exactly what I have to do so!'

At the mention of the Museums, they all stopped looking around the room and returned their gaze to Brenda.

'Mr. Palligria, with the help of Philippe and Maurice has been trying to document some of the items we have found, and brought into this room to keep them safe while building is in progress. Can I get him to show you what he had done so far; I think it is mostly silverware and some of the ceramics? The ceramics are in boxes over here, the art works over in the far corners, that is right Signor?'

Philippe was interpreting for Brenda as she spoke, Poppa looked at her and nodded, still not trusting these people, he would watch them, Philippe and Maurice would watch as well.

Then quick footsteps could be heard in the hall way, heralded another arrival. Brenda wondered if she could cope with yet another negative person, who thought she was wasting their time. She smiled in relief as the cheerful face of Larry came around the doorway, after he had knocked perfunctory on the frame.

'Brenda, glad I caught you, oh sorry you are in the middle of… Fred, my man Fred Austin Healy, how is the family business going?'

Frederick Austin Healy turned as he was addressed, stood stunned at the old Etonian colleague he had lost touch with years ago, walked through the door.

'Larry, is it really you, well I will be bowled over. My god man how many years has it been, no don't tell me, I don't think I want to know!'

The two men shook hands, embracing in the way long lost comrades do when seeing each other after a long separation.

'Well I do not want to interrupt, but can we please see at least some of the 'antiques' we are meant to be valuing, before too long?'

Clearly George was not impressed by the antics of his co-worker. Both Larry and Fred turned at his comment.

'Sorry Brenda, I will just go and see what Norman has been up to and catch up with you when you are free?'

'Norman, don't tell me that reprobate is here as well?' Larry nodded, watched the expression on Fred's face change. He had done what he needed to they would take Brenda seriously now, and he was sure Fred would make sure of it.

Brenda watched him go, advising he would need a hard hat, suddenly feeling that she could conquer Everest, because he was in the house. Talking to Poppa through Philippe she advised him that these were the people from Sotheby's, they had come to check on the artefacts he had been cataloguing, she asked if they had the duplicate disks, Philippe handed over four with a grin.

'I know that you will want to check for yourselves, so will leave you with Mr. Palligira and his assistants, his English is limited, but Philippe and Maurice will assist. I asked them to compile a catalogue, this is the work of two days. They have unpacked, photographed, labelled, re-wrapped and re-packaged every item on the discs. They still have a lot of the boxes to go through, I believe they did the art work and furniture first, they will be on the first disc.'

Maud moved forward and took the discs, this was no fool, she thought. From Mia's initial report that suddenly changed to the phone call of yesterday, had changed her mind on this her first meeting. From believing the rumours, and thinking she was dealing with an Australian imbecile from the middle of nowhere who was wasting her time, clearly this impression was wrong. To do what she was with contacting museums, the cataloguing and how she was recording the same, showed someone who knew or thought she had valuable goods in her possession.

Fred was also doing a quick rethink, this was not going to be the waste of time Maud had said it would be. He felt sure of it now, whatever George and Maud had cooked up on the way here. He went over to Poppa, introducing himself in flawless Italian, asking about the old man's family, clearly winning him over with his direct approach. He went up several notches in Brenda's estimation. She left them to whatever they needed to do, taking Mia with her out of the intense atmosphere.

Chapter 35

S HE TOOK MIA OUT to the conservatory, watching her face relax, as she smiled at the beauty that had been revealed all around her. Brenda pulled up a corner of the padding over the cleaned tiles, showing her what she and Rebecca had discovered under the grime.

'Oh, they are beautiful Brenda, what did Mr. Greenwell say they were I bet he said Marble and Venetian glass?'

'Yes love, but don't worry, I will be quite happy with the basic sandstone or ceramic tiles in the toilets. The fact we have come so far in such a short space of time is amazing, I think I am about out of my quota of miracles!'

They walked down into one of the alcoves, Brenda discussing what they could do, adding that it would have to be double possibly, as there was an identical one on the other side. They wandered down to the kitchen, the garden had started relaxing the tense young woman, Brenda could hear Larry talking to Norman she didn't think she could face him just at that moment. She knew the kitchen would work its wonders on the stressed out young woman beside her. The two tables had been hung with ropes from the beams, waiting for the last pieces of flooring to be put in place.

Mia just gasped at the transformation she saw before her, tears were running down her face, she was sobbing, 'I am sorry' over and over again. Brenda took her into her arms, realising suddenly that this kind of comfort would not be available in her household.

Brenda kept saying, 'It is ok, they were going to fix all the problems, Iris understood, if they all did their best from now on, only good would come out of all their endeavours!'

Mia pulled herself together, gone was the disdainful look that she had greeted Brenda with only a scant week ago. In its place, was a woman who had been made to see she had worth, growing, becoming a stronger person because of the people around her, helping her to reach her full potential at last. The little rich girl gone, because of the company she was now keeping, realising there was more to life, and she wanted her share.

'I am sorry Brenda; I don't know what came over me. I suppose it was seeing my aunt, and the men around her. I know of them, their reputations, of course, they are here because of what I have done. I am so sorry, please forgive me, but I just don't know how to fix the mess I helped to make?'

'I do not think we need to worry too much, I am sure Iris will take care of it for us. Can you not smell that very pleasant fragrance?'

Gardenia was wafting around them, Mia smiled, 'yes I have smelt if before, I thought it was coming from the conservatory?'

'Go and look into the area luv, not one of the extensive Gardenia collection is in flower at the moment. No love, don't be shocked, Iris is just showing that she approves of what you have and are doing, she is trying to get you to achieve even more! Rebecca and you make a good team, are you enjoying yourself?'

'Oh yes, I love working with her, she is so down to earth, has such wonderful ideas, but is encouraging me to chip in as well. I have some of the contacts, she the ideas, we make a very good team. We will make you proud of this place, just you wait and see, but what about my aunt and those doubters from Sotheby's?'

'Nothing at all love, they will see what they want, I am sure Iris will open a few eyes! Come on, it is nearly knock off time for the workers, I have a small celebration to set out, and want to put it in the conservatory. It is Friday, we have all worked our socks off, a celebration is in order, we will invite the Sotheby's team just for the heck of it, shall we?'

Mia took one look at Brenda, and laughed, all pretentions gone, this was one very turned around young lady, boy did she have everything going for her now, Brenda was so proud.

With Mia's help Brenda set up a couple of trestle tables in the cleared conservatory alcove, one for food the other for drinks. Set out the nibbles and extras she had rung Julie to provide, also some of the wonderful exotic food from Mama's Kitchen. Mia's eyes were wide when they stepped back and looked at the groaning tables.

'How did you do all this Brenda? She asked thinking of the agonies her mother had gone through in the past when doing an 'Afternoon Tea' as she called it; when all she did was pick up the phone, waving her hand at the tables, 'all that food, wine and goodies, you have been here all day working, how?'

'It's called networking my dear. This was not difficult, you just have to know the right people. Dennis gave me the contact in the hospitality business for the wine, he has a wonderful cellar, and I will be using him again. Glen's wife Julie and her daughter were in the catering business and will be again if I can help them. Mama wanted to help when she found out I was here. I spent a wonderful afternoon at her café after my first interview for this job!'

Mia broke in to ask did Brenda like her Spanish coffee as much as she did?

Brenda laughed and nodded, 'so never close yourself off from people just because they may not look like you, or walk like you. Life is too short and regret is a very bitter word!'

'Here, here, I second that last remark!' Brenda jumped as Larry with Norman and his team came into view of the alcove.

Larry had been looking for her, took in the spread before him, again that urge to help her came over him. Hearing her words realised that this woman had been hurt badly, would need careful handling, he could smell that wonderful fragrance again, he must ask Norman what it was.

Still not quite ready to talk to him, Brenda turned toward Mia bringing her forward.

'Larry, I don't believe you have met Mia Farrington-Smythe, Mia this is Lawrence Morecombe QC.'

Mia blushed and shook hands, greeting Norman and his group, started to hand out drinks, urging people to help themselves. Brenda moved off to call a halt for the day, it was Friday, time to celebrate what they had achieved. She went into the front room to meet Stan coming to collect Poppa, inviting not only them but Maud and the Sotheby team down into the conservatory for a Friday drink. At a nod from Brenda to the conservatory, a look and smile at Poppa, Stan led them all out of the room. Although the look Maud gave her after nodding her head to her team, spoke volumes as to what she was expecting to receive. Brenda called out to Glen and Dan saying it was knock off time, a yell in return told her they had heard.

Glen walked into a very changed conservatory from the one he had helped discover a week ago. He moved over to Norman and this Lawrence Morecombe QC, he wanted a word with them both, one business and one very private, he had heard rumours.

He had this unexplained urge to confront Larry, that damned fragrance was hanging around. Glen just had this feeling that something was building between Brenda and Larry, he saw the looks between them, remembering the conversations he had overheard the day before, between Mia and Rebecca, did not give him a sense of ease. This feeling in him to watch over Brenda the daughter he never knew, was real, and not helped by that fragrance. He had vowed to watch Larry, and check what his intentions were especially now as Glen knew what some of his history was, his daughter loved to gossip to his wife!

He was going to have a talk with Julie when he got home, seeing what the extra boxes were for, laid out on the table before him. Women, he thought, devious creatures but that is what we love about them, you can never pin one down. He looked with satisfaction at the spread before him, noting Brenda had placed Julie and Gaby's fare on good china plates, showing it all off to advantage. He chuckled, that woman had more sides to her than a diamond, worth the same amount as well.

Norman and Larry were talking to another man who Glen had seen arrive with the Sotheby people, but had not been introduced to.

'Ah Glen, welcome; I believe we are to send thanks to your wonderful wife for most of this spread?' Norman greeted him motioning to the food on the table that was steadily been eaten by all the workmen and guests. Glen nodded and moved towards them.

'I don't believe you have met a fellow Etonian, Fred may I introduce Master Builder Mr. Glen Haddon, he is the instigator of all we see, Mr. Frederick Austin Healy, may I also add Fred, that miracles are this man's speciality!'

Glen took the proffered hand that had a very strong grip, shook it murmuring a hello, 'Have you been in from the start of this madness Mr. Haddon?'

'Please call me Glen, and yes I was in at the beginning. My daughter Rebecca had added to the photographs that Brenda took. I don't think anyone would recognise this place from a week ago, that I put down to one person and one alone!'

'Brenda!' Larry quietly interposed. Glen looked at the man, at the quiet conviction and feeling he had put into that one word; the utter sincerity that came from him, and he began to wonder if he had imagined his fears. There was something brewing here, and then there was that damned gardenia fragrance again.

'Yes indeed, the one and only!' Fred looked a question at Glen, who nodded and continued, 'she has a passion, a feel for what is right and what should be done, she infects everyone, we get to see through her eyes, and want to do what she can see. Yes, she has Pickworths behind her, but even if she didn't I believe she would somehow be doing exactly what she is, to bring this wonderful house back to life. I wondered if you had done anything to assist in renaming the house as "Iris House", Larry?'

'I am looking into it Glen, although she has not asked. I have started the enquiries as when I was here the other day, everyone was calling this place Iris House, I wondered if it was the correct name for the place, just lost in time. I will do everything to get it in place before the grand opening!' Larry looked at Glen wondering, realising he was on trial of some sort here?

Fred broke in, 'you have to realise that the sample of artefacts that Mr. Palligria sorry Poppa has shown me are quite remarkable, as is this project. You say that Sir James Pickworth has a hand in this as well. I am surprised to hear that, I don't think that Maud is aware of that either, or the others. Well we have the discs to work off, and we have been invited back at any time if we wish to check on anything, which is very generous. If you will excuse me, I am going to fill my plate with a few more delicacies, my glass with some of that delicious Australian bubbly, and have a quiet chat with my co-workers. Norman, I will be in touch, Larry do you still play squash?'

Chapter 36

FRED LEFT AFTER LARRY stated golf was more his game these days, when he had time. Norman was called to check on something Ben wanted to clarify; leaving Glen with the opportunity he was waiting for, Larry got in first!

'Ok Glen, get it off your chest!'

'Blunt, I like that. OK I want to know that you will not harm Brenda, not now or ever! She has been through enough in her life, according to Dennis. She deserves the happiness that is coming to her through this house. The legacy that Iris has left her, yes, we know she told us that she was her heir. I just want to make sure she will be ok!'

'Well I was told she has her champions, I knew Norman was one, Dennis also, he is not here?' Glen looked a little shocked but realised it was true, he would always be Brenda's champion, as now most of the men employed on this quest would be. He nodded at Larry acknowledging the truth of his words, saying Dennis had to be with his family over the weekend.

Larry continued with a nod, 'I knew you would be one of the champions Glen, let me say that contrary to all the gossip you may have heard, I intend no harm to Brenda. I don't even know what I feel, I just want to be here around her. As to Iris's Legacy you do not know even half of it, no I will not tell you, I have to tell her first. I was coming to see her this afternoon, saw that Sotherby group passing my window, when I saw Fred in the mix, knew that something was afoot, he was always into things not exactly kosher at Eton. Maud Prendergast I know by reputation, although her niece has changed definitely for the better, and I put that change at your daughters Rebecca's door!'

Both of them turned at the laughter coming from the table where Mia and Rebecca were standing with Ben, Matt and a couple of the foundry workers, looking very carefree and young.

'Were we ever that young and carefree? Any way I left the office telling my secretary to cancel my afternoon appointments, left to help a woman I have only met once, but want to meet again and be her friend, in any way I can!'

'Yes!', Glen said slowly turning to face Larry, 'you do understand, that is the way she has, whatever the request, however outrageous, she makes it sound so reasonable, you find yourself saying yes, while you are secretly screaming no! Then you get that damned waft of Gardenia, and you hear yourself saying yes to things that are totally nuts. Somehow, we have achieved what would normally take four months in a week!'

Glen looked at this man standing in front of him, watching him as he watched Brenda moving around the room, he had the expression of a man surely sinking in very deep waters, and not sure whether to swim against the current or let it take him along.

'Larry, I apologise, you are deeper in than I am, I have Julie for my sanity and the family, if you need to talk to anyone I am here, but I am as much under that woman's spell as you are – let's go and get another drink!'

Larry was a bit puzzled by this salt of the earth man, giving him advice, but he welcomed the bonhomie, it was this group of people, he felt as though he belonged amongst them. There was something going on here, he was enjoying for the first time in a long time, being a part of.

'Tell me Glen, is the fragrance I smell the Gardenia you mentioned, I keep smelling it around Brenda when I am close?' Glen laughed as they moved to the drinks table, proceeded to explain to Larry about the unseen resident of the house.

Brenda stood on a stepladder to address everyone, 'I don't mean to make a speech!'

Ben yelled, 'why are you on a ladder then?'

'Because,' she turned to him, 'if I tried to talk to you from the ground Ben, I would get a crick in the neck!'

Everyone laughed, Ben the hardest of all, Brenda continued, as she had every ones attention.

'I want to thank you all for the hard work you have put in to my dream for the last week. Please do not think I take what you are doing as commonplace. I realise that there is superhuman effort in what had been accomplished. I want to ask for it to continue until the job has been completed. I know I am asking a lot, but I believe that you all have the skill needed to do this, or you would not be here. I thank you, Iris House thanks you, please enjoy yourself in moderation, I do not want anyone with hangovers here tomorrow!'

Everyone laughed Larry moved over to the ladder to assist Brenda down.

'Thank you for your interventions this afternoon', she said quietly.

'No problem, it was my pleasure. I really came to invite you to dinner, if you are free?'

Brenda was suddenly unsure of herself it was a very long time since she had been asked out to dinner. Then came that waft of gardenia again, Larry smiled as he could smell it too, and now knew what it meant. 'I think Iris has just said yes for you!'

Brenda laughed suddenly realising it was just dinner, what was she making a song and dance out of it for, 'I would love to, casual, formal what?'

'Oh, just something a little more upmarket than what you are wearing, will be fine!'

She looked at the clear blue eyes that were twinkling at her, and chuckled.

'I will pick you up at seven thirty, will that be enough time for you?'

'Oh, plenty of time thank you. I was just going to heat up some left-over noodles, this will be a treat!'

Dan and Brent came over checking on what was left to do. The Sotheby people came and thanked her for the invitation, the delicious food and the challenge of checking the catalogued items what they had seen and what was on the discs. Maud advising, they would contact her with an appraisal as soon as possible. Brenda giving her one of her own business cards, seeing an eyebrow raised in response, the four of them left together. Fred giving Larry a nod before going through the door.

Norman ushered his team out after they all expressed their thanks of being included in the afternoon. Norman adding, they would not be back until Tuesday or Wednesday, as they had to catch up on all the seeds and specimens they had taken, besides they could not do anything in the garden until the crane had finished.

Once they had gone, everyone seemed to leave in a rush. Larry left with Brent and Peter, Peter finally going home to his family, his flu gone. Thanking Brenda for her tea, he thought he could even face his boys again, Dan coming up behind him saying only a father could face and love those two demons. Glen clapped him on the back, saying you love those two troublemakers because of the mischief they get into, I have seen you encouraging them.!

The house was suddenly quiet, everyone had gone, she didn't even need to tidy up as Rebecca, Mia, Ben, Matthew and Charlie had cleared away the dirty dishes. Even folded up the trestle tables and put them neatly back in the dining room. She had no excuses, she went up to apartment two, to check her wardrobe to see what she could wear for her first dinner invitation in so long she could not remember when the last one was.

Chapter 37

B RENDA RESCUED ONE OF her lamps from the boxes she had shipped over, the shade not bad, but definitely would not be acceptable to her interior designers, but she had to have some light in the hall, placing it on a fold up table that fitted the space under where the new window would go between the two doors.

Matt had been surprised at her request for power points in the hall, and also in other places throughout the building, but had realised if only used once a year would be of benefit.

When Larry rang the bell at precisely seven thirty pm, Brenda had answered telling him she was on her way, just had to grab her purse, opening the door to let him in the hall. She had been ready since seven, nervously pacing the apartment, checking her attire hoping it was going to be ok?

Larry looked up the stairs to see her coming down into the soft light from the table lamp. The simple black cocktail dress, round necked and three quarter sleeve, would have been mediocre, if it were not for the black lace and jet beads that was the bottom three inches to just below the knee, and around the sleeve cuffs. Brenda had done her hair with care, a loose chignon fastened with a jet encrusted clip, that was one of her family heirlooms, the additions of Iris's Pearl necklace and earrings completing the ensemble. Larry thought her the most beautiful sight he had seen in a long time, he realised he was long gone, also realising he was thoroughly enjoying the experience of falling for this captivating woman.

'Is this alright? It's not is it! I should change!' She had seen the expression on Larry's face and was suddenly worried.

'No Brenda,' he took hold of her hand as she reached the last two steps to stop her running back up them again. 'You look wonderful; I have only seen you in torn jeans. You just took my breath away for a second, you look lovely!'

For a moment, Brenda did not know what to say, she looked at this man that was a stranger only a couple of days before, but she realised he was now something more, someone her instinct, and Iris, were telling her she could trust.

'Sorry, thank you, it is such a long time since I went out to dinner, with after all a complete stranger!'

'I suppose I am, well let's be away. I have a cab waiting, maybe we can become friends over this dinner and you can stop being nervous?'

Brenda laughed, pulling her black cashmere wrap around her shoulders, squeezed the hand helping her down the last steps, as Larry walked them out the door to the waiting cab, thought she could enjoy this evening very much indeed.

In the cab, Larry regaled her with happy tales of being at Eton with Norman and Fred, making her laugh at the antics of what were very naughty schoolboys. They arrived at the restaurant in the Soho district very quickly, as she stood on the pavement while Larry paid the driver, she observed, and was observed by the "Beautiful People" passing by, and also seated in the prime window seats of the restaurant itself.

'Don't let me eat with the wrong fork please Larry, this is way beyond Dennis and his favourite Noodle Bar!'

Larry laughed at her fears and taking her elbow guided her in through the door, the Maître D moved to intercept as he could see people pushing down the line that was waiting for a table, when he saw who was coming down the line, his demeanour changed.

'Mr. Morecombe, welcome Sir and Madam, your table is ready please come this way!'

Larry took Brenda's arm again to guide her after the Maître D as he moved through the tables, Larry nodding this way and that at diners already seated. They were shown to a booth towards the rear but away from the main thoroughfare through the restaurant.

'Prime spot! I take it this is not a random choice of restaurants, judging by that greeting?'

'No,' Larry chuckled at her remark, 'for our first, and hopefully not last, dinner together, I have brought you to one of my favourites. In fact, I have been coming here practically every Friday night for the last several years. That is why Henri dismissed the others when we came in. I am a regular, and (I say not immodestly) a big spender at times when the celebration warrants it. So, I get First class silver service at all times, and I like it. Now a glass of champagne to start, we will try a French one I like, although I did enjoy the Australian wine you served this afternoon!'

'Yes, it is a favourite of mine, when I rang the contact Dennis gave me and asked what sparkling wine he had from Australia, he told me he had a half case of the Andrew Garrett, I couldn't help myself and took the lot. I think he will be trying to find more for me, and some others I asked for. I hope Peter has organised for a wine cellar somewhere (*forgive me Iris*) for me, or I will not have anywhere to store them all!'

Larry laughed, a waiter arrived as if by magic, champagne poured, toasts made, a sip was enough to tell Brenda that this was Champagne from the right region, and delicious. Larry watched as she relaxed a little, taking a look around at the people seated around them, soaking in the chatter and antics of society people showing off for other society people and noting the few curious glances in their direction. He had asked for a booth rather than his usual table, as what he had to tell her, what was discovered in the strong box would be a little startling for her, and he wanted a little bit more privacy to do so. He knew he could have asked her to go to the office, and she would still have too, but she would not be his client for much longer, things had taken a turn, and he was hoping after the disclosure, they could become more than just friends.

'Now', Brenda turned to Larry breaking into his thoughts, 'I think you should get off your chest, what it is you have to tell me? I don't think either of us want our dinner being spoilt by bad news! I know what it is Sir James is not happy with what I am doing and my dream job is gone before I even start it!'

He watched the devils dancing in her clear blue eyes, as she smiled, half-heartedly at him, the diamonds in the pearl earrings twinkling at him as she shook gently. He realised that she was very insecure, and was half way to believing what she had just said in jest.

'You do have a way of knocking the wind out of people, how did you know I had something to tell you?'

'The Booth! It is a dead giveaway, if we were on a proper dinner date, we would be centre restaurant, so all your cronies could see that you have not lost your touch with the fairer sex. Although I think they would be slightly disappointed by your choice in me!'

'Well I am not,' Larry said more forcefully than he should as she had been spot on with her analysis, and it had shocked him. 'What would I do with a dolly bird half my age, if that is what you are implying? No don't answer that I can use my imagination as well, and that is not what I am after, and you know it.'

Brenda had the grace to chuckle; he smiled at her, although once implanted in his way ward brain, the pleasant thought of he and Brenda together would not go away. Then he realised she had again pegged it in one, that if they were on a real date, he would be at his usual table in the middle of the room! He shook his head, and Brenda chuckled again at his discomfort, knowing she was right. Laughing at her fantasies about a real date with Larry, realising that was exactly what she would like, suppressing the sudden longing for it to be so, she took a deep breath and a sip of champagne.

'Ok, I do have something to tell you', they sat back as the entre Larry had ordered was put in front of them, enjoying the food that was wonderfully cooked. 'I hoped that you would like to be told over dinner rather in my office, I do have quite a bit to tell you!'

'Oh, for heaven's sake Larry, please spit it out, just tell me is Sir James unhappy with what I am doing or not?'

'Of course not! 'Oh, for Heaven's' sake indeed, both he and Linda are heaving a sigh of relief that you have taken over this project and are finally getting it to completion! I was instructed by them both to assist you (if needed and contacted). I am pleased to tell you that team of yours handle bureaucrats better than we can!'

Brenda smiled at the praise for what he called 'Her Team'.

'It is just that I have to advise you I registered you with the firm in your own right!'

Brenda turned more towards Larry, very interested indeed. 'You mean that I am not just listed as an employee of Pickowrths but something more?'

'Something more indeed, yes you are still on our register as an employee of Pickworths, which is no small achievement believe me. You are also registered in your own right as Ms. Brenda Chalmers heiress of one Mrs. Iris Fitzgibbon Boerchemeir. You have to realise Brenda, your being named as Iris's Heir has raised your standing up to the equal to that of Sir James, she had a very prestigious family behind her, and was not a nobody, Peerage level and beyond no less!'

Brenda stared at him, trying to come to terms with the truth of what he was saying. She had of course realised from the beginning, but not acknowledged it in her own mind, that she had been given something extraordinary. Knowing as the boxes of stashed bounty had been opened, she had acquired something unique. She was wondering at exactly what was in the box he had taken away. She took another sip of champagne to help collect her thoughts, and smiled slightly as gardenia wafted around.

The plates for the entre were removed before he turned to her and continued, 'Another thing,' she nodded at him, still unable to speak, 'there is no easy way to say this, I am not going to be your contact in the firm anymore. I am recommending you to my boss, Mr. Hugh Pemberton, he is one of the three senior partners in the firm. He is a wonderful chap, and will be able to look after your interests with impartiality. I hope you agree as I have set up a meeting with him on Monday morning!'

Shock ran through Brenda, that she might be losing him, that she may have been right in her first thought of not trusting, the negative thoughts vied with her common sense, and the word 'impartiality' seemed to ground her.

'Why Larry?' she asked more sharply than she should, 'for what reason, and you must have one, have you done this before consulting me?'

'Well you see, when I looked into that strongbox, and realised what it contained, it was though a light bulb went on in my head, and it stopped me going further and I called Hugh in, we discussed the situation, and he agreed to take you on, freeing me from the situation, as I realised in that moment that I would like more than a working relationship with you, and that you would need someone to assist you once everything was checked!' He took a sip of champagne to steady himself, this was harder than he thought.

'When we had checked out just the top part of the papers in that strongbox, I realised I would have a conflict of interest if I stayed as your counsellor, especially once the contents were common knowledge. Do you trust me Brenda?'

Yes, she said immediately and without any hesitation, it was as though she had been waiting for the question from him all her life.

Yes, she had said, just that one simple word, but to Larry it was a whole world, he knew without a shadow of a doubt, that these feelings that had been growing in him all week, were reciprocated even if Brenda did not realise it yet. He had been given her trust, and he knew he would be with her, helping her, looking after her for the years to come, in whatever capacity the fates would allow. He accepted that she would be part of his life and after he had consulted with Hugh, and what a Pandora's Box it was, realised she would need someone of his calibre to help guide her through the next few years at least, without being part of the law firm. He had discussed the fact he realised he wanted more of Brenda's attention than the professional one at the moment, they had both decided that Larry's personal interest in Ms. Brenda Chalmers would leave him and more importantly her, open to speculation and innuendo, if he continued in his work capacity.

'Yes, without a second thought, just yes!' he asked again.

'Yes,' Brenda said again, she did not have to hesitate to dispel the negative doubts, as there were none, and the gardenia fragrance that had appeared, just reinforced the feeling of trust, of knowing this man, that he was strong, trustworthy and sure was at once unshakeable.

'I can hear your questions, so I will try and answer the main ones now, please be patient with me!'

Brenda nodded, both took another sip of champagne.

'The reason I have removed you from my care to the senior partner is twofold, first that I would have a conflict of interest. Our acquaintance may only have just begun a couple of days ago, but I want to get to know you more, as a friend, confidant, or even recently in my dreams something more. I do not know if you feel this too, but I believe there is something building between us, I could not continue as your contact with the firm, especially if you do feel in some part that something is building between us, as it could in the future put you and your reputation in harm's way, and that I will not allow!'

Brenda could hear the sincerity in Larry's voice; see the conviction in his eyes. Never, ever before had someone stated quite bluntly that he liked her and wanted to get to know her even better, to know more about her and get closer to her. It was a new and heady experience, one she thought she liked, but was still very wary.

He continued as she mulled over his words, 'and second we also thought that you would need to have legal representation yourself, to guide you through what we are just learning from those papers, and I humbly put myself forward in that capacity?'

'I understand Larry, thank you,' she put her hand over his resting on the table between them. 'I understand more than you think, you are giving us time; time for you to know me and vice versa. My life at the moment is a new area for me, the job, the legacy and now your interest in me. I am still getting my sea legs so to speak, while I will acknowledge that I like your company, and I feel I can trust you in life, and not just to represent me in a legal capacity, can we please take this slow, and enjoy every phase of this blossoming relationship?'

He put his hand over hers and squeezed in acknowledgment of the agreement just made between them.

'Thank you, and yes I agree, let's take this friendship slowly, the legal side I may need an answer sooner than later.' He grinned as she chuckled beside him, she had understood, 'It is conceited of me to think I am the only one seeking your attention, I must be the latest in a long line of beau's?'

Brenda laughed aloud relieving the tension of the situation, remembering the continual drought period of her life, where her children were the only companions she had, them and her very loved and missed dog.

'No, I must admit this is a novel area for me. I moved here to see if I could regain something I was sure I was missing. I wanted to see a little more of the world before I got too old to enjoy it. I could not do it where I was, so I up-stakes and moved where I could. Hoping to get a job that would allow me to live and travel for a few years, do what I had dreamed about. I was just about to go back to my Uncles for a while when I got the job at Pickworths. Do you realise I haven't been in my new job a month yet; I feel as though I have been with them for years, and I haven't even welcomed my first guest yet. Glen is calling this venture the 'Iris Guest House' and he is rating it as a six-star property!'

'I will happily acknowledge that when it comes to Mr. Haddon and Co., they are definitely your champions, and will be with you in whatever venture you may be in and enjoying the ride, as I am!'

They toasted with raised glasses the statements of the last few minutes, as the waiter came up with their soup and salad.

'Well, I am to meet with Hugh on Monday at nine?' Brenda continued after the waiter had gone, 'what am I meeting him about, you will be there with me please?'

'Of course, I will, I would not dream of leaving you on your own, it is why I have removed myself from your case, so I can advise you as a friend. I have to also advise you that there will be another firm of barristers at the meeting!'

Brenda inclined her head for him to continue, he still held onto her hand, as he could feel it start to tremble, even though she looked outwardly calm.

'This firm,' he continued, 'is one who continues to control Lord Lucas interests,' at her questioning look, 'Lord Lucas was Iris's father. It seems the papers you found in that strong box, were not from Iris, but were from her father and grandfather, not many but what there was were very informative. It seems that whoever Iris names as her heir and inheritor, is also named as Lord Lucas's heir!'

Brenda thought she was going to faint, this is too much, just too much she thought, trying to get her head around what Larry was saying. How, how in this day and age did someone die, and not have anyone around to grieve for them. To help them, she thought of Iris old and alone, dying in that house and her heart broke. Tears flowed down her cheeks, Larry handed over his handkerchief, grateful that he had put a spare in his pocket. He could hear Brenda muttering, I don't believe it, over and over through the tears. He moved to put his arm around her shoulders and pull her more into the booth for some privacy, pulling her into his warmth, glad there was no one at the table next to them. Being the strength that she needed at that moment, and in that instant realising that he would be there for her in whatever capacity he could, and for however long she needed him.

'OK you had better tell me the rest of it, I hope that being named as Lord Lucas heir is just that a name; a phrase on the papers you found, but I think that would be a false hope, am I right?'

'Well there is a bit more, are you up to it?'

She grasped his hand nodding.

'You cannot own the house, because it is part of her father's estate, so as his heir you actually own the street! I should tell you that the title is perpetual, goes from heir to heir – Lady Brenda Lucas sounds good, doesn't it?'

Brenda looked at him, for a moment she could not do or say anything, her brain could not comprehend what he had just said, then it dismissed it as impossible, she laughed.

'All right Larry, who put you up to this? It is a joke right, and a very good one. I nearly fell for it, oh I have had some good one's played on me through the years, but this takes the biscuit. Dennis, no Sir James or no I bet Norman this definitely had the stink of an Etonian prank. Where are they, they should be around to see the result of the jest?'

She picked up her glass and started to look around for the perpetrators. Larry picked up his glass too, and took a sip, trying to understand, he had thought of Brenda's possible responses to the news, but he had never thought it would be of a prank, a jest on his behalf. She just didn't believe him, or, did she and she could not imagine or understand what she was about to learn, her life was not going to be the same.

'Larry this is a joke, right? You cannot be serious! This is me, a month ago I was tending a bar at my Uncle's pub, wondering if I even had enough money to come south and find my dream job. I am a divorced woman with two grown children, I haven't exactly been dirt poor but there were times when I wondered how I was going to pay the bills. Something always happened though, and they might have been late, but I paid them. I haven't been around the world, but I had the children they were reason enough to stay and enjoy life. But Larry, please things like this do not happen to people like me, they happen to someone else, this is a joke!' Just then a hint of gardenia wafted around them, Brenda knew in that instant that her life was never going to be the same again.

'Oh God; oh, my giddy aunt, what do I do, help me!'

Larry pulled her close again, as the tears flowed. After a few minutes, she took a deep breath, giving herself a shake to settle the world around her again, picking up her spoon to start on the food in front of her, immediately putting it down thinking hard.

Larry laughed at her reaction, reluctantly releasing his hold on her because she felt so good in his arms. She felt the tension that had been building disappear, as the smell of gardenia lingered she knew Iris had guided this man to her, so that both of them would guide her through this. She pulled away a little, his close proximity was a welcome anchor in this world suddenly turned upside down, to study his face.

Concern reflected in his eyes, concern for her that she could not assimilate what he was saying. She wanted to scream at him, it was not fair, it was not fair that someone had to die alone and terribly neglected for her to inherit this legacy. That she was the one who had found that journal, and Iris's will was, a million, no a billion to one chance.

'Why me?' she finally asked.

'I don't know, truly I don't; but it is yours. We have consulted with the best, they concur that the way Iris and Lord Lucas detailed their wills confirms that you are both their heirs! Now what you do with this legacy is up to you, but the way you have begun is wonderful.'

Brenda looked at him again, puzzled at the meaning of his words. The waiter arrived to check all was ok with the meal, and they moved slightly apart to begin eating, but still stayed close their legs touching. Larry did not want to lose the physical contact, as he thought she would run out of the restaurant before he had finished with some of the information. Brenda with a puzzled expression on her face asked 'How so?'

'Well the way you have been organising your team. The contacts and contracts gained, used and passed on, the jobs that are now rolling into the businesses because of your use of those men and women with their unique talents. You have to know that all the industries that you are employing are going to have a boon time. Worked right for the rest of their lives and a few more generations to come. Brenda, I can see that you don't have a clue what I am talking about, and that makes it even better, as you are helping people subconsciously, it is your nature to nurture,' she had to suppress a giggle at his pun a little light headed with the praise.

'Yes, well no pun intended. I hope that you will see this inheritance as a benefit and not a millstone. Please I will be there to help you, guide you if you need me. Your trust is important to me, so I make this pledge that I will never do anything to make you doubt me. I will be honest, straightforward and loyal if you will let me?'

'Well I don't really need a puppy,' he laughed at that, 'but what I will need I can see is a friend, one who will tell me when I am being a real idiot, who will pull me back into line. Larry please tell me honestly, this is for real, no doubts, objections how far does this go?'

The waiter came and took the plates away, Brenda knew that what she had eaten was delicious but she could not remember eating a thing. The main course was served and she was hungry, but realised hungry for more than the food. She had just been handed something huge, but she had no idea what it was. The next question she posed herself was, did she want to find out more, if yes, the Pandora's Box that was Iris's Legacy could not be closed, she would have to run with it! Could she, did she want too, that was something she would have to sleep on, wait till the full disclosure on Monday. She was now very sure that Larry was not telling her the whole of it, he was holding something back.

Larry was watching the expressions cross her face, watched as she raised questions, and then answered them without a word being said. He wanted to interrupt, to help her answer some of them, but realised it would be a wrong move. She had to work through some of this in her own space, he had definitely not told her all. Full disclosure would have to wait till Monday, they had really only scratched the surface of this long-lost legacy. His firm were going to make sure that the wills were both watertight, the last thing that anyone wanted was for Brenda to get used to the idea of being Lady Brenda Lucas for real, then for a court case to ensue because of some nut who decided they wanted their share of the good fortune.

'Well, as far as we can tell, and we are still checking, that box you found really caused a stir in our office alone, never mind when we contacted the firm handling Lord Lucas estate. The deeds and writs were incorporated when Lord Lucas bought the land to build Steel Street, for him to showcase his work in steel. The title is made in perpetuity, passed down through nominated heirs of the family, I do believe old Norman Lucas had a premonition in regards to his heirs, that is why the wording is so specific. We are working on finding out more about the title, and of course the monetary aspect of the inheritance. You have a few bank accounts that have not been touched in a very, very long time. All of which have been added to every few months, interest added every year. We have only accessed three of them, we know about, but the estimated worth is over two hundred million!'

Chapter 38

'TWO HUNDRED MILLION, I have inherited…. Larry, please be serious there is not that amount of money in the world. You are serious, please excuse me a moment!'

Brenda rose and made her way to the Ladies, and was very sick, the attendant was a little concerned, but Brenda kept saying she was ok, she had just received some shocking news. She was fine, she just needed to be quiet for a moment, should not have indulged in the champagne. The attendant was reassured, offering her a cold towel, which Brenda gratefully accepted.

Larry did not know what to do. Suddenly realising bringing Brenda to the public place was wrong, he should have told her at the office. He was about to go and find her when she returned, looking paler, but composed. His admiration for her grew even more, he was so proud of her.

'Larry, I am sorry but I am not doing this wonderful meal justice. Do you think we may be able to have a rain check, and a doggy bag, I think I would like to go home!'

Larry chuckled, calling Henri over advising him that there was a family emergency; they had to leave, could they take the rest of the meal with them. Henri immediately called a waiter, sent him off to the kitchen to bag up the meal. Asking Larry if he could get them a taxi, moving off when Larry said yes please.

Brenda could not remember leaving the restaurant, or even the taxi ride home, the only thing she could remember with any sense of surety was the touch of Larry's hand holding hers securely. He was the anchor she clung to as her world was ripped apart, and put back again as a new and improved version. One in which she could do, if she wanted, all she had ever dreamed about, not just for herself but for her children as well. This had to be a dream, she knew it, a dream that someone was going to come up and say 'April Fool', things like this did not happen, especially to her!

Larry was asking for her key, she realised they were back at the house. She roused herself out of her mental fog to open the door, switching off the alarm automatically while Larry paid for the taxi. Motioning him to come in went up the stairs to apartment two. Suddenly an absolute longing for apartment one to be finished assailed her, to be in her own space, which indeed it was; Pickworths may be paying for the building, but she owned the lot, giggling like a schoolgirl she realised she was being paid twice.

Larry had moved into the kitchen to put the kettle on, but came back into the room with a scotch, to find Brenda standing shaking uncontrollably. He quickly put down the glass and gathered her into his arms. Gratefully her anchor came back, warmth from his hands and body seemed to seep into her. This was peace, this was calm, here in this frame of man and woman, she had an island of sanity, in a world suddenly gone made. The scent of Gardenia wafted around them, Larry just kept holding her, until the tremors had passed; it was shock, he kept murmuring, he repeated to her; it will be alright, it would be fine. Finally, the murmured words and comforting arms penetrated the fog that had surrounded her, the scent of gardenia brought her back to her surroundings. She stirred realising she was being held by some strong muscular arms, she hugged back feeling him relax, asking if she was feeling better?

'Hm, I think so, but only if you keep holding me. I am sorry I don't know what came over me, thank you Larry for being here with me,' she looked up into his blue eyes, that clearly showed his concern, and gently tentatively kissed him.

Larry realised that the kiss was a reflex of being held in his arms, and that Brenda did not really know what she was doing. So, he returned the gentle kiss, then put a lid on his growing ardour for later, when she knew what she was doing, and they both could enjoy the intimacy, it would be worth waiting for he had no doubt.

He moved Brenda over to the sofa, retrieving the glass, made her take a few sips.

'I am sorry for ruining your evening. I feel so strange, like I am in some very bad B grade movie. I keep waiting for the director to yell cut!'

He chuckled at her remark, 'I think a good night's sleep is in order; you have had a shock, a really big one. Is there anything I can do for you before I go, I will be back in the morning early? I know that Glen and the boys have a full day ahead of them. Did you realise that Dan and his team had put all the support beams in place for the lift? They only have to wait for the inspectors,' Brenda grimaced in disgust at the mention of 'The Inspectors', Larry laughed at her reaction. 'Yes, well they are important, once they have cleared the work, which I have no doubt in happening, they can install the lift and the glass around it, then get onto your apartment! Now get some sleep, no I am not staying, you really do not want me to. I would be the biggest cad in the world if I did, my mother would not like me, if she were still here. I can hear her yelling at me "Lawrence, you took advantage of that woman when she was vulnerable, how dare you!"

Brenda laughed, taking another sip of the fiery liquid, knowing he was right. She was very glad he was there, but also very glad he was a gentleman as well. She had not met many; most of them had been in the last couple of weeks. Accepting the truth in his statement she saw him out of the building, retracing her steps slowly mulling over the information she had been given, trying to actually believe it was real.

Getting ready for bed, she was exhausted, but something nagged at her, she realised she had to say thank you, retracing her steps to the table/come desk, reaching for her writing paper and pen began:

Dear Iris and Norman,

I hope you do not mind my use of your first names, as
I think of you now as the long-lost family that I never
knew, was never able to be with. Long ago companions
I hope you will allow me to call you that. I have much

to thank you for, you are the family I have never known, but will get to know you in redoing, remaking, rebuilding your visions.

I thank you from the bottom of my heart for giving me this chance. I thank you for your generosity in allowing me, a perfect stranger into your lives. Please continue to be there guiding me, helping me to use these legacies you have put in my path for the good of everyone.

Whether they like it or not, I am here and I will endeavour not to let you down.

In remembrance and loving regards.

Your Humble Servant,

Brenda Chalmers.

With tears running down her face, she put her letter in an envelope and put it in her expanding folder with the other important papers she had gathered. Finally, a sense of rightness came over her, she knew Iris and all the Lords including Iris's father were pleased with her courtesy, breathing a deep sigh, she went to bed.

Chapter 39

THE ALARM RANG AT 6:30, she had forgotten to switch it off. Still she was glad, getting herself into gear and reacquainting herself with a building that had suddenly changed. A life style was going to be hers that was often dreamed about, but completely foreign, she hoped that it wouldn't change her, it had taken a long time but she liked the person she had become. The coffee pot was bubbling when the doorbell rang, a little self-consciously she ran down to let Larry in, he stood there with a slightly silly grin on his face holding an enormous bunch of Iris flowers.

He greeted her with a kiss on each cheek, and then one on her brow, 'thought I would try and appease the unseen resident! How are you this morning?'

Laughing with him, she took the flowers, gestured up the stairs, 'I am fine, I am so sorry for ruining your evening. I cannot remember if we actually ate dinner?'

They had moved into apartment two, Brenda motioned towards the coffee pot and raised an eyebrow in question, Larry nodded, he was very pleased at the subtle changes in Brenda, she had accepted what was about to come. He knew she would ride it out, and enjoy the ride, now that she had gotten over the initial shock. She was going to be able to help a lot of people, if she wanted to, a great many of them in her own way.

He opened the fridge door and showed her Henri's takeaway boxes on the shelf, 'Oh I guess we didn't miss out on the main course after all!'

Brenda knew what she had to do, taking the coffee with them she took him on a tour through the entire house, when they got to the basement, she pulled the hanging plants away from the doorway into the 'Workshop' as Ben and Matt were calling it. To give him full disclosure of what Iris House was offering her. Larry gasped, amazed at the space there was when they walked into the room. Flashlights they were carrying did not do the space justice, but he could see the portable generator and standard lights in the corners, asking whom? Although he thought he knew who would be itching to get into the area to see how it could be reused.

'Ben, and Matt to some extent, Ben because he is trying to pull the plumbing into this century, for use not only in the new powder rooms, and bathrooms in my apartment, but hopefully for the whole building. I am just happy that I have a team that wants to conserve and reuse the good parts of the past. Matt wants to fit this place out with 'modern electric lights', but is happy to wait putting it last on the list. We have not shown Norman down here, Glen thought we should concentrate on getting the building works finished and passed before we start on the restoration works. I agreed, there are just too many things happening at once. Norman did say that they would not be back till Wednesday, didn't he?'

'He said Tuesday or Wednesday, I will give him a call and tell him Wednesday would be early enough to return, shall I?'

Brenda nodded her head as they moved out of the workshop, and back up to apartment two for a coffee refill.

'I am so sorry for the way I behaved last night, I just didn't know how to handle it, my brain sort of shut down. Can we go back again I want to enjoy Henri's hospitality in full next time.'

'It would be my pleasure,' Larry chuckled at her confession, 'you do not need to apologise, it was my mistake. I should have really told you about the details in my office. Let us just put last night behind us as one of those awkward first date things, and forget it!'

'There is nothing to forgive, thank you for being here Larry. I will need your support, but let's not tell the team about my elevated status, shall we? I don't want them to know that the Lady B on my hard hat is for real, I do not even believe it yet!'

He laughed and said of course, as the doorbell rang, heralding the arrival of 'The Team', along with another box of morning tea. At Glen's very pointed look to find Larry already there, Brenda told him to keep his thoughts to himself, Larry had arrived earlier and was already a cup of coffee ahead of everyone. Glen looked at Brenda, there was a subtle difference in her this morning, she had an air to her that was not there before, a sort of confidence he could not place.

'Before I forget lass, Julie wanted me to invite you to Sunday Dinner, tomorrow if you are free?'

'Glen that would be lovely, thank you very much,' Brenda answered, turning from what Rebecca was telling her.

'Of course, Larry, if you are free, you are welcome to come along. Perhaps as you are the local, so to speak, you can bring Brenda, would that be OK?'

Larry looked at Glen and smiled, he knew he would be having another of their chats, but he could have them now with ease, he knew where he stood with Brenda in these early days, and was comfortable they could go on.

'I thank you for the invitation Glen, and readily accept. If you could give me the directions, I will pick Ms. Brenda up and enjoy the drive out to the country!'

Glen did so, Larry then took his leave, saying he had things to organise and would call Brenda later.

'Well lass, did you want to know what is on the agenda for today?' Glen continued after Larry had left.

The agenda, as Brenda found out was just as long as she thought. A new face came into the room as she was listening to Glen.

'Ah Patrick, come and meet your boss for the next couple of weeks. Brenda Chalmers, Mr. Patrick Greenhill, Painter extraordinaire!'

Patrick was a small wiry man, put out his hand and clenched Brenda's in a vice grip. Telling her that he was eager to begin, Rebecca and Mia had filled him in, and he was going to make a start on the front of the building, so the scaffolding could be taken down sooner than later. He was starting at the top, as by the time he got down to the bay window at the front, Charlie should have fixed up the windows ready for him. Glen advised him that the apartment was the official tea room and facilities for the build, Patrick nodded looking around and then ushered his companions out the door to start in earnest.

Matt's team were still crawling over the building, preparing for the installation of the new updated electrics from top to bottom, he had already appraised her of what he thought of the previous electrician's work, that was why they were starting again. Matt advised her the team thought her idea of putting the wires in the existing tubing brilliant so much easier than hacking away at the walls.

The new doors, especially the cavity ones between the hallway and her apartment, she had insisted on for internal access were to be the first job of the day. Ben and his plumbers working overtime to complete all they had to do not only in the bathrooms and powder rooms, but also in the re-found kitchen and laundry, Glen pushing him hard in this space as they had to lay the new oak timber floors, for Patrick to seal. Brenda reminded Ben that Norman would not be back till Wednesday so if he had to work on the boiler he could, he heaved a sigh and wandered off to keep his workers on track.

She watched as they dispersed around the house, she followed Glen and Jack down into the kitchen, asking as they stepped carefully into the room if there was any reason the shutters over the window into the patio had not been opened. Glen shook his head saying they were just waiting for her to ask, and did she want to help?

Nodding at Jack, and with Brenda's assistance they unlatched the middle shutter, with effort pulled back both sides into the niches made for them. What was revealed was not a window, but another set of French Doors, identical to the set from the dining room into the conservatory.

'I suppose you want to reuse these?' Jack said looking first at Glen with a wink, then at Brenda.

'Oh, yes please, I don't see any cracked panes, can we please reuse them. Oh, and Glen can you raise up the old safe, I will definitely want to reuse that please.'

'Already done Brenda, first thing I got the men to do when we redesigned the space with the wall down, and had to raise the floor, knew you would want to use it lass. Ok we have bricks to remove,' he turned to Jack as he spoke, who in turn moved to pick up the tools he had set aside, knowing Brenda would want light at least in the room, if only a window had been found. Smiling and humming to himself he wandered out into the patio to see where he could start.

There would be no Charlie or Dan that day or the following, both of them seeing to projects at their respective workshops and foundry. As the projects were undoubtedly to do with the Iris House Build, she would Glen had told them, understand completely.

'I don't think we can actually do much more until the inspectors give their approval on Monday morning, so; a day of peace on the street before we begin our final push to completion. Now that Patrick is here, he may want to continue tomorrow, while it is quiet and the weather holds. He might want to get a head start on the internal painting. I know that Rebecca and Mia have given him strict instructions on what is going where, so to speak. I think we can give ourselves a break; now what are you up to today?'

'I am claiming Brenda today Dad!' Rebecca came over from the kitchen, cup in one hand, balancing her ever ready notebook and tape measure in the other. 'We need to go through all the things Mia and I have gathered in Mia's warehouse. To decide what goes where, especially once Ben has installed the new gas fires, and Patrick has worked his magic, we will be ready to furnish the apartments quickly and properly.'

Laughing with Glen, Brenda yielded to the inevitable and was laughing still as she followed Rebecca out of the house.

The day was a whirlwind of colour, fabrics and furniture, she thoroughly enjoyed herself. It was a long day, but supremely satisfying as they had laid down exactly what was going where, even down to the towels in the bathrooms. They had divided the space in the warehouse into four sections, one for each apartment. The attic only had two bedrooms, so the style was quite different to apartments two and three. They had, of course all Iris's antique pieces of furniture for Brenda's apartment, which they complimented with some lovely squishy sofa's, and chairs. The dining room was still a work in progress, all depending on if the 'Builders' had arrived at a solution to her request for a dumb waiter from the kitchen. Rebecca and Mia laughed with her as they explained they had at last found a place between the spiral stairs and the back door that was perfect according to Brent.

A raised eyebrow from Brenda asked the question, 'Brent had a major input in where it went as he is supplying the actual dumb waiter mechanism and lift required. I am not supposed to tell you though,' Rebecca said, 'it is supposed to be a surprise!'

Promising she would act surprised, made the girls go off into peals of laughter, it was a nice sound, Brenda was very happy to be in such good company.

She arrived back at the house, which looked a little patchy, she realised that Patrick and his men had gone over it preparing it for its first coat of paint in quite a while. Preparation first, not just slapping a coat of paint over the old, so it would not peel before it should. She looked up and down the quiet street, noting the houses on either side, checking on the paintwork on them both, decided they had both been slap dashed.

Patrick, Glen even Ben and Matt had gone, she realised it was after five, glad that Matt knew how to switch on the alarm, which he was updating with all the rest of the electrics, and had advised the security firm what he was doing.

Brenda let herself into a house that every day was changing. Coming back to life, breathing again, to begin a new era with new people, looking forward to the challenges of a century that had forgotten graciousness, style and manners, Brenda was determined to bring them all back in some measure.

There was a message on the answering machine, and on her mobile, both from Larry. Saying he would see her tomorrow, pick her up around ten thirty, eleven, for a leisurely drive, possibly a ramble so good walking shoes please, and possibly late morning tea, before they headed down to Glen and Julie's. She was to sleep well, and enjoy the peaceful evening.

Smiling at both messages, she realised she missed his company, that thought brought her up short, even after this very short acquaintance. While it would have done her ego so much good to have him permanently around, the temptation of allowing too much licence was very great. She didn't really know yet how she felt, there was an instant physical attraction, but she needed /wanted more than that, as she had been there before, she hoped in Larry she could find the companion she needed. Even so, the small doses of Mr. Lawrence Morecombe she was receiving at this stage in their relationship was definitely all her confused and full mind could take. It seemed a good idea to try and keep some distance if she could; trying to ignore the ghostly laugh she could just hear, with the waft of gardenia, gratefully she moved into the apartment to see what she could finish up before she headed to her bed.

Chapter 40

SUNDAY! WHAT A LOVELY day! She lazed in bed till eight and then decided to do some very necessary housework. Cleaning the apartment and making it fresh for the coming week, a week where most of these apartments would be returned to what they were intended, for the use of very special guests. Linda would be back tomorrow; Brenda was looking forward to seeing her with trepidation. Not secure enough in their growing friendship, she thought was there, to know what she would do when told of the full extent of the finding of Iris's will. Brenda was sure Linda only thought it was a few boxes of trinkets, ah, well tomorrow would tell.

Patrick rang the doorbell, telling her as he bounced into the room, that they would be able to put the first coat on the outside, and see how it looked. Then they would like to check out what there was to do in the other apartments, against the list that Rebecca and Mia had given him. Mostly they wanted to get an undercoat on the new back doors recently installed. Brenda advised him the house was open, and she trusted Patrick to know what was to be done.

When Matthew arrived with his team, he advised her they were all enjoying themselves enormously, hoping the bubble didn't burst. For the first time in a long time he was doing what he had dreamed of. Brenda had let him do that, he would be forever grateful to her.

She was just putting the finishing touches to her hair, after getting dressed for the day in tan dress boots, and moleskins, with cotton t-shirt, chambray shirt and a jumper around her shoulders.

'You look very nice today, did you say yes to Sunday dinner?' Brenda answered yes, but she was going to have a ramble with Larry first and be at his parents' house around five.

'That should be just about the time I get there. I intend to have all the wiring in place today; the blokes are having as much fun as I am. It is so clean and neat not to have to bury the work in the walls, just bend the pipes, drill the holes to put them through, thank you for the idea Brenda.'

'It was not my idea love, you talked to Rebecca, she told you the idea was there from Victorian times. I like the look of the pipe work throughout the apartments, it gives an old-world charm, and an excuse to employ Stan and his crew to keep them gleaming. So, I will see you at dinner?'

'I would never miss one of Mum's Sunday dinners, especially when there is special company coming!'

She laughed and told him he had better get on or he would miss it, he left her laughing as well, saying he would lock up when they were done. Brenda thanked him and tried to get down to some paper work, but she could not settle, she was pacing when her mobile rang.

'Brenda, Larry here, can you just come down, I am turning the corner now. I really don't want to hold up the traffic any longer than necessary. I apologise for not coming up!'

A true gentleman, Brenda thought, and assured him she was ready, just had to pick up her bag. Yelling a goodbye to Matt and Patrick, she heard a rumbled farewell from inside, and a louder one as she ran down the steps.

When she saw, the convertible Mercedes had the top down, she hurriedly put on the jacket she was carrying, ran around the car to the passenger side, smiled to the people in the cars behind as she slipped into the seat. Leaning over to give Larry a kiss on the cheek, he grinned at her.

'Ready for a ramble, thought we would have morning tea/lunch on the Thames, a little spot I know not far from Glen's but far enough away from the maddening city!'

'Ready and eager, it has been a while since I saw anything but concrete and buildings. Dennis and I used to head out to Hampstead

Heath on Sundays to read the papers and relax in the grounds of Kenwood House, when the weather was fine, a wonderful place you could imagine yourself worlds away!'

Larry nodded understanding the need for peace, he apologised for the top down but sunshine and a convertible demanded it. Brenda laughed with him, pulling a headscarf out of her pocket, very old fashioned, he said, very practical Brenda countered with, wrapping it a la Grace Kelly style, tying the corner down at the back. They moved out of the city with ease Brenda realising that whatever Larry did there was an element of expertise, like the way he was handling the powerful, beautiful machine with precision and care. He asked about what she had done the day before, wanting to know if she enjoyed herself. She related the time she had spent with Mia and Rebecca, saying that when the builders, electricians and painters had finished it would not take long at all to get the apartments ready for guests, with the system they had worked out. Larry laughingly saying she had just dismissed a mountain of work in one sentence, but he didn't for a moment doubt it would not happen exactly as Rebecca had planned.

They had a wonderful light meal at an old pub on the riverbank, just on the outskirts of Windsor, then they rambled along the river chatting amiably while they walked.

'Larry, I have to ask,' Brenda could not leave the question of her inheritance alone, 'I am sorry to keep harping on about the miracle that has happened to me; but it is right? Legally I mean, it just seems so far-fetched and like a story, a fairy tale even, that I have to keep asking! I will probably believe when I have to sign all the paper work I am sure there will be a lot of them?'

Larry pulled her hand through his arm, pulling her closer to him, so she could feel his assurances, as well as hear them.

'Yes, it is as legal as it gets, as far as we can ascertain. That is why there are two of the senior partners along with myself; most of the juniors and assistants in the office going through those papers you found and also the additional records we found in the archives, with meticulous care. We do not want you to understand and begin to utilise what you have been given, then have to stop for a crackpot court case or two. Why do you have something in mind already?'

'Well, I have been mulling over a few things since Friday, cannot stop the brain from ticking over. I can wait till tomorrow or even later, to see how my meeting with Hugh goes, who is the other lawyer I will be meeting?'

'Oh, that is a friend of my fathers, his firm was taken over recently, although the company of Lawyers and Solicitors go way back. Mr. Michael Dranish Fawkes QC is his name, the company is called Fawkes Inc.' she couldn't help but chuckle at such a modern sounding name for what she realised was an ancient company. 'Yes, well you want to hear what Michael says about it. Probably will get chapter and verse on it when I get the invite from my father to bring you to dinner, Michael is sure to be invited as well!'

'Oh yes, well I suppose that is inevitable. You only have the one parent alive?' Brenda asked suddenly wanting to hear about something other than the inheritance.

Larry understood the change in topic and gladly told her about his mother, her quick demise through cancer. She didn't suffer, he was glad to say, also didn't realise what was happening. It was while he was at Eton, so he wasn't at home much to see the disease progress to its conclusion. All he could really remember of her was the scent that hung around her and even its scent today brought a measure of comfort. Then there was her smile, a very similar smile to Brenda's, a smile that made everyone smile along. She turned and looked at him, saw the pain still in his eyes, even after all this time he still missed her. She pulled him close and hugged him, 'We all miss our mothers, when they are gone, but we have the memories to remember them by!'

Hugging her back and daringly kissing her on the cheek, he laughed agreeing with a nod of his head.

'Well, my two marriages were something of an anticlimax. I married them for the smile, without realising there had to be a thinking caring person behind it, to make the magic work. Fiona, well she did give me my two boys, both grown now and in relationships of their own. Come to see me occasionally, when they need a place to stay in the city, Andrew is 25 and Ewon is 23. Fiona decided I did not live in the society she wanted, and left just twelve months after Ewon was born, I raised them myself, oh with the help of Nannies of course!'

Brenda laughed, she had not realised that this man had so many sides, she was fascinated and urged him to go on, it seemed he was relaxing with the tale of his life, releasing some burdens held too long in check.

'Lorna, well Lorna was a mistake from the beginning, but I would not listen, the fact she totally dismissed the boys, would have nothing to do with them, should have warned me, but still I would not listen. The marriage lasted just on twelve months, and she took me for a considerable amount of money, thank god for the pre-nup my father had insisted on, or it could have been a lot worse. No children from her, thank goodness, I don't think she could nurture a cactus anyway. I have not heard from her in years, I don't particularly want to either. So, I work, I help Sir James and Linda, her husband Shane is an old Etonian, was a year ahead of me, but we keep in touch. Now though, I have a new project, and I am thoroughly looking forward to pursuing it; You!'

Brenda laughed and Larry stopped them, turning her to look at him she smiled, 'Ahh yes, there it is the smile with care in the eyes, just like my mother, thank you.'

'You are welcome, kind sir, I hope to meet your family soon, I would like to put faces to the personalities you have described. Although I cannot help but wonder what they will think of me, I only hope they like my smile as well?'

'There is no doubt in my mind of that being true,' Larry answered. He realised they had walked further than he thought, turning back toward the inn car park as a slightly brisker pace than the amble out.

Chapter 41

'DO I HAVE TO get a crowbar to find out about you? I know you are not from here, but I have been unable to place you. You are a mystery, Brenda Chalmers, I like that, so I have told you my sad tale, what about yours?'

Larry asked as he put the top up, as the clouds had gathered when they got back to the carpark. Pulling out of the inn Larry checking the directions again, looked at her with a raise of an eyebrow.

Brenda laughed, she told him about the short life she had in England, to which he nodded as the back ground check his office had done for Pickworths had advised this. Before her parents had immigrated to Australia. Her upbringing and life in the outback town, through tough times with some tough people, but worth their weight in gold and she had a childhood that was magical. She had married, straight after finishing school, but it had not been a happy marriage. Met Dennis when he came as a backpacker to work at the hotel, she was working part time in the office. He had been there for the birth of her twins David and Kate, they were now 24, but Dennis had left soon after their birth. They had kept in touch over the years, even when she moved away from the small community, enjoying the nomadic life she led, but always putting the children's education first. David had just been taken on by a prestigious architectural firm in Melbourne, as a junior architect to hone his craft. Kate happily working in a Travel Agency making lots of friends. No partner for either of them yet, so no grandkids, thank goodness, they needed to live a little. It was Kate who had suggested and organised the trip for her it was a complete surprise.

'They could look after themselves now,' she laughingly retold Larry, so here she was and what a ride! She had told them she had landed the perfect job, but was trying to think how to tell them the rest, and was putting that off until she understood exactly what it was herself.

He chuckled, knowing the confusion in Brenda, and wondering at how calm she could appear, chuckling more at his imagined reaction to when she finally did tell them about her and their new and improved lives. He was intrigued to know more, they had done a background check, but only a very limited one, just enough for Pickworths to realise they were not hiring a criminal. He glanced across at her realising there was a great deal in this story that she had skipped over, probably because it was too painful for her to remember. He also realised that a great deal of caution on his part would have to occur, to allow her the time to believe in him, and his feelings.

'Dennis?' he asked, a whole world of questions in that single name.

Brenda wondered when this question would be asked, smiling she turned in her seat to look at Larry's profile. 'Dennis is a friend, a very good and trustworthy friend, and my brother from another mother really. I am not the right kind of lover for him.'

Ah, Larry understood, and smiled again. He had wondered, but could relax. He didn't have a rival, he hopefully had another new friend.

They had been driving through some wonderful countryside before he slowed to pull into what was originally a farm. The original farmhouse was a beautiful thatched cottage, which was picture postcard perfect, with soft lights in the windows, that gave a warm welcoming glow. In the dusk, Brenda could make out a couple of barns, that lights shone through the windows in the dusk, so assumed the whole family still lived on the extensive property.

As the car crunched over the gravel, the door to the main farmhouse opened, Glen stood on the doorstep beaming a welcome.

'Welcome, you have made good time!' He came up and gave Brenda a hug; Larry a firm handshake, taking the bag that clinked from Brenda motioning them into the house before him, calling to his wife Julie, that they had arrived.

Julie was slightly taller than Brenda had imagined her, but still the true earth mother she had conceived in her imagination, warm and friendly, immediately pulling Brenda into an enveloping hug, thanking her quietly for giving them purpose again. Larry received a similar hug, and peck on the cheek, which Glen harrumphed about. Julie just laughed and said she was not dead and would receive handsome strangers any way she wanted. Glen harrumphed again asking if they would like a pre-dinner drink. Ushering them into the parlour where a wonderful fire blazed in a magnificent inglenook stone fireplace, and a very pregnant younger version of Julie sat beside it.

'You must be Gabby!' Brenda said, now understanding the delay in some of the glass projects, as she moved into the room, going over to Gabby and stopping her from trying to get up, 'no don't bother, you just have to sit back down again, and I can see that you are at the stage where that is just as difficult when are you due?'

Gabby smiled, realising everything Charlie and her father had said about this lady was true. She did make you feel wonderful with a smile.

'Oh, I think I am a week overdue, but my OB thinks I still have two weeks. I just think this little one likes having a mum in discomfort. Charlie is a wonder, but he is on edge as well, although he has been grateful that the little one has not come while he has had to be with you!'

At that moment, another door opened and the gentleman under discussion walked in, Charlie brightening on seeing who it was, came over to the fire, saying hello and hovering over his wife.

'Oh, for heaven's sake Charlie, go and help Dad with the drinks, will you please stop hovering' Gabby looked at him pointedly, Brenda grinning knowing it was from the pregnancy not malice she spoke so shortly. She looked at Larry who was grinning, nodded at Charlie who had a stricken, what have I done wrong this time, expression on his face.

'Charlie, I have heard you have a workshop here on the grounds, why don't we grab Glen once the drinks have been handed out and take a look around?' Larry saw the smile on Brenda's face and knew he had interpreted the nod correctly.

Charlie looked at Brenda, then at Gabby who smiled an apology and nodded yes. Glen came in with the drinks, Gabby taking a lemonade, Brenda a glass of champagne, she toasted them all then Larry to keep the peace, asked Glen for a look around the place if there was time before dinner. At Julie stating there was still an hour to go, all three gentlemen left as Rebecca came into the room.

'Glad you made it in good time Brenda, how was your afternoon?' Rebecca said watching the tall figure of Larry going past the window to the outbuildings.

'It was fine miss minx, thank you very much!' Brenda laughed with them all, Gabby stopping short as the baby kicked, the rippling of her tummy could be seen by all.

'Here,' Brenda said swapping Gaby's lemonade with her champers. 'Relax a little, I know but if you don't you will be miserable until this one decides he /she has not enough room in there to play ball, and wants out!'

Julie laughed with her saying she had tried to tell Gabby this but what daughter wants to listen to her mother, Brenda turned to her and they said, with peals of laughter, at the same time 'None of them!'

The evening was wonderful; Ben strolled back with the men, having joined them on the tour. Larry caught Brenda's eye as he moved back into the room, the grin and nod he gave her made her hope he remembered what had gone on, so he could tell her on the trip home. Matt arrived slightly damp from his shower very shortly after, telling the room they had done it, the wiring of the house was complete, they only had to wait for the inspectors to pass it the following day. Cheers rang out, toasts were made to Iris House, Gabby hiccupped and everyone saw the ripple across her abdomen as the baby joined in.

'Charlie,' Brenda caught up with him as they were moving into the dining room, 'you take all the time you need if that little one arrives this week. You hear me, I don't care, Gabby and the baby come first and foremost, understand!'

'But Brenda, you have a deadline, and I am so close, wait till you see Monday or Tuesday I promise the scaffolding at the front will only be there for Patrick. I think I have everything ready for the windows, just need to get it all to the house and install!' He stopped and looked at Brenda, and the glare he was getting stopped him, 'oh, alright, I suppose Rob can oversee the installation, and I really do want to be there when the baby is born, I only hope it comes this decade!'

Everyone heard that comment and laughed. Larry caught and squeezed Brenda's hand in reassurance, as they sat together at the large family dining table. A feast was waiting and enjoyed by all. Anecdotes swapped about children, family and great get togethers. Brenda had not felt so secure and welcome in years. It felt so right to be with these people, to be helping them in return. After dinner Gabby waddled out to her workshop to show Brenda her mosaics and lead lights she was slowly working on.

Brenda broached the subject of payment, was horrified when Gabby casually replied saying just put the cost in with Charlies bill for the new windows.

'No Gabby, I will not "just pay it with Charlies bill", this is your work, your artistic right and talent. I have pride in what you do even if you do not value it yourself. You are a professional artist, and that deserves recognition and payment in your own right. Your husband has his own talents, and I will help him separately, although he does not know it yet, but Charles Waines Glass is going to become a known and respected brand name, but don't tell him yet please, I don't want the head to swell too much before he is finished at my place!'

Gabby giggled and stopped short, 'Come on baby, head down and out please!'

Brenda laughed and continued, 'so I would like a separate bill from you, young woman, and don't cut the costs either, this is your work, your money it should be in a separate account. You are going to need one, you will not be able to stop your talent, and you can work around the baby, so are we agreed?'

Gabby coloured not used to being praised but nodded her head in agreement, 'I understand what you are saying Brenda, I can be Charlie's wife, but also have my own independence. I will send my bill with Charlie tomorrow, all things being equal!' she added pointing to the baby bump.

Brenda and Larry headed back to town a little later, Larry saying they could not stay longer he had a big day ahead of him even if they did not, ha ha. Glen agreed it was going to be just as full as the last couple of weeks, with the lift hopefully, being installed, plumbing finished off, to which Ben just grinned, adding 'Piece of Cake!' His father rolled his eyes at his cockiness, looking at him with another harrumph.

Brenda remembered to tell Glen that she had an appointment with the lawyers, he quickly looked at Larry, who nodded and smiled, to put him at his ease, conveying he had it all under control. Brenda continued adding that she was then going to see Linda at Pickworths, so she hoped they understood her absence when the inspectors were there, they really did not need her did they?

'No lass, I know how you feel about those inspectors! Norman won't be there either will he, ah, well just his name seems to work fine to keep them in line.'

They all laughed at Glen's intentional pun, Larry said to just mention his name as well if needed, he had also been on a few committees with a couple of the inspectors that should be in the group. Glen nodded his thanks.

'All the merrier, so you will be there when we arrive, but gone for most of the morning. That's ok Brenda, we will see what we can accomplish without you, Rebecca tells me the furniture and fittings are already to go, once the inspectors clear all the works!'

Brenda gave him a hug thanking him for his understanding, 'yes and I know the apartments are going to look a thousand times better than what the Gardiner contract was going to throw at Sir James. I cannot believe that man had the gall to do his shoddy work for so long, getting away with it and being proud of it!'

'That is what happens when you get too big for your boots, and people keep telling you, you are brilliant, you start to believe you can walk on water. Me, I have my wife to tell me I am an idiot, and keep me grounded!' Julie was horrified, 'Glen!' she said tapping his arm lightly, with laughter ringing out around them, which was what he intended.

They had settled into an easy pace on the drive home, 'Well?' Brenda said turning slightly in her seat to watch the expressions cross Larry's face, 'well what?' he asked back, a grin appearing on his face, as he knew very well what she was referring too.

'You know, the bit about Glen coming over all "Dad Like", making sure that his surrogate daughter is not being pursued by a cad! Oh yes, I know of your reputation, both Mia and Rebecca are very good gossips and into the social pages as well you know?'

Larry had the grace to look a little abashed, but just smiled at her in a glance in her directions, liking the expression of interest on her face.

'Well Glen knows something is up, but not sure what. He is looking just at my interest in you at the moment, although I am sure he knows there is something else going on, but not the full picture. He said he liked the changes that were occurring, but was going to watch out for you, and yes, I do believe he thinks of you as an older daughter, come back to the fold so to speak. He certainly holds you in high regard, and not just because of the work. He thinks very highly of you as a person of integrity too, he is just worried about you Brenda, thinks you are too alone, but is not sure, because of my so-called reputation, if I am the right person to end the loneliness?'

'What do you think?' Brenda asked into the silence, 'are you the right person to end my loneliness Larry?' The question was out before Brenda could think, realising it had to be asked, for her own peace of mind at least.

Larry glanced at her, slowly he pulled over, leaving the engine running, but he had to look at her to give her the answer she needed, so she could see he meant every word he was saying.

'I hope so, but I really do not know for certain. I would like to think we can go on and become old and grey together, but the factors involved in possibly moving us in different directions are enormous. Brenda, I say again to you the promise I made at dinner the other night, that you might not remember I made. I will be there for you in any capacity, Friend, Business Partner, even in my wildest dreams Lover, whatever you want me to be, just know I will be there for you!'

'You have to find yourself, your new place in this world and that over the next few weeks and months is going to be difficult. I am not going to pressure you into giving me more than you can give, or are not sure off. Can you understand what I am trying badly to say?'

'I understand Larry,' she took the hand he was waving about, 'We have all the time in the world, if this friendship between us blossoms into something more, that would be wonderful. If not I will always cherish your honesty and the friendship we have, and accept wholeheartedly your help in the legal department I am sure to need. Yes, please let us take things slowly, *as much as we can with a meddlesome ghost interfering*, she thought to herself, 'you know they say, good things come to he, or she who waits!' She leant over and kissed him tenderly, Larry responded just as gently, knowing something had grown between them. Hoping that when she was confronted by the full disclosure the following day she still thought him trustworthy!

Chapter 42

Another Monday Morning, Brenda woke at six, not sure how she felt. On the one hand, she was looking forward to the day and seeing work being, or at least attempted to be completed to bring her home, oh what a wonderful term, she realised that 'home' was true more today than last week, back into working order.

On the other, she did not know what to expect, she was sure Larry was subtly trying to tell her last night, that there was going to be more. He just could not tell her, that was what frightened her most, that he could not tell her because even he did not realise the full extent of what this inheritance meant. She showered with care and chose her interview suit, navy blue skirt and jacket, pale blue shirt and court shoes, to give her a semblance of professionalism. If she looked the part of a confident woman in charge and control, it may actually rub off in life. For added insurance she put on Iris's pearl necklace, but her own pearl stud earrings, which matched the necklace in colour and size, for courage and good luck, a waft of Gardenia floated around her to help calm her down.

It was after seven when the Haddon's arrived, with Dan and his foundry men it was just as well that Norman was not going to be there, the house was overflowing already. Charlie came up with a morning tea box, and envelope for Brenda, still with no news, but he had his mobile and Julie promised she would ring him. As Brenda read Gabby's estimated bill, she thought she was going to have to have another very serious word with the girl. She had not listened to a word she had said last night, and totally undervalued herself and work. The bill she had sent was for all of the windows, was a total of seven hundred and fifty pounds, a ludicrously inadequate quote, it hardly covered the materials for the three very large windows and three smaller ones she had already bought, never mind the cleaning and repairing of all the antique ones that they had found. Charlie was talking with Rob and she motioned him over to her.

'I think I need to have a word with Gabby when she has delivered this child of your Charlie!'

'Why Brenda, is that her bill for the windows, she was worried she was charging you too much!'

'Too much, Charlie Waines, have you seen what she quoted?' she asked handing him the sheet of paper to read.

No, he said reading the bill, and shrugging his shoulders, 'she just said to give this to you, what is the problem?'

Glen came over to see what was going on, as Brenda looked quite upset.

'No Glen, no problem, at least it is not going to be as I can fix this. It is just your daughter in the final throws of pregnancy not valuing herself or her work highly enough. Charging me too much, look at this bill,' taking the bill from Charlie so Glen could see what she was talking about.

'I have checked prices online, stained glass lead light windows the size of the one over the new back doorway, plain start at twelve hundred, with a small pattern can be worth fifteen. The smaller plain ones start at five hundred, she is robbing herself blind, and I won't have it!'

'She thought it was too much,' Charlie said looking a little uncomfortable at seeing this different side of Brenda, 'you are family, she couldn't charge the right amount!'

'Oh, for heaven's sake, is that what this is about, Glen and you Dan, who had wandered over to see what the commotion was, 'please don't, I sincerely mean this, cheapen yourselves, please do me some favours, I would like that, but when it comes to your own work, your artistry do not undervalue yourselves. I expect to receive the full bills from all of you, if you want to think of it this way; most of the bills are not being paid by me, but by Pickworths. The company is the one paying for the major building works, but this one is mine, as I requested the work!'

She walked over to the table, pulling the expanding file over, finding her own cheque book totalled the bill to her satisfaction, writing that amount on the cheque she handed over to Charlie.

'Now I think I have robbed her, so put that in a bank account for the little one if you need to, but I will not have her think less of herself. You should not either,' and she rounded on the stunned faced gentlemen in the room all looking at her, 'you should also tell her so, she needs that kind of support as well as the back rubs and hot water bottles!'

Charlie smiled sheepishly, giving Brenda a hug, saying thank you, and I will have to revise my bill now after that episode.

'Thank you, lass, this will mean a lot to Gabby and to us. Are you alright this morning, you seem a little tense, you look good in that suit, but are you OK?'

'I am a little tense Glen, I do not like lawyers, and I have to see two of them this morning!' Glen nodded his understanding it had to do with the inheritance. 'Then see Linda, but I hope that meeting won't be too bad, at least I can tell her we are moving on apace, and right back on track with the rebuild. Matt has done a great job to get everything nearly finished so quickly!'

The house shone with the new brass pipes going into and out of every apartment, matching the antique pipe work in her apartment. The team had cleaned and polished (not to a Nona standard of course) every tube as they added or reused them. Matt moved over to them as he heard his name.

'Wait till we get the ok to continue, Brenda, then I will show you how it all works, it is just so neat!'

Glen just looked at him, thought he had better put him to work somewhere until the inspectors arrived or he would explode. Telling Brenda to take it easy, that they would be here when she got back, organised the work crew, ushering them out, some with cups of tea still in hand.

Brenda arrived at the law offices a little early, presenting her card to the receptionist, she was asked to take a seat, which was the last thing she wanted to do, putting her bag and case in a chair paced the room, trying to keep calm.

The door opened and a silver haired gentleman walked across the room, hand outstretched in greeting.

'Ms. Chalmers, welcome, I am Hugh Pemberton, sorry I am a little late, had to send Lawrence out on a mission, actually he is getting coffee for us, please will you come with me?'

Brenda had taken the hand and shaken it, wondering at the very deep rich bass voice that had flowed from Mr. Hugh Pemberton, which so fitted his appearance. He was a short man same height as Brenda without her shoes, a round barrel of a man, she also assumed he would have a very good palate, and more than likely be involved is some choral society or other, with that rich deep voice it would be a shame if he was not.

He ushered Brenda into a room surprisingly similar to Sir James office at Pickworths, the familiarity easing her fears a little.

'Now, I know this is all very strange to you, my dear, but I need to advise you we are here to help, in any way we possibly can. I am going to ask my Legal Secretary, Sally to sit in on this and every session we have in the future, as she can then record what is said, and you can have a written record of the proceedings as well. I hope you do not mind, it is an old-fashioned thing, but I prefer this to a tape recorder on the table?'

'Mind, no not at all Mr. Pemberton, it would be beneficial to have a written record of what goes on, for I surely will not remember the most of it. I apologise in advance, I am very nervous, so please forgive me if I make a fool of myself, you have to realise I have never even won a lottery prize before, this is just so surreal!'

'Quite understand, my dear, you have to realise that legacies like this are indeed very rare, and yes you can compare it to a lottery win, except this one keeps on going!'

Before Brenda could question his turn of phrase, he continued.

'It will need to be handled with care for the future, I assure you of my, and my firms complete dedication to you and your family in the years to come, I hope you will be with us for a long time?'

Hugh turned and pressed a button on his desk, while Brenda tried to interpret the unspoken words in his little speech, but could not fathom the intent, as she was sure he was referring to what was about to be disclosed. A slim attractive mid-forties lady walked in, she had an air of 'this is my place, I have earned it' about her. Hugh introduced Sally to Brenda, who shook her hand, thanking her for her time. Sally had rarely been acknowledged before never mind the courteous thank you, more used to being classed as a piece of the furniture; she took the hand mechanically, wondering if this person had a clue what was to come.

'Now before Lawrence interrupts us with coffee,' Hugh was saying as Sally seated herself behind a small desk with a stenograph machine already primed and waiting. He drew Brenda's attention to an area in the corner of the room, a sofa and two chairs with a table groaning with papers in the middle.

'Are these all to do with me?' Brenda asked horrified.

'Indeed, my dear, you have opened a legal can of worms. As soon as we think we have all that there is, another lead and more paper work pops out!'

Brenda could not help but give him a rather startled stare, wondering if she was going to have to read all of them.

'Now, don't look so alarmed. Most of them are just agendas for meetings similar to this one. You don't have to read any of them, Sally and her team have already checked them, giving us a concise precis of the salient points.

'Thank you Sally, I owe you big time!' Brenda turned and smiled at the woman sitting upright at her desk, typing away with ease, she looked quite stunned at being addressed directly, but nodded in acknowledgment and smiled.

Hugh handed Brenda a folder, she took it and looked at the loose sheets inside, he motioned her to sit on the sofa.

'I need you to read through this please. It is a more detailed explanation of how you found Mrs. Boerchermeir's will, we have to add this to the paper you signed for Mrs. McGill at Pickworths.

Brenda sat and started to read the contents with more concentration, reading and correcting when she found errors, adding more information where she thought it was needed. After the last page of the account, was a single sheet that just screamed, "Read me VERY carefully!" at her.

At Brenda's raised eyebrow at this sheet of paper, Hugh Pemberton looked and smiled. Yes, he thought, she had picked it, Lawrence had assured him that she would not just dismiss or skip over the disclaimer like so many others would have done, in their eagerness to get their hands on the legacy riches, he had said Brenda was not like that.

He had also said she would stop and ask for explanation, and indeed he had been right as Brenda looked up at him and smiled.

'Excuse me Mr. Pemberton, can you please explain this to me?'

'Of course, my dear, that is a legal document we have to have your signature on. It states that you did not know of the Legacy, or of the Boerchermeir, Fitzgibbon or Lucas holdings or estates, before you arrived in the UK. That you did not arrive in the country to deceive or do fraudulent business!'

Brenda looked at Hugh Pemberton, hearing the steel in his voice, realising his mild appearance masked a very tough cookie, and a very good man to have on your side.

'I can certainly with a very clear conscious indeed sign this Mr. Pemberton. You can check with the Immigration Department, if you have not done so already, that I arrived here nearly two months ago, and that was the only arrival for myself since my parents immigrated to Australia over thirty years before. I always wanted to return and bring my children for a holiday, but circumstances prohibited it till this visit. I also see that my children have been referenced in this document, why?'

'This has to cover them as well. They will be your heirs, I take it, they are also adults, could conceivably have travelled independently of yourself and brought back the information!'

'Ah, yes I see.' Brenda realised what he was saying, again she wondered exactly what she had gotten herself into, he was covering any sort of legal actions against her or her family for foreknowledge of the Legacy. She sat and re-read the page, trying to read between the lines.

Bright Hugh thought, very bright but innocent, guileless and honest, what a refreshing wonderful combination in this day and age.

'Well as my son has never owned a passport, but will I think need one soon?' Hugh nodded and smiled.

'My daughter only recently made a first overseas visit and that was a work trip, I can sign for them with a very clear conscience. I would like to add a couple of things if I may,' again Hugh nodded delighted at this very intelligent woman, urging her to go on, 'my parents or even grandparents would have had no knowledge of Lord Lucas, Iris or any of her kith and kin. They were never servants or indentured staff, they never would have moved in the same circles. Also, you had better add my good friend Mr. Dennis Brookes to this disclaimer, he is British based, also the children's Godfather, but I can guarantee he would have no knowledge of the family either.

Yes, thought Hugh, *I like this woman, nice to look at, great smile, wonderful manners, and a brain that works to go with it. Modest, honest and with integrity, oh I am going to enjoy looking after this account, I only hope we keep it!* He nodded to Brenda for the inclusion, and looked at Sally to see if she had got it all down.

The door opened as Brenda finished reading the paper again, after adding her inclusions, signing it with a flourish. Lawrence strode into the office, with a tray of coffee cups and biscuits in his hands. He put it down on Hugh's desk taking one over to Sally, who beamed at him thanks; going over to serve Hugh and then sitting down beside Brenda with two cups handing one to her with a smile.

'*Oh Ho, that is why!*' Sally thought, as she sipped her coffee. Rumour had been going around ever since Larry had taken himself off this account. She now knew why and sighed, better give up on that dream Sal old girl, he is gone for good, no mistaking a look like that, even if she doesn't realise it.

Chapter 43

'WELL WITH THE LEGALITIES out of the way, we now get to the fun part. I don't know if you realise the full scope of this legacy Ms. Chalmers?'

'Please Mr. Pemberton, if your association is going to be a long standing one, can you please call me Brenda, I would appreciate it!'

'In that case Brenda, please call me Hugh!' they nodded to each other in acknowledgment of the change in status for both of them.

'As I was saying, I do not know if you realise but you are now a very wealthy woman. I know that Lawrence has given you a verbal amount of your inheritance, but I have to tell you that figure is very conservative, very conservative indeed. We are still delving into the legacy from Iris's family; I believe we should wait until Michael arrives for more details on that side. The separate legacies from her two marriages are enough to begin with!'

'Edward Fitzgibbon, her first husband was the last in his family. He died in the war, there were no children left to inherit on his side. I take it you have been reading Mrs. Boerchermeir's journals?'

Brenda nodded unable to speak; she had found time to read about some of Iris's life, but had not realised that there was any sort of inheritance from that first marriage, it had been so short, Brenda had grieved for her loss as such a young age.

'Well there are legacies and a very fine house and grounds involved in the Fitzgibbon Estate, we can go into further details later. We have a little information on her second marriage to George Boerchermeir who was a South African; he arrived to visit the old country. We know he met Iris at a garden party, married her within a month, returning to South Africa, sending for his bride once he had built a house for her!'

Brenda continued into the pause, she had read about this marriage only the night before.

'They had a few years, I read. Iris enjoyed being in the hot land, and interacting with a different culture, everything was so new and strange, though she wondered if she ever really fit in with the expats that were her neighbours, as she treated everyone the same, even the servants. She lamented in her journal that they were never blessed with children, at least living children, she did mention the two miscarriages with great sadness. When her father became ill, she returned to nurse him, she was all the family he had. In the end, she never returned to South Africa, about six months into her visit home, George was killed while trying to capture some poachers on his property, they never found his killers. Iris remained in England after her father had died, with George gone there was no reason to return!'

Shaking off the sadness that wanted to engulf her, and with gardenia around, she smiled at the people listening intently to her tale 'But I am determined that now I am her heir, I will try and begin the work she wanted to do and wrote about in her journals. After all the sadness in her life, she still held great joy and belief in people. I do not have the restraints that Iris had in her era, I intend to help where I can, to begin where her dreams left off!'

Hugh and Larry nodded at the conviction in her statement, both looking at each other with a slight grin, thinking this is going to be one hell of a ride.

'There are estates with both marriages, as I said before,' Hugh continued, 'both here and abroad. We know they have been maintained in some way, due to the fact that royalties are still coming into the accounts and trusts set up for the estates. That is entirely due to the foresightedness of both the gentlemen in question. I believe a tour of the properties should be done, but not quite yet. There will be time enough after you feel comfortable with your new life; it will take a while to be able to see clearly your life ahead!'

He handed Brenda a sheet of paper 'this is an estimate of wealth after only three bank accounts have been checked and verified. We understand that there are at least three more, all to do with overseas interests. They have all been and are still accumulating money on a regular basis, and have also been accruing interest since they were opened. I think you might be interested in the figure at the present date?'

Brenda looked at the figure with a lot of zeros mixed in with the numbers, and didn't know whether to laugh or cry. A wisp of gardenia floated by, she took a deep breath to steady herself.

'Well, huh, whew, it seems a very large and unbelievable sum. I know I am sounding like a broken record, but are you sure of all this?'

Brenda looked at the three people in the room, they all smiled. Larry laughing at her expression and seeming calmness, put a steadying arm around her shoulders. Hugh was beaming like a fond parent. Sally smiled at her nodding her head, she liked this woman, no hysterics, no yahoo, and she deserved every pound of what was coming her way. Her estimation of Brenda went up even higher when she bent and removed a couple of sheets from her attaché case.

'Well I don't know if this is the right time, but I would like to start 'Iris's Legacy' with these thoughts, right now.'

She put the papers into Hugh's hand, the first was a request for setting up companies in Charlie, Matthew, Ben and Rebecca's own rights. Saying that she wanted to ensure the innovations and ideas that they had come up with, and would come up with in the future with the revamp of the house, would be their own recognized work. Wanting to ensure that any patent rights for the new techniques they had already come up with had been lodged where appropriate, on the work already done, waiting approval for them. They had been working so hard, they probably had not time to do it for themselves, so she would.

The other idea, and she smiled softly, was to buy old hotels around the country, even abroad if she had that much scope, turning them into affordable retirement hotels. Fully staffed, medically and hospitality wise, to be facilities for people with no family to look after them, or even for respite care for those that did. She did not want the spectre of Iris being alone in a room with no one to care, did not rear its ugly head time and again.

Hugh beamed, a very interesting time to come, he thought. He took the sheets over to Sally to add into the record.

Brenda continued, 'both of these different legacies I hope will be an ongoing concern. To help people with talent, secure that talent for themselves, especially in this day and age, innovation and talent should not be curtailed due to lack of funds. Or our elderly die alone in a room with no one to care! Of course, I do not want to run out of money, but I like the idea of investing in something that itself provides for its own future. I have no idea if it will work, but it seemed a logical thing to me, and I have been thinking of this for a few years, what do you think?'

Hugh was absolutely beaming, Larry was amazed that she could think so clearly at a time like this, especially as she had not had the full disclosure yet. That she could think of others and want to help, when she hadn't even sorted out what was happening to her, took his breath away. Sally just smiled, knowing this 'Lady' was just warming up!

Chapter 44

T HE INTERCOM BUZZED, HUGH answering, 'send him in Rose, we are expecting him thank you!'

The door opened to admit another silver haired man, this time the exact opposite of Hugh. Mr. Michael Dranish-Fawkes, was so thin he was almost skeletal, looking for all like an escaped monk, complete with tonsured head, hook nose and very dark unreadable eyes. He nodded to Hugh, took the outstretched hand that Larry gave him in welcome, then turned to Brenda who had risen as he entered.

'Lady Lucas, it is a pleasure to meet you!' bowing from the waist in acknowledgement of her new status.

Brenda looked at him, wondering what she should do to answer him.

'It is confirmed then Michael all verified, no doubt!'

'No doubt at all Hugh, the checks we have made were exhaustive and still ongoing, all came back with no doubt at all. Lady Brenda Lucas is the correct title to call the former Ms. Brenda Chalmers, although she may still use her original name if she so desires!'

Brenda looked at everyone, standing around her the men gave a short bow, and Sally a very slight curtsey to accept Brenda in this new area of her life. Her first reaction was of disbelief, this was not, could not be happening to her! This was a dream, a very strange and real dream, but a dream she was sure she would wake from very soon. Then she saw the truth in Larry's eyes, she blinked furiously to stop the tears that suddenly wanted to flow. Breathing deeply, wondering what she should do, suddenly she found the situation so ludicrous that she giggled, then laughed, startling every one with the sound.

Gaining some control, and seeing the looks on the men's faces, she took another breath, 'I apologise, I really do, please Mr. Fawkes, please understand, I mean no disrespect to you or the information you have brought to me. Nor do I want you to think I do not take the title or office that you have offered me in low regard. It is just so absurd, please can you not see!' she held out her hands in entreaty, for them to listen and understand her.

'Ten minutes ago, I was (and hopefully still am) Brenda Chalmers, a middle-aged mum of two grown children. Ten days ago, I was unemployed, wondering if my holiday and dream of living in the 'old country' was over and I had to go back to what I left in Australia!'

'Now because I was disgusted at a society that would let a woman die old and alone; packed what I thought were her few personal belongings; found a will no one could find, because of that disregard, I find myself a very wealthy woman and elevated to the peerage, can you not see how that is so fantastic an occurrence, like a movie script! If your firm knew of Mrs. Boechermeir's existence, how did this incredible scenario come about?'

Mr. Fawkes was very startled indeed, he had no answer for this very astute and he now realised level-headed woman in front of him. He had been prepared for everything he thought, from the vapours to probably vulgar obscenities, knowing a little of her background, but was definitely not prepared for the laughter. He also did not like that she had him questioning his firms conduct, as he could see exactly where she was coming from, and did not readily have an answer to their neglect of their client for her.

'I cannot answer that question I am afraid. As for apologising Lady Lucas, it is I who must apologize to you I should have given you more time. I have no way of mitigating the lack of interest in the wellbeing or situation that Mrs. Boerchermeir found herself in. She did not request anything from us apart from payment of bills. She was a recluse, guarded her privacy jealously. I believe that a certain amount of apathy on our part has to be factored in as well. There

I am being very candid, and can only hope that the events prior to your discovery will not alienate you from our services?'

Brenda, realised they were still all standing, some instinct told her they were waiting for her to do something, motioned for them all to take their seats.

'Sit please sit, thank you Mr. Fawkes, and I request you at this time call me Brenda.' She put up her hand to stop the rebuttal, she knew would come from him, 'in here, in private I give you all permission to call me Ms. Chalmers or Brenda depending on the situation we are in. Including you Sally, I think and hope your services are going to be needed for a long time to come!'

Sally smiled at this woman, who had walked into the room a commoner, but would walk out a Lady of the Realm. She realised that as shocked as she was at the moment, she would do very well indeed, and also realised that she was looking forward to future sessions in this room, they were going to be very interesting she was sure.

Brenda was indeed in a state of shock, realising that this dream could quickly turn into a nightmare, if she was not careful. 'I would also like it if the knowledge of my elevation to the Peerage could be kept somewhat quiet, for the moment! I have to think of some way of telling my children first!'

Michael was bemused, looked at Hugh, then Larry not understanding why this woman wasn't running up and down the room screaming her news to the rooftops. Then he recalled her initial reaction, it was one of incredulous horror, before her natural level headedness and good old common sense had kicked in. He understood in part that she wanted life to be normal, and advise her children, but it could only be for a short while. He would need to get to know this woman, to find out who the person was behind the basic facts they had discovered about her, but the delay could only be for a short while, he nodded to Hugh.

'I think that would be fine for a while, there are things we must advise you of, we can delay your court presentation, it is a tricky thing to organise these days. We have time, I don't think we can do anything before the Windsor Sitting in July!'

Brenda was working hard to suppress the nervous laughter that was building again, under her calm exterior, furiously she suppressed the thought this is a dream.

'Presented at Court, ah, well, I suppose if I must, I must. If I am to-do what I like with this legacy I have been entrusted with, then I will of course do what you ask, but please Michael,' he nodded at the use of his first name, 'give me time to get my breath and also get used to the situation a little?'

Larry was struck by the calmness of the woman beside him. When Michael had walked into the room and addressed Brenda as Lady Lucas for the first time, he really did not know how she was going to take it. She had laughed, even at this early stage he knew her well enough to know that it was sheer nerves that made her do it. But to come back and throw the neglect of Iris in her later years in his firms face, showed him a woman of depth. He could only imagine how many pompous institutions she was going to bring down a peg or two. Now as he looked at her again, realised that although still in shock, she would do very well indeed, he knew quite a few Lords and Lady's that Brenda was going to run rings around. Her innate good taste and common sense would be a breath of fresh air in a staid and nearly outdated society. If given a chance to be who she was and not get sucked in to the pampered lifestyle of the idle rich, she would do what the estate of Lord or Lady was supposed to do, nurture and improve people's lives. He stopped and inwardly laughed at his own notion, it was definitely not what his Brenda was. They already had a sample of what and how she would continue in the papers Hugh had in his hand. He caught his breath as he realised how superior this "Lady" was, that she had depths that were as yet untapped. What did he have to offer her, it was a thought that he disliked, as it was usually the other way around?

Michael had also been deep in thought, knowing that he would have to tread carefully, there was so much they could do to help and advise Brenda of; how her life was going to change, if she would let them. It was going to take a while for him to be comfortable not calling her "Your Ladyship, or Ma'am" that sort of etiquette had been inbred. There were just so many things that would be required of her, with the acquisition of the title, he also stopped and wondered how many she would dispense with as unnecessary. He decided he would consult with Hugh, he would have a better idea, he hoped, of how to move forward.

'Your La…Brenda' he interrupted the thinking silence around him, 'I have some paper work that requires your signature?' he looked up as she chuckled, a deep rich sound, one that he knew he could easily get used to, realising it was Brenda's way of acknowledging irony. Enjoying the warmth in the smile she gave him, yes very different, but he smiled knowing he could get used to it very quickly.

'I realise that is probably what Hugh has had you doing all morning, but I only have two documents that need your immediate signature. One is the acceptance of the fact you are Lord Lucas's heir, also to give us a sample of your signature for our records, and the second is the acceptance of the Peerage!'

'I don't suppose I can avoid it, can I?' again, the shake of the head in denial, 'well then advise me Michael, do I sign Brenda Chalmers, or Lady Brenda Lucas, or both?'

The tension in the room dissipated, a slight waft of gardenia floated around everyone. Iris is very happy Brenda thought, looking at Larry, he raised an eyebrow, he had caught the fragrance as well knowing what it meant.

With the signatures on the papers completed, Brenda looked for the first time at her signature as Lady Lucas, she could not help but give a small ironic smile. *Life it seems, just keeps giving me curve balls,* she realised that she liked the feelings running through her. Now there was purpose, this was what she was meant to do, she could now realise the dreams she had held secret for so many years.

Then Michael cleared his throat, to drop another bombshell.

'I need to tell you also that your estate and holdings as Lady Lucas are quite extensive, in England and in Europe. The accounts set up have been accumulating funds for a very long time, without being tapped in any measure apart from Mrs. Boechermeir's small requests for expenses. I believe that Larry has advised you that you own the row of houses named Steel Street?' Brenda nodded at him wondering what was coming next, could she take any more in one sitting? 'Well the whole block is owned by the Lucas Estate, you own quite a bit of real estate in this part of London, in fact this building we are in at present is on the books!'

The room spun, Brenda gasped, grasping Larry's hand for comfort and support. Readily his arm came around her, holding her till she could focus on the faces around her. Concern was first and foremost, Sally was up giving Hugh a glass of water to pass to Larry.

Michael holding back on the rest of the information there was time. This lady would cope, he knew deep down that she would cope magnificently, but not with all the information at once. He had what he had come for, her signature and to see the integrity and calibre of the woman who would inherit and use the legacies his firm had been nurturing all these years. He was very pleased indeed, a genuine smile formed on his face, it transformed him, this was a rare occasion indeed he was a happy man, for the first time in several weeks.

Brenda shook herself, settling the darkness back where it belonged, she was in control again, sipping the glass of water, thanking Larry for his support, she looked at Michael.

'That is one hell of a piece of information to throw at someone Mr. Fawkes! I will want to see exactly what, how and why, but not today. My life just got very complicated and very exciting. I have a challenge, which I love, and a purpose, but I have to ask, are you,' and she included Hugh and Larry, grasping his hand tightly, in the question, 'up for the journey we are about to take?'

Michael was even more shocked at the question, the smile that he had started, turned into a grin that lit his eyes. Looking at Hugh, then at the clasped hands of Larry and Brenda, the look that passed between them, realised something was brewing in this a new relationship, could only nod yes.

'Well in that case, you had better have these other ideas of mine, and liaise with Hugh, there are more, but until I realise the full extent of what I can do. Please do not tell me now,' she interrupted as both Hugh and Michael started to speak, 'I have a House I am transforming and need to see how it is progressing. Do you have everything you need at present Gentlemen?'

Michael bit back the words that were waiting to be said, that she should now have someone else take over the rebuild for her. Realising with a start, that she would never think about doing that, it was just not who she was, anything she started she would definitely see through to completion.

Hugh looked at Michael wondering what was going through his mind, as he was sure he stopped himself from saying something. 'I think I can fill Michael in Brenda, we know where you are. We are quite looking forward to seeing what you are doing with the house!' Michael adding a most certainly, to Hugh's statement. 'Oh by the way, this if for you, it is the document confirming the name of "Iris House" to you. Perhaps I can set up an appointment with Michael for next week?'

Brenda nodded, taking the paper from Hugh and gently putting it in her case. Larry rising with her, she turned as he walked her to the door, 'I have to see Linda, can you come around later. I think I need a little space to breath!'

Larry said of course, as he opened the door and walked her out to the front steps, she gave him a peck on the cheek, walking down the street to meet with Linda head high and back straight.

Larry returned to the men, Sally having left to type up the meeting. He poured more coffee from the thermos jug he carried into the room for them all.

'Well is she, all right?' Hugh asked Michael as he took the cup offered to him.

'I think she will adjust, given time.' Michael said, 'I was impressed with her demeanour. Not what I expected but pleasantly surprised; I think she will do well, very well indeed!'

'She is definitely shell shocked at the moment, 'Larry said, 'the information about owning land in the city was a body blow. Do you know the full extent of her holdings Michael, or are you still checking?'

'Still checking, my boy, the late Lord Lucas was a very inventive and far sighted individual, years ahead of his time, the same as his father before him. We have a good idea, don't get me wrong, but some of the investments put in place seem to have strayed off track.

Perhaps a good thing in some cases, I will be interested to see what the new Lady Lucas, sorry Brenda; that is going to take some getting used to, thinks about them?'

'I think there will be a lot of things we will have to get used to in the new Lady Lucas. She is not one to sit back and let others do work for her. I foresee a new and invigorating time for us all.' Hugh said sipping his cup, 'I do not think we will be disappointed by her either. Guidance is what is needed, we can give her that, I think she will do very well!'

Larry nodded, realising he could add very little. It would be better if he just kept out of the firm's way at present, listening and making sure anything done, was in Brenda's best interest. He was looking forward to seeing her later and hearing about her meeting with Linda.

Linda was making a cup of coffee when Brenda walked in with a couple of takeaway cups in her hand.

'Wanting one of these?' she asked, laughing at the 'how did you guess?' that was the reply.

Linda looked again at a subtly altered Brenda. There was something apart from the suit she could not put her finger on the change, but it was there.

'You look well rested; did you enjoy your break?' Brenda asked, as she sat down in the seating area of the room at Linda's gesture.

'Oh, it was wonderful, the weather was fine, and we were pleasantly surprised at the way the alterations are going to the house. We are rebuilding an old Farmhouse in Tuscany, my husband Shane is an architect, he is responsible for new design,' Brenda smiled and nodded, 'so how are things at your building site?'

Brenda laughed, 'yes you could call it a building site, although the changes have been drastic, they are moving on. Second inspection should be long over, so they could make the final push this week, which gives them and me a week to tweak everything into place, I hope!'

Linda laughed pointing to a note on the table, 'Grandfather wanted to know what was going on, especially with all the phone calls he has been getting. He is a bit restless, so is coming home this afternoon, what can I tell him?'

'Why not come around and see, I also want to introduce you to the people who have made it possible. How about coming for morning tea at eleven, Julie Haddon is sure to send her best if I tell her the CEO and Owner of Pickworths are coming around. I do have some news I want to tell you both.

Linda laughed again saying fine, she was itching to see what had been going on. This new friend of hers had subtly changed in the short time she had known her. She did not know whether this inheritance was a good thing, not understanding exactly what it was, but she was sure Brenda would tell her more, when the time was right. Leaving the other itch about Lawrence Morecombe, she had heard about that from Shane, there was something going on, but she bit her tongue and bided her time.

Brenda left when the coffee was gone, looking forward to seeing them in the morning. She walked slowly back to the house, looking around for the first time seeing the substance of the inheritance, wondering if she could really take it all in. She longed to see her children they were the sanity in her world, the people who with a smile could bring her back to reality. She wanted to see their reactions to this new and improved life she had acquired, laughing at the imagined answers they would give. *I had better tell Kate to organise David's passport, he will need one,* she thought.

Chapter 45

A NEW AND IMPROVED IRIS House greeted her, it took a moment but she realised she could actually see the house, the scaffolding was gone, she had to pinch herself to realise that Patrick had finished the painting of the outside of the house, it glowed. The bay window had a second skin, just like the windows above, with the same treatment for the basement window completing the front of the house. Standing in amazement, realised she was being hailed by Glen coming down the front steps to his van; she turned to him with a Cheshire Cat grin on her face.

'Brenda lass, what do you think? Makes a difference doesn't it!'

'Difference, Glen that boy's blood is worth bottling! I just cannot believe the difference, and I was only away a morning. The whole feel of the house is different, it feels lighter somehow? Where is he I want to give him a hug, he deserves one!'

'Home, Julie called about eleven thirty, Gabby is in hospital, the baby decided to come. I am waiting on a call to tell me if I have a grandson or daughter! How did you go, is everything all right?'

'I am fine Glen, I have had some good news, I will tell you about later, that is great news about Gabby. They will certainly understand what life is all about once that bundle of joy arrives. By the way, before I forget, Sir James and Linda will be coming for morning tea tomorrow. I want to show them the house and of course introduce them to my ace building team. I hope you don't mind?'

Glen nodded, 'no problem Brenda, I am sure Julie will be happy to bake a few extras for the occasion. Thank you for your concern about Gabby.' He could sense something had changed, he liked the confident feel that was coming from this woman whom he held in high regard.

'Well want to see what else has changed? The inspectors arrived just after you left, thought they would catch us unprepared. That one that disliked us so much was not with them, this group were very happy with the work, and all the improvements. I don't even think they stayed for morning tea, just signed everything off and left!'

Glen was guiding her into the house through the apartment door, she stopped short. There in place of the old timber stairs was a wonderful gleaming black ironwork staircase, complete with timber treads.

'Dan did this while Brent was doing the lift. He wanted you to see it first, he said he was going remove the treads until all the work boots were no longer using it, but he wanted you to see the timber in place. I have to hand it to that man, he gets an idea, and then gets it done, they really do fit in with the overall scheme better. What do you think, do you like them?'

'I think I had better go for the afternoon, you will have finished, that is what I think Glen Haddon. I am changing your business cards this instant to "Haddon & Sons & Associates, Builders and Miracle Workers INC." I didn't realise Dan was anywhere near finishing that, I thought it a week or more away?'

Glen laughed shaking his head as he steered her down the hallway, 'may look good but still not quite usable, just yet. Any way I have a better way for you to get to the apartment to change!'

They moved through the back door, with its ruby red undercoat, out onto the landing. Where Dan was beaming, Brenda went over and pulled him down to hug him.

'I take it you like the stairs?' she nodded, 'yes well not bad for a rush job. Greg had to go back to the foundry, forgot a couple of uprights, that is why you cannot use them yet!' Anyway, why not use the lift!'

On cue the lift glass doors that he had been shielding opened, Brent stepping out with one of his workmen, the grin on their faces echoing the ones around her. She couldn't help it and gave a hoot of yahoo, skipped around doing a little dance.

'You did it, you have actually done it, complete nothing missing, nothing else to do?'

Brent was grinning at Brenda, nodding his head at every question. He just grabbed her and pulled her into the lift, hitting four on the panel. Slowly the doors closed and they rose up, Brenda taking in the details of the efficient space around her. The lift had glass walls, clear to see through. Below the grab rail were steel panels echoing the same Iris design that was in all the glass panels in the building. Brent pointing out the control panel, advising they had numbered the floors as B for Basement, then one, two, three and four, very simple. Smoothly they rose, at four the doors opened and a smiling Matt and Rebecca were waiting to meet her.

'It is so smooth, it is wonderful, thank you, oh thank you so much Brent, you and your team have done an excellent job. I don't think you realise what this means to me!'

'Oh, I realise Brenda, it has been a pleasure working on a site as organised as this. These two have on hell of a dad, he has been an inspiration to work with. Hope I can work with him again. Now I will leave you with these two, I have a dumb waiter to install!'

With that he stepped back into the lift pressed the B button going down, his smile she could see all the way down to the basement.

'It is not really finished yet Brenda!' Matt was saying as she looked around, 'still have to put the glass in and enclose all of this!' He was moving his hand pointing out the steel beams surrounding the stairs, landings and the lift, all in its gleaming blackness, prepared and waiting for the glass. 'Marcus said they would start tomorrow, the crane would be arriving at seven, he arriving with it or before!'

'That I believe,' Brenda came back to the here and now, from the daydream she was having of the finished house, 'any news from Charlie or Julie?'

'No, but we expect any minute. Come and see what we have done, I hope you like this?'

Rebecca pulled her through the back door, this one had a rich ruby red gloss coat of paint. 'Don't touch any of the paint work Brenda, Patrick has just finished, it is still wet!'

Brenda walked into a different apartment four from what she had left that morning. The laundry was now finished, although the fresh wet paint smell permeated the area, new appliances all set back into their positions. Rebecca could not wait in her excitement to show her the finished apartment, pulling her through the rooms, showing how she had arranged the furniture as they had planned in the warehouse. It looked wonderful, Brenda pulled her into a hug, saying thank you, Mia and you have done a wonderful job.

Matt tapped Brenda on the shoulder, 'Can I show you my part?' He moved the ladies back into the laundry pointing to the keypad on the wall. 'The keypads here and same at the front door control the flat!' Pulling the unit from its holder on the wall saying both of them were the same. Remotely unlocking or locking doors, switch on the lights, heating or cooling, even operate the oven or microwave if you want!'

They had moved as he spoke pointing out things that had moved the standard of the flat to that of a six-star hotel. In the lounge, Brenda wondered at the space they had, even with all the furniture in place, the wonderful bronze glow from the windows, now without the scaffolding to hide them. 'Watch this Brenda!'

He touched the pad again, music surrounded her, it was a full rich sound. He moved and opened up a cupboard door, showing the music and entertainment system inside. He tapped again, the curtains at the window closed, at the room darkened the lights automatically came on, 'I have put sensors throughout the place, for lights to come on if there is movement in a space,' he told her as they watched the wonderful country scene in the picture over the fireplace dissolved being replaced with a welcoming message, it was a TV Screen!

'Oh Matt,' was all Brenda could utter. The entire system was housed in the built-in cupboard in the alcove beside the fireplace. It was efficient and up to date, exactly what she had wanted. 'You too Rebecca, this is wonderful, elegant, modern with a refined twist; a definite improvement on the shoddy work Mr. Gardiner and his cronies were going to do. Where is Mia, did she help with this?'

'She had to get back to the warehouse Brenda, she wanted to make sure everything was ready to fix apartment three, now we have the deliveries out of it. We wanted to know if we could get Stan with Nona and Poppa here, although it looks good, this place needs a Nona cleaning touch!'

'Didn't they come this morning Stan said he at least would call in? Let me go and get changed then I will call them. You have all done wonders, I know that there is more Matt. I need a cup of tea and a change of clothes, then you can give me instructions on all of this!'

Matt nodded, flicking the switch to reset everything, the smile would not come off his face, it all worked he had not shown Brenda the half of it yet. Rebecca stopped Brenda saying now she had shown her around the apartment four, she would go and help Mia prepare for tomorrow, then go and spell Julie at the hospital.

Brenda wished her good bye, and good luck, telling her to ring if they needed anything, giving her a quick hug at the door to apartment two. Brenda was shocked at the quiet in the space, going into a peaceful place for once, moving into the bedroom, closing the door as she wanted to be undisturbed for a little while.

Chapter 46

Dennis's voice penetrated her retrospection, she had been deep in thought about her life to come, and reflecting on the life that had been for Iris. Now with the added complication of Iris's father Lord Norman Lucas, she wiped the tears from her eyes.

The reality of her situation had struck when she had seen apartment four brought back to life. Yes, it was not a complete restoration, but that would be impossible. Too many years of shoddy handling had destroyed the chances of that, but Rebecca and Mia had returned a muted elegance and grace to the room. It incorporated the white walls of a fortnight ago, the replacement of the original fireplace surrounds and mantle, with new gas inserts helped, with subtle colour additions in the wallpaper, gave a relaxed atmosphere and made the whole place welcoming.

Dennis's voice rang out again, she yelled 'hello I am here' turning to splash some water on her face, grabbing a jumper to put on tucking her shirt into her jeans opened the door moving down the hall way to a flat full of people having a late lunch.

'Hey there,' Dennis said, going over to her with a plate of sandwiches, 'these people do not know when to stop. What a transformation in a week and half! Hey are you all right, you have been crying. What's up, knew I should not have gone away!'

Taking her arm, he steered her back into the bedroom, closing the door on the noise, she dissolved into tears again, he pulled her into his familiar comforting hug, so welcome at that time.

'I am sorry Dennis love, I thought I had gotten that out of my system!' She said as she pulled out of his arms sitting down in the chair, while he perched on the bed, he asked what had happened in the last few days.

'A lot has happened over the weekend. How are your Mum and Dad by the way, did you have a good time with your family?'

'Never mind my weekend, what happened to you! That is the first time in a long time since I have seen you in tears. Come on own up, what the heck is going on? I bet it has something to do with Lawrence Morecombe, come on give what has our dear Larry been up to?'

Brenda laughed at the proprietary note in his voice, and the dire consequences he projected in his words. Assuring him that Larry was indeed the catalyst for the tears, but not in the way he thought, assuring him he had been a wonderful help over the weekend. She told him about the dinner with Larry on Friday night, the Sunday dinner at the Haddon's, he nodded as he knew that was going to happen, but made a mental note to ask about the Friday dinner, as that was news. Then she told him of the meeting she had that morning, with Hugh Pemberton and Michael Dranish-Fawkes, that she had just been told she was a very wealthy woman, then her connection with Lord Norman Lucas, which was the extra part of the inheritance. After she had finished she looked at Dennis as the silence was unusual for him, she thought he looked just like a hooked fish, mouth open and floundering.

'You are serious, Brenda, there are no candid cambers in here, no one to jump out and say April Fool!'

'Now you know how I feel and have felt since Friday, when Larry told me part of the story, and that I had my meeting today. It is real Dennis, but apart from the people in the law firms you are the only other person to know that the Lady B on my hard hat is for real. I would like it to stay that way for the time being as well!'

He jumped up, pulling her into another hug, a real "I am so proud of you" hug.

'You are going to do and be just fine, I know it. If you need me I will be right at your side. All you have to do is holler and I will be there you know that. Do the kids know?'

Brenda laughed again, the lingering doubts that had brought on the tears a thing of the past, she hugged him back. Saying she had just found out herself had not had time to formulate how she was going to tell Kate and David, but she had better email Kate that David will definitely need his passport now.

Dennis laughed nodding in agreement, they moved out the door, to find Glen in the hallway, his face one of utter shock. Brenda took the phone out of his hand to hear Rebecca shouting down the phone.

'Brenda, thank goodness, is Dad all, right?' she asked, Brenda assured her he looked just like a stunned mullet, 'that is ok then, so you know the reason why he looks like that is Gabby just delivered twins! Boy and Girl, mother and babies are doing fine, Dad is still in shock. No wonder they didn't want to arrive they were having so much fun!'

Brenda whooped sending congratulations to mother and father, from both herself and Dennis, putting an arm around Glen's shoulder to bolster the shocked man, reassuring Rebecca that she would look after the new Granddad, after hanging up put the phone in his pocket.

Moving him into the midst of the workers enjoying lunch, handed him a strong cup of tea that Dennis had made. When he announced the births a cheer went up and he was backslapped and congratulated by everyone.

After the initial euphoria, Glen did his usual harrumph to get everyone back to business, started handing out the afternoon work assignments.

Ben looked at Matt who nodded, 'Dad, we can handle the jobs this afternoon. Mum would appreciate you at the hospital, as well as Gabby. Why don't you take the afternoon off, we know where to reach you if there are any problems, go and visit your new Grandchildren!'

Glen looked at his two sons, realised that they could do it he had raised them right; besides it was only for an afternoon. Jack added his words of encouragement, then everyone chipped in, Dan included told him to go. Brenda came up with a bottle of the Andrew

Garrett, 'this is for Julie, Charlie and yourself, but this little one is for Gabby. Doctors' orders, when I had my babies, the doctor arrived the following morning with a little bottle of champers, just like this, just for me! Relaxed me and then of course relaxed the babies, it works. Just go man, you know you want to, give Gabby all our love, she did well, very well!'

Glen laughed and accepted the bottles, knowing the work would be carried out even better with the good news, marvelling that his Gabrielle had produced twins!

Uncle Matt and Uncle Ben then made sure everyone moved out to do the work promised. They were in advance of the already tight schedule and they wanted to keep it that way. Brenda could not help feel very proud of them all, she was already thinking how she could organise a bonus for each and every one of them, they deserved it, suddenly suppressing thought and chuckle, she could also now afford to do so.

'Dennis is Poppa alright? I thought that Stan was going to bring him over this morning? You haven't heard anything bad, have you?' Brenda asked as they were clearing and washing up the lunch dishes.

'Sorry Bren, I forgot to tell you. I needed them today, oh it's all right I had a sedentary task for Poppa. Philippe and Maurice had lectures, so I put them off till tomorrow, I am sorry I forgot is it ok?'

'Of course, it is ok, they are your cleaning team, I just usurped them for a while. I mean to usurp them again in the future as well. Dennis this job will be an ongoing one, hopefully they can fit us both in, it is actually probably better they are here tomorrow.' Dennis raised an eyebrow in question, 'well I have invited Sir James and Linda for morning tea, they need to check on the progress of the build. I need to tell them about the inheritance, they don't realise exactly what I have inherited, Linda I believe thinks it is just a few teacups!'

Dennis laughed, 'are they in for a rough awakening. I wonder how they will take it?'

'Well make sure you are here at eleven tomorrow, and you can see. Dennis, do I have your support?'

'You have mine always!' came Larry's voice from the doorway. Dennis turned and looked at this man that had appeared in Brenda's life wondering what to make of him. Dennis of course knew who he was, and his reputation, even apart from the gossip from Mia and Rebecca. The circles his job took him in allowed entry into some areas of 'The Establishment' the general populace knew nothing about, and between these people gossip was an art form, and sometimes particularly viscous. Then he saw the concern in Larry's eyes, hearing the sincerity in his voice. Yes, he could trust him, a whiff of gardenia passed him, ok Iris I will leave it alone you know best, he thought.

'That makes two of us then. Afternoon Larry, how are you?' Dennis walked over and shook the outstretched hand, conveying without words his acceptance of Larry in Brenda's life. Larry smiled taking the firm grasp, recognizing his acceptance into the deal as long as he continued to treat Brenda right!

'Larry,' Brenda went over and gave him a hug, his arm staying comfortably around her shoulder, 'have you heard the good news?' He shook his head in a negative, 'Gabby has had twins, a girl and boy, we just sent Glen off to wet the baby's heads!'

'That is great news, twins; well you would know what that will be like. What hospital is she in, I need to send flowers?'

'That I don't know, but we can ask Uncle Ben and Uncle Matt, they are still here "in charge" so to speak!'

'They will both love that. By the way what are you putting in the tea around here, I have never seen anything like this. With the scaffolding, down I nearly walked past the place. It was only when I saw Greg replacing the front fence I realised this was the house. It sure looks different, and I love the new stairs, they fit in so much better than the timber ones!'

Brenda exclaimed she hadn't realised that Dan had finished the steps or even had the replacement fence. She dragged the two men with her on a tour of inspection, as she wanted to know what was going on.

Out on the front pavement, the replacement railings gleamed gloss black, looking as though they have never been missing. They seemed to finish off the front of the house, they tied into the peculiar ramp that had been put in place, to give wheelchair access for the first time. With a ramp going from side to side across the area, steps for able-bodied guests running up the middle, putting a platform at the intersection of step and ramp, it was very neat.

Brenda could not wait to see what Norman's reaction would be, but could see that he must have left instructions with someone, as there was not a weed in sight, and she could definitely get a whiff of compost. They walked into the hallway for the apartments, seeing the new ruby red sliding doors into apartment one, closed and complete, walking down the hallway again sniffing that fresh paint smell, to the back door. Brenda took Dennis and Larry out onto the landing, hearing them gasp as they saw the working lift. The ramps in place seemed to be expecting people to promenade up and down, the only incongruity was the boarded-up entrance into the Conservatory, the timber panel would be in place till all the glass pieces to enclose the stairwell and that entrance were fitted.

Brenda told the two men to go and see what Rebecca and Mia had done in apartment four, while she went to have a word to Dan. She watched as two of the three important men in her life stepped into the lift, fleetingly wanting to be a fly on the wall, smiling as she went down to see Dan, to make sure she had the names of all the workers here and at his foundry.

Chapter 47

'Brenda has told you Dennis, about the inheritance?' Larry asked as they were smoothly and silently moved upwards.

'Yes, I really cannot believe it, this is not some kind of prank is it Larry? It is in sick taste if it is, that Lady, and I have to tell you that in my eyes, she has always been a "Lady" she deserves all of it and more. She has more than earned every penny, her life has not been easy, what has she told you?'

Turning to Dennis, wondering if he would give him a few pieces to the puzzle that was Brenda, perhaps to fill in some of the gaps that had been in the talk they had by the river took a gamble, 'she told me that she is divorced, has the two children Kate and David, twins. You were there when they were born, weren't you?' With a smile Dennis nodded, 'she, sort of glossed over the father!'

Dennis could not hide the grimace as he remembered those time, and his chagrin that he had not done more to help his dear friend. 'He needs burying not glossed over. You know what I am, I am no threat, although I guard my friendship with Brenda jealously, she is the sister I never had. She took me in when I arrived in Australia, I got on the wrong bus, and ended up in this country town standing on the pavement outside the hotel she was working in. No money, she persuaded them to give me a 'jack of all trades' job, bar work, restaurant, handyman,' he shook his head remembering.

'Brenda did everything, answering the phone, organising raffles, housekeeping and stock takes, then she would help out in the kitchen when needed, making the tastiest meals out of the simplest ingredient, oh yes she can cook. Not the fancy West End or Soho restaurants with their pea sized meals on oversized plates, but the ones that put meat on the bones of shearers. When I arrived because of her pregnancy she was in the office organising bookings and basically running the place.'

'Well he!' and the tone in Dennis's voice left no doubt of his opinion of the ex-husband, 'took it into his pea sized brain that we were having an affair. Which was laughable because everyone knew, even Brenda, that he could not keep it in his pants, his womanising was legendary in the town, 'at Larry's raised eyebrow, 'small town gossip was rife. Wouldn't take it out on me though, took it out on her! I didn't want to but I left, Brenda arranged another job for me. So, I toured around, but always rang her to see if she was ok. Managed to make it back for the births, oh did those babies scream, but Brenda just looked even more serene, cuddled them even tighter. I will never forget the look on her face when the babies were in her arms. Well when he came to the hospital, which thank goodness was not often after the first visit, started throwing his weight around as though he had birthed them, I tried to shield her but look at me!' pointing to his skinny frame. 'I was no match for him, so on Brenda's insistence left again. I am sorry I did, she took the beatings shielding the children for two more years. I knew she had begun saving to get away but had to delay because of the twin's birth, saving and planning became the norm for her. Oh, people knew what he was like, and even what he was doing, but small town remember, you don't interfere, overtly helping was acceptable, not outwardly interfering that is a no-no. Eventually she organised with the manager of the hotel a transfer to the coast, I was back in the UK by the time this happened or I would have been there to help her. One day she decided enough was enough she had everything organised and left. She hid from him until she could file for divorce, kept moving around, but always put the children and their education first. I doubt he missed her for long, his sort of rugged handsome outback looks and charm would have someone looking after him quickly!'

'Then out of the blue, Kate emailed me to say he had been looking for Brenda again! Asking around in the town and next one over, the girlfriend that Brenda had stayed with for a couple of weeks had tracked Kate down via the Travel Agency, and told her he was checking. I told her to buy her mum a ticket, I would pay half, she arrived nearly two months ago, and the rest as you can say is history. You realise Larry that I have no intention of letting another mongrel into her life, and I know of your reputation, apart from the gossip Rebecca and Mia have been listening too, so are you, a mongrel that is?'

Larry was appalled, but not surprised. It was what Brenda had left out of her information the day before. He looked at Dennis, put his hands on his shoulders turning him so he could see the sincerity in his words.

'Destiny my friend, has brought this singular person to me, for a reason, whether for her benefit or mine, I do not know. I would rather rot in hell for ever than harm a single hair on that woman's head. Yes, I know I have a 'love-them' and 'leave-them' reputation, but I think that is because I have been searching for the right person. I think I am falling very much in love with her, although with what is going to happen to her in the coming weeks and months, I do not know if I will be enough. But I can assure you, I only want the best and will wait, behind the scenes if necessary, helping where and when I can. Is that a good enough assurance for you?'

'Thank you, yes, I can see that you admire her, and are probably falling very hard. Welcome to the club, she seems to have that effect on everyone bar the scumbag that she married. Still he will get his just desserts, Karma will out one day!'

She walked into apartment four a short while later, to easy chatter and a relaxed atmosphere. Larry was telling Dennis that he had been in the house briefly before. While Iris was still alive, although he didn't realise there was anyone living in apartment one. He was asked to check out what was going on for Sir James; Bill Gardiner had brought him up to the top to show off the almost finished apartment. Larry had disliked it on sight, but now he was shocked at the changes it was a completely different place. He turned as he heard Brenda come through the back door from the lift. 'How have you done this, you have given this place back its soul!'

'With the help of two very bright and intelligent young ladies, with a little colour and fabrics do the trick!' she said, going up to the men standing in the middle of the lounge.

'It also helps to have the right person to guide them of course!' Dennis added, with a here, here from Larry.

'I didn't do much,' Brenda nodded to them, 'but I must admit that this place feels good, looks good and everything now works correctly!'

Matt appeared coming into the room still with his Cheshire Cat grin, asking if Larry had heard the news about the twins.

'Yes, indeed I have, Uncle Matt, what hospital is your sister in, she deserves two bunches of flowers for twins!' Larry asked him, laughing with them all. Matt gave them the name of the hospital, asking if Brenda was ready to be shown how the gadgets in the apartment really worked. Confessing that she had not really taken in her first go through, asked if he could go over all the wonderful things he had achieved again for all their benefit, gave him a hug in apology. He then proceeded to show his captive audience the finer points of the new technology updating the old building schematics into the twenty second century.

'This system is going to be available in all four apartments, but controlled from the office going into your apartment Brenda!'

'Office, what office, where, this is news to me!'

'Oops, I think I have put my foot in it. Please don't tell them you know. I think it is one of the surprises planned!'

'Surprises huh, ok well I suppose I cannot expect to have so many people crawling all over this place and not expect someone to expand on one of my ideas for me. At least I know the work will be top class, and fit in with the feel of the building. It is ok Matt I promise I will act surprised when it is sprung on me!'

'Thanks Brenda, now I did come to find you, want to come and see the kitchen, the bones are finished, still need a couple of days, but come and see.'

'Dennis, you go with Matt, I want to close up here. I just cannot wait to see this after a Nona Clean, it will sparkle!'

Both of them agreed, leaving to use the lift down to the basement. Larry went to the front door making sure it was locked securely, coming back to find Brenda standing in front of the fireplace deep in thought.

'Penny for them, how are you, I haven't had the chance to ask. How was Linda, did they have a good break"

'So many questions, yes, good, ok and fine!' she replied.

'I guess I asked for that, seriously are you ok?' he went up to her, put his arm around her, pulling her close, a daring move he knew, but he thought she needed the support.

Her anchor was back, she sighed a thank you. This hug so different to Dennis's, but she liked it, although still wary, she thought finally that these were the arms of a man she could trust.

'I am getting there, I have invited Linda and Sir James over for morning tea tomorrow, that was what I was asking Dennis for his support and you giving yours.' He nodded unwilling to let her go, she felt so good in his arms. 'I hope Glen remembers to tell Julie, I had better ask Mama that I need morning tea tomorrow from her, I think the Haddon's are going to be busy people.'

He laughed agreeing with her comment, as they moved out of the apartment securing it for the night. Calling the lift Larry marvelled at the smooth silent workings. Brenda telling of her conversation with Brent, about silent running machines and the reason why. He was laughing when they reached the basement, a very different basement from the one she had found four days before.

The French doors from the kitchen were uncovered and in working order, the black steel frames still looking brand new, the glass thankfully untouched, open and folded back flat against the wall on either side.

Dan came through them, smiling at them both, 'That was a great idea you had with the AGA Brenda, will work a treat, but I see the need for the extra gas range!'

The room they walked into could not be the same one, she thought, it had changed so much. Instead of two separate rooms there was now one large kitchen. Where the wall had been between the Butler's Pantry and the main room was now a half wall, with the original butlers sink, and a smaller one in steel with timber draining board, replacing the rotted wooden sink. She could also see the space for a dishwasher, and when she looked across the room a second one, under the prep bench along the laundry wall. With the cupboards that had held the crockery for so long, standing in the hallway waiting to be replaced once the new timber floors had been sealed, to be used again.

The new timber floor had been sanded, waiting for a coat of varnish, that Patrick told Brenda when she walked over to him, would happen when all the feet had gone home. She laughed, the new floor was not high, just enough to run the pipes through, the AGA now looked settled in its place. Ben was busy with fixing pipes into and out of the carcass of the gleaming machine. The laundry wall had also been prepped for the new large fridge/freezer, as well as a smaller sink that she could see had been fitted with a constant hot water tap, and a new gas range. Quickly checking into the new laundry space, seeing the original copper had been turned into a sink, complete with copper tapware to match.

Walking back into the new kitchen space, checking the two original tables were still secure hanging from the rafters, she was amazed at the amount of work done by these men in so short a time. No one could tell her from then on, that all British Workmen were lazy. They just had to be given the right working conditions to do the best work they could.

Turning to them all, telling them to pack up for the day, to give Patrick and his team time to get at least one coat of his special varnish on the floor before anybody tried to use the taps in the reworked kitchen. Patrick advised her that there would need to be at least three coats and would take a week minimum to cure before anyone, and he looked at Ben and Matt, could walk on it again, without damage. He assured her though if she did give him the time, it would be a wonderful finish. Ben and Matt, she told to go and see their new family members, be sure to give Gabby a big hug from her. Dan promised that once Marcus began with the glass outer skin, it would not take too long to finish it all. At least he hoped so; as the weather had been too good for too long, it was bound to change, hopefully Mother Nature would give them one more day.

Chapter 48

D INNER THAT NIGHT WAS a very companionable trio, at the local fish restaurant. The piano man in the bar area was plunking out very easy to listen to tunes. Both Larry and Dennis were determined to keep Brenda's mind off the legacy for at least one night, but were failing.

She was proving resilient as she asked questions that had been running around her mind, the main one being "Where exactly did she stand in the hierarchy of the life she had now assumed, what exactly did she do about her job? She didn't need the money that was true, but what was she going to do?"

'Your job Brenda, you are not making sense, what about your job. I thought you liked your job, even though you haven't even started it yet, I think!' Dennis answered a previous question, he was on his third glass of red, a very dangerous area for his thinking, as it was at this stage he started to relax.

'Ah, Den, my boy, I think I know what she means,' Larry was on his third too, but was not addle brained till his fifth, so he told them, 'our dear Brenda is taking a salary from Pickworths, for the job she has been employed to do, but she actually owns the street, so Pickworths is actually paying Brenda rent!' Dennis look at this piece of information, was of wonder, looking at the smile on Larry's face to the worried look on Brenda's made him sit up and nod for Larry to continue. 'In effect, she is being paid twice, that will mean a dilemma for our Brenda here. She wants to do the job, but she can't take if is she gets paid, and in this country, you cannot work unless you do! See what I am getting at I hope?'

Brenda looked at both of the men in front of her, Dennis itching to know more, Larry who was trying not to give too much away, she was on her second and last glass of wine for the night, looked at them both and could not decide which on she pitied most. Both of them in the morning were not going to be happy the way they were going, especially as they ordered another bottle of red!

'That is exactly my problem, I still want to work I will go stir crazy if I don't. I know what is expected that I look after the Iris House Legacies, but I would make a balls-up of them, I have the ideas but not the expertise to run them!'

Larry held his breath, realising this was where Brenda would decide who was moving forward with her in the handling of the legacies and accounts, taking a sip of wine waited for her to continue, and then breathed again.

'Why would I take anything away from the people who have handled the details for decades successfully, made more money and are still making money when I want, no need that to continue, so I can expand my ideas. So, at the moment I want to work; I know I will still work for Pickworths, they can pay the salary I would earn into the trust fund for the Respite Care Hotels I am hoping to start. Then Pickworths will not be paying me twice, I keep my job (and my sanity) the help stop the elderly dying alone. That's it, thank you gentlemen you have been a great help!'

Dennis and Larry looked at each other, and shrugged, 'Glad we could help', they both said at once.

Brenda put them both in a cab, giving the driver directions, waved them off and walked back to the wonderful looking house; a little while longer please be patient.

The next morning Brenda decided she would give up red wine for good. Her mouth had an old overcoat in it, she was glad she had come home alone. She was awake, showered and the urn boiling merrily when Marcus rang the bell at six thirty, heralding the beginning of another busy day.

'Marcus welcome, you are early. Is everything ok, you are not worried, are you?'

'Me, I am always worried Brenda, all the time. I keep thinking of all the things that could go wrong today. I intend to have all the glass pieces in place by three, oh ok,' as she gave him a startled glance, 'at least five. I want to see this dream of yours a reality more than you do, it is so neat and practical and such an exciting use of my favourite material. What time do you expect the Haddon's, and Charlie?'

'I really don't know Marcus, they are usually early as well, but you do know that Gabby, Charlies wife had twins yesterday?'

'Twins, oh my, no I didn't. Ok well we will just have to rely on Ron, he is my master glass man, he and Rob work well together, just like Charlie. I must go and ring Charlie and say congratulations.'

'Marcus, I would hold off on that it is only six thirty, I don't think you need to disturb them just yet. Come on have a cup of tea, and we will go and inspect the preparation work your teams did yesterday, have you seen that the lift has been installed?'

Ron arrived on the heels of Brenda's speech, she nodded to the kitchen for him and the others to get a cup of coffee or tea, while she distracted Marcus. He nodded and mouthed "Thanks" as she walked Marcus to the back-door cups in hand, out onto the landing to watch the beautiful sunrise mature, waiting for the crane to arrive.

Dan and Greg arrived next, joining them on the landing watching as Ron and his team manoeuvred the crane into the right position, so the trucks with the glass could roll up one way offload and then just keep going, no annoying reversing beeps required. Very efficient Dan sad blowing to cool his coffee. Brenda made a mental note to ask the Kew people to check the commons after all the heavy machinery had rolled over it, to repair any damage that might have been don.

Ben and Matt made an appearance with Charlie in tow.

'Just what do you think you are doing here Mr. Charles Waines? Why are you not at home with your wife and family?' Brenda rounded on him shocked that he would leave his lovely wife at a time like this.

'She kicked me out Brenda, said I was no use to her, seeing all I could talk about was the glass going in here today. So, she told me to come and see that what Marcus and I had figured out was going to work, then go back with more champagne!'

Brenda had to laugh, her irate mood at him dissipating, as she could imagine Gabby heaving a sigh of relief when he had gone. She pulled the embarrassed man into a hug, congratulating him for his immediate family, asking if he had any pictures? All three men pulled out their phones to show her the latest ones, everyone laughing with them.

'Well I can supply you with the champagne, and a little something I picked up for Gabby. There is not much you really can do at the moment anyway; babies at this stage need mum most. New mums need their mums next, and at the end of the line is the father of the children, just as another pair of arms really!'

'A wise woman this is men, she has just said it straight!' Glen walked out onto the balcony with a cup in his hand.

'Hello Grandad, how are you this morning?' Brenda went over and gave this gentleman a big hug. 'How is Julie this morning, has she stopped smiling, or is she worrying over the fact you only bought one of everything, although you have enough baby gear to fit out a shop!'

Glen looked at her shaking his head, 'Definitely a wise woman, how did you know?'

'First daughter; having first grandchild, sorry grandchildren, with very doting parents on both sides of the family; then Gabby with too much time on her hands when she got too big to work the only thing to do is waddle around baby shops!'

All of the men around her laughed, the married ones nodding in agreement realising that Brenda had just described their wives to a 'T' in the later stages of their own pregnancies.

'Well you are right lass, that bottle you sent over went down a treat. Talking of treats, I brought the morning tea box, extra special because of the added guests. Anything I should know about Sir James and Mrs. McGill?'

'They are people like you and me, they may have a little more status in the world perhaps, but they are people Glen, just treat them like everyone else. Be the gentle man I like and admire very much, then they like me will not be disappointed in the founder and head of Haddon & Sons!' Brenda gave him a kiss on the cheek turning and walking back into the apartment.

It was about nine thirty when the first of the panels, outside apartment four went into place, perfectly. The first raised a cheer, everyone breathing a sigh of relief that the measurements were right. Brenda had been in the garden hardhat on, silently wishing it into perfect place. Then it was a procession of trucks with the glass specifically numbered that matched the numbers chalked onto the inside of the steel supporting beams. They had a great system working to put the panels in place. It was more efficient for Ron's team of glaziers to put the sealant around the pieces as they were held in mid-air by the crane, in front of the actual places they were meant to be positioned,

There were four men, and Brenda was happy to see a woman, all wearing harnesses suspended from the latticework of ropes that had been strung across the area. Brenda now understood the reason for the closed hooks that were welded onto the steel beams, seeing the riggers confidently moving from place to place swinging with ease in the space. The crane inched each piece into the right place after the sealant was applied, with the workers making sure it fitted snugly. Marcus said they would use more sealant than less, just to make sure, his team would tidy up the edges once it had gone off, before they put the face plates in situ, and before they took the ropes down.

Brenda's camera was working overtime as she recorded this newest twist on a conservatory going into place.

Dennis arrived with Philippe and Maurice, about ten thirty, with Stan, Nona and Poppa, the rest of the crew hard on their heels. Poppa beamed a hello, Brenda going over to give him a hug, hoping he was feeling a little better Phillipe translating for her. He nodded smiling, 'Fine, Lady I am fine', and smiling still; gathered the two young men, Brenda giving them her laptop and extra discs watched them going down the stairs. Nona had been looking around and coming back with Stan after viewing the aerial gymnastics that were happening outside, coming back to look at Brenda in awe.

'How are you doing this? What have you done to the establishment of the British Builder, you realise that Glen is making a rod for his back, and every other builder in the country when word of this,' and he pointed out the back door, 'gets around!'

Brenda and Dennis laughed at his comment, he had a grin on his face as well. Nona came back into the room talking animatedly to Stan; she was clearly asking what they were doing there.

'Please tell Nona that I am pleased to see her again, thank her for the work on the silver, and the cleaning of the kitchen the other day. It has changed again, I will need all of you once the work has been finished to go through the whole house, but as I have guests coming today to see the progress, would like her and the team to concentrate on apartment four which is the only one finished at the moment.' She stopped as Rebecca and Mia came through the door.

'Hi you two, wondered where you where, well I will hand Stan and Nona over to you both. You know what you want, better than I, so go to it. I have a morning tea to organise!'

Mia went over to Nona taking her hand explaining in flawless Italian what they wanted her to do, leading her out and up the stairs with the rest of the team following behind.

Brenda with Dennis's help then moved the tea room from the kitchen of apartment two down into her apartment, putting a note on the back door so everyone knew the right place to head for a cuppa. She was going to leave it there, as Rebecca and Mia would need to get into apartment two to repair the damage very soon. Putting up trestle tables, to hold the urn and coffee machines, Mama arrived with her contribution, thanking Brenda saying she was very good for business. Hoping that she could see the finished house, as she loved what Brenda was doing. Dennis agreed that it was good for the street, but watch this space as it was only just beginning.

Brenda could not settle, she walked the house, out into the conservatory, always with her hard had on, so Glen could not stop her, watching her and Iris's dreams become reality.

Chapter 49

HER MOBILE RANG, 'BRENDA, its Larry we are out on the pavement, want to come out and meet us?'

Grateful that he had walked around with the others, she moved through the front doors to greet Larry, Sir James, Linda and a very striking gentleman in a wheelchair!

Linda was looking everywhere at the building, trying to take it all in. What an achievement this lady had wrought, she turned to the group, 'Brenda you are a miracle worker. What you have done in so short a space of time, well it takes my breath away. Perhaps we should employ your services on the house in Tuscany, what do you think Shane, shall we give her the job?'

Shane McGill laughed at his wife, put out his hand, 'Better introduce us first love, I think Ms. Chalmers is a little shell-shocked. Shane McGill, Ms. Chalmers it is a pleasure to finally meet you. My wife has talked about you constantly since you joined Pickworths!'

'Shane, please call me Brenda. I apologise for my staring, but I was not expecting the wheelchair!'

'Brenda, it is alright, an accident a few years ago. I was glad I was in an industry that allowed me to continue working. I do like what you have done here,' and he pointed out the new front steps and ramp, 'not many people would think of wheelchair access!'

'One of Brenda's best attributes, I fear,' Larry interrupted, 'always thinking of other people first!' He turned and gave her a quick hug to take the sting out of his words.

Smiling at him, she turned back to Shane, 'you get to be the guinea pig Shane, trying out the improvements, if you don't mind?' Brenda asked motioning him to the edge of the ramp.

'Mind, no I don't mind at all, thanks for the courtesy Brenda. Sir James, you have been very quiet what do you think?'

Sir James had been silent, just looking at the building in front of him. Comparing it to the ones on either side. He could not believe the change, thinking that he had watched this place for six months, get worse and worse, then, what had Linda called Brenda, a miracle woman, yes, she was that and more, had come along and is making it the best house in the street, and he had not even seen the inside yet!

'I am struck for words. Dear Lady how have you achieved this miracle in such a short space of time?'

Linda laughed and put her arm through her grandfathers, motioning him to the steps, why don't we go in and find out, I want to see what has been happening inside. I remember my one visit of a dark and smelly place, I bet it is not like that now!' Linda was impatient trying to get everyone inside she wanted to see everything now! They all watched as Shane easily manoeuvred his wheelchair up the ramp, waiting at the top for everyone to join him.

'Well it has definitely changed and for the better I hope you agree,' Brenda said as she ushered everyone through the apartment front door, 'come and meet the people who have made all our dreams a reality. We are working on a project at the back of the house. I have documented the changes, before, during and am looking forward to adding the finished photos as well.'

They followed Shane, in through the red sliding doors into apartment one, then through the door into the sitting room. Saying as they were working at the rear of the house they could get a good view from the dining room in her apartment. She introduced Dennis who had come to meet them welcoming them all to Iris House.

'Iris House, I like that, is it official?' Sir James asked taking Dennis's hand and shaking it firmly.

'Yes,' Brenda replied, 'as from Friday last week, that's right isn't it Larry?'

Larry nodded as he was introducing Shane to Poppa, who had risen as the guests had come into the room. Sir James went over and greeted him, again in flawless Italian.

'I am going to have to learn to speak Italian, Spanish and French,' Brenda said, everyone laughing at her quietly spoken words. 'You will,' said Dennis.

Linda looked at the boxes around the room, turned to Brenda, 'There was more to the legacy than I thought, have you had this checked Brenda?'

'Oh, sorry my dear, Linda did ask me for a name, but I plumb forgot!'

'That is alright Sir James, Mia Farrington-Smythe; you will remember she was the interior designer with the last team. Well I retained her services after I kicked the other incompetents off the build. She contacted her Aunt, a Maud Prendergast at Sotheby's, she arranged for an inspection. I am waiting for the results of the first lot that was catalogued, but would be grateful if you could check for me. I want to reuse these items, and cannot until I know the true value of them?'

Poppa came forward, motioning to some paintings he had placed along the wall, Dennis translated for Brenda.

'Poppa thinks these three portraits may be of interest to you Brenda, but you will need more light to see them properly, and they definitely need a professional clean!'

Brenda was moving over to the paintings when Glen and Matt walked into the room, she introduced them to everyone, asking if they could open the shutters on the bay window.

'Of course, Brenda, don't know why you haven't done it before, this room is nearly ready to use again, apart from taking the plastic off the floor, but I think Stan has a time frame for that!'

'OK Matt, Larry and Dennis let's get some light in here!'

The four men moved and pulled with ease the shutters back into their niches on either side of the window, flooding the room with light and rainbows. The smell of gardenia floated around, the feel of the room lifted with the golden sunlight flooding into every corner.

'Oh, my this is wonderful!' Linda exclaimed, 'what a beautiful room. What have you planned for here Brenda, that sunlight is just marvellous!'

Brenda had moved over to the pictures, resting on the wall, sunlight now allowing them to be seen properly. Iris at the age of about twenty was looking at her, a wonderful wistful smile on her face, and Brenda realised it was her that she had seen in the Conservatory on that day what seemed a life time before. The scent of gardenia's hovered around Brenda for a few moments, Larry coming over to her side, catching her hand and squeezing it gently. 'Ah Iris, very pleased to meet you. Hope you like what Brenda is doing?' He then caught the gardenia wafting around, 'thank you,' he quietly said, only Brenda heard.

The others gathered around inspecting each of the portraits, smiling as they realised who was painted. 'Hey this one is of Lord Norman Lucas, I wonder which one, is he Iris's father, grandfather or great, would be good to find out. Oh, this handsome devil is someone called Fitzgibbon?' Dennis was reading the plaques on the bottom of the paintings.

Sir James walked over, tut tutting the state they were in. 'I can help you here Brenda, to make amends for my forgetful memory. I know a wonderful group of people that just love restoring old masters. That is what these are, very beautifully painted, but they are in a very sad state. Never mind I will get Duncan and his fellows onto these and I know they will come up like new, where are you planning to put them once they are clean?'

Brenda knew that Iris and Lord Lucas would be going back on either side of the fireplace, in the spaces made for them, but said to the group that until everything was finished would be put out of harm's way, until Sir James contact came through. Poppa put the dust covers back over them, telling Philippe and Maurice to move them to safety.

They all moved through into the dining room, seeing the crane moving another piece of glass into place. Shane, Linda and Sir James exclaiming at seeing workman hanging from the rafters so to speak.

After watching in stunned silence the placement and fitting of the huge pane of glass Sir James turned to Brenda and Glen.

'I have to meet the people involved in this scheme! When I was here last, I had no idea that the conservatory or the staircase was still in place. How did you know my dear, who has designed all of this?'

Linda had been standing at the French Doors, watching as Ben and his team worked on the powder rooms in the conservatory, 'what a clever idea, yes grandfather, I want to meet the people who thought of this!'

Glen, Matt, Larry and Dennis all turned to Brenda, who blushed as she realised what the men were doing. Sir James, Shane and Linda all shook their heads smiling.

'Might have known,' came from Linda, going over and giving Brenda a hug, 'don't you be upset, please; this vision is amazing!'

'Thank you, but I had a lot of help and ideas. Ben came up with moving the powder room into the conservatory. Glen with Dan, that is Dan Jones he is the steel man and our surveyor, came up with the design of the glass enclosure for the stairs!'

'We were and still are, being led by the ideas coming from this lady though,' Glen put in, 'she is the one who has given us the inspiration to do this. Her vision of what this house could become, has been what has driven us all. Ah, Dan, come and meet Sir James Pickworth, his CEO Mrs Linda McGill and her husband Shane McGill.

Dan and Greg had come in from the back-landing walking to the group with outstretched hands.

'What do you think, already half done, Marcus is jumping all over the place, but he will get it all done by five or before he is positive. Is it morning tea yet, I am parched seems a long time since my cuppa at seven?'

Brenda laughed, saying yes, it is definitely time for morning tea, or even an early lunch break. Putting her hard hat on went out onto the landing and called tea break for everyone, down in apartment one.

The workmen arrived singly and in groups, Brenda making sure she introduced Marcus and Ron, to Shane and Sir James. Dennis had taken Linda to meet Rebecca and Mia, who had brought Stan, Nona and Poppa and the boys into the apartment for morning tea. The numbers swelled in the room but they were never cramped. Brenda checking them to see that no one missed out, and Sir James met all the people who had wrought the change in the once neglected house. She was also checking the numbers, filing away the information of how many would fit comfortable, also where they all congregated so she could allow for this when the soirées began.

Everyone kept checking what was going on in the back garden, Brenda went up to Charlie, who had been hovering at the French Doors all through the break.

'Are you eager to disappear Charlie love, I can get the basket for Gabby if you do want to go?'

'Not yet Brenda, I am waiting on the truck from the foundry, they are bringing the new skin for the conservatory, as that has to go in before we can finish the glass. It should have been here half an hour ago, what is that, yippee it is here! Dan, Greg, Marcus the truck is here, ok boy's tea break is over, come on!'

His enthusiasm was infectious, Brenda laughed at the mass exodus, saying to the retreating backs, that ok what is left will be afternoon tea! With smiling faces they all quietly but efficiently moved out to put the new skin on the conservatory.

It was in two pieces, once in place it would fit like a glove, being supported by the upright pieces that had been welded onto the original frame as they cleaned the glass. The new outer shell rested on those five-millimetre steel supports, similar in principal to the new windows, the frame was beautiful black steel. Once it was in place, the roof of the ramp into the conservatory was put in place it was fixed to the bottom of the landing at apartment two, sloping down to the conservatory, where the panel had been removed, and once in place looked as though it had been there for years. This effectively gave the conservatory an annexe; the bronze tint to the glass gave the impression of everyone working in sunshine. Everyone in the dining room, clapped and cheered when all the glass pieces were in place, Brenda asked Glen if they could take her party out onto the landing, as she wanted Shane to test the lift for her. Glen asked for a few minutes break on his walkie-talkie, nodded to her when he got the affirmative. She and Linda went first so she could direct, then Sir James and Shane.

'What a wonderful idea, that you can see the whole scope of the commons is great, you really get a sense of space in this home. Brenda that lift is so smooth and easy to use, I have to take my hat off to you, you have thought this through right to the home comforts!' Shane congratulated her as he moved into the apartment with ease. Larry, Rebecca and Mia came up the stairs to show everyone around. Nona and the team had worked wonders and the whole apartment shone. The sunshine coming through the windows touched every surface and all the rooms glowed. The smell of gardenia and lavender pervaded everywhere, the girls had decorated with the final touch of flowers to give life to the rooms.

Linda looked across to Brenda who had moved the girls into the lounge room, to take the accolades they richly deserved, moving Matt into the room when he arrived with Glen, letting them take centre stage while they told everyone about the rooms fixtures and fittings. Linda could see that she was as proud of these young people as if they were family. Then she realised to Brenda they were, a new family, who had come to her aid, and helped her overcome adversity. Strangers no more, they would continue as a family for the future. Linda had no doubt that Brenda would be there to help if needed, to encourage and give ideas if asked. Glen standing beside Brenda looked as though he could burst with pride, as his children explained what they had accomplished, he had the right to be proud, the ideas and execution of them was sensational.

'Well Grandfather,' she turned to Sir James, who had just been shown how the electronics worked, 'I don't think we have to worry about the guests at Iris House getting shoddy treatment. I want to move in here myself, what do you think Shane, shall we move in?'

Shane was also talking to Matt, asking about his ideas, he turned, 'if we hadn't spent all that money on updating our place, I would have jumped at coming here. I still wonder if we got value for money. Matt, can you spare a few minutes to come around and check it for us?'

Matt looked at his father, shrugging his shoulder, everyone laughing at the gesture. Glen thought, so here it begins, all due to this lady, and I thought we were heading to bankruptcy, how can I repay her. He looked over to Brenda who was trying to blend into the background, to be unnoticed, she doesn't handle praise well, or like being in a spotlight, keeping in the background, out of view, he realised was second nature to her, and it made him wonder why. Then remembering a comment of Dennis's about her ex-husband, began to understand, no one in her life had ever told her she had done good work. Well that was about to change, if he judged the character of the people around her at present.

Sir James moved over to Brenda and put an arm around her shoulders, 'knew I had the right person from that first meeting. Not many people would sit and talk to a crotchety old man, but I never felt as though I was being pampered to. Now my dear, don't colour up, this is a triumph, you should be enjoying this!'

Glen beamed; he liked this gentleman very much. His granddaughter was a delight, and she had reason to be bitter, with a husband in a wheelchair, they were all good people. Charlie appeared in the door way.

'Sorry folks, I am off, cannot do anything more, in fact I am in the way. Rod and Marcus can complete the finishing of the conservatory skin. Dan just kicked my butt, Brenda did you say you had something for me to take to Gabby?'

'Yes Charlie; Charlie's wife Gabrielle gave birth to twins yesterday. She kicked him out this morning so he could be here to check on the rebirth of this place! Gabby is also Glen's eldest daughter, so we have a new Granddad amongst us!'

Sir James went over and gave Charlie a handshake and slap on the back to congratulate him. Brenda turned to everyone, 'How about you all move down through the building? Mia and Rebecca, with Glen and Matt can show you what we have planned in the apartments, I will meet you all in apartment one.'

She moved out with Charlie, as Sir James went over to Glen, gave him a handshake, with another slap on the back saying 'Welcome to the club!'

Chapter 50

B RENDA SENT CHARLIE OFF with a basket of goodies for Gabby, a couple of outfits one pink, one blue, with another bottle of the Andrew Garret, hoping that Dennis contact could get her more.

She was in the dining room, waiting for the visitors to arrive, Marcus she could see was pushing his people to finish before the black clouds they could see gather on the horizon turned the commons into a quagmire, bogging the heavy trucks. She could see a two-pronged attack; Rob was working with some of the men, putting the individual panes into the new conservatory skin, working from the garden towards the house, to keep out of the road of Marcus's team working on the enclosure for the staircase.

Dan came up to her, 'told you the weather could not last Brenda. I like your group of people, down to earth aren't they! Have you shown them around your place yet?'

'No not yet Dan, I am waiting for them to finish the tour of the other apartments, but I think,' she could see that Marcus had waived for a halt, 'this should be them coming down now.'

She watched the happy faces of Shane and Sir James as they came down in the lift, moving into the apartment beside her, the others coming down the stairs in a chattering happy group. They all congregated beside Brenda and Dan in the dining room, watching the changes nearly completed.

'Will he make it before the rain, do you think?' Linda asked Dan who she was standing beside.

'I think so; I have never seen so many large panes of glass assembled in so short a time. Yup, there is the last of the big ones just coming in now!'

They all stood in awe at the ease in which the riggers handled the sheets of glass. A cheer went up as it was secured, the last truck and the crane packed up and moved out, job well done. Marcus with his team now out of the climbing gear they had spent most of the day in, walked into the room accepting the accolades that were their due, they in turn had smiles that would not disappear from their faces.

'We did it, all of them in place, not one broken pane and look it is not three o'clock yet! All we have to do is finish off a few panes that are needed in the conservatory, Dan did you check the door section?'

'Yes Marcus, it is in place working perfectly. Matt here only has to add his technical wonders and all will be finished.'

'Can we go out onto the landing Marcus, it is safe? I want to take everyone down?'

'Yes Brenda, all is safe now, wait till you go out, it is the most surreal experience, gives the impression of perpetual sunshine, great idea using that type of glass!'

She moved everyone out onto the landing, a very different landing to the one of that morning. The whole area down to her apartment was enclosed in steel and glass, a weatherproof coat to ensure the staircase and lift could be used in all weather conditions. The pieces of plywood that had been covering the doorways to the conservatory and garden things of the past; replaced with two solid glass sliding doors, framed in black steel, the bottom half of both with more of the cut-out steel panels that matched the ones in the lift. Brenda was astonished, as she had no idea they were in the design, she also stood and wondered how much man power would be required to open and close them, they looked so imposing and heavy. Shane wheeled himself over to inspect the workings, gently pushing the door out to the garden to one side.

'Wonderful, simply wonderful Dan, Marcus this is spectacular, yes you do feel as though you are in perpetual sunshine! What did you mean Marcus by 'that type' of glass?'

Marcus had moved up to watch Matt attach the fixtures for the automatic door control, he turned to look at Shane, as he also watched Matt with interest as well.

'Well it means using a stronger type of glass, layered to be almost bullet proof! Brenda asked for it to be energy efficient, safe and secure, so we made a new laminated glass to be energy efficient, and in the end, you could say it would be bullet proof. Looks good, doesn't it?'

Linda was standing next to Brenda; she put her arm around her giving her an admiring hug.

'I knew you were the person we needed, knew it first time I saw you. Although you didn't know it. I gave you the job, as you were sitting in the waiting room at the very first interview. Yes, I was watching, Erin my secretary also; she pegged you when you came in, helping her pick up the files and sorting them back in order with her. While the other two bimbos watched, and sneered. Then grandfather wanted to meet you, so we set up that little charade in the waiting room. Yes, I knew you belonged in this job, right from the start!'

Brenda chuckled, finally at ease with this woman, who she knew would become a lifetime friend, even after she told her and her grandfather about the legacy.

'We still have to see the rest of this apartment; Sir James did you ever see this or any of them?'

'No, my dear, unless you count the front porch, I was never welcomed in to any of them. I don't think anyone was welcome into this one at all. Do we go back into the lift, I like this thing, so much easier on the knees!'

Brenda nodded and moved everyone down the stairs, as Sir James and Shane used the lift. Patrick was standing to one side of the basement French Doors, apologising to everyone, as Brenda made it to the bottom last of all. He was telling everyone that he had put a second coat of varnish on the floors, as he had completely forgotten that they were coming, but they could look through the doors to see the space; this everyone did gasping at what they could see.

Mia and Rebecca urged everyone in through the basement door, ushering them all into what would be Brenda's bedroom; would be that night, as Brenda came last into the fully finished and furnished room. Wallpapered, painted and black plastic taken off the wonderful original carpet, that had been cleaned, it in turn showing off the beautifully made up big king sized bed that had looked so neglected a fortnight ago, back in pride of place, facing the window with its view into the conservatory. Curtains hung, side table and lamps all gave the room a warm glow, helped by the subtle light filtering through from the conservatory. Mia and Rebecca were showing off the bathroom and wardrobe in the back of the room, as Brenda caught her breath. Larry went and put his arm around her shoulders, realising that Brenda had not known this surprise was waiting for her today.

Mia was telling Sir James and Linda, that Brenda had not been told they had completed this room for her, 'we thought it was about time you were living in your own apartment, at least sleeping in it. The kitchen will take a few more days, but you can always use the one in apartment two, what do you think?'

The girls watched the surprise and shock cross Brenda's face to be replaced with a calm, this is right look, she walked over and gave both of them a hug apiece.

'Thank you, both of you; it is exactly right, you read my mind, it is perfect. I do have one question though, it is a new mattress, isn't it?'

Everyone laughed as the tension that had been building in the room left, the familiar smell of gardenia wafted around. Nona, Stan and Poppa beaming from the doorway, Brenda knew that Nona had cleaned in here for her, she nodded as Brenda gestured cleaning the furniture.

'Si Bella, is for you I do this, it is right you here!' Nona said in halting English much to the surprise of everyone. Stan moved forward saying they had to go, but would be back on Friday, as they had nothing really to do, they had done a basic clean in all of the flats. Saying goodbye to Sir James, Linda, Shane and the team they left, happy chatter following them out of the house. Everyone moved back into the dining room for another cup of tea or coffee. Stan and the boys had put out some of the dining chairs that had been covered in the corner of the sitting room. Dennis then took Philippe and Maurice off saying he would call later. Mia and Rebecca also said their goodbyes, after advising they had moved Brenda's things down into the new bedroom, officially moving her into Apartment One; they would see her in the morning, looking forward to finishing off the other apartments.

Glen took Dan and the men that were left off to check on what was left to do. They could not work in the kitchen, due to Patrick's embargo and letting the floor cure. Marcus had already said goodbye, once the final touches to the conservatory were finished the work for the day was done.

Chapter 51

S HANE WAS STILL SHAKING his head at the marvel in steel and glass that was the now fully enclosed fire escape and landings. Sir James and Linda were chatting to Larry who was explaining that the conservatory still had some work on the inside to make it complete.

Brenda realised that now was the time to come clean, 'I do have something else to tell you all. I hope you do not think less of me when I tell you, but I really don't know where to start!'

Turning to look at her new friend, Linda realised there was tension, and doubt in her whole demeanour. She moved over and made her sit on one of the chairs, sitting beside her, 'come on Brenda, just spit it out how bad can it be? After the miracle you have wrought here, whatever it is just say it!' Larry positioned himself between Sir James and Shane, directly opposite to her, smiling encouragingly at her.

'Well it is to do with the legacy!' She looked at Sir James who nodded, letting her know he knew about the will. 'Iris's Inheritance, there is a little bit more, well a lot more to it than what we can see in here, pointing to the bounty stashed in the front room, and we first thought!' Brenda then told them in a quiet voice, with a whiff of gardenia around her, the full details as given to her by Messrs. Pemberton and Fawkes the previous day.

Sir James was the first to recover, looking at Larry beside him, asking the question with his eyes, and receiving a grin and nod from him to confirm what Brenda was saying. He rose and moved over to Brenda, taking her hands in his pulling her to her feet. Bowing from the waist, taking one of her hands, raised it to his lips kissing it gently.

'My dear Lady Lucas, welcome to our world. I think you will be a breath of fresh air to this staid institution. I hope you will ask for my assistance at any time, know that my family is there for you if you need any help.'

Linda was next, pulling her into a furious hug, 'Lady Lucas, oh that does suit you. I am so very, very pleased for you. Now I know what was bugging me last night, knew that there was something different. I wish you the best, and as grandfather said, we will be there for you if you need us!'

Shane wheeled over, taking her hand raised it to his lips, 'I can't give you the requisite bow you are due, but please know Lady Lucas, that I am your most humble servant from today on!'

The tears were running down her face, as she realised the acceptance of her into this society was complete and utter from this group around her, and that was all she needed. Larry was beside her, handkerchief at the ready and his steadying arm around her, telling her not to be upset, see he had told her all along it would be all right.

She smiled at him, wiping away the tears, looking at everyone in turn, 'Sorry everyone, but it has been quite an emotional time over the last few days. Since I walked into this house, I have the feeling that I belonged here. It has been a strange but comforting feeling, and I know this will sound silly, but it is true, Iris kept opening up surprises for me, and the rest of the team. I feel as though I have been here all my life, but it is less than three weeks, can you believe that!'

Sir James, Linda, Shane and Larry looked at the tear strewn, happy shining face and realised that Brenda would do all right, she chuckled wiping away the last of the tears and doubts smiling at everyone.

Larry chuckled, releasing Brenda as she did a little hop skip and jump of joy, he turned to the group, 'I am sorry Sir James, I know your injunction about alcohol and the workplace, but as this is actually Brenda's home I don't think it really applies, and this is a special occasion.'

Moving over the to the kitchen bench pulling a cover off a bottle of champagne in an ice bucket, started to fill the glasses beside it.

'Mia and Rebecca did this to celebrate the completion of the lift and apartment four, they didn't realise I endorsed it for a different reason entirely!'

Larry continued as he handed out the glasses, Linda moving over to help him; when everyone had a glass, he turned and toasted 'to the new Lady Brenda Lucas, and the speedy completion of Iris House!'

All raised their glasses to the toast of Lady Lucas the scent of gardenia surrounded them all. Sir James raised an eyebrow in query "Iris", Brenda said. He just looked around in wonder giving a chuckle.

'I need to ask you Sir James; may I continue with this job?' Brenda asked the question that was in the forefront of her mind.

'Well my dear, from what you have told us, you will not require a salary, although I would be loath to lose your invaluable services!'

'Good, because I do not want to leave, please hear me out,' both Linda and Sir James had started to speak. 'I have not done all of this to walk away. I would like to stay on as Chatelaine of Iris House, for as long as I can. What I propose is that my salary be put into a trust fund for an organisation I am starting. It will assist the elderly and their families with easy and affordable care. I keep the expense account to run the Guest House, as Glen calls it, but you would not be paying me twice!'

At Sir James perplexed stare, Larry interrupted, 'that is the second part to the legacy sir, Brenda owns the street, you are paying rent for this place to the Lucas Estate.

He looked at her, shock hitting him, realising that what Brenda had told them was only part of the story, then he started laughing, a deep hearty laugh, that had everyone chuckling with him.

'Oh, my dear, you have only told half the tale, I can hardly wait for the full disclosure. I think that would be best given over a very long dinner, and hope that you will be my guest along with all of you on Friday night. Then we can hear the tale in comfort and in full!'

He looked at her still chuckling, Brenda smiled back realising that he would enjoy the full disclosure even as she had squirmed.

Linda came over and gave her a hug, saying they would work something out, as she didn't want her to go either. She was also looking forward to dinner on Friday, as she wanted to hear more details. They were bidding her goodbye, she realised as they moved out, Shane taking her hand saying she would have to come to dinner at their place as he wanted to pick her brains on some of the things that were not working at the build in Tuscany. In fact, she would need to come and visit with them next time they were over there, so she could get a feel of the place.

Brenda was moving to bid them goodbye at the front door, when Ben arrived looking for her.

'Don't worry Brenda,' Sir James said turning to Ben, who stuttered to a stop, 'Ben tell that father of yours he has a good group of workmen. I will be recommending you all to more of my colleagues who need extraordinarily good builders.'

Ben thanked him, watching them leave, wondering just what was in store for all of them. Knowing that whatever happened, it was tied into the fortunes of this house, and the happy lady that walked back into the room.

'What's up Ben, you look like the cat who has just been given some cream!'

'Sorry Brenda, Larry I was miles away. Can you both come into the conservatory, we have something to show you!'

They moved out through the open French Doors and down into the conservatory. Rain was tapping on the completed new skin; the light still had that bronze hue even in the rain. Glen was there with Dan, with the arrival of the rain, all the other workmen had left for the day. Larry went back into the dining room, returning with glasses of champagne for everyone to celebrate.

'I think a celebration is in order gentlemen. Sorry Marcus had to leave early, but I think he will be in bed by now, he was absolutely bushed.' Larry moved around to Ben, 'so what's up Uncle Ben!'

Ben laughed and took the glass motioning to the powder rooms behind him, 'these are finished plumbing wise, we just have to wait for the tiles and painting to be completed. Mia and Rebecca are hoping that will be done tomorrow, it has all been plumbed back through the workshop, as neat a job as I have ever done!'

'Oh Ben, that is wonderful,' Brenda exclaimed going over to give him a hug, inspecting the very compact and functional silent running amenities. 'I don't know if you gentlemen realise this but you have all impressed Sir James and Shane McGill enormously. I think you may find a little more work coming your way from now on!'

'No doubt about that,' Ben interrupted, 'I was just warned by Sir James himself that he was going to tell all his pals about the first-class work being done here and he hasn't seen half of it!'

Matt appeared asking where his glass of champagne was. Larry dutifully handed him a glass, asking in turn where he had been and what had he been up too.

'Had to make this place secure, I was just finishing off the controls for the sliding glass doors, they work a treat come and see!'

They all moved out of the conservatory up the new ramp onto the landing area. Although the rain was now coming down quite heavily, it didn't take away from the sunny feel the tinted glass gave the area. Matt had in his hand what looked like an IPhone but just slightly larger, the icons filled the screen, and he was touching them in order showing how they worked, the door at the garden ramp dutifully opened and closed at his tapping, saying that it was the master for all of the keypads that were now throughout the building.

He turned to Brenda with his hand out, 'Can I have the unit I gave you before Brenda?' she pulled it out of her pocket, handing it over. Matt in turn handed her the new one, looking at him with a quizzical expression.

'Well you will need this, I am affectionately calling the "Iris Phone", it is in fact a phone, and you can use it for the business, but it also has all the apps and controls on it to operate the new systems round the whole house. 'Also, the bill has been made out to Pickworths, I have added in the phone numbers I thought you might need, ours of course, and Sir James, Linda and Larry,' he threw a cheeky grin in Larry's direction. 'I have four of them, with spares if needed, all coded to individual apartments, but yours is the master control, you can access all of the apartments from this or via your linked computer, which is not connected yet. But the security now works on this, the security people have welcomed the updated system, it will be more efficient. They can now keep track of you, it was getting difficult wondering where you were all the time!'

Brenda laughed taking the control from him, asking him to show her again the sequence, marvelling at this miracle of modern technology, saying she had not realised they were this close to finishing.

'Closer than you think lass. Do you realise, now we have the glass in place, we only have some tidying up to do in the other bedrooms, finish off this dining room of yours, and wait for Patrick's floor to dry properly before we install the new appliances, and that is it! We have done the job, and we will definitely have finished well within the four-week deadline, not much, but a couple of days at the least!' Glen added raising his glass to the accomplishments of the day.

'Only a couple,' Larry said, 'I heard a rumour that all you needed to do was put in the dishwashers, and fridge, put the tables back on the ground and you were finished!'

'Don't know where you got that information from Larry, but it could be right. Any way, we had better get off home, tidying up tomorrow. I will bring Rebecca with these two Brenda, I doubt we will have Charlie with us.'

'I hope not Glen; Brenda said as they walked back into the apartment, 'he needs to spend time getting acquainted with his family, however much he wants to be here, there is not much for him to do, although I will be happy to see the Iris Windows back in place. So, you give that daughter of yours a big hug from me, and hopefully I will get an invite down this weekend to give the babies a cuddle?'

'You are welcome at any time lass, you know that no invitation is required. Now can we give you a hand with anything before we go?'

'It's ok Glen, I will stay and give Brenda a hand, in the nicest possible way of course.' Larry added as Glen gave him a searching look.

'I don't think we will be here either Brenda,' Dan put in, 'unless something falls apart or Iris uncovers another room?' everyone laughed, 'I think our job is done as well, but we will keep in touch, may even see you at the Christening?'

'Before that I hope you big lug, come here!' Brenda pulled him down into a hug and kiss on the cheek, 'all your men did a terrific job, be sure to thank them for me.'

'I will, and they know it anyway, but I will tell them your thanks,' he said giving her his usual rib cracking hug in return.

Matt gave her a sheet of instructions in regards to the system, 'just in case,' he said as he ran down the front steps out to his van. Ben waived a goodbye and Dan slapped Larry on the back saying, 'enjoy!'

'Enjoy, wonder what he meant by that?' Larry said as he and Brenda moved back into the house.

'I think he was referring to the serenity this house has found. It is breathing Larry; can you not feel the peace in here?' He nodded, they moved back into the dining room, taking a couple of the chairs and putting them so they could watch the rain make patterns on the roof. Listening to the sound, enjoying the smell of the rain after the warm days, and the last of the champagne.

'I am not staying, I have to be in the office early tomorrow, and then possibly away for a couple of days with work!'

Larry said as helped Brenda clean up, he pulled her into his arms, savouring the feel of her, the scent that came from her, a heady mixture of gardenia, musk and something he could not put his finger on. Desire rose in him, but he knew he had to be cautious, if events of the last few days had taught him, and his talk with Dennis, it was that. It would have to be Brenda who made the first move, and he could be patient, the wait he knew would be worth it.

'Besides I think you have to finish this house before you can think of anything else, although Glen tossed off the things that still need doing, there is still a lot of work to do. Norman and his gang will be here in the morning; I will be interested in hearing how he likes the 'new skin' on the conservatory. So, I will bid you a goodnight, and sweet dreams, I will call you tomorrow OK?'

Brenda was on the brink of asking him to stay, but realised he was right. She could not give him the attention he deserved, so she held him close, thanking him without words for his support during the day. 'I know, thank you, ring me tomorrow, call around if you can, its Wednesday, middle of the weekday. Lots of good things seem to happen to me on a Wednesday. Larry, I was thinking, could we get away from this madness for a weekend perhaps. I know I am being forward, but I think I would like to see what being alone with you could be like, without meddlesome ghosts or burly builders around, what do you think?'

He laughed, 'I love the idea, and will hold you too it. We will work it out Brenda, I know we will, we have Iris on our side remember?'

She smiled and walked him out to the door, to the cab he had called. Waving goodbye as it disappeared down the street. Brenda sighed and closed the door, checking on the Iris Phone that all was secure. Moving through her apartment, she would have to make sure that Linda and Sir James were aware that this was her place, her town house. This was home, more surely than any place before in her life. It was in this place that she had found meaning and purpose, had found a means to do the things she had dreamed about for years. With like-minded people who would be along for the dreams and nightmares; she was sure there would be a few of those as well. She only wished she had the two people that meant the most with her, she missed her children so.

Duncan would like to come around this morning to take a look at your paintings, would that be alright?'

After Brenda assured him that it was more than alright, and very welcome, 'I am glad my dear because I told him it would be, they will be around to you by ten. Don't forget dinner on Friday, Larry I am sure will pick you up, see you then!'

The call finished Brenda looked at her watch, it was a quarter to ten, wily old coot, she thought, I wonder how many strings he had to pull for all of this?

She had moved into the front room, asking Tristan, one of Normans team to help, putting out a line of chairs to place a picture either on or leaning against, then thanking Tristan for his help, as some of the larger ones were very heavy, walked the row, taking a good look at them all, where she could, they were very dark and dirty. She could also see the beauty and artistry that each one had, Iris smiled at her again, Edward Fitzgibbon looked wistfully at her, she also found a small one hidden in behind all of them of George Boerchermeir, his haughty expression she knew from Iris' writing was just a façade. Moving onto the large one of Lord Lucas, whichever one he was, reminded her somewhat of Sir James, he had the same haughty air. The doorbell rang, and was echoed by the mobile in her pocket, laughing at what she thought of Matt's overkill of technology, she went to let Duncan and his team into the house.

'Ms. Chalmers?' Duncan was as wiry as Michael Dranish-Fawkes, but not so gaunt, he had a ruddy disposition with a very prominent Adam's Apple, which bobbed as he frequently swallowed. Brenda nodded a hello, 'Duncan Rogers, Ms. Chalmers, from the National Portrait Gallery, Sir James said you would be expecting us?' Brenda looked behind him to three other people, two ladies and another trim and neat gentleman looking at the house with wonder.

'Sorry Mr. Rogers, but Sir James just advised me you were coming. I appreciate you arriving so promptly, if you and your companions will follow me?'

Brenda led them into the front room, watching them as they saw the paintings displayed around, Duncan moving over to the one of Lord Lucas.

'May I ask where these have been, Ms. Chalmers, they are in a shocking state!' Clearly, he took his work very seriously, and was moving from painting to painting tut tutting and moaning at the state they were in, coming back to the one next to Brenda of Lord Lucas, seeing the stricken expression on her face.

Which was also noted by one of Mr. Rogers companions, 'Nonsense Duncan,' a late fifties woman, slim in build with clear green eyes moved forward, 'Doris Worth, Ms. Chalmers, pleased to make your acquaintance,' giving Brenda's hand a firm shake, 'these are just dirty. I can see little damage that a good clean will help bring the colours in these back to life easily.'

Brenda explained what had happened and how the paintings had been found, with nods of understanding going around the team, Duncan thawing visibly when he realised that Brenda was a saviour of the paintings, not the one who had inflicted the damage. Doris looked at Duncan nodding 'I told you so!' look passing between them.

'We will need to take them to the Gallery, Ms. Chalmers, we cannot do anything to clean or restore where needed here. It will take approximately six to eight weeks, but I assure you they will be returned in immaculate condition, and we can appraise them for the artist, and value them for insurance purposes. Can we take them with us, we have brought the right crates to transport them, Sir James gave us a rough number to do so?'

Brenda agreed, reluctant to let Iris leave at first, but realising she was being silly, especially when a whiff of gardenia wafted around her. She knew that Iris was happy to go, so she watched as the men and ladies crated with great care her paintings, giving a detailed receipt of each crate. Telling her that she would be informed with progress, and they would also keep in touch with Sir James.

Suddenly the house seemed empty, even with all the workmen around. She picked up her bag telling Glen she was going out for a while, it seemed that she had been in the house for years, without a break, she just could not breathe. She walked around the streets just letting her mind wander, not taking much notice of where her feet were leading her. She was pulled up short when someone grabbed her from behind. 'Watch it love, you can't go much further or they will arrest you!' She realised that she had nearly wandered right through the gates of Buckingham Palace! Thanking the man for his intervention, he walked away shaking his head, Brenda just stood with the rest of the tourists looking through the railings at the activity behind the fence, wondering what it would be like to meet the Queen. It was with a shock she remembered that she was going to meet the Queen, laughing at her own sense of folly, she realised she had been walking for nearly two hours, she had missed morning tea completely, hoping she had not missed anything else, was turning to find her way back home, when her own mobile rang.

'Hello Brenda, Hugh Pemberton here, are you free, wondered if you could pop around we have some information for you, and some more papers to sign?'

'Of course, Hugh, I am a few blocks away, I can hop in a cab and see you in about ten minutes, will that be ok?'

'Perfect my dear, see you soon.'

Now with a destination, Brenda gave a shake of her shoulders and hailed a cab to see what Hugh had come up with.

After the papers were signed, he gave her the details on the patents she had asked to be arranged, also gave her the basic concepts to put into practicality of the ideas she had given him for the business set ups for the Haddon's and the Respite Hotels.

The best part of the meeting, was when Hugh gave her the details of the everyday bank account and the amount they deemed a meagre allowance for her from the legacy for her personal use, she just looked at Hugh, and shook her head in wonder at the amount in the account, also the little plastic cards to let her use it. She could now use some of the money she had inherited, as she left the office she rang Linda, as she did not really want to go back to the house just yet.

Erin answered, 'Pickworths how may I direct your call?'

'Erin, its Brenda Chalmers, is Mrs. McGill free?'

'I will check, Brenda, please hold,' after a few minutes, 'I will just put you through.'

'Lady Lucas, this is a pleasure,' came Linda's voice over the phone.

'Don't you dare Linda McGill, you can stop right now!'

'Sorry Brenda, just had to gauge your reaction, won't happen again I promise, now what can I do for you?'

'Lunch I hope, if you are free? We do have a few things to straighten out, I am just walking in the door!'

Another thing that she really had to stop was when she entered Linda rose from her desk and dropped a very elegant curtsey to her.

'Please do not do that either! I expressly forbid you to curtsey, call me Lady Lucas, Ma'am or do anything that Brenda Chalmers, that is myself would think very crass!'

Straight-faced Linda rose, 'I have been instructed that this is the correct way to address you from now on!'

'Who told you that?' Brenda asked not sure how to react to the greeting, and wondering if Linda would show her how to curtsey with such grace, as she realised she would surely have to learn.

'Grandfather!' was Linda's quick reply, still with a straight face, but eye's twinkling with devilment.

'Sir James, huh, do you always do what your Grandfather tells you to?'

'Now that you mention it, never!' She laughed and went over to give Brenda a hug, 'sorry but I just had to do that and see your reaction, it was what I expected, you didn't like it. But Brenda you will have times when this will be the norm; and your reaction will have to be appropriate, which I can help you with. Grandfather wanted to know how you would react, I can now report to him, that you did exactly as he expected, but', she looked into the clear blue eyes of her new friend to show her sincerity, 'we are going to be ok, we will be here to help you, just remember that ok?'

Brenda breathed a sigh of relief, knowing that she would have people who cared about her and would be there to help her through this transition period. She could relax, relaxing even more when she realised they had agreed to her way of employing her. Then Linda took her to her favourite Day Spa, for a couple of hours of pampering and a very delicious lunch.

Sitting in the comfortable Japanese Zen garden surroundings of the Spa, the world seemed to click into place, but there was a question she had to ask.

'Linda, can I ask you a question?'

'Sure Brenda, you can ask me anything right now, isn't this wonderful, an afternoon of pampering will put the world to rights in no time at all!'

'Well, how do I dress for your grandfather's dinner? Is it an ultra-formal occasion, I realise jeans will not be acceptable, but I have no idea how much or little he requires?'

'Good Lord, I had completely forgotten, you would have no idea, and probably not a dress to wear. Thank you for bringing it up, I should have thought of it first. Hm, well to answer your question, Grandfathers dinners are done in the "Grand Style", the ladies with floor length dresses and diamonds, the men in tuxedos. Woe betide anyone who does not conform or check.' She began to pack up her things and motioned for Brenda to do the same as she spoke. 'I remember once a very famous film star was invited and he arrived in a suit, a very nice suit and very expensive from Saville Row, but Grandfather would have none of it and made him leave, it was just not the done thing. Heavens what is the time? Kimi, Kimi?' The slim oriental owner of the Spa arrived at the call of her name.

'Mrs. McGill, is something wrong?'

'No Kimi, nothing could be wrong with your expert care and wonderful place. Please can you check if Clarissa is open and to what time? If she is open please advise her I am on my way with Ms. Chalmers.'

'Certainly Madam, please do not undo all the good with unnecessary stress!'

Both Linda and Brenda laughed, relaxing in the face of such calmness, but with dressing finished headed out into the real world again, to find a Taxi. Brenda rang Glen and advised him she was going to be back a little later than she thought, asking if Matt could lock up for her please. He advised that they were packing up as they spoke there was not much to do if they could not get into the kitchen. Ben and Matt were still busy of course and he would leave them to finish, while he took the rest of the team off to look at another job that had just come in. He also wanted to be home early as Gabby and the babies were due home from the hospital that afternoon. Wishing him well, she hoped the boys were not working too hard, and to drive safely, see him in the morning.

The ladies taxi deposited them outside a house just off Mayfair, Linda grabbing Brenda's hand to pull her into the showroom on the first floor, Clarissa moved forward at the tinkling of the bell at the opening of the front door.

'Mrs. McGill, what a pleasure to see you, it has been too long. What can my humble establishment do for you today?'

The friendly false smile and limp handshake Clarissa gave to Linda was not lost on Brenda, especially the sideways put down glance that took her whole appearance in, in one look. Disdainful and dismissive with a where did you crawl out of sneer, instantly had Brenda wishing she was dressed in her suit and not her work jeans.

'Well, Grandfather is having a dinner party Clarissa, we both need dresses for the occasion,' at this Linda brought Brenda forward and introduced her. Clarissa openly eyed Brenda up and down, taking in the work boots, jeans and paint daubed shirt, no makeup, but good skin, hair just tussled up into a ponytail. Clarissa, made up her mind that this personage was not really for her establishment, and her countenance showed her disdain, she spoke rather haughtily to Linda, turning her shoulder at Brenda to say 'Australia, right?'

'G'day mate, how d'ya ever guess?' Brenda gave right back with a thick Australian brogue, going forward to take Clarissa's hand in a vigorous hand shake.

Linda looked stunned at first, wondering where this was going, of course she knew that Clarissa was a snob of the very first order, but she was an expert milliner, knew exactly what cut and colour would suit any shape and size of body, she was very exclusive, hence the snobbery. Linda had always wondered how and who would give her the set down to bring her head back to normal size, if it was possible, hoping she would be there to see it when it happened, it looked as though her wishes were coming true.

Brenda realised that this woman had worked hard for the prestige she deemed her right, and she must have earned it over a long time, but that had also given her the impression she had the right to judge others. Knowing the best set down would be a swift one, and best done by the final bill of her purchases, she hoped that Clarissa would still be helpful, as she really liked the few dresses she could see.

'Well of course, we can see what is possible, but you must realise Mrs. McGill,' again she spoke around Brenda to Linda, raising Brenda's hackles even more, 'that this is an exclusive establishment, and we can only do so much to assist such cases, and go so far!'

This was said with a wave of the same limp hand in Brenda's direction.

'Well, ya know, if you don't have the fancy frocks to suit, Linda and me will just toddle off to Harvod's, isn't that the place we need to go Linda? The Sheila's back in Bourke, said that was the place for the real fine duds!'

Linda at this stage could not help it, turning to look at one of the dresses displayed trying to suppress the laughter bubbling inside. The expression on Clarissa's face was one of ultimate disdain, looking between Linda and Brenda, in an effort to understand what was going on.

'I apologise for my little joke,' Brenda said, drooping the charade, continuing on in her normal voice, 'but I would be most grateful if you could assist me in the purchase of a few outfits, as well as a gown suitable for Sir James's dinner, please.' Brenda could not keep up the charade any longer, as this woman was so ingrained in her persona she would not see the joke if taken any further. She would be shown that what you see is not what you think you get, in the purchases that Brenda was going to make, that she realised was the best way to get her point across.

Clarissa was stunned for a moment, at the transformation that this person went through before her eyes. Still in the same clothes, but with an altogether different demeanour, she could be Nicole Kidman's older sister for her looks and refinement, suddenly she realised she had been on the end of a joke, at least that was the only way she could take it.

'Ah, Mrs McGill, you nearly had me there. A joke you played on Clarissa!'

Then all business and without a break in her countenance, turned to Brenda, 'now, let us see what we have to work with? Anna, Anna come immediately we need to measure and see what we that will be suitable for the ladies!'

Brenda was taken into a fitting room, complete measurements were taken, Clarissa took in the old scars on the lovely skin, realising this woman had not had an easy life. Her brain working overtime wondering just who this person was, and would she be able to afford her services. Still, she was with Mrs. McGill so she must have some standing, especially as she had an invitation to one of Sir James Pickworth's dinners, those invites were very exclusive. She was miles away thinking of what they had that would be suitable when Anna suggested the Lavender and Teal. Yes, she thought perfect, sending Anna off to bring them into the fitting rooms, also a couple of cocktail dresses she thought of, and the lovely burgundy set of jacket, trousers, skirt and dress that would work wonderfully on Brenda's more mature trim figure and skin tones.

The teal dress fitted like a dream, V-necked and draped around the high waisted bodice, gave what Brenda thought was an indecent amount of cleavage, the empire line style draped and moved around her, she felt like a fairy princess. Linda in the lavender halter neck creation looked just as lovely, both of them just looked at each other and smiled, they were a world away from the work clothes they had walked in wearing.

'This I could get to like!' Brenda told Linda as they left Clarissa's not only with the dresses, but with multiple bags apiece.

'A little of Clarissa goes a long way, I have found. But she does know what will suit, I love that teal on you, makes you look taller! Anyway, come on how about dinner back at my place, Shane is cooking, so it will be very edible!'

Brenda was breathless, as never in her entire life had she spent so much on herself. Trying to realise that she now could, although she would restrict her visits to Clarissa's establishment to a must needs basis. Giving a small smile as she realised the normal high street stores would always be her favourite places to shop, she turned to

Linda, 'I don't want to impose Linda, I have already taken up too much of your day!'

'Nonsense, I have enjoyed myself, it was worth it to see Clarissa taken down a peg or two. What are you going home to, heated up noodles that Dennis has left you? We are just a short taxi ride away, here's one now!'

Brenda nodded a yes thank you it would be a welcome change. In the cab the Iris phone rang, a message appeared – *"Brenda all finished for the night, hope you had a good day. See you tomorrow, all locked up tight – Matt"* followed by the security code telling her the building was secure.

'That is one very neat system Brenda, you should have heard Shane go on about it, he was very impressed. He is going to have a word with Matt when things get quieter, wants to incorporated some of his ideas in a couple of builds he is working on!'

'I am sure Matt would be happy and very willing to discuss anything that allows his imagination free reign. It is about time all four of the Haddon children were in their own businesses, I mean they can still work for their father when needed, but they also need their own companies, and I mean to help them achieve just that.' Linda just nodded as the taxi had pulled up at a very modern warehouse conversion.

Night had fallen Brenda appreciated the warm welcome glow from the building they had stopped beside. Walking into the ground floor apartment, Shane called a hello from the kitchen, 'is a glass of wine required?' at them laughing at the immediate yes from both of the ladies. Brenda realised she had not switched on her own phone, to check messages, if any, there was a voice message from Larry.

'Brenda love, sorry but I have to go into the country for a couple of days. Don't worry I will be back in time for Sir James's dinner on Friday, would never miss one of those, will pick you up at seven. Hope you also were ok with Hugh today, and that Linda did not lead you too fare astray with your new cards? Ring me if you need me!'

Shane was a great cook, the meal was first rate, the company even better; Brenda enjoyed sitting there in the middle of the banter between them. Exactly what it should be between married people, she shut away the thoughts of the life she had with her husband. It had taken a while before she realised that it was not normal for the male to take his frustrations out physically on the female. It was good that she had left that relationship, but she had been lonely ever since. Ah well, the challenges ahead, the possible relationship she was building with Larry gave her life excitement and purpose.

As she switched on the Iris phone in the cab to open up and turn on some lights, making the house welcome, a message appeared – *'Check the Dining Room!'*

Wondering what that meant, but sure that there was nothing wrong, she had memorised that code, she paid off the cab, carefully carrying the bags from Clarissa moved into the house. Mia and Rebecca had liked her initial idea of a table and lamp in the hallway, they had replaced her temporary set up, with two more identical ones in the right style for the house, one in the apartment side hall, and the same on her side of the hallway. The soft glow as she opened the front door into apartment one was very welcoming, moving down the hallway, deposited the bags at the top of the stairs turning to read a note stuck to the door, pulling it off and reading as she moved into the room.

'Brenda sorry about leaving you with no kitchen, slight oversight! Hope this temporary area will work, no stove but noodles heat up fine in a microwave. Hope you had a good day, see you tomorrow. Love Mia and Rebecca.'

She switched on the lights to find the dining table in place, at its smallest setting, still large enough to fit eight of the dining chairs around it, placed in the old kitchen/new dining room area. The cupboards were completed a couple with glass doors, enclosing the area and giving a lot of storage in the space. They looked functional and gleamed with polish, a mixture of Nona's special and of course gardenia floated around. There were individual notes taped to the doors – *"Open Me"* – she went to the first note, folding back a door that hid a bench with square miniature butlers sink, complete with working taps. Yippee Brenda thought no more filling the urn from the powder rooms. In the cupboards beside it a small refrigerator, stocked with all the food items from her fridge in apartment two, also with a couple extra boxes of noodles with a note – *"Love from Dennis"* – she laughed. Next was a microwave, and then the next had been turned into a makeshift pantry with the rest of the food from apartment two. Next to that was what would be the dumb waiter, with yet another note – *"Not Quite Working"* – attached. Her stereo had been put on a new bench that was placed under where the still missing Iris Window would be re-instated, beside the bench were stacked boxes holding her other bits and pieces, to place where she wanted them. She laughed again, well it looks as though I am moved in here alright. She made a cup of tea in the microwave, took it to sit and sip in the finished window seat, that looked out over the newly enclosed staircase, finally at peace; the familiar waft of gardenia came again, *'You like?'* thought Brenda *'I like too!'*

Chapter 53

THURSDAY GOT OFF TO a hectic start, Patrick arrived at seven and immediately began the final sand on the kitchen floor; his workmen now took over from Glen's crew, finishing the painting and wallpapering. Ben and Matt were back, saying that Glen would be up tomorrow, but his side of the fit out was complete, they would only have a few things to finalise when they could walk on the kitchen floor. Though there was still a ton of work to do, especially in the conservatory with Norman.

Brenda then voiced the problem she had been mulling over to them both, 'I think it is about time we told him about the workshop, don't you?'

They both nodded at her suggestion, relieved that she had said it, as they were both itching to get back into the space, to finish off correctly their own tasks, as well as complete the ones discussed with Norman.

'I need to get back in there today, Brenda, if you want me to fix the hot water problem. I need to double check all the connections; I did do it a bit hastily. I cannot connect the other bathrooms until it is checked.'

Brenda nodded in agreement, then thanked them both for the mini kitchen set up in apartment one. Ben advising that once they had found the original kitchen in the basement, he had reorganised the plumbing set up, and would also add a single dish washer drawer as well, it would be useful in the space, but he was still waiting for Rebecca to bring him the fittings to finish it off properly.

Rebecca hearing her name came over and thumped him on the arm. 'What was that for!' he asked, 'Because I could,' she answered. Suddenly Brenda missed her two, and laughed at the banter going on between the brothers and sister. Rebecca was checking on what Brenda had planned asking for her help in setting up the larger apartments, after Norman and the team from Kew arrived.

Norman was full of news, as he saw the group together, his team had headed out into the garden the day before; Norman saying the rain had been a godsend, as it loosened up the soil, they could easily dig up the garden beds. Brenda asked if he could send the team ahead, as they had something to show him.

Curious he nodded, telling Tristan he wanted the check on the commons work done first, then to continue finding and clearing the paths until he caught up with them. Brenda smiled taking him out onto the landing, down to the basement, Norman exclaiming about the light and space in the new conservatory.

As they walked down the stairs to the basement he looked around, 'I really must get to this area, you know Brenda this place will look lovely. I can see a small table and chairs outside the kitchen, with a fully stocked herb garden and flowers in the terraces, what do you think?'

Rebecca answered that they already had the perfect setting in the warehouse, they would be bringing it over when the kitchen was in use, sometime in the next millennium!'

'Patience love, Patrick knows what he is doing, the finish will be worth it, won't it Patrick?' Brenda told Rebecca, motioning to the man in question as he worked hard in the kitchen.

'When Patrick please?' Rebecca yelled at the back of the man, through the open French doors, that were allowing the fumes out as the men worked.

He paused, resting on the long-handled roller he was using on the floor, with a sigh of knowing, turned to her, 'the way this is drying Becca, you can get in here on Monday, as long as no one, and I repeat no one walks on it over the weekend, hear me!'

'Oh ok, but we have so much to do in there! I want to see it finished and give Brenda her space and life back!'

'Thank you love, but you have given me so much, I love the mini kitchen upstairs, and it works very well you know,' Brenda gave her a hug, turning around to face the terrace wall.

Norman was perplexed wondering what was going on, Ben and Matt just grinned at him, nodding in Brenda's direction. Matt moving the orchids out of the way, as Brenda took the key off the key ring, opening the secret door. Rebecca and Ben then pulled the cleaned and greased door back into its position cradling the stairs, then caught hold of Norman's hand pulling him into the workshop, all the while he was gasping in wonder.

Gob-smacked that was what he was, lost for words as he moved around a piece of living history. He looked at Brenda, then at the three Haddon's smiling at him, he didn't know what to say.

'How long have you known about this gem?' was the first question that popped into his head.

'I am sorry Norman, but I have known from the first week. I apologise that I have not shown you before, but it was just too much at once. Please forgive me, but now is the time for you to know about this, we have taken photographs, and not disturbed too much. Ben has been the only one down here, please, please do not think too badly of me!'

Norman took a slow turn around on the spot, noticing the ceiling, and the glass inserts in the floor now made sense. He was on the verge of ripping into these unthinking people, to keep a discovery like this away from him, and Kew, was unthinkable and unworthy of them. Then he listened to what Brenda was telling him, and realised that they had no choice but to keep this a secret, for if it had been known, they would surely never have got the planning permission for the work around the fire escape stairs, and the new skin over the conservatory that he admired so much.

Ben was saying that Dan and Glen had checked the new foundations that had been put in and they had missed the original terrace walls, in fact they could help, as they could use the new foundation posts to help anchor the terrace more securely. Matt and Rebecca stood looking at him concern on their faces, these young people were trying to explain to him, and Brenda looked stricken.

The look on her face was what brought him round. He could not bear to see the strain, the worry on her face, this place was going to be a legacy of Kew, she had promised, he realised that she had made that promise with the knowledge of this; what did they call it "Workshop" existence.

He took another turn around and sighed, 'it is alright my dear, all right,' he took Brenda's hand and patted it. 'I may not fully understand the reasons, but that you have shown me now, and not disturbed anything is wonderful. Come on all of you give me the guided tour please!'

They all seemed to breath at once, Brenda tucked her hand in the crook of his arm, Rebecca taking the other side. Matt stopped them going too far.

'I have to work on a new lighting system before you can see everything Norman, and I want you to see something first, can you and I go back upstairs for a moment? Stay here he said in an aside to Rebecca, Ben and Brenda.

They stood in the main body of the workshop, suddenly there was light from above. They could hear Norman exclaiming, calling his team back from the gardens to help them uncover the floor, allowing light to come through the glass panels. They both arrived back with Tristan and Fred, who exclaimed at the workshop fixtures, Norman saying he wondered why glass had been put around the outside of the tiles, it now made sense.

Matt was smiling, saying he would still need to put lights in the space as the during a bright day the light was almost sufficient, they still had to compensate for rainy days and night time. Ben slapped his brother on the back, everyone laughing, 'I will be working down here most of the day Norman. You were asking about a watering system, well if you can loan me Fred here, he can help me utilise what is already here. It is still in good working order, apart from a few perished hoses. I have already converted the original boiler to gas, but it still has a few kinks in the system!'

Norman could see more and more as the light improved, pulling Brenda into a hug doing a little jig on the spot. She had never seen anyone so happy, saying 'Am I forgiven?'

'Forgiven, for giving me a treasure like this, yes, forgiven for being a caring soul, who wants to restore this for use, not just to sit in a museum, not necessary. Now let's see how we can help Ben and Matt, Fred who do you need from Kew, call them up!'

Rebecca and Brenda made a discreet exit, nodding to Matt and Ben as the team from Kew surrounded them. Norman standing in the middle of the astounded group beaming in all directions at once. Matt mouthing 'Will update you later!' at them as they moved back into the house.

She spent the morning with Mia and Rebecca, organising the removal of the temporary furniture from apartment two, calling Dennis to see what he wanted to do with the bits and pieces he had given her to use; having it carried down into the sitting room, to wait for collection.

When Dennis arrived at lunchtime with the orders, he wanted to know what was going on, astounded by the changes being wrought in such a short time. He knew Brenda could work miracles, but this was the fastest damn miracle he had ever seen, he also wanted to know why there were three vans with Kew logos on them disrupting the parking in the street.

'You remember when we found the kitchen, I told you that we had discovered something else?' He nodded at he, 'well come with me!'

Leading Dennis down into the basement, through into the workshop, the once lonely and neglected space now teaming with people, cataloguing and checking all the tools, fixtures and fitting, cleaning as they went. Norman came out from the wine cellar, a very dirt encrusted bottle in each hand.

'Where?' was, all Dennis could croak.

'Over here,' Norman nodded back at the doorway, 'I know a little about wine Brenda dear, and I can say that this is very good indeed. I can recommend a firm that can check it all for you, and help you continue to keep it.' At Brenda's intake of breath, he continued, 'Oh very discreet, I would only be asking the head man of course, you did want this checked?'

'Of course, I do Norman, thank you, but can we leave this wonderful cellar to a later date. It has waited this long, it can wait a couple of weeks more. You would then be able to assist him, wouldn't you?'

Norman beamed, of course he would that was a very good idea. Brenda then made his smile even wider by suggesting that he take a couple of bottles with him to show his contact what had been discovered. Nodding, he advised he would find a box to secure them in, and with her permission and Denis's help,' Dennis nodded in eagerness, 'would move a few bottles into the dining room wine rack that had been so helpfully installed by Glen and the boys into her new mini kitchen; might as well have some of the finest in there, what did she think?

'As long as you assure me it is drinkable, why not. Perhaps we could open one up before you leave tonight, just to make sure?'

'You are a woman after my own heart, what a wonderful idea! Come on Dennis, let's just see what we can move easily. I do not want to disturb too much until Edgar can see this wonderful place!'

Leaving the two men enjoying themselves enormously, she wandered around the workshop, seeing industry and order coming back to the once neglected area.

Matt had added some temporary lights and the generators to use them, until appropriate ceiling lights could be installed. His team happily adding electric cables by threading them through the pipes Matt had discovered in the ceiling, the possibility that they were originally installed for gaslight but never used occurred to him. He would soon be finished; the hold-up was Rebecca supplying him with sufficient fixtures that were in keeping with the era to complete the job.

Ben was whistling happily off key, as he and Fred fine-tuned the born-again boiler. They had swept and cleaned the floor so you could see that the tiles were the same as in the conservatory floor above them, green marble as the surround instead of the glass. The smell of gardenia floated in the air, everyone was walking around with big grins on their faces.

At four o'clock Norman called a halt to the work, he and Dennis had checked on some of the wines, moving a few bottles into the wine rack. They were opening three bottles as the group around them grew, began to decant them into separate carafes. They had put a cloth over the padding on the antique table, forever looking like mad scientists conducting an experiment, the sight imprinting itself in Brenda's memory, and Rebecca's camera recording the event.

'I bought the carafes and glasses Brenda, I know you will have some in the boxes downstairs, but I did not want to disturb them too much. Perhaps you will accept them as a gift from me to you, and this remarkable house. We will need them in the cellar, when we check the wine anyway.'

Brenda laughed with everyone, saying she was happy to accept the gift on behalf of the house. She was handed the first glass, the rich ruby liquid swirled and coated the glass. She tipped the glass to smell the notes in the wine, watching the expression on Norman's face light up on seeing that she knew the right way to check this bounty. Taking the first sip, she could feel the velvet liquid smoothing her throat, leaving the taste of blackberry, she could almost smell the moist earth the vines had been in, many decades ago.

'Oh, Norman, what a treasure, please everyone, please take a glass and try, what do you think?'

Dennis and Norman had matching expressions after the first sip, they looked like a couple of well-fed cats that had fallen into a vat of cream, didn't know whether to sink or lick it up!

When everyone held a glass, Norman turned to them all, 'a toast people, to Iris and her family, a group of very forward thinkers, a big thank you!'

The toast of Iris going around the room made Brenda realise that they all knew who Iris was, and she was content. Little steps, soon Iris's legacy would be known around the world, not Brenda, she would be in the engine room, but the name the world would know would be Iris Fitzgibbon-Boerchermeir, she had promised.

Norman and Dennis looked at Brenda startled, they had both smelt the gardenia realising that iris was giving her benediction on the opening of the stored bottles. Ben and Matt were enjoying the wine, but realised it was a lot stronger that they were used to. Mia and Rebecca were enjoying the companionship of the people who had worked so hard during the day. Patrick and his painters were enjoying the lovely red wine with the rest, looking forward to finishing this project that had been quite different from the start.

Chapter 54

B RENDA WOKE ON THE Friday morning, with a big grin on
her face. Everyone except Norman and Dennis had left
shortly after their celebration glass. They had dinner of warmed
up noodles, the first meal around the wonderful dining table in
many decades, and of course a few glasses of the red wine. Brenda
had called a cab for them about nine, watching as they disappeared
around the corner. She had put the remaining carafe of wine back
into the bottle, she knew that Norman would have given her a set
down if he had seen her do it, but she could not see it going down
the sink. Gently washing the glasses and leaving them to dry on a
tea towel went down to bed humming a merry tune.

Glen with the boys arrived first, he telling her the babies and
Gabby were well and at home trying to get into some sort of routine.
Charlie sent a message that he would see her to finish everything off
later. Brenda asked where John and the rest of the team were?

'Well they are visiting a friend of Sir James, I went around
there yesterday, with John, apparently, this chap was having trouble
with some work that he had just had done, and he needed a second
opinion of if it was correct.'

'Bill Gardiner strikes again, I take it!'

'Got it in one, Brenda lass, so we checked it out, John and the
lads are around there working on the problems. In fact, it is a good
job this work is nearly complete, we have so much work on the
books, I will need more men!'

'That is great news Glen; I am so pleased for you, and the business. Now did these two fill you in on what we did yesterday, and our disclosure to Norman?'

'Oh, they told me about Norman all right, how is your head this morning?'

'Mine was fine, I don't drink that much, but I think we had better tip toe around Norman, and please do not shout the lunch orders to Dennis today!' They all disappeared down into the workshop to show Glen what had been done as soon as they all had a hot morning cuppa in hand.

Stan with Nona and Poppa arrived shortly after, Nona beaming that Brenda was in her own place. They were claimed immediately by Mia and Rebecca to help put the finishing touches moving out with Nona, for a second opinion, leaving Poppa and Stan struggling to come to terms with the changes being made. Stan came over to Brenda, asking if she was ready to take up the black plastic on all the floors. He had been pleasantly surprised with the condition and state of the carpet in her bedroom, but he needed to check the rest, so he could have them cleaned or advise Rebecca and Mia to replace.

Brenda agreed, she was also curious and wanted the plastic the last piece of the puzzle gone. So, dragooning Ben and a couple of the Kew workers to help, they rolled the black plastic off the floors in the dining room, right through to the bay window in the sitting room; opening the shutters around the window, allowing light to spill on carpets hidden away for decades. Brenda was not really surprised at the quality of the main carpet, in excellent condition according to Stan, but also the parquetry flooring that appeared in the old kitchen area, now dining room under the table. Then as they completed lifting it out of the sitting room, four beautiful rugs appeared, sunlight came through the windows and they glowed. Beautiful blues, rich reds, greens and gold, Stan held his breath, never had he seen such quality. He turned to Brenda, but he didn't need to say anything, seeing the tears running down her cheeks. He nodded and took the helpers down the stairs, to remove the plastic in the other two bedrooms.

Brenda spent most of the day in the conservatory, keeping out of the way of the carpet cleaners. Helping one of Norman's team re-pot some of the plants; they had carefully removed the spider orchids draping over the workshop door, replanting them into large pots that were placed on either side of the steps from the dining room. Saying they had never seen such rich deep colours before, giving Brenda the flowers that had broken off during the re-potting, telling her they would keep in water for weeks.

Work by consent finished at four, it was Friday after all, everyone was looking forward to a quiet weekend. Patrick and his team had finished by lunchtime, and already taken their leave. Patrick reminding Brenda that he would be back on Monday, but to not, under any circumstances, let anyone walk on the kitchen floor. Assuring him that there would be no one in the house but herself, there was no need, as the only job left for completion she realised was the kitchen. Glen, Ben and Matt were very happy, Ben declared the refurbished boiler now worked a treat, judging by the hot water that was now flowing all over the building, and he hoped the kitchen too, but he could not check that due to Patricks embargo.

'Don't you even think of it Ben, I promised Patrick no one on the floor till Monday, so patience please!'

Matt wanted to be sure that he had everything ready for Monday, Rebecca had assured him that all the lights that she and Brenda had picked out for the Workshop would be delivered on Monday morning, so he was raring to go. Glen laughing at the enthusiasm coming from his two sons, said he would take everyone away till Monday, enjoining Brenda to enjoy a peaceful weekend, if she was free on Sunday to come down and see the babies and have dinner.'

'Coming to Sunday dinner could become a habit Glen, I like visiting your family!'

'The family likes the visits Brenda. This is a lot better without the black plastic over it, glad to see that gone. Stan has done a great cleaning job, not much smell either!'

'it is a secret of the trade my friend,' Stan said as he joined them walking back into the house. 'Yes, the rooms definitely are better without that black plastic, but it did its job wonderfully. Nona likes it gone too, did you see what Poppa did?'

On the question, he opened the folding doors between the rooms to show the majority of boxes had been moved out, at Brenda's look, 'we put most of them down in the basement hallway, at least the ones that originally came out of there, as we will need to put them back in the kitchen when we can. Some are here to be put into the cabinets that Rebecca and Mia has assured us are to arrive, then also be put back on the shelves either side of the fireplaces, once you, Rebecca or Mia decide what it is you want to display?'

As they moved into the room, she saw that individual pieces of furniture that had been under dust covers were now in position in a room ready for use. The end tables, desk, love seat, were positioned around the room and in front of the fireplace, no sofas or comfy squishy chairs yet, but the space just screamed out for them to make the space complete. The timber furniture highlighting one of the rediscovered rugs, laid out in front of the fire, she could see the others rolled up, standing in the corner waiting for Brenda to decide where to put them. The original wallpaper glowed with dappled sunlight the room seemed to breathe again, gardenia and rainbows floated in the air.

'Oh, Stan this is wonderful, Rebecca what do you think?'

'I think it is about time we left and organised for Monday to return this whole place back to what it should be, a home and a home away from home. I love it, I cannot wait to add the extra pieces from the warehouse to complete the transformation, thank you Stan!'

No one said anything as everyone could see the tears in her eye, matching the ones in Brenda's. After the hugs of farewell the workers left; Norman and his team were the last ones that day. Norman not working to full capacity, asked Brenda to remind him of this day when he brought Edgar around; that wine of hers packs a mean punch. The house was silent, peaceful and Brenda loved it, so did Iris judging by the scent floating around, it could not all come from Nona's mixture.

Chapter 55

S HE SPENT A LUXURIOUS time having a bath christening her new tub, enjoying the sensation of the now very hot water, and peace. Getting ready for the dinner she had put her hair in a lose chignon, tucking in a couple of the orchids, fixing them with jet clasps, a little make up, it was a special occasion after all. Then she had to decide whether the emeralds or sapphires would better match the dress, grateful that she had not had a chance to put any of the necklaces back into the safe, as she would not have been able to access them in the kitchen. Making a decision on the emeralds were the correct choice once she had put the dress on.

She had searched for a box to put two of the bottles of wine, carefully keeping them flat, nestling them in a bed of paper, wrapping the whole thing in a paisley scarf, tying the ends so she had a handle to carry the box with. She was ready when Larry rang the bell, putting on the jacket that went with the dress, this with a high fastening mandarin collar, that hid the neckline and necklace from view, fastening under the bodice, to flow over the dress with a satin sheen, she now really felt like a fairy princess.

Larry had worried all the way back that afternoon, wondering if he should have made sure that Linda or someone had advised her on the dress code for one of Sir James evenings. Kicking himself that he had not called Brenda that morning to advise, but the time had just got away from him. He rang the bell, trying to think of tactful ways to get her to change, if she had not managed anything but the little black dress of a week ago. He heard footsteps, and stood wondering at the vision in swirls of green and blue that stood before him. The little black dress a poor rag compared to this creation, it took his breath away.

Brenda smiled at his confusion, kissing him lightly on the cheek, moved out on the doorstep, as he mechanically closed the door behind her. Moving to the waiting cab, trying to get his brain to work and say anything at all, 'You are so beautiful!' was what his confounded brain could stammer. The taxi driver had to agree, as he waited for instructions on where this very handsome couple wanted to go all dressed up. Larry pulled himself together as he climbed into the cab after Brenda, turning to give the address in Mayfair.

'Yes,' thought the cabbie, 'definitely where this couple should be going, he wouldn't have been surprised if they said the Palace!'

Larry was sitting looking at this vision beside him, as far away from the torn denim and flannel shirts as you could get. She shimmered, from the emerald and diamonds in her ears, to the gentle folds of the floor length coat and gown. He noticed the orchids in her hair, matched the dress in shades of teal, a delicate perfume tantalised him, he wanted to explore to where it was strongest!

The cab pulled up suddenly at the lights, jolting him back into the here and now. Looking at Brenda, clear eyes shining in the street lights, smiling at him, she knew exactly what effect she was having on him, and was enjoying every second.

'Did you have a good time, last few days?' she asked, holding and balancing the package as the taxi moved off.

'It was busy, sorry I have not called you, but most of the time I could not get a signal. How was your time spent?'

'Oh, we got a few things done,' he nodded at the package, 'for Sir James, I hope he likes it, Norman and Dennis sure did!'

They had pulled up at the entrance of an exclusive Mews, Larry helping Brenda out of the cab paid the smiling driver, who wished them a good night. Larry took the package from her taking her arm to help her walk over the cobblestones to the well-lit house, Brenda happy that she did not have to tell him to keep it flat. He handed it back at the top of the steps waiting for the door to be opened.

'Giles, good evening, how are you tonight?' Giles bowed at Larry, opening the door to allow them entrance, the epitome of an aristocratic family butler, thought Brenda.

'Giles, may I introduce Ms. Brenda Chalmers.'

'Ms Chalmers welcome,' with a bow in her direction, he motioned them further into the hallway, 'may I take the parcel for you?'

'Thank you, Giles, but I wish to give it to Sir James myself, but he will need your services, will you follow us in?'

'Certainly madam, but can I at least take your coat?'

'Oh sorry, of course,' she handed the precious package and her purse back to Larry, while she slipped the coat off her shoulders, handing it to Giles who accepted it with another slight bow.

Larry took an inward breath, seeing Brenda now revealed in the dress and showing off that and the emerald and diamond necklace to perfection, beautiful, the thought breathing again, for both the necklace and the wearer. Brenda smiled at both men, taking back purse and package, moving at Giles request through the double doors to the left of the hall.

Linda and Shane were already in the room, with Sir James; Brenda was quite unaware of the stir she caused gliding across the room to where Sir James was holding court.

He watched the vision in green and blue walk towards him, with a start realising that it was Brenda, Larry following with a bemused expression on his face. Oh, yes, he thought, that is one man in way over his head, and why not, this was one amazing woman, and what an unexpected beauty.

'Good evening Sir James, I am continuing an outback tradition, if you don't mind. It is customary in Australia to arrive with a bottle of wine when invited to dinner.' She turned to Shane and Linda, 'sorry you two but I will bring two bottles next time I get an invite!' They nodded in understanding, smiling at the happiness that was radiating from her. Turning back to Sir James as Giles appeared at his side. 'I hope that you can enjoy the contents, I have tried to carry them prone, but cannot vouch for the handling that Norman and Dennis may have given them when they brought them up from the cellar!'

'The Cellar?' Sir James said, 'yet another of Iris's surprises I suppose?'

Brenda nodded and smiled, he looked at Larry standing beside this lovely creature with a very proprietary smirk on his face, understanding what was going on from his perspective anyway. If he had been twenty years younger he would have given him a run for his money. Still he could and would enjoy the friendship that was blossoming between them all. Taking the parcel gently, nodded at Giles, with Larry's hands underneath the box, he undid the tie at the top, the scarf flowed away from the box revealing the two dirt encrusted bottles nestled in the paper. 'Oh, my dear, what a way to begin your entry into this world. Giles please check them for me?'

Giles moved over and raised an eyebrow at the bounty nestled in the box, the eyebrow the only thing that gave away his surprise.

'I tried not to jostle them too much, they have not been tipped upright, hopefully they may decant well, but I will rely on your skill to advise us Giles?'

Brenda told him as he took the box and scarf away, saying he would put the scarf with her coat, moved out of the room, wondering at just what had arrived into the house.

Sir James moved beside her giving her a hug of welcome, with a peck on the cheek, taking Larry's hand asking how the trip went. '

'Nice diamonds!' Linda said as she moved next to her glass of champagne in hand, holding out a second one to Brenda, 'Iris?'

'Who else,' Brenda said accepting the glass, 'want to borrow them sometimes?'

Linda blinked and then laughed, realising Brenda meant it, giving her a hug, moving her around the room to Shane who was talking animatedly to Hugh Pemberton. He took her hand and kissed it, telling her she looked lovely, introducing her to his wife Phyllis. Small talk and chatter flowed around the room, there were twenty people all checking each other out, Brenda was being introduced to all of them either by Larry, Sir James or Linda. At one stage Brenda excused herself moving to the powder room, coming back down the hall she met Giles.

'May I ask a favour of you please, 'she said as she came beside her.

'Of course, Madam if I can assist.'

'Giles, I am not much of a drinker, two glasses of wine at the most. I would appreciate it if my glass is not topped up over and over please?'

'Would you prefer sparkling or still water, ma'am?'

'Still would be fine, thank you for your understanding Giles.'

'Certainly madam, I think we can accommodate your request.' Giles liked this woman, first the wine, then the civil request, yes he liked her very much and his first impressions were usually correct.

She had been reliving her experience and fears in Hugh Pemberton's office too much laughter from Sir James and disbelief from Linda and Shane, when Giles announced, "Dinner is served!"

Sir James took Brenda's hand pulling it through his arm and guiding her through the doors into the dining room, the table beautifully set with a lot of glasses and silverware. Brenda leaned into Sir James, 'Please do not let me eat with the wrong fork!' He and Larry, who was escorting Linda, laughed and nodded encouragement. Shane following behinds smiled as he heard the comment as well.

Dinner was progressing, waiters were filling glasses and bright happy chatter could be heard. Giles walked to the head of the table, a carafe similar to the others in his hand, but the wine inside was decidedly darker in colour. Sir James had put Linda on his left, with Shane beside her, Brenda on his right with Larry beside her, to which Brenda was very grateful. Giles bent and said something to Sir James, who looked at Brenda and smiled.

'I take it the wine was deemed fit to drink, Giles?'

He bent down to speak so only the people at the end of the table could hear.

'Madam, I have been serving wines to Sir James for many years, I will not tell you of the number of so called vintage wines he has been given over those years. The bottles you have given him this evening, are vintage; very, very beautiful wines. That is why the one bottle I have opened is in this carafe, and is intended only for this party; the second bottle I am reserving for Sir James to enjoy one evening when he is alone. Madam, I thank you on his behalf!'

Brenda was moved by the sincerity in his voice, he was genuine in his praise. Pouring a small glass for each of them, he moved behind Sir James and waited, Sir James raised his glass in a silent salute, as the others raised theirs in reply. He looked at the wonderful deep rich colour in the glass, noted how it coated the inside, moving to his nose inhaling the fragrance and rich notes, taking a first sip, he sighed. Looking at Brenda, 'thank you my dear, for thinking of an old man, this is a treasure, you are being careful with it I hope?'

'I have Norman and Dennis on my case already Sir James, I think my cellar is in very good hands, but I will watch them both like a hawk!'

He laughed and said non-better, taking another sip of the wine savouring the richness and bouquet. Looking at Larry, Linda and Shane whose faces showed their appreciation of what they were drinking. The evening was going splendidly, and he smiled, the food was wonderful, laughter and bright cheerful chatter filled the room, he was a very contented man.

Chapter 56

THE DESERT COURSE HAD been removed, when Linda rose, the gentlemen standing as she did.

'Ladies we shall retire, to allow the gentlemen to their port, and if required cigars!'

Brenda smiled and could not help but think she had been transported back into a very old movie, again waiting for the director to yell cut. She stood, as all the ladies did, Larry pulling out her chair, briefly taking her hand and squeezing it tightly, as though he could sense her inner confusion. She moved back into the parlour with the other ladies, where tea, coffee and little petit fours were waiting.

Sir James motioned for more of Brenda's fine wine, a look of disappointment crossing his face when he realised Giles was pouring the last of it into his glass.

'You have one fine woman on your hands there my boy. A little bit of fatherly advice, don't let her slip through your fingers!'

'I don't think I can call her my woman just yet Sir James. We have only known each other for two weeks; you have only known her for three! But you are right, I would be a crazy man to let a jewel like Brenda slip away from me, but I intend to go very softly, I even think my father would approve!'

Sir James roared with laughter, a gasp and nodding of head from Shane echoing Sir James answer, as he knew the type of woman Larry had been linked with in the past.

'After the last fiasco, oh yes, I heard all about her from your father, Finder, Fiore what was her name, oh never mind, not in the same class or universe my dear boy,' and he bent towards the two men sitting close, 'and I am not talking about the legacy either, without the legacy she is worth ten of some of the so called 'Ladies' I know. Just look at what she has done for me! With the events to come, I think we should just stand back and watch the fireworks, oh the future is looking bright and lots of fun!'

Shane nodded, was about to comment when the other gentlemen moved closer to the head of the table. Grateful that the last of the good wine was in his glass, Sir James motioned for the port to be served.

The atmosphere in the drawing room was a little tense, the ladies of this age not sure what to do in a room full of ladies. Linda moved with Brenda over to Lady Dorset, a matronly, yet sprightly woman, nearer to eighty than seventy but still looking very youthful.

Hoping to dispel the tension that was in the room, Brenda asked the question she had been mulling over through dinner, realising the company she was in. 'Your distant relations were not responsible for the Tea Dances in Bath, that I used to read about in my favourite Georgette Heyer books, were they Lady Dorset?' She asked, the haughty visage relaxing immediately at the unexpected question.

'Well you know Ms. Chalmers, I think they could have been. Vincent and I have been doing some research; the Internet can be quite fascinating, have you found?'

'I must admit that I have not had the time lately to do much checking, but there are a couple of things that I am interested in researching, perhaps you could help guide me,' at a nod of her head she continued, 'I am interested in some of the customs to do with the Peerage, the do's and don'ts really, would you know where I could find the most comprehensive information?'

Linda looked at Brenda, realising that she was still worried that she would put her foot in it, but the tension in the room had relaxed, as the other ladies, who had heard the question (Brenda had not exactly been whispering) came around them to offer their own pieces of advice, which was what Brenda had intended. By the time the gentlemen joined the ladies, they were having a high time. Lady Dorsett had been regaling them on the etiquette of the day, how the ladies in the drawing room would find out what was going on, all the juicy gossip, of the world they lived in, by gossiping to their counterparts.

Larry moved beside Brenda as Lady Dorset said, 'Of course the ladies would have to show off their skills at these evenings.' At Larry's questions look and 'how so' comment, 'all these evenings were organised for only one thing, to allow the eligible young people a way to meet and possibly attract a suitable marriage!'

'Ah, I understand, but what type of skills?' Larry asked the obvious question, as he did look extremely handsome in his tuxedo, Lady Dorset decided she could accept the question, from a man; she had thawed to the women, not to all of the men.

'Well, there was the playing of the piano forte, or reading of texts or poems. It was an unwritten rule that a lady had to be accomplished in a great many ways, for the time, they seem very old fashioned today. Painting, drawing, embroidery, well the days were never long enough to accomplish everything!'

'I suppose,' Linda added, 'the days were never long enough, because they only had oil or later gas lamps to do things by, so were in bed very early!'

'Probably so my dear, until the gaslights were everywhere. Now then I am going to ask all of us to do a little piece, recreating a little of a bygone age, as we have been reminiscing. Linda, would you give us a song, it has been a long time since I heard your lovely voice?'

Linda was a little shocked at first; it had been a very long time since she had done any singing. In fact, she realized that it would have been before Shane's accident. She blushed, but Shane looked at her and smiled, 'I will accompany you?', moving over to the baby grand piano in the corner, Larry and Hugh quickly moving the piano stool out of the way. Brenda watched as everyone moved to sit or stand and listen, the music that came from Linda and Shane, as he was as accomplished a pianist as Linda a singer, was wonderful. The applause that flowed after their finish was very genuine for both of them. Shane stayed where he was, tinkering the keys, now and then playing a few lines of popular songs.

Linda motioned to Larry, 'Duet?' she asked.

He looked around, ready to say no, it was an even longer time since he had felt like singing, although he, Shane and Linda had often sung together at evenings like this, he was decidedly rusty. Then he saw the smile and challenge in Brenda's eyes, suddenly he felt like singing. Moving over to the piano and checking with Shane, the popular song was performed all the while watching the expressions on Brenda's face.

Lady Dorset herself stood next, motioning Linda into her seat, accompanied by Shane, she sang a very lovely country song, that had everyone singing along with the well-known chorus. Another gentleman said he would read a sonnet from a book he had pulled from the shelves. Sir James was amazed, he hadn't realised that they were reading books, and thought they had been placed there for decoration! Everyone laughed, the gentleman took his position at the fireplace, following Lady Dorset's direction. Gentle applause followed his expert reading, Lady Dorset then turned to Brenda, 'Your turn my dear, what will you do?'

Brenda was stunned for a moment, but then she realised that these people were going to be companions for a long time. She would need some of them to help her through the months to come, especially Lady Dorset. Even as her counterpart had the ability to make or break people in Victorian/Georgian Bath, this lady had the same influence, it was a shock that she realised this was what Sir James had intended with this group of people, to introduce her to people who would be able to help her.

Brenda stood at the fireplace; she didn't think the songs she had sung for the shearers would be acceptable for her first oration.

'An Ode!' she began

I come from the sun, the surf, the heat and cool crystal aqua water.
The Light and the Amber.
I come with sadness, dreams turned to nightmares
That were ripped and shattered asunder.
I come from the times of sadness and mourning
To a new place. A new day dawning.
I come to begin again, a fresh start.

I come to the green and cool water.
I come to begin again to meet new friends, make a new family.
Out of the darkness, out of despair.
To renew what was old, what was neglected
To begin again, a legacy long forgotten, a promise long hidden.
With colleagues who see with my vision, believe with my heart
I come with hope of a new world, a beginning, a new start.
I come, I come, I am here.

Silence, crisp clear silence, Sir James started clapping, the others joining in. Lady Dorset stood asking where she had learned her ode? Brenda told her it was an old aboriginal poem, she had heard it many years before, that she had adapted with her new beginning, working for Sir James thought it was appropriate, Lady Dorset agreed, giving one of her quick mercurial hugs.

Linda was asked to sing again, accepting only if her grandfather and Hugh would sing with her. Larry moved over to Brenda, 'old aboriginal huh?' Brenda nodded, watching the banter going on between the four people at the piano, she just knew Hugh would have a rich voice. 'I have never seen such a beautiful old aboriginal; the ode and the teller are very wonderful people!'

Brenda blushed and looked into his clear blue eyes, much the same as hers, realising at last that yes this was a man she could trust. Could read her poems and stories too, who would understand her dreams, her frustrations with the world around them. A very lively four-part ditty was being sung, it broke the mood, everyone joined in to help with the chorus, laughter and high spirits surrounded them, squeezing her hand, Larry turned them both to help in the sing along, enjoying the atmosphere for the remainder of the evening.

As the cab pulled up in front of the house, Brenda turned to Larry, 'Coffee?', Brenda turned on the lights and switched off the alarm as Larry paid the cab. Making their way up the steps, Brenda laughed at his confusion as the lights were not on in Iris Guest House, only a soft glow came under and around her apartment entrance.

'There have been a couple of changes since you were here!'

She opened the door into the sitting room; the lamps either side of the fireplace giving a soft glow, giving a cosy feel that was definitely better than two weeks ago. Larry, standing in the hallway, was looking around in wonder, the timber parquetry floor that had been revealed under the black plastic, gleaming down to the circular staircase, he could still see the section still to be patched, but the original was just magnificent. He followed Brenda into the sitting room, and in its starkness, not fully furnished yet, with the odd bit of antique furniture here and there he could see what it would become, a beautiful relaxing room. He could see people in here, happy people, he could hear laughter, he turned and walked through the open doors into the dining room as he heard faint music.

'Did you hear that?' he asked Brenda, as he went over to stand in front of the fire place in the dining room, admiring the work done, loving the feel of the carpet that had been revealed, and imagining how it would look when Ben had replaced correctly the fire and surrounds that were propped beside the spaces for them in both rooms.

'Hear what?' Brenda asked

'Laughter and music!'

'I have been hearing laughter, smelling gardenia and seeing happy people in these rooms for the last couple of nights; I think we are doing something right!'

'You; it is you that is doing something right. Brenda none of this would be happening if not for you! I bet the blonde you thought had this job; oh, yes, I know about that, Linda told me, would never have realised what a treasure she had, or the empathy to actually understand. She would not have been down in that bedroom packing up the trinkets, she would have hired someone, they would have just gathered everything and tossed it all in the garbage. She would also have seen nothing wrong with Bill Gardiners refurbishment of the building either, and that would have been a monumental disaster!'

He moved over to her, as he wanted to be sure she understood what he was telling her. Taking the coffee and spoon out of her hands, putting his hands on her shoulders, his thumbs absently playing with her skin around the necklace.

'A beautiful piece of jewellery for a very beautiful woman, thank you for your company tonight. I enjoyed every minute, I don't normally enjoy Sir James' evenings, I especially enjoyed the old aboriginal ode,' as he moved closer 'and don't I know you made that up on the spot!'

He kissed her then, a kiss of promise, a kiss of desire, she responded then pulled away slightly.

'Larry please stay, I don't want to be alone tonight!'

'Are you sure?'

'Yes, I am very sure, I want to share this magical night with you; please stay with me!'

He pulled her back into his arms, this time it was not a gentle kiss, but a kiss of need, passionate, bruising. Brenda pulling him closer, wanting to be part of him, wanting him to realise that she knew what she was doing.

Chapter 57

Morning; the sun was up, Larry moved, coming up from the depths of sleep. Wondering where he was, then realising the dream he had been having for so long was not a dream, but real! Brenda was snug in his arms, her back to his chest, the covers pulled up around them, only her lovely shoulders could be seen, the rest of her warm against him. He slowly looked around the wonderful bedroom seen through the light coming through the slightly ajar shutters. The pink glow declared it early; *'oh God he thought, Glen, they will be here soon, he will kill me!'*

As though reading his mind, Brenda spoke, turning to see his reaction, smiling at him, 'no workmen today, we have the weekend to ourselves, do you mind?'

'Mind; you to myself in this wonderful place, it is my idea of paradise!'

Brenda moved, pointing to the bathroom. Larry nodded falling back to the pillows to watch her move, it was nice to watch. Although he could not help be angry at the old scars on her lovely skin, that could be clearly be seen even in the half light. How any man could strike a woman was foreign to him, to beat someone you love, incredible. Brenda returned and snuggled back into the bed, in turn watching Larry move into the bathroom. He was surprised, but then not surprised when he found the men's toiletry kit on the shelf, thank you he yelled, receiving a your welcome, with a dry chuckle.

He moved back into the bed, after opening the shutters to allow the filtered light from the conservatory into the room. Brenda moved into his arms; snuggling into his side, loving the feel of him. His scent excited her, contentment stole over her, this was meant to be. Lifting her head for his morning kiss soon gave into his loving hands and enjoyed this way of saying good morning.

'I will have to go and get a change of clothes, will be fun going through town in my tux, but it will not be the first time I have done it!' Larry said as they lay side by side watching the world awaken.

'If you don't mind, I did bring some of David's casual clothes in my boxes, I brought some of Kate's as well, in the hope that they could visit without having to lug a huge suitcase with them. You would be about the same size as him, I think Mia and Rebecca were going to put David's bits and pieces in the middle room, Kate's in the front. Why don't you check while I go and make us the coffee we didn't have last night?'

He came up the stairs, looking at the rooms with fresh eyes; they had done wonders in so short a time. The smell of coffee took him into the dining room, classical piano music flowed around him and he smiled, it just made the morning even more complete.

'I bet you cannot wait to have some furniture in these rooms, or out in the conservatory. I can see you reading the papers out in the sunshine and wonderful atmosphere!'

'It will be lovely, but I am making do at the moment,' Brenda replied, 'I forget you have not seen the place since Wednesday, two days is a long time in my world. Can you open the shutters in the front room for me please?'

Larry walked through into the sitting room, there was something missing, but he could not quite put his finger on it. A lot of the boxes that had filled the room were gone, he walked across an exquisite rug, his bare feet testifying to the quality of it, easily opening the shutters back into their niches. Turned and looked at the room again, noting the original furniture set out, just waiting for a sofa and a couple of comfortable arm chairs; the gas fire parts waiting to be replaced in the gaping hole that was there at the moment, to finish the room. He walked back into the dining room still puzzled.

Pictures, they were missing, 'Pictures, where have all your paintings gone?' he asked taking a cup of coffee from her and motioning into the front room, 'and all your boxes, there were more than these?' he pointed at the six boxes lined up along either side of the fireplace in the dining room, a bottle of Nona's mixture and rags on the top of one of them.

'Sir James pulled in a favour from the people at the National Portrait Gallery, they evidently do quite a lot of cleaning jobs, either that or Sir James promised them something that I may have to deliver on!' Larry chuckled taking a sip of his coffee, nodding for her to go on, 'so they arrived on Wednesday morning, taking them all away to be cleaned and returned hopefully in six to eight weeks?'

'Nona and Poppa did the arranging of the furniture after the carpets were cleaned. Most of the boxes have been stacked in the downstairs hallway waiting to be put back into the kitchen once we can get in there. Would you help me today Larry, I would like to clean the recent building dust off those shelves,' pointing to the shelves either side of the fireplaces in both rooms. 'To see what we can put back on them, make them come alive again, to start showing that this place is a home. I know that whatever I do, I will be tut tutted by my interior designers and cleaner, but I do not care, I want to decorate at least one room myself just a little bit, using the pieces I have inherited!' He chuckled as he pulled her into a hug.

'What do you want to do for breakfast? I am afraid the main kitchen is out of bounds, Patrick has spoken, and I don't fancy warmed up noodles this morning!'

Larry laughed pulling his wonderful woman to him, wanting her close. Hold up partner, don't go too fast, his woman, one night does not make a forever. He had thought her truly his, his heart leapt at the thought, he realised that he did want to make her his permanently, but caution was needed. Slow down, his sensible side said, small steps take small steps and let her lead, as she had last night, which would be a change for him!

Brenda watched as the thoughts crossed Larry's face, fascinated by the expression of want and need still there. Caution came across; he was wondering how fast they should take this new relationship. It made her love him even more, that he was slowing himself down, not rushing things, not rushing her. She had made the decision that she did want him around she could not think of a time without him, but she still had to be sure, and only time would help her decide that. Life and love had not been kind to either of them in the past, she was damned sure it was not going to go pear shaped now, even without the trace of gardenia floating around them, as she stood in Larry's arms, she was going to make sure of her feelings.

'Well breakfast,' he was saying, 'as I am suitably attired,' which he was in linen slacks and matching cotton jumper, 'your son has very good taste. I will produce breakfast and organise dinner if that is ok with you? I think we can make inroads on those noodles in the fridge for lunch. I am hoping that we can open another of those delicious bottles of red that you gave to Sir James last night?'

'Perhaps,' Brenda laughed, 'but you will have to be very,' and she stretched up to give him a gentle kiss, 'very good!'

They both pulled away, looking at each other, aware of the feelings between them, but both of them being hurt so badly in the past, being cautious.

'Right then, I will be away to get the meals organised, can't wait to use that kitchen of yours, when anyone can, if you will let me of course. I will be right back!'

He arrived back, changed with a bag of groceries, and a bag of clothes. 'I had to go back to my place, so thought I would change, to give David back his things, do you mind?' he held up the overnight bag.

'Mind of course not, why not put them downstairs, I have already hung your tux in the wardrobe, you will find some empty drawers as well. I hope this is not the only time I will enjoy your company overnight?'

His heart soared, 'I was hoping the same thing!' he said passing the groceries to her with a kiss on the tip of her nose, moving down the stairs whistling a happy tune. Gardenia floated around him, *you approve Iris*, he thought, *'oh so do I.'*

'Dennis rang while you were out,' they were seated around the dining table, eating a breakfast that had turned into brunch. 'I told him you were here, and he had the nerve to chuckle!' Larry just nodded smiling broadly at her, 'I invited him over this afternoon, you don't mind, do you?'

'Mind, how could I mind Dennis, he can show me the cellar, I also would not mind a look around the workshop, now that it has been cleaned up a little, and it is common knowledge. Now!' and he dusted his hands, taking a last gulp of coffee, stood up and turned looking at the shelves, 'how do we tackle these shelves, have you decided what you want and where?'

They had taken the dishes and platters out of the boxes, seeing what was there before deciding what pieces should be put on the shelves, carefully wrapping up the rest and putting them back in the boxes.

'Less is more,' Brenda said, 'I don't want to clutter the shelves, just show off the pieces, and I can always rotate them!'

They used liberal quantities of Nona's mixture once the vacuum cleaner had removed the most recent building dust, they also washed the shelves down. Time moved on, both of them learning more about each other, exchanging anecdotes about their lives, becoming friends, talking about their dreams, hopes and fears. Settling into an easy companionship, that could only become deeper as time went by. Brenda was putting a silver platter on the top shelf, in the middle of two beautiful ceramic bowls, when they heard a rat a tat tat, on the front door.

'I will get it,' Larry said starting to move away from the ladder.

'No need,' came the reply from Dennis, 'it was unlocked! Hey Brenda look what I found on the doorstep!'

Dennis came into the room; followed by the two people Brenda thought were many, many miles away following him in.

'Hey Mum, if we knew you were slumming it, we would never have come!' David said with his familiar lopsided smile crossing his face.

'Why did you not tell us you needed us, we would have been here sooner!' Kate said enjoying the look of utter shock and surprise on her mother's face.

Brenda could not move, fearing the people before her were another apparition, she had wanted them both here for so long, she could not comprehend that they were indeed in the house.

"Oh, my god, oh my god, it is you, you are here I am not dreaming, how are you here? I don't understand how on earth did you know?'

Brenda turned to Dennis and Larry, seeing the same 'oops I think we had better leave' expression on their faces.

Kate and David moved then, helping her down from the ladder, handing the platter to Larry, pulling their mum into a wonderful hug. They were real, they were really here; tears were flowing not just from her but everyone, all Brenda could do was mutter, thank you, over and over as she enjoyed the closeness of her children again.

Larry and Dennis made a discreet withdrawal, Larry asking to see the new and improved workshop, while the family reacquainted themselves. They came back to find the three of them around the dining table, coffee and teacups in hand. Brenda had finally gotten over the shock of seeing her children where she had dreamed them to be, loving the fact that her children, her sounding boards were back in her life, to help her enjoy fully, this new phase of all their lives, to be able to share this legacy with them.

'Did you like my surprise Brenda? I emailed Kate to organise a sabbatical for both of them, did I do, right?

'Dennis my love, apart from nearly giving me a heart attack, you did very right. Now can I please introduce, Larry my son David and daughter Kate, you two this is Mr. Lawrence Morecombe.'

'Larry, finally we get to meet, so glad Dennis gave you our contacts. It has been great being in the loop so to speak, finally succeeding in surprising Mum!'

David stood going over to Larry hand outstretched, Brenda's mouth dropped open at the familiarity between the two men. She had hoped they would get along, but it seemed that they were lifelong friends already. She looked at Kate, who also went over to Larry giving him a hug to say hello, she suddenly felt out of the loop, just a little disconcerted that she had missed something. Dennis was watching her reaction to her children meeting Larry as though he was a long-lost relation, he smiled at her, going to check the kettle, coming back with a cup of tea, sitting beside her taking one of her hands.

'I knew you were missing them Brenda. I watched you with the Haddon's; Kate and David need to be here with you. Kate realised once you had taken the job, you would not be going back to Australia. She also realised, and she is one very smart cookie, that trips back to the UK for both of them would be happening sooner rather than later, so organised for David to get his passport. Larry saw the loneliness too, so he asked if he could help, and who better. You are going to need them to help you, what were they doing in Oz, not much. There is an empire here that you will need your strengths to run, they are your strengths, the three people over there! Yes, I include Larry, for he is going to be in your life, even if you do not see it, everyone else does, and Iris definitely is meddling! We haven't told them anything, just that they needed to be here. You have to decide how much you tell them, personally I would tell them the whole story, it is not as if they are going to believe it anyway, and I would tell them soon'

Brenda turned watching Larry with her children, he was showing them what was in the boxes, she enjoyed watching the easy interaction between them.

'And you my friend; my dear, dear friend, I will need you as well. Don't think you can disappear on me again. I have a role for you in this enterprise, or what did you call it 'Empire' I am building. I will need your organisational skills even more!' Brenda looked at this friend of many years, and smiled; the doubts, the uncertainties erased for the time being. Hugging him, wiping the tears from her face asked if anyone wanted a top up, brining everyone around the table soaking up the happy atmosphere, gardenia fragrance was in abundance.

An inspection of the house, started in the bedrooms, where the bags were deposited. Brenda started to apologise that the rooms were not quite finished; she had not checked them since Wednesday.

'I hate to see what you classed as finished mum?' David said as he opened the middle bedroom door, Brenda shook her head, those girls had done it again. Kate echoing her brother's sentiment as she walked into a fully finished front room; beds made with side tables and an easy chair in the corner, a desk in another corner, lamps on bedside tables; all the towels and accessories required in a modern bedroom. The smile on her face would not go away, after a tour of each bedroom, they moved over to the kitchen, seen from the open doorway, as Brenda would not let them walk on the curing floor. Brenda telling them of the friendly fight between Glen, Ben and Matt with Patrick in regards to the time frame for putting the finishing touches to the room.

David turned after making suitable noises, 'I am looking forward to meeting the people Dennis, Larry and you mum, have been talking about in your emails. This looks like a nice place down here, cosy as well. What's out here?' David asked moving through the basement back door and onto the patio.

'One of your mum's triumphs!' Larry said with a chuckle.

They moved out into the courtyard, tidy now after the Kew people had been in the terraces. They were clean but bare, waiting for the herbs and plants to return it into the kitchen garden it once was. Moving out from underneath the landing to look up and view the enclosure around the stairs fully appreciating the new structure they could see enclosing the stairs and landings to the roof.

Dennis nodded and called for the lift, both of the children gasped then smiled, hugging Brenda again, laughter followed as the three elder members of the party showed the newest recruits the secrets of the building.

Dennis after the tour excused himself, saying he was having dinner with Lulu that night; he needed to tell her just how right she had been about the job for Brenda. Brenda laughed and told him to tell her that she was invited to the "Garden Party" she was going to throw to launch 'Iris House', at least the Iris House the public would know about, as her home.

'Thanks Uncle Dennis, for getting us here, we will see you through the week, won't we?' They both asked him.

'Yes, give your lunch orders to your Mum!' he threw back at them as he went out the door.

Both of them turned and with identical quizzical expressions, asked how so? Laughing when Brenda explained Dennis role in the epic adventure that was nearly complete. Larry stood to say goodbye as well, both Kate and David looked at him with a smile.

'Please do not go on our part Larry,' Kate said looking at David who nodded, 'we did not mean to spoil your weekend, and if you don't have any other plans, please stay. Jet Lag is sure to hit both of us early, even though you kindly booked Business class seats for us,' she turned to see her mum's raised eyebrow at that disclosure, 'so please stay!'

Brenda laughed, saying you had better run now! Larry looked at her, and it was a look not lost on either Kate or David. There was a different vitality to her, she was complete he liked even more what he saw. He didn't really want to leave he would feel very empty as he had been looking forward to the weekend, and hoped when he knew the children were arriving they would invite him to stay. 'Well if you are sure, I had better up the order I made for dinner to four, steak ok with you both?' Laughter rang out from everyone.

Brenda and Kate finished the cleaning and placement of the pieces selected for the shelves, with Larry and David then carrying the boxes down stairs adding them neatly to the others in the hallway to be replaced into the kitchen. They spent the afternoon going back over the house, both children exclaiming in delight over the decor in apartments four and three, agreeing with Larry the disaster that was apartment two, looking forward to helping in any way they could. Most of Larry and David's time was spent in the workshop and poking carefully around the cellar, Brenda took time to reacquaint herself with her daughter, but avoiding the main topic of the conversation, why they were there, and Larry.

The evening passed with a meal delivered from Larry's favourite restaurant, 'Henri insisted the best, hoping that you enjoy this one fresh!' Larry advised them as they sat the table to enjoy the food, Brenda laughed and had to give an edited version of the first meal she had at Henri's. They had finished off the decanted wine she had put back in the bottle, which was enough for a glass with the meal, it was as both men said 'Superb!' Kate and David started yawning about nine, and called it a night.

'As per usual, they go off to bed, and Mum cleans up after them!' Laughing with her, Larry helped her clear up, pulling her into his arms as they closed the dishwasher.

'I like your two, hope you like mine when I can get them to visit! I am going home tonight, no I am not staying; you need to wake up in the morning, just the three of you here. One day, and I hope soon, I will be able to stay; they have to get to know me, know who I am. At the moment I am the interloper, I will tread cautiously, for your sake as well as mine; you don't mind, do you?'

'I understand, of course I do, thank you for your understanding, and caution Larry. Thank you also for your help in getting those two reprobates here for me. You will come over tomorrow though wont' you, oh I was invited to the Haddon's again, I did want to see the babies!'

'It should be alright; those two need to be kept awake so a lovely drive in the country should do it. I will ring Glen and ask if it is ok that we bring a couple of overseas travellers with us!' With that he gently kissed her and left, Brenda waving him a goodbye from the front door.

She finished tidying up, preparing the coffee machine and kitchenette for breakfast the next morning, just as she had done all her life, her routine was back; the feeling of completeness surrounding her, gardenia floating around as well, she had her family back in her life, all was right in the world.

Chapter 58

IT WAS A LAZY start for her to a Sunday. Brenda made the coffee and was working on her laptop set up on the end of the dining table, getting up to date on her paper work. Wondering where she was going to set up her main computer, remembering Matt's promise, relaxed a little, the laptop at the moment would do. Kate was the next to come up the stairs, stretching and going to give her mum a morning hug, filling her cup came and sat beside her.

'I like this mum, very much. The house suits you, it doesn't smell like an old house, I keep getting a scent, oh what were the flowers you kept trying to grow and not succeeding?'

'Gardenias my love, and get used to it. Iris is just saying hello and welcome!'

At Kate's raised eyebrow, Brenda explained in more detail from the day before of what happened after she had got the job with Pickworths. David coming up for air, around the time she went for the second interview, giving both an edited version of the Iris Legacy, but not about the money or the Lady Lucas bit, seeing Kate's shock at the reveal of the furnishings being part of the legacy, thought it wise and one shock at a time would do.

Both children listening with rapture at a tale worthy of a Hollywood film script. They both were amazed at the photographs when she showed them the albums, both hers and Rebecca's. David also being a disbeliever when she reiterated that all the contents of the flat were their mums as per the will; made Brenda doubly glad she had not made a full disclosure.

Brenda telling them they were going out for a drive in the country, then to Dinner at the Haddon's, to meet the Family, and also cuddle the new babies.

'Larry too?' David asked with a smile on his face.

'Yes, Larry to, in fact he is the one with the car. You do realise that I have not driven anywhere since I got here!'

'Oh, poor deprived mother, what will become of your famous (ha ha) driving skills!' He laughed being closely followed by his sister.

They both then asked questions on what was happening, where did she see them helping her. It was something that Brenda had been wondering as well, knowing that the question really could only be answered once full disclosure had occurred. She again had that hesitancy, so she put the question back on them asking how they saw themselves helping?

Kate had been thinking, saying she would love to help in the running of the Guest House, that was what she had been told Mr. Haddon had called it. Brenda laughed, yes love, I would like to have your help here. I have a few ideas of how you two can help, but they can wait till Monday, today is Sunday let's just leave all decisions till then, and enjoy the weekend.

David had been wandering around the rooms, opening the shutters in the front room, then the French doors to the Conservatory, letting the rich smells of the indoor garden into the house. They all took a walk around the conservatory, Brenda explaining what she would like to do in the spaces if Norman agreed.

'You know mum, you could make one of these wings into a Gentleman's Area', I bet that there was a billiard table in one of these originally. I have been checking on the era, since Larry and Dennis began emailing and calling us. There is enough space, also why would you need two sitting areas, besides with the smoking rules around at present, you do not want people smoking in the house, you could ventilate one of the areas very well, making it a smoking zone!'

Brenda was taken aback that her son had been thinking the spaces through, although with his architectural background, what else could she expect. 'I will introduce you to the people who will help with the organising of that, as I think it will be a good idea. We will definitely meet Rebecca, who is one of the interior designers, she is in her final year of University, specialising in the Victorian and Georgian periods. She will be the one to check for us, Matt and Ben her two brothers will be the ones arranging the mechanics involved. What are you doing?'

They had walked back into the house, David walking around tapping on the walls, 'well as I said, I was reading some books I got from the library, yes sis, I know what a library is!' He turned and made a face at his sister, then continued his minute scrutiny of the walls, especially a blank section from the walls flanking the bookcases on either side of the fireplace. He tapped again, and a very hollow sound ensued.

'This was just the sort of thing I was looking for. In the books, it stated that anything that was useful, but not used in everyday life, was put into cupboards, or hidden closets. From what you have said about Iris and this house this just seems odd, why don't the bookcases go all the way to the edge, as in the front room?'

'You know I haven't spent that much time in here. You do realise that I have only been in this apartment full time since Wednesday! Now that I look at it, you are right, that does look odd!'

The doorbell rang Kate went to let Larry in the house.

'I brought croissants, if anyone is interested? What's up?'

'Iris we think, show Larry what you have found, David love!

David explained what he had read again, as he was still taping the flat areas going from side to side on both sides of the wall. Larry turned looking at Brenda, not again, he said. She just looked at him and shrugged her shoulders, she could not speak, all of them getting a whiff of gardenia, and hearing the faint sound of laughter. Shocked Kate and David looked at Brenda and Larry, who were smiling at their reactions.

'Ah ha!' David said as he put his finger into what seemed to be a painted over knothole in the timber, but what turned out to be a ring pull, similar to the Workshop door. Slowly the panel with persuasion moved open, revealing three inserts and supporting legs for the dining room table. Larry following his example opened the other side in the same way, to reveal one more insert plus another set of the supports to hold them once installed. Brenda just stood and looked at the timber, Kate helping David and Larry remove them from the frames that held them in place, swinging out from the cupboard, dirty and covered in cobwebs, they were still magnificent. Everyone moved then by mutual silent consent, moving to the table and clearing it, David and Larry finding the catches underneath, pulling it apart, putting the extensions with support legs in place, giving a seating for twenty or more people for the first time in decades.

Kate had been on her hands and knees at the edge of the carpet, 'Mum, I think this parquetry goes under this carpet. You know it would be nice to have it all the way across. In fact, I think the carpet is a new addition, I think the parquetry goes throughout the apartment!'

Larry moved over to Brenda, putting his arm around her shoulders, as he could see the shock on her face, she looked at him. 'I wondered where the pieces for the table were; I knew they had to be somewhere. Nona and Poppa said as much the other day, after they set the apartment up, Stan told me, they were worried as there were many more chairs than the table as it was, could accommodate. I thought that they might have been chopped up in the mess I found in your bedroom that first day David, I am so glad I was wrong. This is just magnificent, even in its present state', she put her hand on the table in benediction, enjoying the feel of the ancient timber, and marvelling at its beautiful design. 'Just wait till your mate Fred sees this! She turned to Larry, who was admiring the fully extended length of the magnificent mahogany, he chuckled.

Larry laughed with her, pleased she could bounce back from yet another one of Iris's disclosures, so easily. Realising it was the steady influence of her children that made the difference. The men were just going to put the timber back in the slots, but Kate; thirty seconds before Brenda could say anything, stopped them. First, she took photographs of the table complete, then the sections as David and Larry held them, then the cupboards. Kate directing them to give them a vacuum and inside of the cupboards, Larry stating he would not like to step on Nona's toes, as whatever they do would not be good enough, before returning them to their hiding spots.

Brenda agreeing with Larry's sentiments, that whatever they did, Nona would not like their efforts, but she could not put them back in their original state. '*Thanks Iris*,' silently, hoping there were no more to come, she again heard the faint sound of laughter, and the whiff of gardenia, that they all looked around for. Laughing again, Brenda watched as cleaning duties done, Larry and David put the table back to its size of the morning, then she and her children, went to get ready for the trip into the country.

Kate came up the stairs with a couple of parcels, wrapped in baby paper, one blue, one pink, Brenda looked the question.

'Well, Dennis did let slip in his last email that there were new babies, and you know how I love to baby shop for friends. I thought these might be useful, and a couple of outfits, you can see them when we get there!'

'I think you are a wonderful daughter, and love having you here,' giving her a hug of approval, Brenda turned looking around, 'ok where are the men?'

Brenda picked up her own basket of goodies, moving Kate out through the front door at the toot of a car horn, realising that Larry and David were waiting in the car.

Looking for the Mercedes, was interested to see them seated in a dark green Range Rover, Larry waived them over, David already ensconced in the passenger seat.

'It might rain, and I never get the chance to take this out, so thought it would be good for today, there is a little more room for four passengers!'

Brenda laughed, moving into the back seat with Kate, who punched her brother on the arm, 'I get shotgun next time!'

'Sure Sis,' from David laughing as they pulled out into the traffic.

Chapter 59

THEY HAD AN EARLY lunch at the same pub on the river, David insisting that he should pay for the lunch, as Larry was driving them. The friendly bickering lasted the meal; David prevailed by the expediency of going up and paying, when he went to the bathroom before the end of the meal.

They arrived at the Haddon's on time, both David and Kate exclaiming that this was what they expected, the thatched roof and farm buildings, in the middle of some glorious country, the friendly glow from inside the farmhouse very welcoming.

Glen came out hand outstretched to Larry, giving Brenda a hug, turning to see the children of the woman he admired, hoping that they measured even half to their mother. He was not disappointed, David immediately took his hand.

'Mr. Haddon, thank you for the invitation, sorry we imposed on you at short notice!' Kate going over, giving him a kiss on the cheek, 'we feel we know you already Mum, Dennis and Larry have been emailing us about your progress at Iris House. We want to thank you for all you have been doing for mum!'

Taking the thanks with a nod of his head, ushered them into the house, Julie coming from the kitchen receiving the same type of courteous greeting, and a hug from Brenda and Larry. A wail from the front room, told the visitors that chaos had arrived in the shape of two very small bundles. Brenda moved over to Gabby and Charlie, giving them a hug apiece, asking how Gabby was fairing.

'Wonderful Brenda, now I know what was going on, I still cannot believe I have twins, all I have to do now is get back into shape to cope with them!'

Brenda signalled to Kate and David who came over to stand beside their mum, grinning at Gabby and Charlie as they did a double take, realising that Brenda's children were also twins. Charlie liking what he saw even more, he couldn't help it and shook his head chuckling to himself.

'You didn't realise I had twins Charlie, well, let me tell you to enjoy the time now, because before you know it, they are this big and you wonder where the years have gone, now where are they I want my cuddle!' They all watched as Brenda moved over to the large bassinet picking up the baby what was squirming, just about to yell.

'Mum always gets clucky with new babies!' Kate said as she gave a parcel each to Gabby and Charlie. 'We brought you a gift from Australia, hope you will accept them, from one set of twins to another!'

Gabby and Charlie hugged the two of them saying thank you, then unwrapped the two sheepskins, one blue one pink, held up the outfits for each of the babies. Gabby saying, they were wonderful, just what they needed. Glen and Julie enjoyed seeing the pride in Brenda's face at how her children were being accepted.

'I can't keep calling them 'the babies' haven't you two come up with names for them yet?' Brenda asked as she heard the familiar burp from the unhappy bundle on her shoulder that immediately settled down once the burp was released.

Gabby looked at her, smiling at the sight of Brenda with the now contented child asleep on her shoulder, looking at the children and Larry with a wonderful smile on her face. The glow of contentment was palpable; she relaxed people, made them see that life is to be enjoyed, at any time. Charlie came over to them with the other baby, nodding at his wife to answer Brenda's question.

'Well the little man on your shoulder is Edward Lawrence Waines; this little cutie here is Iris Brenda Waines! We hope you like and don't mind?'

Like! Brenda was stunned, not knowing what to say, Larry equally stunned looked at the Waines with incredulity. Charlie continued, giving them both time to compose themselves.

'We wanted names that meant something, the fact we have twins was significant, it was Glen that suggested what we should do.'

It was then that Brenda realised that Glen had known about her children's arrival and kept it secret.

'Also, the fact that they have arrived when we were working on your job Brenda, that our businesses have gone through the roof, since we teamed up with you and the crazy venture we have nearly completed, led us to one conclusion, that we needed names that would mark this period as a milestone, meaning a lot to us, and you do!'

'Charlie, Gabby thank you I don't know what to say, but thank you,' Larry moved over to give Gabby a hug, took Charlies hand, taking Iris from his arms, 'welcome to the world Iris Brenda, you and Edward Lawrence are in for one hell of a ride!'

Everyone laughed at his comment; Brenda coming out of her shock went to stand beside him, his free arm coming around her shoulders, steadying her while she added her thanks.

Ben, Matt and Rebecca arrived with Champagne for everyone, enjoying the looks on Brenda and Larry's faces at the news of the baby's names. Brenda introducing her children to the newcomers, she in turn enjoying their looks when they realised Brenda's children were twins.

There was laughter and good spirits in the room, but as Iris started to yell in Larry's arms, the younger Haddon's decided that taking Kate and David around for a tour of the complex was preferable to sitting waiting for dinner in the front room with the babies.

After they had left, Charlie turned to Larry, 'Of course you realise, that we are also asking you to be Godparents to the children; Gabby and I both hope you will accept?'

Larry looked at Brenda who was still a little stunned, then at Glen who was beaming at him, nodding his head in confirmation. 'I would be honoured, I am sure I speak for Brenda as well.' He looked again at Brenda still with the sleeping Edward on her shoulder, the look of contentment and peace on her face made him melt; she nodded and smiled.

'He does, thank you both for the honour you have given both of us, we won't let you down.' Brenda finally found her voice, looking over at Glen smiling at him, he harrumphed at the room in general, then offered a toast, turning to Julie asking when dinner would be ready.

Brenda had warned Kate and David that the workers arrived early, they were struggling up the stairs the next morning, when the Haddon's with Charlie and Patrick arrived at seven thirty. Brenda had the coffee on, urn bubbling merrily and was waiting to see what was to happen that day.

Patrick had tut tutted over the kitchen floor, but deemed it ok if Ben and Matt put something over the top to stop it being scuffed by their work boots. Patrick had already made sure there were pads on the kitchen tables that were still suspended from the rafters, so they would do no damage when they were lowered into place. Thanking him profusely, both of them pulled out some of the padding and black plastic saved from the carpet reveal taping it down over the entire floor, Brenda heard Patrick muttering 'Overkill' as he passed her. The two boys could be heard whistling merrily as they completed the tasks in the space, opening all the doors, even the basement front door to allow for the kitchen appliances that were due to be delivered.

Charlie and Rob were eager to move on, finally replacing the restored and revitalised chandeliers back in to the rooms waiting for them, to see that the additions they had made worked with the structures in place. Norman arrived, Brenda introducing him to David and Kate, he beamed like a long-lost uncle at the two of them, saying that they had one very talented mother, he hoped that they appreciated her, both of them saying oh they did.

Brenda asked where his team was?

'Oh, they are out in the garden Brenda, we have very little to do in the house today. We really need to concentrate on the walkways, especially the garden around the ramp, then finish off the work on the commons. We need to check on the gate out to the area, possibly talk to Dan about installing a new one, to match the steel work and finish everything off!' He turned to David and Kate, 'have you had a chance to check out the gardens yet?'

Both of them said they had walked the conservatory, and were most impressed with it, but had not yet ventured out into the gardens, they were looking forward to seeing what the end result was. Dennis and Stan arrived with the cleaning team breaking into the conversation; Norman acknowledged the new arrivals left saying he would love to give them a tour, once everything was at that stage.

'I haven't been out in the gardens yet,' Brenda said to her children, 'so don't go without me!' Both of them assured her they would not be going on their own, turned back to give Dennis a hug, who then introduced them to Stan, Nona and Poppa. Rebecca coming over to say hello, what were the two of them up to that day?

'Apart from trying to get over that wonderful meal your mum cooked last night. Thought we would see if we could not add something to this endeavour?' David said moving everyone into the dining room.

Rebecca and Stan looked at Kate and David a quizzical expression on their faces. Kate laughed, 'well Iris left one last surprise for us to find yesterday!'

As she moved to one of the bookcases, David moved to the other, like magicians they revealed the hidden sections with the table inserts, Nona gasped, Poppa smiled and Stan just shook his head, translating when Nona started speaking.

'Nona says that she wondered where the rest of Bella's table was, it was so small, so incomplete, but now she is happy, but they need a good clean!'

Everyone laughed, the men taking the table sections out of their holders, Glen coming over to see what the commotion was laughed 'Not again!'. Brenda looked at him nodding, 'Iris had to keep something for the kids to find, and what a treasure they found!'

They then checked out the cupboards, Glen marvelling at the ingenuity of the swing out holders for the sections. Making sure everything was sound to continue to be used, stating apart from being dusty and full of cobwebs, everything was in perfect order. Pico and Bella were moving the pieces into the front room so Nona could advise them how to clean them. Moving the big industrial vacuum cleaners into the room to clean out the cupboards.

Brenda took Stan and Rebecca over to the dining table.

'What do you two think, if I am going to put the dining table this way, it makes sense that the flooring is the same. We think the parquetry floor runs throughout the house, under all the carpet, can we lift it? If we use the two matching rugs, end to end while the table is extended, only one while this size, storing the spare in the cupboard with the extra leaves, it will then define the room, what do you both think?'

Stan nodded, looking at Rebecca who turned to Brenda 'I was wondering what to do in here!'

David came over to them, followed by Kate, 'we think the carpets are a new addition, shall we find out, if we are careful we can always just put them back if we are wrong?'

The ingenious expression on his face had everyone laughing. Glen called Jack and Matt to give a hand; they moved the table as far back into the small kitchen as it would go. With many willing hands carefully removed the edging on the carpet, rolling it and the underlay from the French doors to the folding doors between the rooms. Everyone just stood and looked in wonder at the parquetry floor with a beautiful inlay appearing in the middle of the room.

'That looks like the pattern on the steel work, made into a coat of arms!' Mia said coming into the room. Matt nodded, looking at the beautifully crafted inlay, 'Looks as though it was only put in place yesterday, it looks in great shape.'

Stan turned to Nona who had been talking very animatedly with Poppa; he turned and left the room to get the rest of the cleaning team.

'Poppa said no one is to walk over the floor till it has been cleaned, and he can check it thoroughly.' He turned to Brenda, 'Do you want to take the carpet up entirely Brenda, never know what we may discover in the sitting room? If you want to leave it I need to call my associate who cleaned the carpets downstairs to come and finish off the edging of the carpet that is staying correctly?'

'I don't know, truly I don't!' Brenda said, her mind in a turmoil at yet another treasure found. A whiff of gardenia floated around her helping to calm her mind, 'how about we leave the carpet in the sitting room, that would be cosier Rebecca, that will fit in with your plans wont it? Brenda said going and sitting on one of the dining chairs in the kitchenette, looking in wonder at the dusty floor in front of her, looking at both Dennis and Glen who were also shaking their heads. Kate and David had been talking to Rebecca who in turn had introduced them to Mia, Stan going over to add to the conversation.

Matt shrugged, 'we need to know how and what so we can finish the wiring, where do you want power points, in view of furniture placements? David want to come and give me a hand, I will explain what we were planning, to give your mum time to chat with Rebecca and Mia and sort things out?' David smiled looked at his mum, who nodded at him with a slight wave of her hand; he went off with Matt, bending close eagerly listening to what he was saying. Rebecca, Mia and Kate headed off into the front room to see what furniture had been delivered. Dennis walked over to Brenda, two cups of strong tea in his hand, giving one to her, Glen following his own cup in his hand.

'Lass,' he said, 'I just don't know how you do it, just one thing after another!'

'I hope it settles down now Glen, I don't think even I can take much more! Now while I have you two on your own, I need to talk to you both. I am going to be holding a "Garden Party", I want to invite all the workers that have helped make Iris House this thing of beauty. Many of them have been in at the beginning but not seen the end result, and I want them to see what they worked so hard for. I think the weekend after next, we should still have some good weather; I would like to put a marquee over the central part of the garden just in case, but have the gates open to the commons. That gives space for the families with children to run off steam, but still have cover if we do have to endure a summer rainfall, can I ask both of you for assistance?'

'You have mine, I think I know of a place with a large enough Marquee, I will go and check with Norman, to see how we can put it up, without too much trouble. In fact, I don't have much to do at the moment so will just wander over and check with him now!' Glen saluted them both with his cup, wandered out through the conservatory whistling a happy tune.

Dennis was chuckling, 'I take it I am to organise tables, chairs etc.'

Brenda saluted him with her cup, 'yes my friend, I think a little assistance from my two drop ins would be good. Hopefully they will find their feet, while they are helping?'

'Good idea, oh, here come the cleaners. I think we had better get out of the way! I will call back with lunch, need to go and check what awaits me in the office. You did say you had a job for me in your new empire? Let me know when I can give this place the boot, sooner rather than later please!'

Brenda laughed sending him on his way with a promise of soon, and a hug. She walked him out to the front, then was roped in by the girls to help place the final pieces of furniture in apartments two and three.

The house hummed, the smell of Nona's Mixture pervaded everyone's sense, mixed with liberal doses of gardenia floating around. Brenda could not help but smile, a serene peace had descended on her, she could not help but say thanks every time a rainbow crossed her path; the day was filled with rainbows.

She would get a hug from her children as they passed her, happy to be helping. Charlie had warned them to stay away from the basement, while so many people were trying to finish off her apartment. They wanted a surprise of their own making, not one that came from Iris.

Glen came to tell her that the inspectors were due at two pm to do a final check on the building for the building certificate. Brenda thought that would be an ideal time to walk David and Kate around to Linda's so she could introduce them. There were just too many people in the house; she didn't want to be there when the inspectors arrived.

Chapter 60

LINDA WAS AT THE reception desk with Erin when Brenda walked through the door with Kate and David.

She instantly knew who they must be; the stamp of their mother was undeniable. Once the introductions were made she ushered them into her office, to find out more about them. Brenda had just started to advise Linda about Kate wanting to help her run Iris House, when the door opened and Sir James walked in.

'Brenda my dear, what a lovely surprise, sorry to interrupt but Erin just told me you were here!'

Brenda laughed going over to him giving him a kiss on the cheek, introduced him to her children.

'I had no idea they were coming, Dennis and Larry cooked it up between them, but I am so glad they are here.'

Sir James looked at the two-young people who stood at his entrance, pleased with the courtesy, showing that they at least had manners. Took the firm handshake of David, the clear look in the eye that told him this was a young man who loved his mother very much, and would never knowingly let her down. Kate took his hand in a strong shake, smiling and showing a younger version of Brenda, he could see the same strength of purpose that was in her mother.

As they took their seats around the coffee table with coffee cups filled, 'What do you plan on doing my boy, or is this just a holiday?' Sir James asked David, after Linda told him Kate wanted to help Brenda with Iris House.

'Well Sir, I have just finished my final exams, I was working as a junior with an architect firm in Melbourne. If I can find a firm that would take me on over here, then wonderful, otherwise it is just a holiday at the moment. That is if Mum does not need me, what I have seen her achieve at Iris House, I think I would have been better working with her all along, forgetting the University degree!'

'Oh, no my son, you need that very vital piece of paper in this world, to be able to give you the practical experience in this day and age. I am just very glad you stuck to it!' Brenda put in laughing with them all.

'Well I know that Shane can use an extra pair of hands so to speak. He was just telling me that they were losing a staff member, he is going to do some Charity work in South America. Shall I see if he will see you, I don't mean to push you out into the work force immediately, it will be another month or so before you can begin; what do you think?'

David looked at Linda, he had been told by Larry the story of her husband, liking what he had heard; wondering at his good fortune, nodding his thanks, 'I would love to meet him Mrs. McGill, whether a job is in the offering or not, thank you!'

'It is Linda, David; you and Kate please call me Linda. Now all three of you must come to dinner tonight, I insist,' this as Brenda started to speak, 'anyway Brenda has promised me at least two bottles from her cellar!'

'I am inviting myself as well then,' Sir James stated, turned to Kate, 'What of you my dear, do you really want to help us out?'

Kate had been sitting taking in the conversations, wondering at the kind of world her mother had landed in, so far from the life she had known, but she liked the feeling it gave her.

'Well Sir, I was working in a Travel Agency, I liked the work very much, but was feeling a little stuck and frustrated, as though I was missing something. So yes, I would love to help Mum, this might be what I was missing; she is great at the feeling side of running a place, making sure of the creature comforts. I would love to help with the organisation side, the flights, cars, bookings etc., that will be needed; that is if she will let me of course?'

'I think that is a very good idea, Brenda; it will take some of the load off you, at the moment, also give Kate a chance to find her feet. Well I think Pickworths has found another employee, what do you think Grandfather?'

Linda gave Sir James a look, and he chuckled at her, 'I think I had better go and make sure I don't have anything planned for tonight, leave you lot to your dynasty plotting! I will see you all later, I am looking forward to it.' He left the sound of his chuckling following him out. Brenda turned to Linda a question in her eyes; Linda just shrugged her shoulders in a "don't ask me" manner.

Linda had been thinking that Kate could be the solution to a couple of problems that had cropped up the previous week, turned to Kate.

'I think you will be getting a little more work than just Iris House; if you will accept, once we have the guest house operational of course. I would like to see if you will help us here at Pickworths, I found out last week that our Travel Organiser is leaving as she is going to have a baby; so, if you want, and once we check your paper qualifications, the job is yours. I then don't have to advertise it and go through the vetting process. We can give you at least six weeks' holiday, before you come in here to work with Jane, until she leaves; time enough to learn the ropes, also leaves enough time for Iris House project to get off the ground. What do you think?'

Kate could not believe it, oh yes, I could get to like this place she thought. Jumping up to give Linda a hug, 'Thank you, I promise I won't let you down.'

Linda looked at her, then at Brenda who had a grin a mile wide on her face with pride in her children shining through. 'I have already got that promise from another person in your family, I know I have nothing to worry about!'

They talked a little more, Brenda telling her, with help from both Kate and David about finding the table sections, then the parquetry floors. Linda realising that neither of the children had been advised specifics of Brenda's Inheritance, so kept quiet on that score. They were visiting because the 'Inspectors' would be at the house, Brenda did not want to face them, as she believed she would jinx the proceedings.

Linda took a phone call as they were leaving, pulling Brenda aside, 'that was Grandfather, he said he had just been contacted by Sotheby's; apparently, Maud Prendergast was wondering if he knew what was going on at Iris House!'

'Trouble?' David asked instantly alert, seeing the colour drain from his mum's face.

'No David, Sir James will handle it, just leave it in his hands; he said he would tell us about it at dinner, so see you about seven; I wouldn't like to spoil his fun!'

They both looked at Brenda, who was chuckling; realising that Sir James would help keep her safe, what from neither of her children knew, but there was something going on, but they knew Brenda had the right person on her side.

They walked back to the house, Brenda wondering if she should tell the full details of the inheritance, not just the job and the furniture, while they walked, but her courage failed her. She was still unsure about it herself, realised that they were going to have the same trouble with the fact that she was a very rich heiress, when she did tell them, as she did.

Tristan and Mary were in the front garden, putting in Rose Trees and lavender bushes, the scaffolding completely gone. They told her that Mia and Rebecca had said there were no more deliveries to the basement, so could finish off the front garden. Still marvelling at the new and improved Iris House, she just nodded as they told her Norman had gone off with Mr. Haddon, left them to finish one of the last jobs to do, adding to Brenda that it had been a privilege working on her gardens, they were sure that Norman would ring her later.

Going up to the front door after somehow saying goodbye, Brenda realised that there was something different. It took a moment, with David and Kate holding her back to look properly, she realised that the timber panels were gone. New stained glass windows flanked both doors, and in the doors, themselves, one giving light into the apartment side of the building, and one into her apartment. At first, she thought that one was the original Iris window, but quickly realised that both were very good copies, with the plain glass having a bronze tint, they were both beautiful.

She moved with the children into her apartment that had light coming from the back through the original window back in pride of place.

'Don't tell us, Iris?' they both asked her. Brenda nodded, tears were running down her cheeks, both children put arms around her, David giving her a handkerchief.

'Must find that man, he has missed out on two hugs, Charlie Waines, where are you?'

Brenda walked down the hall to the stairs, she could not stop looking at the window, it seemed to glow, shimmering in the light coming from the back of the house.

Charlie came up the stairs from the basement, 'you like?' was the question he asked, looking at the smile and tears on Brenda's face. He was given a hug and kiss on the cheek to show how much she liked what he and Gabby had done for her.

'You are both geniuses, I love the ones at the front, how?'

'Well, when Gabby heard Glen talking about what they were doing with new doors and windows, she had the idea to use the original window as a pattern for the new ones. The only trouble was she had the twins in the middle of it, so sorry but they were delayed. Gabby also did a thorough clean of the big one and told me how to clean the others that are in situ, she hopes you like it all?'

'Like them, that woman of yours is extremely talented, and a miracle worker that she has completed them so well in the time she had. How are they doing downstairs, I can't hear any cussing, where is everyone, I know Glen had gone off with Norman, but where is everyone else?'

'We are down here Brenda, come and see?' Bens voice came floating up the stairs. Laughing Charlie went back down them, followed by Kate and David, Brenda slowly following behind.

Brenda gasped, she had her kitchen back, sparkling new and up to date. The tables were set back on the floor in pride of place. The floor gleamed; all the new appliances set into the new cabinets gleamed. Ben was next to the AGA, Matt, Rebecca and Mia in front of the new Stainless French door fridge. Stan was coming from the Laundry, Cheshire cat grin on his face at Brenda's surprise.

Ben moved forward to give her a hug, 'Dad said to show you how everything works, he will call you later; it is all finished, and so are we!'

'Finished, how can you be finished?' As the words were spoken Brenda realised that she didn't want them to be finished, she had enjoyed all the company over the last four weeks. The professionalism and friendship of these people had wormed its way into her heart, it was with a wrench that she realised they would not be back, no more six am wake up calls, in their professional capacities at least.

'Rebecca came over while Mia moved a tray with champagne flutes onto the table; Ben and Matt wrestled the corks out of a couple of bottles of champagne.

'Well the inspectors have given us the full Building Certificate, so all is done. We will pull up the last bit of plastic, Stan is taking that away, all is finished. All that is left, as dad said to say is to pay the bills!'

Rebecca gave her a hug, 'we will still keep in touch, and I want your opinion on the finishes in all the apartments.'

'Well this is a shock, of course I realised that you would be gone once the work was finished; but I thought it was going to take a few days longer. Your dad promised me less than four weeks, and he was a man of his word. Oh dear, I don't know what to say!'

Ben handed her a glass, when everyone had one raised his, 'To Iris House, may rainbows and happiness shine her into the future!' The retort of Iris House had everyone looking a little teary, Ben turned to Brenda, 'now that the toast has been had, let's take our glasses and give you the final guided tour of the new and improved Iris House!'

They turned surveying what had been two rooms, now it was one big kitchen, the smaller table back in place, matching the larger one in the main room. She checked all the cupboards out, now restacked with the contents of the boxes.

'Nona and Poppa replaced everything Brenda, they wanted you to know that they would be very happy to come and clean for you at any time. You have touched their hearts with what you have done here, they are very happy.'

Brenda gave Stan a hug, as he showed her around, asking him to pass on her thanks to Nona and Poppa the rest of the family as well. Stan moved her into the laundry, a million miles away from what it was when she found it, new washer and dryer the copper now a laundry sink; a sliding door led to a small but functional powder room. Back out into the kitchen, past the prep-bench with a smaller copper sink, the gas range, next to the fridge beyond which was another sliding door. Ben with a huge grin on his face pulled it back to show her a very compact and efficient looking office. Matt with a huge grin splitting his face standing next to two top of the line computers and office chairs in place.

'When we heard that Kate was on her way with David, we tweaked this space for two, as we thought she may be joining the firm so to speak!' He bent down and whispered in her ear as she passed him, 'told you there would be a surprise!'

'I am sufficiently surprised, thank you from the depths of my heart, this is just stunning!'

Matt in a louder voice continued, 'we put the office here so you could see Gabby's windows, it was the best place for it.' He then showed Brenda and Kate, with David watching over their shoulders what had been put into the space, to make it a very efficient hub of business, everything that was required was there.

'I was wondering where I was going to put my computer when I bought one, but this is wonderful, you will have to show me how I transfer from the lap top, so don't go too far away you and your expertise I will need a lot longer!'

Kate smiled, saying she could help, if Matt would explain it all to her as well. Matt smiled at her, saying it was easy, giving them a demonstration of how to log on and the programmes he had already installed so Iris House Enterprises could officially begin.

They moved out into the clean and neat patio area, and outdoor setting for six in pride of place. Looking back into her house, Brenda sighed; the house seemed to echo her, the whiff of gardenia floated around, everyone realising that Iris was giving her approval.

Mia urged them back into the house and up the internal circular stairs now finished with carpeted treads. Stan taking the lead, moved everyone down into the sitting room to show what a lovely space it had been transformed into.

Sofas, comfortable arm chairs, were now arranged amongst the antique furniture, the pieces arranged in front of the now fully installed gas fire, the ancient mantle and fire surrounds sparkling back in pride of place. New curtains and one of the found rugs completed the décor. Stan apologised about the curtains, the original ones had not survived the cleaning, but what they had rescued they had made into cushions that were in pride of place amongst the others piled onto sofa and chairs.

Matt then showed everyone where the sound system and DVD player was housed in one of the original cupboards next to the fireplace, pointing to the remote controls neatly placed on the top, but asking Brenda for her Iris phone, she handing it to him with a question in her raised eyebrow. He turned back to the cupboard, turning to hand Kate and David their own Iris phone apiece; they turned to Brenda looking confused, then back at Matt and the expression on his face was ingenious.

'These are mobile phones yes, and function as a mobile does. I have loaded relevant phone numbers in them already, your mums of course, a few others and most importantly ours, if you need us we are here. You will also need these as they operate the security measures, and most of the electrical appliances in the house!'

'You are kidding me!' David stated, 'how, show me, this is great!'

Matt smiled enjoying showing off his skills to them both, 'Yep these are you front door keys, as well as allowing remote access to the sound system, lights and TV's in your rooms.'

We have a TV in our room, where?' both of them said together. Everyone laughed at that, Matt quietly saying that he would show them before he left, but there was so much to see. Before the tour continued, he switched Brenda's phone on, taping the screen a couple of times, suddenly the watercolour painting over the fireplace, in an antique frame, came to life, welcoming Kate and David to Iris House.

'Oh Matt, that is exactly what I wanted from you, this is superb!' Brenda was slightly overwhelmed at what she was being show, but knew this was exactly what was needed to take this enterprise from being just so, so to extraordinary.

Once the watercolour was reinstated, Mia and Rebecca urged the group in to the dining room, splendid in all its glory. The dining table extended to its fullest, set with candelabra, silver and glass ware, as though dressed for a dinner party. The three of them gasped, the floor glowed, showing the design in the floor now free from the dust of decades in all its glory. As Brenda had suggested two of the rugs had been used under the table, looking as though they were made just for that place, not hiding the wonderful floor but enhancing it. The whole place was breathing again, living again; Brenda could hear the sound of ghostly laughter, see people seated around the table.

Stan broke the moment by taking Brenda's arm, urging her into the wonderful room.

'Nona and Poppa thought you would like to see the table set, in all its glory.'

All Brenda could do was nod, the centre piece of the table was one of the crystal oil lamps that had been found in the kitchen, sparkling now in the light flooding into the room, being echoed by the crystal glasses and cutlery; the Iris pattern dinnerware in pride of place, just waiting to be used again.

The temporary kitchenette a thing of the past, the space now stocked, as it should be as a secondary serving area for the dining room. A door hid a large microwave, the little fridge replaced with a wine fridge, and the fully operational dumb waiter. Matt was showing Kate and David how it worked, Rebecca and Mia asking if she liked the setting of the table and chairs, apologising that there were only twelve and not the twenty the setting could accommodate.

Brenda shook her head, wiping the tears she had not realised she was shedding from her face, smiling at the anxious faces in front of her, laughing her thanks giving them both a hug of approval, she was very, very happy she told them both. She didn't need the scent of gardenia that flooded the area to realise that Iris was very happy as well, the whole house was alive and breathing again.

'I think we may have to commission someone to make the replacements, as I am sure you will not be able to track any down, although you can try, perhaps the Sotherby people may be able to help you in that. But what you all have done is wonderful, just wonderful thank all so very much.'

The girls and Stan, with help from the boys then showed her and Kate where to put the table ware when not in use, in the new glass topped cabinets that were on either side of the folding doors. Now that she had seen the setting in pride of place, she could see where the pieces could be stored, but she could change them if she wanted, Brenda could see that apart from being functional the cabinets kept the pieces safe, allowing them at last to be seen not hidden away again.

The boys had reduced the table down to a setting for six, putting the inserts back into their niches, rolling up the second rug, putting it in the same place, as though it was meant to go there. The oil lamp had been left in the middle of the table, it was then that Brenda realised the second one was in pride of place in the centre of the restored and working fireplace again as though meant to be.

Mia interrupted her thoughts, 'the other dinner service we uncovered, my aunt said would be for everyday use, we put back into the kitchen. I also bought a white set for you to use every day, if you did not want to use your antiques!'

'Thank you all of you, I appreciate all you have done for Iris House and me over the last four weeks. Especially the herculean effort you made today to get us to completion, and I really did not realise we were that close! As Glen said, all I have to do is pay the bills!'

They all laughed, Matt came over, 'I do have one last thing to show you, can I have your Iris phone again, she handed it over watching as he tapped on the screen, she could see that he had updated the system there were a lot more icons appearing.

Tapping one, watched with everyone the curtains closing over window and doors, making the room very dark, he handed the phone back to Brenda, saying tap the icon with the Iris in it. Brenda did as she was asked and gasped.

'I had the team put lights along the bottom of all the stained-glass windows in the entire building, they deserve to be seen as the works of art they are. When your paintings are returned, let me know and I will come and light them correctly. Go into the conservatory when it really gets dark, use the same icon, but tap the Gardenia flower, let me know what you think?'

Brenda nodded giving him a hug, as he restored the room back to daylight, putting the phone back in her pocket once done. Rebecca, Mia and Matt then took Kate and David back to their rooms downstairs to show them how their own Iris Phones worked, while Stan helped Brenda get acquainted to where everything was in the kitchen, before taking their leave.

'We will be on our way as well,' Mia said, 'we have to check on the surplus, and see if we can return any of it!'

'Can I make a suggestion girls?' Rebecca and Mia looked at each other and nodded, 'hang onto everything. I like the stuff you have showed me, but not used here, as it would have been too much. I think the surplus is going to be very useful to you, as I can see that you are both going to be very busy in the future, the less you have to source to give your joint business a head start would be useful, don't you think? What I think you both should do is sit down and talk about a partnership between you, as you do work very well. Then come back to me once you have decided, I will see what can be done, I have a very good lawyer I can recommend!'

'We will, and we are seriously thinking about it. We know that you will always be here for us, thank you for that. We appreciate the faith you have shown in both of us!'

They turned then saying goodbye to everyone, Rebecca turned back to Brenda, 'we thought we would take Kate and David out on Friday night, didn't think you would mind. They have to see the nightlife of this town; they should be rested by then! Besides I thought Larry said he was taking you out to dinner on Friday, at least he said he was to me!'

'No, I don't mind I would rather they be with you lot, than me. I am too much of a fuddy duddy anyway. Whether I get the invitation or curl up with the wonderful TV in the front room, I don't care. Thank you for caring about them.'

'Our pleasure,' the girls yelled as they went up the stairs taking Matt with them, joining the exodus out the front door.

Brenda, Kate and David explored their new world for a while, before Brenda asked David to show her how her Iris Phone could do all the things Matt had said. From times past, David knew he only had to show her the basics again, then she figured out the rest from there. Then they made the first cups of tea and coffee in the new kitchen, everything working perfectly, all was right in the world.

Chapter 61

THEY ARRIVED BY CAB at Linda and Shane's at seven, the rain falling in a light mist, carefully keeping the bottles in their snug nest flat. Linda opening the door ushering them into the welcoming room, David looking around as he walked assessing the large open space of the warehouse conversion. Sir James waited, looking very relaxed moving forward to assist when he saw David with the precious parcel.

'Careful my boy, they need very careful handling you know!'

'I know Sir James, I did a six-month stint in the Victorian Hills, helping a vigneron one long university break. As soon as Larry and Dennis showed me mum's cellar I thought I had died and gone to heaven. Do you know what she has down there?'

'Alas my boy; I did not have time to see it on my last visit, but I hold you to show me when I get an invite to dinner, promise!'

'A dinner invitation, Sir James, you know you are welcome to come and share the spare boxes of noodles Dennis keeps leaving me at any time; you don't need an invitation!'

Brenda said, hearing the end of the conversations, walking into the room, going up to Shane, who wheeled forward to be introduced to the children, and meet the son who his wife had recommended for the job in the firm. Brenda kneeling to give him a hug, he looked at Linda coming into the room with Kate, smiling at her startled reaction to seeing Brenda on her knees.

'A proper hug, I worked out how to give you one! Shane, may I make the formal introductions, the young man attempting to untangle your wine from the box, is as you may have guessed my son David, this is my daughter Kate!'

Both children smiled at the introduction, Shane taking the firm handshake, Kate gave saying she hoped that was ok, but she was not dressed to give him a Brenda hug, but acknowledged it was a good way to give a proper one. Shane laughed and shook his head, saying the handshake was fine, going over to David asking what he needed, retrieving the decanter and items requested putting them on the bench beside him.

Linda moved Brenda and Kate over to the sofa, while the men struggled with the wine in the kitchen. She asked how the rest of the day had gone after they had left the office. Brenda with Kate adding bits, along with the occasional comment from David in the kitchen, told Linda about the house, what the Haddon's, Mia and Stan with his family had done.

'So, it is finished!' Linda asked incredulously.

'Did I hear that it is all finished, the workmen have finished completely?' Sir James walked over to the sofa, sitting next to Kate.

'Yes, Sir James, all mum has to do is pay the bills. Sorry, I mean all you have to do is pay the bills, which I am sure will be coming in very soon!' Kate said, then laughed at the expression on his face, the eyes of which twinkled at her.

'Just like your mother, you know that the first thing she asked when I gave her the job!', at Kates raised eyebrow, he continued with a chuckle, 'was how much was she allowed to spend!'

'Sounds about right,' David said coming over to the group, Sir James looked a question at him, 'have to let it breathe for at least five minutes' sir, patience it will be worth it. Yes, the first words should be how long and how much, do you know what the answer is?'

'All right,' Shane said as he moved over to everyone, a tray with glasses and a bottle of white wine in his lap. Kate jumped up to help him, carrying them to the coffee table, 'I will bite, what is the answer?'

'A piece of string!' David said completely stone-faced. Everyone looked at him; Kate was trying to see the reaction to her brother's very warped sense of humour. She had heard it before of course, but this little icebreaker sometimes went down like a lead balloon.

Sir James kept saying 'a piece of string', puzzled he looked at Shane, then Shane looked at David and started to laugh.

'A piece of string, oh I get it. Yes of course, very useful that piece of string,' continuing to chuckle as he filled the wine glasses. Watching the straight face looking at Sir James, who was even more perplexed.

'A piece of string sir, is as long as you need and you use as much as you need!'

The old man chuckled, looking at the young man in front of him, he had a brain this one. 'Oh, my boy, very funny, very funny indeed! I can foresee an improvement in the level of conversation at the garden parties!'

'Garden Parties, what Garden Parties mum?' David said, looking at Brenda who was handing out the wine to Linda and Kate.

'I am holding a Garden Party in a fortnights time, love; I will need help from you and Kate's to organise it. That is if I don't ship you up North to see your Uncle, if that is the level of jokes you are telling these days!'

Sir James realised almost at once that the children did not know the full extent of Brenda's inheritance, if they knew anything at all. He immediately turned the conversation to Linda and Shane's house in Tuscany, asking how the renovations were going, earning a grateful smile from Brenda.

Shane invited David to view the plans, and to judge his level of competency for the role in the firm, they went off into the study / workroom speaking Architect jargon. Linda asked if she could have a word with Kate, saying that there were a couple of things to talk about with her new role, going off into Linda's study, leaving Sir James and Brenda talking about the Haddon's, but when they were all out of earshot, Sir James turned to Brenda.

'My dear I had a rather interesting phone call this afternoon, did Linda tell you? It had to do with Maud Prendergast!'

'Just as we were leaving her office, she said you were talking to someone from Sotheby's. Trouble Sir James, what should I do?'

He smiled, took her hand patting it in reassurance. 'Trouble, yes it could have been, but I have been waiting to take that family down a peg or two for years. Seems that Ms. Prendergast has been putting it around that you have stolen goods!' Brenda gasped, so it begins she thought, 'Is anyone listening to her talk?'

'Oh, I had a good talk with her boss, Sir Charles Ashton, who had called me in regards to the report that Maud had submitted. He is the head curator, a partner in Sotheby's, and an old whist crony of mine. I don't think anyone will be taking her seriously for a long time! I hear she has taken a job at an archaeological dig in Turkey; it will be a very long and very back breaking time!'

'Sir James, how did you manage that?'

'Well when I told him that the new Lady Lucas, who was a very good friend of mine,' and he smiled nodding at her, taking a sip of his wine, 'would be very unhappy that her confidentiality with Sotheby's was being impinged by an employee of the company, while having been retained to evaluate the inheritance, he was most aghast. My dear don't look so down cast, you are going to have to accept that you are now Lady Lucas, may I also add that you will need to tell those two sooner than later. Charles also told me that the reason for Maud's allegations is that the pattern on the dinner service is very rare and valuable. It was registered for exclusive use of the Lucas Line, there were only two sets made. One you have, and it is complete, the other has vanished; so, what you have is very, very valuable. He asked me to pass on his assurances that this will never happen again, he will personally bring all the valuations over to me. I also pointed out it was not only Maud but the others in her little group, bar one, a Frederick Austin Healy, I believe his name is, were spreading the malicious rumours, he promised he would make everyone aware of the huge mistake they had made. He hoped that he may be introduced to you in the near future!'

He patted her on the arm, 'I will do everything in my power to help you through this time, you know that; it will work out, just you wait and see!'

He turned the conversation to asking about Gabby and Charlie's twins, as he heard Linda and Kate returning, being very surprised when Brenda told him the names they had given the babies, he nodded saying very fitting. He had been inundated with calls from people that had passed the new and improved Iris House, wanting to know the name of the company that had done the renovations in such a speedy time frame; they were all going to be very busy people, very soon.

Dinner was a wonderful success, with Brenda regaling the group with anecdotes of the build, and the company was wonderful. Brenda was helping Linda bring out the desert, Linda asking if she had heard from Larry, she had tried to call him to invite him for the evening, but had no reply.

'Oh, he was meeting with his father, apparently, he had come up to town, but was only here for the one night!'

'So, why are you not with him?' Linda asked bluntly.

'Because I am having a wonderful evening, introducing my children to the new friends I like very much. Who don't make a fuss, besides why would Larry want me there visiting his father?'

'Brenda my dear heart, for a start he probably came up to town to actually meet you! He would have heard the rumours about you even in his country retreat, you are big news, oh no,' as she saw her stricken face, 'not for the Lady Lucas that is definitely not common knowledge, but for what you have achieved with Iris House! As for Larry, I am sure he would want you everywhere if you get my drift!'

Brenda laughed, looking at her new friend, hoping she would not say anything more. Wondering if she could voice the concerns she felt about the relationship, to this wonderful self-contained, supremely confident woman.

Linda realised that there was more going on in this new relationship than met the eye. 'Ah, well it is a waiting game, huh? OK wait but not for very long my dear; there are an awful lot of women interested in our Larry!'

They moved back into the dining room with the desert and coffee, Brenda grateful that Linda had not said more, but she was more than a little unnerved with the conversation., and that Larry had a string of women after him, so to speak.

Everyone had enjoyed the wine with the meal. Brenda much to Sir James disgust, not opening the second bottle of wine, advising it was for Linda and Shane only. She placated him with a bribe of half a dozen bottles out of the cellar, once it had been properly catalogued. Giles and David could pick out the best for him, he laughed, the mental picture of Giles in the wine cellar, kept him chuckling all the way home.

Brenda left Linda and Shane, telling them both to come and see the house themselves the following day. It was quite amazing the peace, without the hordes of workmen around; also for them to keep Saturday night free, as she was going to christen the kitchen with a small dinner party. Although she was so rusty, they may have to resort to reheating Dennis's noodles. Kate and David looked at her, then muttered, yes mum sure that would never happen.

Chapter 62

THE REST OF THE week was a whirlwind. It began on the Tuesday morning with Linda and Shane arriving to view the finished house. Linda came armed with the files on the prospective guest for the apartments, Kate laughing, saying she would have to show her how with the new equipment now installed they could transfer all files electronically, much to Shane and David's amusement, Brenda stating she still liked the paper files at the moment, thank you very much. Linda smiling at Kate, saying that she would have to convince Sir James as well, he liked the paper files, then she asked if they could both check over them over now she had brought them, and pick their top three, and see her later in the week.

Shane and David discussing the work now finished, confirming that they would not have done anything differently. Shane asking David to come into the office to see him, as he wanted to discuss what would be expected of him, he also wanted to introduce him to the other partners. Also, asking Brenda for all the contacts of the people that had done such spectacular and magnificent work, especially the Haddon's, all arms of that group, Dan and Peter's as well, as he wanted his firm to get to know these talented people better, and use their expertise in a couple of projects coming up.

Brenda and Kate then organised themselves, to check on the prospective tenants; making up information folders, sending them out with a request list to advise preference, room requirement, number of people using the space, this they found very easy to assemble with the equipment Matt had installed in the office. Kate also saving the information sheets in the individual files she started in the computer, if the prospective tenants required a digital copy to fill out, being more efficient she told her mum.

They also rang the personal assistants of the top three on the short list they made, to see first if the accommodation was still required, and to advise that further details would need to be advised and to ask how they wanted to receive this by mail or electronic. Brenda also asked Kate and David to sleep in each of the apartments for a couple of nights, to give an independent rating on the spaces.

Friday dawned, the end of one hectic week; eight days before the first guest was to arrive, confirmed by email the night before. Brenda still could not believe they had succeeded in getting everything ready. Sitting in her office watching the photo's flick through on her computer screen (of course Matt had downloaded all the photographs taken and turned them into a roaming screen saver, (as if she could ever forget those frantic weeks), still she had to pinch herself that this beautiful building was her home.

The afternoon saw Brenda in Linda's office, to give her the top three names on the list. Saying she hoped Linda agreed as she had already confirmed the booking; first tenant to arrive in one week's time.

'Mind, why should I mind, they will be your guests. I am curious to know whom you have chosen though?'

Linda moved them to the sitting area of her office, where she seemed to do most of her thinking, Brenda realising she avoided her desk as much as she did. After discussing the guest chosen, then lining up the prospective tenants for the next group, Linda said she was satisfied that Brenda and Kate knew what they were doing and to carry on.

Laughing with her as Brenda said she intended to do just that.

'You are ok for dinner tomorrow night? I am having the house to myself tonight; the kids are going out with the Haddon's, I don't really expect to see them till the morning!'

'Yes, it is still ok, have you heard from Larry this week? You have been very quiet on that front?'

'He has been away, work I believe. I got a quick message and email telling me to enjoy the peace of the house while I can, before the madness begins, I am not sure when he will be back?'

Linda looked at her friend, for the first time saw doubt in her face, realising that Brenda was still very unsure about her relationship, "Ah well, just in case I will get in some of Dennis's Noodles, if I get a last-minute call postponing dinner tomorrow, as you may have a better offer, when he does get in contact!'

Brenda laughed at the comment, and after checking that all was good with the arrangements she and Kate had come up with left very shortly after. Walking slowly back to Iris House, wondering at the silence from Larry. Wondering if she had done something wrong, or if perhaps having her children close had somehow pushed him away. Perhaps one of the other women in his life was claiming his attention.

'*Get a grip Brenda*,' she said to herself, '*he is a free agent, just as you are, you would not give up your independence and freedom, why should he. Independent people living independent lives, wasn't that what you said you would do, if you ever found someone who you could care about again?*'

It had been a long time since she had even thought about a relationship, thinking about her word of caution to Larry, asking for him to take some time, she shook her head and tried to put Larry out of her mind.

Thinking of the night before when Dennis had been over amazed and wondering that they had settled in so well, so quickly; although as he said, with an apartment like this anyone not settling in would have to come from outer space!

He had come to give Brenda the information for the set-up of the "Garden Party", she also asked if he could find a String Quartet to play, wanting them to be set up in one of the alcoves in the Conservatory, there was space as the billiard table David had sweet talked Rebecca into buying would not be arriving for a month or two. They finalised the details of tables and chairs, crockery and cutlery etc., checking that Glen had also organised the Marquee to be delivered on the following Friday, Dennis adding that Glen and some of the boys would be with it to set it up.

'So, when do the first official guests of Iris House arrive?' he asked as he sat at the big kitchen table, savouring a glass of the vintage wine.

'First guest arrives on Saturday next, day of the party. I have warned his PA of what was happening, but he had to be here that day he has a meeting in the morning he cannot miss. It is the way Sir James and I want to continue; it will be the normality of life that will make the differences to whether the guest returns or not, this is my home and I will not change my life for a guest. It could be interesting around here in the next six months or so!'

She smiled and picked up the pace of her walk home, the drizzle had started to get a little heavier, breaking into her thoughts, and she wanted to get back home before it developed further.

Music was playing when she arrived at the house, Michael Buble, one of Kate's and her favourite singers. She yelled I am home, going down to the study to put the files and her briefcase on her desk, to check on any messages.

'Back so soon?' Kate said putting her head around the door, 'What did Linda think of the choices, do you want a cuppa?'

'Yes, to the cuppa please, Linda said to go for it, just as well she did as we have already organised the arrivals!' Brenda said, going out joining her daughter in the kitchen, moving out to the patio, the rain had stopped, enjoying the sunshine coming into the courtyard. David had laughed when she told him that the glass was bullet proof, he shaking his head at the way his mum's brain worked, and how the ideas she had just worked as well.

'Where is David?' Brenda asked.

'He had to go to Shane's office, something to do with a design needing a fresh perspective or something, I don't know. He will be back later, the Haddon's are coming here first before we go out tonight, you don't mind mum, do you? I even offered them accommodation for the night, if that is ok, we would get some opinions on the flats if they can remember using them of course!'

'I don't mind love, might as well use them, I want a lived in feel to them anyway, not the sterile hotel room feel. I will be getting Nona and the Family to clean them all before Friday. Oh, we did send the invitations out to them, didn't we?'

'Of course, we did, in the first lot, you would not forget them. We have had confirmation from them, all of Mr. Jones's, Glens, Marcus workers along with all of the Kew Gardening Team, we have even included the neighbours who when I invited them were very, very happy that the building works were finally finished, and eager to see the finished product. Everyone we have invited will be here, it is going to be so much fun!'

Kate left her mother to her tea and to digest the information, going to see if she had received a reply on a couple of bookings Linda had asked her to look over, as she was not sure Jane had already left the office in organisational skills if not in body.

Brenda finished her tea, then changed from her business suit, putting on jeans, shirt and cotton jumper; even with the sun warming the air it was still a little chilly in the basement. She had wandered around making up some nibbles for the hoards that were to descend on them in the shape of the Haddon family, pottering around filling in time, but she could not put her finger on what was bothering her.

The doorbell rang, 'I'll get it,' Kate called, 'probably David forgot his phone!'

She was leaning on the door frame looking out over the patio, wondering what the plants would look like when they had a chance to grow, when a pair of strong arms came around her.

'Penny for them, you were miles away?'

'I was wondering if I should pull the weeds in the terrace, then I realised I would not know a weed from a herb!' She turned and smiled at him, returning the kiss he gave her, suddenly wanting more.

Shaken she moved slightly to look at him, as handsome as ever, with his crooked smile. Dressed like her in jeans, shirt and jumper, with a jacket she could see he had thrown over a chair.

'I have missed you,' he said looking at her smiling face, 'do you realise that there are areas in this country that you just cannot get a mobile signal. I felt like I was on the moon at times!'

'Oh, that would be a nice place to be, not to feel guilty because you physically cannot ring anyone, it is just not your fault!'

'Good, I am glad you think so, let's go!'

'Go Larry, go where?'

'Well I have been thinking on your request, I have found the perfect place for a weekend away, which you said you wanted to do, so let's go!'

'But, but I have Shane and Linda coming for dinner, the kids just arrived..I.I.I don't know what to say!'

'Here you are mum, all packed! See you Sunday or even Monday! Don't worry David and I will be fine and promise to keep everything under control. What little there is to do anyway!' Kate stood at the door to the kitchen, a jacket over one arm, holding a packed weekend bag in the other.

Brenda looked at both of them, Larry seeing the look pass over her face, 'don't get angry at Kate love. I rang earlier to speak to you, Kate told me you were at Linda's, but I just missed you when I called her, she said something about 'Noodles'?'

Brenda looked at him, then at Kate, smiling suddenly as all doubts were erased in an instant, a hint of gardenia floated around, 'why not, come on let's go before I change my mind, this is so reckless of me!'

They went out to the Range Rover, Brenda looking at Larry who had a smile on his face as though he could not believe she had said yes. 'We need this to get to one of the blank spots; I promise it will be worth it, trust me?'

'Absolutely, I have missed your company this week; more than I can say I also missed your counsel at times. Although we have managed to arrange everything, and I think the children have both settled in really well!'

'I have missed you too. The number of time I wanted to ring and hear your voice, to give me encouragement and a bit of common sense, but was unable to do so. I can also believe the children have settled in with your encouragement.

Chapter 63

THEY HAD MOVED OUT into the flow of traffic, it wasn't too heavy, but due to it being rush hour, it was already busy enough for Larry to concentrate a little harder, to get into the right lanes for the direction he wanted to go. Soon they were leaving the city behind, heading out on the Salisbury road, continuing up towards Bath; they had been driving for a little more than two hours, the evening was beginning to settle in around them.

Brenda enjoyed the companionship, the easy banter between the two of them once the city had been left behind. Larry relaxed, as he always did while in Brenda's company, he felt that she was a long-lost friend, now reunited back to becoming something more than a friend, to be the companion that he needed, to complete him.

This was the decision he had made on the lonely nights he had been away, that Brenda had that quality he had been searching for a very long time, someone he could trust. He had been traveling to find out more of the Legacy, the firm realising he was the only one that could check everything out for them, and be thorough in doing it, as he had Brenda's best interests at heart, he had been following a lead from Michael in regards to the Lucas estate, but had found some very interesting results indeed.

Eventually he turned off down a country lane, Brenda turned from looking at the beautiful countryside they were travelling through, admiring the cottages of the villages as they passed, turning to look at Larry when he said, 'the villages look pretty but the inhabitants find them very difficult in modern times to live in.

Laughing at her raised eyebrow, and comment of one 'of the many dead spots, I take it!'

He wondered how she would take this next piece in the Iris Puzzle, 'almost, well I found this little place, realised it was your perfect weekend retreat that you asked about. So, I booked us a room for the weekend, it is just the most marvellous place; I loved it immediately I hope you do too?'

They had turned into a driveway, although not really late, Larry turned on the headlights to see the road ahead clearly. Not far off the main road, it broadened into a parking area, big enough for several cars, although there was only one other parked. Larry pulled into a spot, in front of a two-storied manor house; picking up both their bags led Brenda inside to a foyer, hearing a female voice saying, 'I am coming!'

A spritely elderly lady, grey haired but ramrod straight moved from a doorway to the left of the magnificent central staircase.

'Mr. Morecombe, welcome back, I have your room ready; this must be Ms. Chalmers, welcome I hope you enjoy your stay at Fitzgibbon Manor!'

Brenda looked at her in shock at hearing the familiar name, stammered a greeting, seeing the devilish look on Larry's straight face, thought to herself his is enjoying this entirely too much.

'Thank you, Mrs. Chambers, I hope you are well?' Larry asked as the lady in question picked up a room key, once the register had been signed, motioning for them to follow her.

'How was the drive down, not too much traffic I hope? We are light on this weekend, only yourselves and one other couple, they are not due till tomorrow morning. Unfortunately, dinner is over, but I can see if Mr. Chambers can rustle you up something, see you in the parlour in about half an hour say?'

'That would be wonderful, the traffic was horrendous, but it was pleasant once we got out of the city. Thank you we will see you in half an hour.'

Mrs. Chambers had turned left at the top of the stairs, going to a set of rooms at the front of the house. She ushered them inside showing the room, where everything was, leaving them with a 'see you downstairs.' She went down to advise her husband that a small supper was required, wondering at the silence from Ms. Chalmers and her reaction to the house, as she had been trying to see everywhere at once on her journey up to the room.

'*Ah well,*' she thought, '*if there was one think in life she had realised, always expect the unexpected from people!*'

'Fitzgibbon Manor?' Brenda stated in a flat questioning tone as the door closed after Mrs. Chambers left.

He could hear a world of questions in that one phrase; Larry turned and watched Brenda put her bag on the very large, comfortable looking king sized canopied bed. He could not stop his wayward imagination thinking of them both in that bed, at least he hoped so after he had told her about his finding of the last few days.

'Well yes, now let me explain, please. One of the things I have been doing over the last few weeks is checking on the details of your legacy, at least Iris's part, you know that?'

Brenda nodded watching the expression on his face.

'This was the first place, and easiest place I found. The Fitzgibbon Inheritance is quite substantial; this was the original manor house, it was turned into an exclusive B&B only has eight guest rooms, in this its latest incarnation. It is quite an extensive area, you can fish, ramble, play tennis on the championship equipped courts, although don't try and book the month before Wimbledon, as the place is booked out with tennis players, practising for the main event! You can even take nine holes of golf, and there are plans to expand that to the normal eighteen, shortly. The day spa in the grounds, does very well all through the year!'

He came to a halt, not knowing how Brenda was taking this, as she had moved round the room as he was speaking, finally coming to a halt in front of the bay window overlooking the grounds. There was a wonderful arrangement of flowers in the centre of a table placed in the window alcove, with a bottle of champagne in a bucket and two glasses, standing with her back to him, she absently played with the flowers, her mind a world away. She was trying to fit this new place into her life, also wondering what else was to come!

'Hmm, well I think you have done extraordinarily well, of course my estimation may go up, with the quality of the service this evening, of all kinds!'

Larry laughed, going over to her pulling her into his arms, loving the feel of her, the smell of her fresh and vibrant, she moulded to him, returning his kiss.

'Thank you, Larry, thank you for caring, I do appreciate your efforts. Now how about some food, let's leave the champagne till later shall we?' Brenda said looking towards the bathroom, with a raise of her eyebrow.

Larry gave her a devilish grin, looking at the bathroom, his imagination again running riot, 'oh I believe we can definitely enjoy it later. Come on let's go and see what Mr. Chambers has for us; one of the reasons this place does so well is that he is a five star Michelin Chef, he runs very successful cooking weekends here, as well as his restaurants around the country!'

The food was exquisite, with a glass of champagne to start, then a red that went with the veal steaks and fresh vegetables. Mr. Chambers came in at the end asking if they wanted any desert?

'Desert, I could not even fit in another sip of wine! Thank you, Mr. Chambers, that meal was delicious for something you just threw together. Are you by any chance running a class this weekend and if so do you have any spare places?' Brenda asked, might as well go in for the whole experience, she thought, I am also going to arrange at least one pampering session at the day spa, to check that out as well.

'Ms. Chalmers, I think we can squeeze you in. We only have one couple booked for the class this weekend, a second couple cancelled at the last minute, we were going to have to tell them it can only be run with a minimum of four, so if you and Mr. Morecombe would like to attend we can now run it?'

Larry was hoping to do some fishing, but saw the look on Brenda's face and decided the fishing could wait for another time. 'I would like that very much Mr. Chambers, when and where please, so we can fit in whatever else Brenda has in mind!'

He laughed at Larry's prompt reply, liked the smile that his lady had bestowed on him, wondering where he had seen her before, as she was most familiar. Yes, one very nice couple, he told them that they would be expected in the foyer at two pm for a ramble through the grounds, then back into the kitchen to cook for dinner at seven. Checking on their likes and dislikes or allergies hoped that they would enjoy the remainder of the evening, to help themselves to port or liqueurs that were on the sideboard. With a nod and smile left them to their choice and the warmth of the fire burning merrily in the grate.

Brenda leaned over to Larry, said very quietly, 'I don't think I want the port, too heavy. I was thinking more of something with bubbles!' Smiling at the look on Larry's face added, 'give me ten minutes!' Larry watched as Brenda rose, moving across the room and up the stairs, remembering the champagne in the room, and the very large bathtub, slowly finishing his glass of wine, anticipating an interesting soak in the tub.

As she got to the top of the stairs, a light down the opposite corridor beckoned, she thought she heard her name being softly said, thinking it might have been Mrs. Chambers said 'Hello?'. Gardenia surrounded her with a ghostly laugh her feet moved her towards the light and a painting.

The couple looked so young, Iris would only have been seventeen or eighteen, Edward in his early twenties. They smiled at her, Iris holding onto her husband's hand as it rested on her shoulder, in the light Iris had dark hair, and a fanciful notion came to her that it could have been her sitting in that chair, they looked similar.

With a laugh at her ideas, gave the couple a small curtsey, turned back to her bedroom and to continue the evening.

Brenda woke in an unfamiliar bed, wondering briefly where she was then realising that the very heavy weight across her was Larry. Carefully she moved the arm, going into the bathroom, enjoying the solitude in the very opulent space, which was a little different in the morning and without the candles. Coming back, she moved over to the window, where she could watch the sun just rising across the gardens, seeing the scope of the land they had driven through in the gloom the evening before.

Larry stirred, she scuttled back to be beside him when he woke, watching him wake seeing the smile in his eyes when he saw her watching him.

'Morning, do you know how many mornings I wanted you here with me?' at her negative shake of the head, 'all of them!' She laughed and snuggled closer into him, he pulling her as close as he could.

'Would it be forward of me to say that I wanted that too?' Brenda whispered still a little of that lingering doubt, but now very sure of her feelings toward him.

'No, it would be honest, I hope we can at least be honest with each other. Let us enjoy this weekend, and see how we go shall we?' Larry realised that the admission of Brenda wanting to wake up with him, was a big one. *One step at a time Larry my boy*, he thought.

They enjoyed a morning ramble, after a light breakfast. Brenda telling Mrs Chambers that she was still working off the wonderful meal of the night before, ignored Larry's raised eyebrow. As they walked Larry pointed out the holdings of the property. They passed the Day Spa, already with outside visitors, Brenda ducking in to make an appointment. The Golf Club, already with people on the greens, then the working farm which was in itself a rarity in these days. The proposed new area for the villas, as extra accommodation, to enhance the B&B not to replace it. Brenda hoped they would be kept in keeping with the style of the original manor buildings, arriving back for a light lunch.

She arrived back from the Spa, in time to start her cooking class with Mr. Chambers, and the couple that had arrived while they were out walking. The afternoon was fun, going and picking the vegetables out of the home garden, walking around the farm, picking out from the cool stores the meat to cook with the vegetables. Mr. Chambers saying that most of the produce from the farm was used in nearly all his restaurants, he was very happy to have the source so close to his home base.

The afternoon was full of laughter, rainbows danced in the very up to date commercial kitchen that the class was held in. Brenda realised with a gasp that the sunlight streaming into the room was coming from a series of stained glass windows, the focal point of which was a repeat of the Iris Window in London, but multiplied, as the Irises were in bunches.

'Ah yes Brenda,' Mr. Chambers said as he realised what had taken her concentration away from the sauce she was making. 'The window is original to the Manor, when we applied for planning permission to build this cooking centre, we were advised we had to save the window, reusing it in any new building. We were very happy to do so, in fact we rebuilt the new structure with all the elements of the original replaced, in situ almost. It has always been a boon with the light that it brings, we have the history of the house printed up if you are interested, I will get Mrs. Chambers to put a copy in your room.'

Brenda nodded and smiled her thanks; the sunlight was a benediction, she knew, the slight waft of gardenia confirmed that what had happened to the Manor was meant to be, and had Iris's stamp of approval. They all enjoyed the cooking class, Mr. Chambers was a very good and patient teacher; the results of the afternoon were enjoyed in the restaurant that evening, which had quite a few more patrons, being a Saturday than the night before.

Once Brenda and Larry had left on the Sunday morning, Mrs. Chambers was helping put the room to rights again for the next set of visitors. As she passed the painting in the hall on the way to the linen closet, she stopped and took another look, wondering at the resemblance between the young woman and Brenda. The likeness was remarkable, shaking her head at her fancy, continued on to get the towels from the cupboard, reminding herself to mention the painting to her husband, to see if he agreed.

Chapter 64

LARRY TOLD HER THEY had some driving to do on the Sunday, it was with a wrench that they checked out, driving down the lane way, Brenda looking back at the first piece of the history puzzle that she had been given. Hoping that all of them would fit in so well, but realising that would be a false hope, knowing the attitude and greed of people. She had told Larry about Maud Prendergast, he had been concerned until she told him about Sir James's solution.

'He is right you know! You should tell Kate and David about all of this, they would be all right. We need to have them in the office very soon anyway; they have papers to sign as well!'

'I know, but I am still trying to get used to it all. I received a parcel from Mr. Fawkes the other day; I opened it and just put it aside, not knowing how to deal with it!' At Larry's raised eyebrow in question, 'it was information in regards to the investiture, and a Debbretts Guide!'

'Oh well I can go through it with you if you would like me to? I will have to know what to do as well that is if I am invited?'

'Hmm, well I will have to think about that,' she mused not looking at him, 'of course your past performances will be taken into consideration, but you do realise that once I become 'a Lady' well we will just have to see!'

This was spoken in the most regal and condescending voice she could muster, Lady Dorsett would surely have approved, and she held the rigid pose to go with the voice for a moment, before turning to look at Larry's stricken face, she could not hold it, bursting into peals of laughter. Larry took a quick glance from the road to see who had magically appeared in the car, then he realised what Brenda had done and burst out laughing as well.

'Oh, you had me then for a moment, oh my god, you sounded just like my Great Aunt Alice; please do not do that again ever, and never around my family, some of them would not get the joke, and you nearly gave me a heart attack!'

The devils were dancing in her eyes as she laughed along with him, 'Larry I am so sorry, but I could not help it. This life I am now living is so like a play I once was in, amateur dramatics stuff, but my part called for an arrogant noble woman, when I went to rehearsals I scared the life out of half the cast. I am sorry I promise not to do it again, unless uncontrollably provoked, want to join in next time?'

He laughed again, she was the most fascinating woman, he thought he knew her, but there were sides to her that were just amazing.

Brenda sobered, turning in her seat slightly to see his profile, 'To answer your question, of course you are invited, you are my anchor, the sanity (along with my children) in this crazy world I have landed in. I would have been lost without you the last few weeks, you must realise this?'

He was watching the road, but his heart leapt at this confession, he took a hand-off the wheel, took hers and kissed the back and palm.

'Now I do, I thank you for the trust you have put in me; I won't knowingly let you down, but I am only human so you will forgive me if I occasionally slip?'

She laughed, her hand still tingling where he kissed it, watching his smile light his eyes, enjoying the feeling of trusting someone again.

They had driven through some quintessential English countryside, beautiful in its spring colours; he slowly turned the car off the road into a very run down driveway. In amongst the overgrown trees and foliage you could just make out the shape of two sandstone pillars that would have formed a magnificent gateway, they in turn attached to what would be a rather substantial sandstone wall, stretching both ways into the distance on either side. The wrought iron gates you could just see, were still attached, to the supports blocked by the mass of foliage covering everything, were open to allow access. He pulled the car to a stop just inside the gates, next to the shell of a large gatehouse that had its roof fallen in and walls partly demolished. Turning in his seat, looking at her bemused expression.

'Brenda, before we go much further I have to tell you something. When I found Fitzgibbon Manor, I also on advice and information from Michael, found 'Broadmeadows!' at Brenda's raised and quizzical eyebrow, 'it is the family home and estate of the Lucas side of the inheritance!'

'Ah, ok!' Brenda said on a sigh, unsure of what was coming but the neglect she could see around her did not bode well.

'This is the Broadmeadows of today; it has been like this for many years. I was unsure if I should bring you here, but you have to see it; I am sorry love, but it is not very good!'

He put the car in gear and slowly, avoiding debris of all kinds moved up what was once a magnificent drive way. It still was magnificent in it dishevelled state, lined on both sides with majestic oak trees, a couple had fallen, one across the road, he had to go off road to the side to go around it. The park they were driving through was magnificent and large; she could see deer in the tree line across a field, up a rise that only showed more overgrown jungle ahead, after driving for nearly fifteen minutes topping another gentle rise, when they turned through a break in the foliage, in front of them was the rubble of what was once a great house.

Brenda caught her breath on a sob. She was out of the car almost before Larry could put the brake on, racing across the dividing ground to a set of magnificent sandstone steps, all that was left that proclaimed it a building. Piles of rubble were everywhere, half walls, burnt shell proclaiming a large and imposing structure once stood on the site. Tears were flooding down her face, she was weeping for what was lost, walking around touching the stone where she could.

Larry watched as she made the pilgrimage, wondering what he should do. A whiff of gardenia passed him, realising that he should just be there for her, when she realised he was waiting. He turned the car around, parking it beside a magnificent oak tree, getting out and moving over to where she sat on a piece of the sidewall. Brenda saw him coming, getting up and meeting him, tears were running down her face, he gathered her into his arms, consoling her, giving her his handkerchief, holding her while she composed herself.

'Why Larry, why did this happen? What happened to all of the Lords Lucas forward thinking, here of all places?' She said as she turned again to look at the ruins, still with his comforting arm steadying her.

'We are not sure love, but there is a small piece in one of the bundles from the safe,' he turned her then to look at her, 'we don't have all of them, do we?'

Brenda looked at him, explaining there were still papers and other things in the safe; she hadn't been able to get to them till the kitchen was finished. Glena and Dan had moved it into the new study, behind a false door to conceal it; she had not had the chance to check it out yet, was not sure what she would find.

'Well we will have to read them all, and any other papers in there! The piece we have states that Lord Lucas had begun the removal of Broadmeadows. We don't know really what that meant,' he answered her questioning look, 'but it talks about a new beginning and the goods being moved to a safe place?'

The rain started to fall again, so he moved them back into the warmth of the car, as he continued.

'We do know that this place was hit by at least one stray German bomb during the Blitz, then there was a fire, but the locals say that it had been a shell for a long time before that. They thought it had something to do with death duties or land taxes, the family were long gone as well, so it was forgotten in time.'

Brenda shivered, snuggling down into the seat, looking around the estate, seeing off behind the oaks, through a gap made by a fallen one, another structure, almost hidden by overgrown foliage.

A summer house, the thought came to her, it looked to be made out of steel if she was to believe her eyes, she smiled through her tears; a ray of sunshine broke through the clouds, illuminating the structure, she realised that it could be larger than she first thought, as there was a very large area under all the foliage, not a summer house, more a large green house perhaps. The familiar scent wafted over them both, suddenly Brenda knew this was foolish; there was nothing to do but rebuild, and rebuild better than before if she could, this she knew was what the inheritance was for.

Larry watched the expressions cross Brenda's face, wondering what was going on behind those beautiful blue eyes. He put the car into gear when he asked if she was ready to leave, and got a nod yes in reply. Moving slowly out through the open gates back onto the road. Brenda was silent as he drove, he suggested a counter meal at the next pub, he knew it would be good; she nodded again, he was a bit perplexed by the silence, but at least the tears had stopped, so he left her to her thinking and drove carefully through the rain.

Brenda pulled herself together while they had a lovely counter meal in a quaint pub in the village on the edge of the estate. Larry was telling her that although the house was a ruin, the village and land around it was not, explaining that the tithes from the land were very good indeed. They chatted amiably as he drove them back through the fitful afternoon weather, sometimes in blazing sunshine, sometimes in drizzling rain back to the London house, and whatever mess the children had left after their impromptu party over the weekend.

Larry laughing at the visions that Brenda shared with him, of previous times she had gone away, then the carnage she had been greeted with on her return. It was quiet when they arrived back in the late afternoon, no sign of life, a note on the fridge said the children had been invited to the Haddon's for dinner, they would be back later, don't wait up, see them in the morning.

'Them?' Larry said, looking at Brenda, a bemused smile on her face, she looked at him, an eyebrow raised as he slowly caught on, 'Oh!'

'Looks like the children have definitely accepted you into our lives, love, didn't take as long as I thought! Do you want to stay; I would like your company?'

'Of course, I want to stay, can't disappoint the kids in the morning, can I? What are we having for dinner, 'Dennis's Noodles?''

Brenda laughed and hugged him, Larry took their bags into the bedroom, as she moved into the kitchen to see what there was left in the fridge to make up for dinner, and to put the kettle on. A damp drizzle had fallen over London, it suited her mood, she had not successfully shaken the dismals since they had left Broadmeadows, but she would work through them. She could hear a mobile ringing, thinking it might be hers, went to find her bag; stopping as she heard Larry talking. They had switched off both of them while away, another thing to like about this man, he hated mobile phones as much as she did!

'Sorry love, but I am going to have to go. That was Andrew, he and Ewon have been trying to get me all weekend; apparently, father had a fall on Saturday morning, it's nothing really serious, but serious enough,' he saw the worry cross her face, 'he is in the local hospital, with a broken leg! So, I am afraid I will be away for a few days, is that ok?'

'Larry of course it is, don't be silly, we can at least keep in touch. You need to be with your dad, go on, don't worry about me or the kids; here take this with you.'

Brenda turned and gently pulled a bottle of wine from the wine rack at the door, handling it carefully, she wrapped it in a new tea towel, handing it over to him. 'Tell him it is from me, and that he has to drink it in small doses as a tonic, for medicinal purposes!'

Larry laughed, thinking about the hysteria that he had with previous women in his life when he put his family before them, then the calm acceptance of this woman in front of him; carefully putting the bottle down on the table, moved to put his arms around her.

'We are not joined at the hip; Larry if this relationship is going to work we need to be flexible. I am probably going to explain this badly but please listen. I have enjoyed our weekend, and I want you in my life. I realise though that you have your ways, I have mine as well. We have been independent people for so long, I think we would drive each other crazy if we jumped into living with each other now. Perhaps in time, whether short or long, we will live in the same place, but at the moment, I think we should be independent; am I making sense?'

Larry sighed, oh yes, he understood, the fact that she had accepted him was wonderful, that she didn't expect him to drop everything in his life for her even more so.

'Thank you, Brenda love, I understand and I thank you. You don't know what it means to be able to say things to you and you not take them the wrong way. I want you in my life permanently, I want you to know that now. I could not think of going through life not hearing your voice or being able to hold you. I realise that we have known each other only a month, but I don't want to lose you. Thank you for being cautious for both of us, I like my life as it is as well, we are both busy people; you even more so in the coming months, but we can still be together.

Brenda was in his arms and holding him, sealing the pact just made with a wonderful kiss of promise. The kettle whistled, she broke away, but not before Larry wiped the tears of happiness from her face with his thumb. Accepting the cup of tea before he left to drive down to see his father and the boys, wondering just what he had been doing to break his leg.

Peace descended on the house; Brenda was enjoying the solitude of her home, still fresh from the workers, enjoying the feel of the space. Putting on some music, the mellow jazz was a soothing backdrop to her thoughts. She had reheated some of Dennis's Noodles for dinner after Larry had left, was in the study cup of herbal tea in hand, standing looking at the safe. Iris's presence was there, she felt her smiling, Brenda shook her head she could almost see Iris smiling at her, telling her to get on with it. This was very silly she wanted to know what had been going on in Lord Lucas's head. He and his forbears before him were not the kind of men that would willingly sacrifice or leave to rot a place that had been in the family for generations, she knew deep down that there had to be something more.

Clicking open the panel, opening the door she pulled out the envelope from Michael Dranish Fawkes, putting it at the back of her desk. Kate's space had a notepad, with stick it notes on it reminding her to do a few things on Monday, Brenda checked them and added one more for her to do. Then she pulled out the remaining bundles and a few more journals, she also found another flat large jewellery box, that had been hidden under all the paper work, checking that she had cleared the safe out completely.

The box she opened with a gasp, in the strong down lights the diamonds sparkled brightly, the gems in the intricate design were dazzling. She knew what it was immediately having seen the same on the television many times, it was one of the Lords Original Order of the Garter, and it was magnificent, but very dirty. Touching it gently she thought about the man/men that had worn it, not often judging by the newness of it. Slowly Brenda closed the lid and put it safely back on the bottom of the safe, adding the other jewellery boxes retrieved from her bedroom on top; she then closed the safe door, clicking back the panel breathing a sigh took the books and papers up into the sitting room, settling in for the night.

When she put the bundles on the coffee table, one slipped off and clunked to the floor. Brenda carefully picked it up, a set of keys slid out into her hand, one large, three smaller and two very small keys on a now familiar hinged key ring; puzzled but not able to think about yet another conundrum, she carefully put them down, looking at the paper work they were wrapped in. There were several rolls of paper, tied with ribbon and sealed with wax; they were lists, most of them with ticks beside them, all had a letter L, M or P next to them; on closer study, she realised they were the items you would expect in a large ancestral family home!

Picking up the top journal, intending to sit back and read about the life of a country gentleman, but was stunned to be looking at the house she had seen that day in ruins. A fine drawing of the house from the driveway, it was magnificent; there were front, back and side views; top views of each floor from the basement to the attic.

Then sketches of each room how they looked what furniture was in each one, and where each item was placed. Pen and ink drawings that were clear and concise, you felt you could touch the paper to move the chair printed on the page. Brenda enjoyed the tour of the ancestral home, wiping away the occasional tear for what was lost. The clock on the mantle chimed the hour, it was late; Brenda knew she had all the time to read and understand the information she had been given, but she had a busy week ahead. Gathering up the papers and the keys, moved back down to her room, putting them all on the window seat to put away in the morning, went to bed, not hearing the children returning a short while later.

Chapter 65

S HE WOKE TO SUNSHINE coming through the window, she had not closed the shutters the night before, the sunlight was a warming benediction to the start of the day. She briefly thought of Larry and wondered how he was faring with his father, she got the impression of a crotchety old man, that was used to getting his way; she may be wrong, but it was the impression she had.

Smiling, she showered and dressed moving into the kitchen to put coffee on; closed bedroom doors indicated that her children had indeed returned home, so they would welcome coffee. She picked up another of the journals, moving into the peace of the conservatory, sat at the table and chairs perfectly placed in the green space, which was flooded with sunlight, folded herself into one of the comfortable chairs to read.

She had begun with the earliest of the journals, these in a much rounder hand, judged them to be penned by one of the earliest Lord Lucas. It contained the daily round of what a Lord of the Manor dealt with, and recorded his thoughts of his days. Brenda was engrossed in the minutiae of what he did, his thoughts were on the small things; his pet dog had a sore paw, the butler told him one of the grooms had been struck by his best hunter, and what measures had been taken for both animal and handler. His wife kept appearing in his writing in endearing terms throughout the journal, and to Brenda's surprise her name was Iris; the affection he held her in was in no doubt.

Her phone rang.

'Good Morning,' Larry's cheerful voice made her smile, 'I knew you would be up. How are you, I missed you last night!'

'I am fine, how is the patient?'

'Not very happy, he has just been told he has to be here for another day. Hold on he wants to speak with you, sorry!' he added in a whisper.

Brenda could hear the phone being handed over and a deeper voice to Larry's saying 'is it her?' Larry replying 'Yes sir, Brenda is waiting.'

'Humph, Brenda my dear, I hope I shall be meeting you soon?'

'Mr. Morecombe, I hope you are well sir, all things being considered. I hope that son of yours gave you the medicine I sent down with him. He has a habit of enjoying it himself, but that is his good taste inherited from you I think?'

'Oh, I like this one my boy,' she heard him say to Larry, hearing Larry chuckling in the background, 'yes my dear, I thank you, please call me Norman, I cannot think why they are keeping me in here, I am well enough!'

'Sir, they probably realise that you would not be able to sit quietly, and let that leg heal, unless someone watches you like a hawk. Now please stay put, I am sure Larry is going to find you the prettiest nurse to come and be at the house when you are released. You also have my Garden Party to attend, Larry has given you the invitation I know, so I will expect you, wheelchair and all on Saturday, please take it easy till then for me!'

'All right my dear, till then I will. I want a look around that cellar of yours, if what Larry gave me is a sample of the contents. Larry had told me about your amazing enterprise, and I can hardly wait to see the results of the work. Have been passed the place many times, I thought James mad when he told me had taken over the lease. Ah well better go, Lawrence is wanting you back, can't blame him either sensible woman with good manners! Looking forward to meeting you on Saturday, my dear, wheels and all!'

The phone was handed back, Larry with a chuckle asking what had she said, as he was as meek as a lamb.

Brenda told him and he chuckled, 'thank you, I will be back tomorrow see you then.' He was gone with a 'Father, I will get that, remember what Brenda said!' before the phone went dead.

She heard movement downstairs, thinking it would be Kate, relaxed a little and finished the coffee in her cup, reading a little more. Sure, enough about ten minutes later Kate appeared in the doorway to the conservatory, Brenda saying a good morning and come enjoy this beautiful place with me.

'This is where you are hiding, good spot. Can I ask a question Mum?' at Brenda's nod, she put her coffee cup down, beside it the envelope from Mr. Fawkes, 'what is going on? This is addressed to you but inside is to Lady Lucas?'

The time has come, Brenda thought, she took Kate in her arms, giving her a good morning hug, 'better go and wake your brother, you both have to hear this, and I am not saying it twice!'

Picking up the journal and the envelope she led Kate back down into the kitchen, fixing herself another cup of coffee, while Kate went to rouse David from the depths of sleep. A grumble and what's up came from his bedroom, Kate in an irritated voice, said for him to get up, he had to be at Shane's this morning, and mum has something to tell us.

Brenda had pulled from the safe Iris's will, with the information from the lawyers about the legacy; she was sitting looking very composed when Kate returned, she looked at her mum, she was different somehow, she could not put her finger on exactly how, what was going on here, where was Larry? She liked him, he and her mum matched, she was so glad she had found someone after such a long time alone.

David stumbled into the room, taking the coffee mug from his mum, giving her a peck on the cheek.

'You look all right, how did the weekend go, or shouldn't I ask; is Larry here?'

'The weekend was wonderful, but Larry had to go last night. His father had a fall and broke his leg on Saturday morning; he is ok,' both children had gasped and started to speak, 'I just talked to him he will be here on Saturday wheelchair and all; Larry will be back tomorrow.'

She took a deep breath, 'OK Kate has found this,' and she pushed the envelope towards David who looked at the address on the front, then the letter 'Who is Lady Lucas?'

'Me!' Brenda said, and sat back to watch the reaction from her children.

Kate and David both looked at each other then laughed.

'Good one mum,' David said, knowing his mums liking for practical jokes, 'yes nice now can I go back to bed!'

Kate looked at him, the serious sensible one, three minutes younger than her brother, but wiser in years. She had stopped laughing; looking at Brenda seeing that there was no laughter on her face she meant what she said.

'You are, hey mum be serious. You are being serious aren't you, this is not a joke?'

Kate looked at David, who sobered immediately, looking at his mum again; there was something, he could not put his finger on what.

'No joke, my loves, this is too serious for all of us, our lives are about to change in a very big way. I told you that when I came to the house the previous tenant had died. The alterations had begun on the other apartments, but not in here. Things were not going well, so when I got the job I was given the task of fixing everything up!' They both nodded, having accepted that part of the story already.

'Well you know that the lady who died was Mrs. Iris Fitzgibbon-Boerchermeir, that I found her will and became her heir, inheriting the contents of this house, you are aware of that,' at her look they looked at each other and looked around the room as though seeing it for the first time, understanding that the inheritance was substantial, 'well there is a bit more too it!'

'Ok, let me get this straight; can I have more coffee please sis!' David said holding out his mug to Kate.

Kate stood and brought the coffee pot over, filling all three cups. Looking at her mum, sitting beside her, realising there was a peace, a calm to her that was not there before, she had lost some of the worries that she had carried for years. Putting an arm across her shoulders, 'ok', she said quietly, 'you are Iris's heiress, that is wonderful and will take a while for us to understand that, but what has that to do with Lady Lucas?'

'I am getting to that love; if you think this is hard hearing, think what it was like for me living this!'

Kate nodded, David coming to sit on the other side of his mum, his arm coming across to support her. They waited knowing that they would now be getting the full and unedited version of events, not the watered-down account that Dennis and Larry had given them.

Brenda then went into detail, about finding the will, then the uncovering of the treasures in the house, the meeting with Larry, then Hugh Pemberton; then she turned to the envelope lying in the middle of the table.

'At that meeting, I met Michael Dranish-Fawkes, don't laugh Mr. Fawkes is going to be very important man in our lives from now on. It seemed that when I found Iris's will, it linked me to the will of her father, and numerous fathers before him. When Iris died in this house, she was the last in a line of the aristocracy, she was Lady Iris Lucas, therefore I became Lady Brenda Lucas, as the heiress of the Lucas Estates!'

'No way mum, are you serious, things like this do not happen to people like us! You mean to say you are this Lady Lucas, how? I mean just like that,' David snapped his fingers to emphasise his point.

Both he and Kate had come to help their mum, knowing that if Dennis had asked it was serious, because she never would. She was always taking on responsibilities without asking for help, not wanting to impose herself on their lives. Wanting them to be their own independent people, to make their own triumphs and mistakes, without her help or hindrance, but always there with the support they needed. He brought his thoughts back to his mum, and the strength there was in her, as she continued.

'Yes, I am Lady Brenda Lucas, in name only at the moment, that envelope contains the information in regards to the investiture, which I think is taking place in a couple of months' time. I will then be confirmed in the order and allowed, legally, to use the title; until then I am plain Brenda Chalmers, working mum, and mum to two very special children!'

Both Kate's and David's arms tightened around her shoulders, supporting her without words.

'We are here, definitely not going anywhere. Don't think you can shut us out, we want to help, right Sis?'

'Too true Mum, don't cry, or I will start as well. OK what's next that is not all of it, is it?'

'No love, thank you both of you; you don't know how great it is that you are here, you don't know what it means to be able to tell you about this, I have wanted to all week, but just couldn't. Larry said over the weekend that you needed to be told; let me finish to the end, you had better sit down, this is the real kicker!'

She then told them about the terms of both legacies, then some of the monetary side of the inheritance. Both of them did a double take when she showed them the statements from Hugh, in regards to Iris's legacy, holding back on the Lucas side, she did not believe that yet. They were stunned to silence at the figures on the statements, looking at each other, then their mother. David whooped and jumped up from the chair, laughing and yelling, catching Kate up in a merry dance, pulling Brenda into the three-way jig. Laughter and wafts of gardenia surrounded them; stopping them suddenly as they all caught it.

'Iris?' Kate asked, catching her breath, looking at her mother a smile on her face.

'I think she approves of MY heirs!' Brenda said, stopping both of her children in their tracks. They had not thought that far ahead, here comes the realisation, the bombshell neither one of them had seen.

'Heirs, what do you mean mum?' David asked, already an inkling of what was to come, sobering him, but he still denied the truth.

'Well, you are my children, I also have to make a will, so when I go, all of the Iris House Legacies, go to my heirs!'

David put up a hand, 'Iris House Legacies, what are you talking about mum?'

Brenda nodded and quickly outlined what she had asked Hugh to begin the paper work on a couple of ideas she had, David nodded, not quite understanding, but realising that full disclosure would be coming.

Brenda continued, as David sat back and looked at Kate, both sipping their coffee and thinking hard. 'So, with those projects I am beginning, my will, once drawn will stipulate that these "Legacies" will be bequeathed to my eldest child, to continue into the future, which it so happens David is you; Lord David Lucas think you can handle it?'

He had risen to put his cup in the sink, but sat down with a thump next to his mum, not exactly sure of the whirl wind of thoughts going around his head, he looked at Kate who had the same confused expression on her face, that he was sure was on his.

'Sorry Sis, if you want I will abdicate and you can be Lady Kate Lucas?'

'No thanks bro', it doesn't sound right, besides I think you will be the right choice. Of course, you are going to have to wait a long time, Mum is not exactly going to pop her clogs any time soon, are you?'

'Not planning on it, oh this is such a relief; I knew I had raised two level headed children for a reason, thank you both of you. Now I know when Larry returns tomorrow he will want to see you both, with Hugh in the office. I will contact Michael and see if we can see him as well before the end of the week, will that be ok? Where are you going?' she asked as David rose from the table and moved out to the door.

'Well since I am, sorry we are so wealthy, I am going back to bed, don't have to work anymore!'

Brenda just looked at him, mouth wide open in shock this was not what she had expected.

'Seriously mum, I am going to have a shower and get dressed, I have to be in Shane's office at eleven; you may have money, but I still want to work for mine!'

Brenda ran and hugged her tall handsome son, 'I love you, have I told you recently both of you?' She pulled Kate into the hug, enjoying the sensation of them in her arms.

'We love you too mum, now let us get this day on the road. I am going for a shower as well, don't use all the hot water Dave!'

They left her in the middle of the kitchen, thanking whatever gods that were listening for the good fortune of having two very level headed children. The laughter and gardenia were around her again, in benediction and in acceptance of the new family in the house.

Chapter 66

B RENDA WAS PREPARING BREAKFAST while the children showered, her phone rang, she knew who it would be.

'Brenda love, just escaped from the old man; sorry about before, but when he saw the wine he wanted to speak to you. Brenda love are you all right, what is wrong?'

She laughed, only known the man for a month, he could read her breathing!

'Sorry love, I just told the children the truth, not the whole truth mind you, I have to leave something for Hugh and Michael to tell them. I guess I am just so relieved that I have two very level headed and smart children, wonder where they got that from?'

'I know where, don't you dare sell yourself short. You are one hell of a remarkable woman, and have raised two fine children on your own. I am so glad that you came into my life; how is your unseen resident taking this?'

'Laughter and Gardenia all around, lots of both!'

'Good; father was most impressed, he is now being a lamb with the carrot of the Garden Party and a look see at your cellar, hanging over his head. Before I forget, again, I have an invitation to a play on Thursday, want to be my date? The theatre is walking distance from my place, you can stay the night if you would like, you have not seen my place yet?'

'I would love to, are you coming around tomorrow? I think I should have the kids in your office sooner rather than later, do you think?'

'Definitely, I will ring Hugh, probably tomorrow afternoon; want me to ring Michael as well, see if he can make it?'

'That would be wonderful, thank you love, have to go, the troops have massed for breakfast, I will pass on your love. See you tomorrow!'

Larry looked at the now silent phone, doing a little jig of his own, that Brenda was now out from the cloud of deception. It had not suited her, and he could hear how happy she was. He wished he could have been there with her, but perhaps not, they had to work through this period themselves. He knew now that he was accepted as Brenda's partner, but the true trust would take time. He meandered back into the hospital to see about that pretty nurse that Brenda had promised his father, whistling a happy turn.

David also wandered off to his meeting with Shane, whistling a happy tune. He had finally accepted his part in what he thought of as a TV drama, and just knew instinctively that there was more to come. Thinking about what his mum had said while they had breakfast; what she could and was going to try and do with some of the money realised that it was a good plan, he could see himself helping in so many ways. He had immediately dismissed the life of the pampered child, he had not been raised that way, you worked and earned what you were paid for, that way you understood the value of things. He had been disgusted seeing the waste and so called society goings on while out with the Haddon's on the weekend, he knew that Kate had been as disgusted as Rebecca, as they went around some bars and clubs that Mia took them too, finally he hoped that they had opened Mia's eyes as to what was good and what was not. No, he decided stopping on the thought, he wanted to be useful, knowing the profession he was in, he would be able to help his mum in so many ways, in her quest to help the elderly, while earning his own money that way whatever he did was his responsibility. He also knew that until Brenda told him to, both he and Kate would keep this a secret, wondering if Linda and Shane knew?

Kate had been stunned to begin with, but like her brother had realised that she could and would be able to help her mother enormously. She was so glad that she had been offered the job before she knew of the inheritance, as she had dismissed the life of a lady of leisure, she had decided like her brother, that although they now had enough money to be the idle rich for the rest of her life, that it was not a life she could see herself living. She also wanted to earn her own future, to do with as she pleased, but she still wanted to be useful.

Breakfast had been one of speculation and promise, all of them putting down some ideas they had brainstormed to help Brenda put her initial thoughts into practice. After David had left, both of them had gone into the study to check on the details for the coming very busy weekend. Kate picking up the note from her mum that was stuck on the pad at her side of the desk.

'What's this you want from Matt, mum, I can't quite make it out?'

'Oh', she looked quickly at Kate who had the same raised eyebrow that she used at time, when she was being sceptical.

'It is for another Iris Phone a spare one for our place, oh all right if is for Larry, ok. Don't make a fuss!'

Kate laughed at her flustered mum, going and giving her a hug. 'It is ok to love someone apart from us you know, we don't mind, we like him too!'

'Thank you love, it is still early days yet, neither of us are rushing into anything, but he is wonderful and caring!'

'Oh, all right no need to go on and on,' Kate laughed, 'what is this?'

She had turned her chair, which had touched the panel in front of the safe and it clicked open. Brenda moved beside her and pulled the door open to reveal the contents.

'Sorry love, yet another thing to disclose to you and David, I will show him when he gets home. Let me show you these, perhaps it will put things into a better perspective and allow you to see that the inheritance is just not words!'

Brenda lined up the boxes with the emerald, sapphire and ruby sets, the diamonds surrounding the precious stones, shimmering in the lights. Kate just looked at her mum, 'yes love they are real,' she said to the unspoken question.

'They are in the same pattern as the steel work, they look wonderful', Kate murmured hardly breathing, at the quality she could see before her.

'Picked it in one,' Brenda said, 'seems they liked the pattern so much they worked it into just about every aspect of their lives.'

Picking up the box with the two sets of pearls, showing them to Kate who gasped, sitting down heavily, these were precious items she really knew the value of.

'Beautiful mum, just beautiful; two sets?' she asked breathlessly.

'One for you, and one for me love!'

Tears were running down Kate's face as the reality of what her mum had said hit her. It was all true, not a fairy tale, the Pearls were the truth, as she could not at that time comprehend the value of the diamond sets. She remembered fondly the single drop pearl necklace she treasured, and had worked very hard to buy.

Brenda on impulse and with gardenia floating around, picked up one of the strings, putting them around Kate's neck, there was a sigh and breath of benediction with another waft of gardenia. Brenda looked at Kate, the beautiful strand being set off by the teal dress that she was wearing. Yes, that is right, this set for Kate, Iris had just given her approval of the giving, and the other set, which Brenda assumed was Iris' mothers for her.

Kate ran out to see how they looked, returning into the study carrying her jacket, asked if she could wear them as she had to go and see Linda and do some running around for her.

Brenda laughed, 'Of course you can, they are yours, Iris has given her blessing; but I don't think you should wear the earrings during the day, just a bit too flashy, we should see if we can get you some pearl studs to match!'

Kate nodded, smiling and saying out loud 'Thank you Iris', laughter could be faintly heard, picking up her case, kissing her mother went out for the day.

Brenda was putting together the papers, shutting the jewellery boxes to move back into the safe; disturbing the papers already in there, the keys fell from the shelf, picking them up studying them wondering where these fit in. Suddenly the visions of furniture under dust covers came to mind; she then knew what these keys were for. Moving into her bedroom, turned to the beautiful ornate desk that Rebecca and Mia had put in there for her to use, it had a note stuck to it *"locked or stuck/need key or Stewart to check"*. Pulling the note off, she knew that Stewart the Locksmith would not be required.

Flicking on the elegant reading lamp on top of the desk, looking at the keyhole, then the keys in her hand. Picking one placed it in the lock, turning it with a satisfying clunk, pulled out the supports for the desk part when it opened and dropped down into place. The smell of old leather and paper, with a faint scent of gardenia and lavender wafted out of the desk. There were letters wrapped in ribbon, bundles of documents similar to the ones found in the safe. Bending down she could see right at the back another keyhole; taking the same key opened this section, pulling out the panel, revealed two stacked boxes. Pulling them out the deep red leather was dusty, but in pristine condition. Curious Brenda pulled up a chair and opened the first one, gasping at the jewels a gentleman of fashion would have used, just tumbled inside.

The larger box had a couple of smaller ring boxes tucked inside, Brenda opened one to find woman's wedding band and ruby and diamond engagement ring, in a very old elegant style. A second smaller box held a lady's signet ring, embossed with the same crest that had been uncovered in the floor of the dining room. Realising these were probably Iris's ancestors looked at them in wonder; on impulse, she took the signet ring slipping it onto her little finger right hand, it fit perfectly. Perhaps, she thought, she should not wear it till after the investiture; she caught a whiff of gardenia hearing the ghostly laugher, as though to say don't be silly, shrugging her shoulders accepted the benediction looking at the ring in place on her finger, it was right to be there.

She turned to the box they had been in, this held jewellery for a gentleman of fashion. Inside were cuff links, plain embossed in various metals, she found cufflinks to match the necklace sets she had just put back in the safe. There was a single wide male wedding band loose in the box, she quickly put that in with the female engagement and wedding band, a sigh went through the house.

Brenda was sure she was doing right, the presence of people from the past were around her, urging her to continue, to complete what they could not. She smiled a wry smile, as she pulled out the jewellery laid it on the desk, looking at each piece in wonder. She stopped when she pulled out a solid heavy gold ring, gasping as she realised that although very grimy, it had the faint outline of an anchor embossed in the top, but until it was cleaned could not make out what else was in the design. She looked up and smiled, could not stop the tears running down her cheeks, one of Iris's ancestors had an anchor in her life too. She wondered if she would ever find out which one. Would they mind if she bestowed this on another who was an anchor, and friend to the family, she asked to the house in general. Feeling a breath across her cheek, taking that as a yes, grabbing a tissue to dry her eyes, looking in wonder at what she had found. Putting the ring in the small box that had contained her signet ring, now in place on her finger. Replacing everything turned to the second slightly larger box, which was in two parts, the top shelf had cravat pins, chains and dress rings, even a couple of ornate shoe buckles. The bottom had a plain gold watch and chain, everyday use Brenda thought; with next to it nestling in a handkerchief, an exquisite enamelled and finely wrought fob watch, something to wear in an evening to proclaim your place and wealth, again the thought ran through her head. She pulled that out of the lace edged handkerchief, turning the wheel at the top, watching in wonder as it started to work, with the cog primed. Shaking her head, she knew that David would love looking through this box, wondered if there was and where it was, an equivalent signet ring for a male, as there should be.

A picture of the substantial desk that had been placed in the sitting room, flashed before her, she realised that she had not checked the desk upstairs, suddenly realising that these pieces of furniture may be all that was left of the Lucas Estate, perhaps that was what those cryptic notes meant, that they had removed the furniture from Broadmeadows to the London house. This sudden insight that this desk was not just the previous Lord Lucas property, but one possibly two or three generations removed made Brenda stop. She picked up one of the papers lying on the desk realised that the very smudged date, in copper plate handwriting was seventeen something, she looked in awe at the history she was handling. Carefully placing all the papers on her bed, closed the jewellery boxes back into their safe compartment, she closed up the writing desk, looking at the two drawers underneath that made up the rest of the desk. Putting the same key in the lock of the top drawer opened it with shaking hands; there were more papers, diagrams and drawings similar but on a larger scale to what she had seen in the journal the evening before. She looked at these and shook her head, taking a moment to think about them. Removing them from the drawer, carefully rolling them, tying them up with a ribbon from her dresser, putting them on the bed with the others closed up the desk. Moving with all the papers into the study, putting what she could inside the safe, unrolling the longer papers lying them flat on her desk, a plan was formulating, with a satisfied nod of her head, answering the phone that rang as she closed the safe door.

Finishing the call, moved out to find something for dinner, having invited Dennis who was on the phone, over to christen the kitchen with the children that night. She also bought, while she was out, a couple of file boxes, white cotton gloves, and lots of paper all sizes.

Spending most of the afternoon with her scanner and at the photocopier, blessing Matt that he had set the office up with all modern office requirements. Making copies and computer files of all the papers and diagrams all the scraps of paper she had recently found. She knew as she had walked around the shops earlier, and her plans had crystallised that she would need to refer to those plans and diagrams in the near future, so copies were going to be needed. She did not want to damage the original now historical documents, putting the originals in plastic sleeves till she could get further advice in how to store them correctly.

Kate and David arrived back to a house that immediately transported them back to Australia. 'Mum's Casserole', they both said. Moving down to the kitchen to find Dennis sitting with a cup of tea. Kate going and hugging him, saying what a nice surprise, he smiled back, seeing the pearls, smiling even broader knowing that some disclosure had happened. Dennis started ribbing the children asking what they were going to do, now they knew?

At the look, he received from both of them, 'Well it wasn't my place to tell you why you were needed,' he said, 'I just had to get you here, and I am so glad I did!'

They both laughed, David putting his bag on the table, taking out a very expensive bottle of champagne.

'You can help us celebrate then Uncle Dennis, how about you open that and I will find us some suitable glasses!'

'Less of the Uncle please, just call me Dennis, I get tired of reminding you now you are both adults!' he said, smiling at the children's attitude, knowing that although they had both had quite a shock, and that they did not know all, Brenda had told him what she had said before they arrived, they would not be changed by the revelations they knew and were yet to come.

Chapter 67

BRENDA WOKE SUDDENLY, THE sound of male laughter waking her with a start; she looked at the clock eight am! What, she had slept in, the first time in a very long time she had not seen the sun rise; she felt guilty at first, then laughed she was allowed to sleep in once in a while, she didn't have very far to go to get to her office. Chuckling at herself, thought of seeing Larry that day, wondering who had woken her; showering and dressing quickly she walked into the kitchen, David was pouring coffee, Kate sitting with Peter at the kitchen table.

'Morning sleepy head, I was just about to wake you; want some coffee?' David asked waving the coffee pot around.

'Yes please. Peter this is a pleasant surprise, what brings you to town?' Brenda went over and took the outstretched hand, pulling the young man into a hug. He looking a little embarrassed, Kate just laughed, 'don't worry she does that to everyone, you should see the looks she gets giving Shane a hug!'

Peter laughed, liking this family of the woman he admired, enjoying the friendships that had begun while they talked during the end of the Iris build. He liked David, talent just oozed from him, was looking forward to being involved in the schemes he had rung him about the day before, just wondering where this family were taking him, but he was just going to enjoy the ride. The wackier idea the better David liked it, then he made everyone around him see the reason for it, the ideas of course usually worked out, just like the ideas they had from his mum in the update of Iris House.

'I am here to talk to Shane, we,' and he pointed to David and himself, 'have a couple of things we want to show him, David told me about the Care Hotels. He rang me yesterday to discuss what you had proposed, how we could make them work. Apparently, Shane's firm has a building that might be right for what you want, and the owners are in financial trouble, you don't mind do you? I also did a bit of internet searching, I was amazed at the number of old hotels that are up for sale, been on the market for a while, infrastructure good, just very run down. I have if you are agreeable Dan and Glen on standby to help me check them out. All of them are ripe for what you want to do, but we will check them all out and pick the top one or two at this stage!'

So, it begins in earnest, Brenda thought, the dreams are about to become a reality; she smiled at the two young men in front of her, proud that her son had jumped in with both feet, let the roller coaster ride begin.

Over coffee and breakfast, she answered their questions in more depth, giving a fuller sense of the visions she had been carrying for years. They both understood, David because he had listened to his mum talk about the lack of care given to people we love, to people that we needed to cherish because without them, we would not be here. It was a thought that stopped him in his tracks at times. Peter understanding this woman as he had watched her transform the house with care from ruin to wonder. They both went off with a hug apiece, and encouragement to do what they could.

Kate had left shortly after, telling Brenda she was meeting with Rebecca and Mia for lunch, after seeing Linda. Brenda had told her to keep in touch as Larry was making an appointment for them all that afternoon. Saying she would, went out the door with a cheery goodbye.

The morning wore on as Brenda worked on the couple of research projects she had given herself. Larry called to say he was back in town, would see her at the office with the children at three. She invited him back for dinner, as she was sure the children would have many more questions after the meeting; he accepted saying he hoped it was not Dennis's Noodles!

She was still chuckling at three o'clock as she made her way up the steps to the offices, to find that Kate and David were already with Hugh, she was ushered straight in. Larry coming to give her a kiss on the cheek and a quick hug.

'Please don't mention Broadmeadows, just yet,' she whispered quietly in his ear.

He nodded at her, knowing she would explain why later. She moved over after saying hello to Sally, sitting at her desk, already typing up the minutes of this meeting. Introducing into record Kate and David's initial comments, this was one very unusual family, she had been acknowledged by both children, as startling as their mother, she had thought.

Giving Kate and David a quick hug, Brenda moved to the empty chair around the coffee table, accepting the cup that Hugh handed to her. Hugh in turn looked at this most unusual family; yes, he could see the stamp of their mother on the two children, polite and courteous they had been brought up with manners. Direct and not afraid to ask questions, as they had when he had asked for their thoughts before Brenda had arrived. They had quite bluntly asked if this was a hoax, a joke at their mother's expense, they were worried that their mother would be hurt by it all.

He liked that, looking from David, tall, athletic probably got his looks from the father, but his attitude and morals were all from his mother. Kate was a younger version of Brenda, matching in temperament and in looks. He looked at them both, then at Brenda, noticing the matching sets of pearls the ladies were wearing, guessing rightly they were from the inheritance. Larry had mentioned something about jewellery being found; he made a note on the pad in front of him to check if valuations had been done on the pieces being worn, wondering if they would be able to find an insurance company willing to cover them!

'Have you shocked them sufficiently Hugh?' Brenda asked bringing Hugh out of his thoughts, he chuckled advising that they had not yet started and were waiting for her to arrive, just finished putting their signatures on file.

Hugh then gave them the information about the accounts Brenda had requested to be set up for them, along with the cards to use them. They both looked at their mother with a question, Hugh's estimation of them went up several notches.

'What is this mum?' Kate was the first to speak, a split second before her brother, who could not comprehend the information on the paper Hugh had given them.

'I think there may be an error on this Mr. Pemberton!' he said as he turned the sheet back to Hugh, who chuckled, yes, he did like this family, he motioned towards Brenda. 'I think it is quite obvious, you are both going to need access some of the money I have inherited, you will be working with me, with the trust I am setting up. I know you both; you know how I work, how we keep track of what is spent, what we have, just as we have all our lives so far. We just continue doing the same, but on a slightly larger scale!' Brenda smiled at them both, as they nodded in agreement, 'I know that you will be setting up your own accounts, when you start earning your own money, but you can also use these accounts, and I agree reasonable usage is fine, you will do the right thing. I doubt you will be having wild and extravagant parties at the Ritz!'

David laughed, swallowing hard, there was more money in this account than he had ever seen, and it was for his personal use! Although he had thought he understood what was going on, reality was much more. He looked at his sister to see how she was doing, about the same as me, he thought, that's all right then. Then smiled at his mother, finally realising she had strengths he had never seen or even thought about while growing up. She had been dealing with life and now this alone, suddenly her life came into perspective, wow.

Then he saw the look Larry was giving her, seated off to one side, but watching to make sure she was all right. He knew that she had a champion at last, he could relax a little; to be able to live now without having to be his mother's only hero, she had found another and he was glad. Of course, whether she accepted the situation and help would be interesting to watch.

Kate was also working through the sudden finding of wealth; wondering if she could ever be as strong as her mother, she had known through the tough years while they moved around the country she had strengths seen and unseen. Here she was just sitting there with the same seeming calm acceptance of the situation that she had graced every good or bad situation they as a family had lived through. Kate suppressing the feeling she just wanted to explode in happiness for her mum, she deserved this. Wondering if her mum had experienced the same spurt of fear, the knowledge that the life she had been living would be changing, big time. Would have to change, she was not the same girl that had arrived only a week ago; she was definitely not in Kansas anymore!

The intercom beeped, Hugh going to the door and opening it for Michael; Brenda rose, the children following her lead, went to meet him.

'Lady Lucas, sorry Brenda,' he looked at her. She had changed, he liked the change; gone was the unsure woman of a fortnight ago, here was a woman of substance in every way. The reason for most of the change stood behind her, he took the hand she had put out in welcome, taking it gently, raising it to his lips in gentle salutation. Brenda nodded in acceptance, turned him towards the children

'Michael, may I introduce, my son David, and daughter Kate.'

Brenda beamed with pride; he could feel it pouring out from her. With right, he thought, outwardly these two-young people would make any mother proud. Both tall and good looking; he would wait to see if the moral calibre was the same as the mother, but he had little doubt on that. Taking the firm handshake of the young man, who moved towards him, dressed in a navy-blue business suit, '*off the peg,*' he thought, that fitted the tanned athletic body without advantage; but it was neat, and appropriate to the business at hand, hoping that he was going to update the look, wondering if he could take him to his tailor! So, glad that he had not arrived wearing the ubiquitous jeans and sneakers that so many people thought were business attire these days.

Turning to look at Kate, taking her hand giving it the same benediction as he had with Brenda, she neither giggled or jiggled, taking the salutation as it was given, a greeting of peers, which is what they were, from now on. He approved of the teal dress and jacket, with the simple strand of pearls, which matched her mother's burgundy outfit, he mentally noted. The quiet assurance, much the same as Brenda gave, a good sign for the future, he sighed.

In fact, although they had no idea this family were about to become higher in station, on any scale than anyone in the room, he suddenly realised that this was a point that they would never think of themselves in that way, he smiled. He liked their mothers company very much, and was looking forward to enjoying the children's now that they had arrived. Looking at Brenda, he nodded, shaking Hugh and Larry's hands, moved over to the desk and opened the briefcase he had brought.

He checked with Hugh he had completed his part of the information, and had collected from Kate and David all he needed. Then he gave out three sets of folders; explaining where the information had been derived from; his firm going back into the oldest of the archives and records they had. Brenda looked at him, this was far more details than she had received before, she could see where the papers she had discovered would help to fill in some of the blanks, but she kept silent for the moment.

There were of course more papers to be signed, Kate joked that she would have writer's cramp shortly. The mood shifted, the three men felt the lessening of the tension in the room; this family had accepted the changes that were to come, more importantly were willing to deal with the consequences and gains that would certainly come their way.

Michael continued to outline what they could expect once the investiture had occurred; telling David as the elder child he would then be Brenda's heir, with Kate being, 'Backup?', she cheekily inserted into his hesitancy, he smiled and nodded at her comment. Backup, he added, continuing to describe the scope of the inheritance and the legal aspect of acquiring such a vast and ongoing fortune and land.

David looked at his mum, as he tried to digest what Michael was telling him, 'could have told us about the Lucas side of this, and the property mum, missed that didn't you?'

She laughed and ruffled his hair, 'had to leave something for Michael to tell you, anyway I still don't believe it myself!'

They all laughed, Michael advising them that the investigations were still ongoing; Hugh piped up that he also had men out in the field, so to speak, checking on Iris's Inheritances. Both men advising these searches could take weeks if not months to complete.

'I think,' Michael continued, 'that it may take years to actually compile exactly where you stand Brenda. Because of the meeting of all the legacies in yourself, and the children, you may also have some legal battles to deal with. This is a very complex situation, you need to advise us; do you, and you David, Kate want us to continue to guide you so to speak?'

The question threw Brenda for a moment, looking at David and Kate, seeing in their faces the trust they had in her, motioning for her to speak for them all, turned back to the men in front of her.

One had a slight crooked smile on his face, giving his fate into her hands, knowing that even with the personal attachments Brenda would make her own decision, and that he would stand by her whatever she decided. Hugh and Michael were anxious, they both wanted to continue to work on this inheritance, helping this remarkable woman to achieve the goals they already found amazing. But it was crunch time, she either signed the papers both of them had, to continue in the roles set by the original owners of the legacies, or she flicked them off and started afresh!

Brenda did not really need to deliberate, as she had been thinking of the future, especially now with the children around. The decision she had made was easy, and she knew without the whiff of gardenia, she could not be in better hands. She was going to keep both firms on, they would check and counter check each other, that was exactly what she told them, seeing the relief on all faces around her, even Sally smiled and nodded.

'Why, gentlemen,' she said as they passed around the refilled cups, after the signing of the papers, 'would I change from firms that have only had the best interest of their clients in mind for decades, to some upstart company that is all flash and no substance. I trust that you will both, in your own capacities assist my family and myself for many years to come. Of course, to do that, you will have to assist us to grow, not diminish; I want to use the inheritances I have been given. A little for myself, I will admit, I can be a little greedy at times!'

David and Kate looked at each other then, at Brenda and laughed at that last statement. Hugh, Michael and Larry looking at them in question.

'Greedy for mum, gentlemen, means that she will eat the whole of a chocolate bar, feeling very guilty once she had finished it. Going out to buy two to replace the one she ate immediately!' Kate explained, the gentlemen in front of her realising that this woman did not have a deceitful bone in her body; avarice for avarice sake was something foreign to her. For her children, family and friends she would be generous, to a point, but never exceeding that which she had.

'But', she said smiling at her daughter, 'to do that we need to use this inheritance wisely. I do not ever want to go bankrupt, or exceed what I have been given. I would like the setup of the Iris Trust, for the Care Hotels, also the other projects when they go ahead to be carefully monitored, and to be in the most part self-sustaining. I do not believe in throwing good money after bad, can I rely on you all to do this for me, if the answer is yes, I do not see the need to move anything anywhere!'

The three men looked at each other, each one realising that Brenda, although being told she was a very rich individual, her life of hardship and struggle up to the finding of the will, giving her a reticence for spending, she really did not have an idea of how truly wealthy she had become. Or, that whatever ventures her convoluted brain dreamt up, would never impact on the funds she could access; but they also knew that they could help her by making sure that she could do what she wanted, without jeopardising their relationship with her. They suddenly realised that although Brenda had accepted the legacy; and gone were most of the doubts, not completely gone were the fears of her past life, realising that they never would, but they could help her, they could prove they were worthy of the trust she was putting in themselves and the firms they represented.

Larry looked at the group in front of him, watching the scenario from the sidelines, he would from that day on, although still part of Hugh's company in other capacities, but mostly be the voice in Brenda's interests, within the workings of both companies. He would be there for Brenda, as partner, friend or just legal associate, giving her the best advice he could, making sure that his assistance was in her and the children's best interest, and of course the Iris House Legacies.

Brenda could feel the tensions in the room, she had given all of them a challenge. It would she knew take some time for them to shift through the can of worms she had opened, by finding the will, she would be patient, knew she had the right people to help her. Making sure that Hugh and Michael with their partners had their invitations to the Garden Party on Saturday, saying goodnight to Sally, gave her an invitation as well, smiling at the stunned expression accepting the thanks she stammered. Larry saying, he would check in with both of the men in the morning, left with the family, enjoying the feel of being in such a harmonious group.

Chapter 68

DINNER WAS A SUCCESS, because of the company not just the food. Brenda had decided to use the kitchen with all the new-fangled gadgets, she put a roast on to cook on a time delay, it was cooked to perfection by the time everyone had washed and changed into comfortable clothes for dinner. Larry laughed sharing his vision of the differences between Brenda and Sir James and the versions of dinner parties he had attended at his house. He turned a cheeky smile on Brenda as she bustled around the kitchen asking if she with her newfound status going to the whole hog and demand evening dress and diamonds.

Brenda shook her head, 'There is a time and place for all that, but not at family dinners, I prefer the casual option, thank you very much!'

Kate took the hint and started to lay the small table in the butler's pantry for dinner, opening up the French doors onto the patio. David was opening up a bottle of wine, one of the lighter Australian reds to go with the lamb roast. Dennis had taken him to the pub, introducing the owner, realising that the two Australians would hit it off famously. David had bought a few bottles of wine to supplement the ancient ones found in the cellar. They could not use the heritage wines for everyday use, too much of a good thing and you lose the special feel to them.

Kate finished setting the table, while watching the interaction between David and Larry, going to jump in if she thought her brother was going too far. He was behaving himself at the moment, but she knew him, she did not want him to screw up mum's chance for happiness by being crass. Her vigilance was not needed, however, dinner progressed while Larry kept on with the dinner party theme, telling wild tales of dinner parties he had attended.

'We should host one of those 'diamond and evening dress' dinners, when you become Lady Lucas mum, what do you think?'

'David, love I doubt I would be able to match Sir James for style, he has been hosting them for a lot longer than anyone, but, we can look into it, I am sure he will be only happy to give me advice!'

Larry raised his glass in confirmation of that.

'Of course, you will have to be dressed for the occasion, and you too Kate. Perhaps Larry you can introduce David to your tailor? I realised that the suit you wore today while appropriate really did nothing for you. Kate will need some evening and cocktail dresses, you will need a couple of good suites and your own Tuxedo, that will get some wear, wont it Larry?'

'Certainly will, both you and Kate need to be dressed appropriately, just like this do we are going to on Thursday,' he stopped as Kate asked the question, what thing? 'Brenda and I are going to the opening of a play, it is a black-tie affair. Tuxedo for me, after five wear, I think for your mum, possibly evening wear?'

What is the difference, David asked reacting to the puzzled expression on Kate's face?

'After five, is cocktail dress, knee length or mid-calf, evening wear is the full-blown floor length dress and bling jewellery!' Larry explained, with a nod to Brenda, 'anyway I am getting my assistant Jo to check for us, I know what to wear.'

'He looks very nice in it too!' Brenda put in.

Larry smiled in memory to her, not seeing the looks the children exchanged, 'as', he continued after clearing his throat, 'it will be very remiss of Brenda to arrive to the function in a cocktail dress if evening dress is expected. She would be the laughing stock of all the papers!'

'Papers?' Brenda asked, sitting up straight a worried look in her eye.

'Sorry love, it begins on Thursday I am afraid. The society papers will be at this event, as you are on my arm it will be remarked on,' he faltered a little not sure of how to explain.

'Oh!' Brenda said, understanding, both children looked at the pair of them, looking at each other, an unreadable expression on both of their faces.

'How many of these events do you attend Larry?' Kate asked to break the silence.

'Oh, there is the season, I am sure you will all start to get invitations once the news gets around.' At that they looked at him again, a please explain eyebrow raised from all of them, he laughed. 'You have now become hot property. I guess you haven't realised yet but you both, and your mum, are very eligible matches; good looks, breeding and of course money!'

David and Kate looked at each other laughing, then looked at Larry and Brenda, realising that Larry meant every word. *Oh, dear this could be interesting*, Kate thought; *this could be fun*, was David's.

'But I still don't understand,' David continued, 'why would the society papers be interested in mum and you going to the theatre?'

'Because you, dork,' Kate put in, 'Larry was not a monk before mum arrived into his life, he is a very eligible bachelor, as least that is what you would have heard from Mia and Rebecca, last Saturday, if you had been paying attention. So, Larry arriving at this shindig with mum on his arm, a complete unknown will be remarked upon; so, it begins!'

'It begins, what do you mean by it begins, don't call me a dork!' he shot back. Brenda just looked at the two of them, then at the embarrassed face of Larry, realising that he had been the topic of discussion not by Brenda, but by Kate, David, the Haddon's and Mia.

'It you idiot, Notoriety, in the nicest way of course mum,' she raised her glass to Brenda, who returned the salute, Larry hurriedly refilling the glasses all round. Wanting this conversation to continue, because he realised that the three of them needed to work through this before the papers and photographs started.

'Oh, you mean like a film star, don't be silly Kat, what would the paparazzi be following mum around for much less you or I, grow up!'

'I did,' Kate replied evenly, 'pity you are going to take a decade longer. Think about it Dave, just put that brain I know you have in gear. Think about what we went through in Mr. Pemberton's office, then think aristocracy even royalty. Larry here may not be royalty, but he certainly has aristocratic connections; he is good looking and single, not many of his vintage around,' to which she gave him a sly wink, he laughed enjoying this. Kate had really grasped the situation quickly, but he could not tell how Brenda was assimilating the information. 'So of course, he would be invited to all the 'A' list parties, would also have to appear most of the time with a partner, right?' He nodded yes, taking a sip of wine intrigued as to where she was going with this dialogue. 'Then of course if he is seen more than twice with someone, the society papers would have a field day, almost to setting a wedding date; am I right?'

'Essentially you have the gist of it Kate. I have to admit, that I have not been a monk, as you so eloquently put it. My social calendar starts in March, then goes through the year; I find Christmas is the most difficult time, so I usually head off to my house in Tuscany, for the whole month of December, it was found for me by Linda and Shane and is quite close to their place. It can get crowded as I usually have visits from both my sons, and their partners, it will be even more so this year, Andrew just told me his partner Beth is pregnant, baby due in November!'

'Oh, Larry that is the best news,' Brenda jumped up pulling him up from his seat to give him a hug, 'does Beth need any help at all?'

Larry smiled at the offer he knew she would make, at his news. Kate also jumping up to bestow a hug and asking if there was anything she could do, and she had not even met his son yet, even he was not sure if he was ready for this new responsibility.

David offered his congratulations with a raise of his glass, shaking himself out of his introspection, he just could not believe what Kate had said, it was just too foreign a concept. Anonymity was what his life had been, a nobody, one of the dreamers, still he realised that what had happened that afternoon was going to turn his life upside down. He just had to mull everything over, it was clear that they could never be what they were. It was how they moved forward that was the question, especially what he did; the idea that had crystalized the previous afternoon after his visit to Shane, but he had been thinking about for months, he wondered if now was the time to ask the question.

He came out of his revelry as Kate gave him a glass of champagne to toast a healthy and problem free pregnancy for Beth.

Larry nodded, 'they have accepted the invitations I gave them for the Garden Party, I would have liked them to meet you all before the madness begins, but they will be here!'

We are looking forward to meeting them as well, both Kate and David spoke together.

Chapter 69

D AVID MADE A SUDDEN decision, now was the right time, 'Larry, can I ask you something?'

'Sure David, of course the answer depends on what the question is, but fire away!' He shrugged his shoulders, sitting back down in his chair to listen.

'Well, I know this is sudden, I also haven't discussed it with mum, but things seem to be moving apace, the disclosure this afternoon just had me thinking. We are all going to be calling London home, I have already called and written to the firm I was with in Melbourne, tending my resignation!' Brenda looked at her son, at the determination to get through this little speech, and inclining of what was coming next. 'So, what I would like, what I will need is going to be a place of my own!'

Brenda looked at her son, finally his desire to move out to his own place now out in the open, realising that he had matured especially in the last few days. Perhaps coming to England with the added responsibilities had helped him grow. She also realised that this was an outcome she had been waiting for a while, even back in Australia she had been waiting for her chicks to leave the nest, leaving them on their own while she travelled back to 'the old country' had also given their ideas and wants a foundation. She had wondered which one of them would be first, also that what David was saying was not easy for him to say, so soon after arriving.

Looking at his mum, with an unspoken plea of understanding, David continued, 'let me explain. I am going to need space, I will have to put up my drawing boards, and I cannot do that here, or anywhere in this apartment. You are also going to need the extra room; there will be visitors coming, hopefully one lot at a time! I had been thinking of moving out back in Australia, but it never seemed the right time, but I will have to here, to help you continue the legacy, there is just not enough room here for me to be creative!'

'You are thinking of buying something David, or renting, have you already got a spot picked out?' Larry asked not sure if Brenda was happy with the conversation.

'Well when Peter and I went to see Shane yesterday, he was bemoaning the fact he had to call the police as vandals has gotten into the deserted warehouse beside them, he told me that it had been empty since before they had moved in and was just a prime spot for vermin both four and two legged. I saw the potential immediately, it is just a shell really, looking through the windows. Planning permission is in place not only for an apartment, but also an office, with access from the car park, if I wanted to go that far!' He turned looking at Kate, and then Brenda.

Swallowing hard, Brenda went over giving him a hug, 'I think that is a wonderful idea love, you need to spread your wings, although I did not realise that you had made so many decisions in such a short time. Perhaps I should not be surprised, I realised you were restless in Australia too, I had put it down to finishing University and starting the job. I can see the last forty-eight hours have been an eye opener and catalyst for you; so, the decision is made in your mind, I hope I don't sound as though I am kicking you out of here, but when did you want to move?'

'Thanks mum, for understanding, you are the best!' he said giving her a rib cracking hug in return.

Larry watched the brave face Brenda put on this astounding news, knowing that she would not stop this move from happening, but would probably have some tears later on. 'Well,' he said, 'that is a shock, but not entirely a problem, we will have to contact the agents, or sellers and see what they are asking for the property, if it has been on the market a while, then perhaps we can negotiate. There will be no problem transferring the funds, I can get onto Hugh in the morning, perhaps it might be better if he did the negotiating as well.

We may even be able to clinch the deal by the weekend; will that be soon enough?'

David's face just glowed, he nodded, 'that means I could move in at the weekend, if I can get a bathroom up and running? I only need to buy some drawing boards, oh, and a bed, I can still come here for my meals, can't I mum?'

Larry laughed, turning to a very bemused Kate sitting quietly watching the scene play out, she had known David was restless, but to move out so quickly? Perhaps he had also seen that his mum didn't need his services as a hero, or rock anymore, having seen the interaction between Brenda and himself. Hoping to lessen the shock by moving quickly out of her sphere, not dragging it out.

'How about you Kate, want to spend some of the inheritance on a piece of real estate as well?'

Kate was still looking at her brother with a mix of pride and wonder on her face. Pride that he had taken a step for true independence by moving out; wonder that he had taken the step at all, realising that he was indeed 'growing up', he had also realised that he no longer needed to be 'Mums Rock'. He could with a clear conscience, move out and be his own man, something he could not do in Australia. She looked at her mum, hugging her brother, suddenly realising that she could leave as well, if she wanted, mum would not stop her. Then it hit her, she did not want to leave, she knew in her heart of hearts that she was in the right place, this was home. Like her mum this place made her feel welcome, she had a sudden insight of her in residence, and her mum being the visitor, blinking at the sudden vision, as Brenda came and put her arms around her. Larry repeated the question, giving her time to look at everyone.

'Me! Do I want to dabble in real estate, no not yet at least Larry? I think I am going to be needed here for a while, the guest house once up and running I think will need me. Besides I like having a central London address on my business cards (when I get them)!'

They all laughed, toasting to new beginnings, Brenda and Kate clearing away the dinner things, putting coffee on, while David and

Larry got down to the nitty gritty on requirements for another place should the warehouse deal fall through.

They took the coffee up into the sitting room, everyone enjoying the relaxed atmosphere and cosiness. Brenda remembered that she hadn't checked on the desk in the room, realised that this was the desk that was in the corner of Iris's bedroom, checked the key that she had put in her pocket. Once the coffee tray had been deposited on the table in front of the fire, moved over to inspect this larger desk, removing the note about a locksmith required, that Rebecca had put on it. Kate moved over to see what her mum was doing, while Larry and David continued to discuss real estate.

'You had better come and see this?' Kate said to the two men, as Brenda opened the desk to find more paperwork and more journals. Carefully removing the papers, Larry and David began sorting through them. As in the desk in her bedroom, there was a panel at the back, with the same key Brenda unlocked it, she was not surprised to see more jewellery boxes tucked in the space. Motioning to Kate to check if there was anything else, Brenda took the boxes back to the end of the sofa, beside David, to look through this treasure, Kate sitting on a foot stool next to her.

Inside the larger of the boxes were several smaller ring boxes, with shaking hands Brenda opened the first, it contained and engagement ring and both male and female wedding bands, the second held the same, but the difference was in the engagement rings. The first was a sapphire and diamond oval set, quite simple in its beauty, the second was a stunning very large square cut champagne diamond!

'These must be Iris's from her two marriages!' Brenda said, Larry nodded at the comment looking at the rings and smiling.

Kate had opened another box, 'I think this might be for a male?' handing it to Larry for him to check.

'That is a family signet ring, passed from Lord to Lord; David my friend that is for you!'

David took the box from Larry, looking in awe at the heavy gold signet ring. It had the Lucas crest engraved in the top, 'can I wear it now?' he asked slipping the ring onto his finger, a perfect fit. Then he looked at his mum, noticed for the first time the ring on her little finger, 'hey when did you find that?'

Brenda laughed at her son, showing everyone her signet ring, 'I found this in the desk in my room; I also found some fine gentleman's jewellery. I will need it all itemised and valued, did you ever contact your friend for me Larry?'

Larry looked at her, shaking his head, 'sorry love, but I clean forgot. I will get onto it first thing in the morning. Hugh was also asking me about valuations, when he saw those pearls you were both wearing today!'

'Hey mum, look pearl stud earrings, just the type to wear during the day, I am sure they will match the strand I have been wearing, can I use these?' Kate said, she and David were going through the jewellery pulling out the pieces, placing them on napkins Kate had brought from the dining room. There was an assortment of chains, bracelets, broaches, single rings and diamond studs. The everyday wear that a woman, or man, of substance would need, they were in desperate need of a clean, but would look wonderful once done.

'Would it be possible for you to ask your contact to come here and value everything Larry, could they also clean them while they value?'

'Of course, I will ask, and if they can come very quickly, especially if you are going to be wearing some of it out and about.'

He picked up a bundle of papers, sat back in his chair to read the minutiae of a recluse. Brenda told both of children to take what they wanted, putting the lot in napkins to be cleaned, looking at David asking if he wanted to check through the other jewellery she had found, as it was nearly all for a male. He shook his head; later perhaps, he had his signet ring, giving it back to his mother in the box, asking for it to be cleaned for him please.

David and Kate, after a while of perusing the bundles of papers decided to call it a night, going and giving their mum a hug and kiss, Kate going and doing the same to Larry, much to his surprise; Brenda smiling as David clipped him on the arm going out with Kate. At Larry's look Brenda shrugged her shoulders, he moved over onto the sofa beside her.

'Are you staying tonight?' she asked

'If I can,' he stopped as Kate came back into the room.

'If you are staying, then you might need this; sorry mum forgot to give it to you earlier. Rebecca brought it up with her this morning; Matt sends his love, by the way.'

She disappeared with a wink at her mum, humming a happy tune as she quietly closed the door behind her.

Larry looked at the box Kate had given him, opening it to reveal his own Iris Phone, there was a note explaining its operation, with a *"congratulations, hope you will be happy together"*, scrawled on the bottom in Matt's distinctive handwriting.

Larry laughed showing Brenda the note, she chuckling as well, 'I guess it was bound to get out sooner or later, he said.

'What?' she asked, devils dancing in her eye as she looked at him.

'That we are definitely an item, of course that will be common knowledge after Thursday, but at least our families and closest friends found out first! Thank goodness I told the boys about us.'

'And what, exactly have you told them pray tell!'

'That you are a witch, and have bedazzled me to the point where I can think of nothing else but you; spending all my time with you, holding you close!'

He moved then putting action to his words, the papers slipped form her hands, as she surrendered to his kisses, enjoying the feel of him the scent of him the quiet strength of him.

Chapter 70

L YING CLOSE TOGETHER IN the early morning light, Larry
knew Brenda was awake. She had been restless for some
time; he thought she might be upset.

'Want to talk about it?' he asked quietly.

'Sorry love, did I disturb you. My mind just will not shut down,
I keep thinking of things I need to do, questions I need to ask, but
when I get up, they disappear. I will have to start putting a pad and
pencil next to the bed soon to write them down!'

He chuckled, pulling her closer, enjoying the warmth that came
from her, the calming effect she had on him.

'Like I said, want to talk about it?' he persisted.

'I don't know where to start. David gave me a shock last night,
although I don't know why it should have. I have been expecting him
to say he was moving out for a long time. I can see his need for the
space; it is just so hard to let him go. I have to of course, I see that,
but I was just enjoying his company. I know that won't end, and he
will be a lot closer, being in the same city, but it is different when
they are not living under the same roof!'

Larry let her ramble, as the words tumbled out as though unable
to stop once the dam had been opened. Knowing it was the best
way for her to come to terms with one of her chicks leaving the nest.
He was not surprised last night when Kate said she did not want to
follow her brothers example, this place was going to be hers really.
He knew, with a sudden insight, that eventually, Brenda would
be so busy with her trusts, that she would not be able to run the
guest house project. That baby was going to be Kate's, he knew she

447

was going to be very successful, especially after talking to Linda, who had been impressed with Kate's credentials both written and practical. Pickworths had needed Brenda to get this scheme off the ground, but it would need Kate to run it efficiently, and others he knew that were in the pipeline.

'You will check that all this is legal and above board with the warehouse, won't you Larry? I understand that you will, but I just have to say it; I wonder if Dan and Glen would be free to help him, oh, and Rebecca and Mia to help with the furnishings. I had better see if I can organise a bed for him and sheets!' She made to get out of bed, to write everything down, but never quite made it.

Larry pulled her to him kissing her, she forgot everything as they said a proper good morning to each other.

Brenda looked at the clock on the side table, 'oh my god its quarter to seven!' Larry looked the question at her, 'Norman and the Kew team are coming around today, and they will be here all week, to finish the gardens, getting them ready for the Garden Party. Glen and Dan are coming to set up the Marquee on Friday; sorry love I meant to tell you, but I have had other things on my mind!'

He laughed, what a glorious way to start the day, he thought, with the woman of my dreams and laughter.

'It is fine love,' he said as she moved to the shower to get ready for the arrivals.

They were sitting having breakfast waiting for David and Kate to emerge, continuing the conversation, 'I will be gone for a couple of days, dad is having his plaster checked, I should be there. I will be back on Thursday, pick you up about seven; did you want me to take a bag of casual clothes back to my place for you. It is only fair, I have my stuff here?'

Brenda laughed, said what a good idea, don't think it will be wise to carry a weekend bag to the opening; she went to organise it as the children came in in for breakfast. They greeted Larry without fanfare; picking up the conversations from the evening before, just another family member, and he liked it.

Brenda had just returned with the bag, when the doorbell rang, saying I will get it, moved up and escorted Norman and his team through to the conservatory. Norman was beside himself as he realised all the work on the house was finished, insisting on a guided tour when she was free. Brenda agreed, saying that as no other workmen, no morning tea from the Haddon's, but she had organised with Mama to bring some, and to take lunch orders which she was happy to provide to the team; this was greeted with smiles and thanks as they moved out to complete their tasks.

As she came back into the kitchen, Larry advised her he would make his escape, picking up her bag, saying he would call with details of the jewellery appraiser when he had set it up. He and David went out, with a kiss on the cheek from both of them, Kate yelling a goodbye from the office. Soon Brenda and she were engrossed in the fine details for the coming weekend.

Mama arrived at eleven with the morning tea, enjoyed her look around the building as promised by Brenda. Norman tagging along to check on the details offering options for plants for the apartments if she wanted any. Brenda thanking him as she had forgotten plants but had organised for flowers to be delivered for when the guests arrived; a local contact of Mama's, but plants would be ideal for in-between times, to give life to the areas. As they moved down into Brenda's apartment, he also pointed out, with a gasp from Mama the complete lack of plants or flowers in her apartment. Mama saying yes that was what was missing, there should be a floral arrangement on the table in the bay window, and something on the dining table to bring light and life. Candlesticks and lamps were all well and good but you needed growing things as well. Norman and Mama were in such harmony that she sent them both off to the conservatory together, to let them organise plants needed to bring the building to life.

Telling them both that what they started they had to continue with, so to organise deliveries and give her the details to make the payments. She thought they heard her, but could not be sure, as they were deep in discussion in regards to what hardy specimens would look good but be easy care. Norman being delighted that Mama told him she was a "Friend of Kew", Brenda chuckling to herself as she made her way down the fire stairs to the kitchen for a cuppa and more work with Kate.

Just after lunch, again delivered by Mama herself as she just wanted a few more words with Mr. Greenwell. Kate yelled a goodbye see you in a little while, and there was a call on hold for her.

'Good afternoon, Ms. Chalmers,' a female voice with just a hint of an accent came down the line. 'My name is Jo Seymour, I am Lawrence's secretary, he asked me to ring so you would recognise my voice in the future!'

'Ah yes, thank you for the call Ms. Seymour, and where is Lawrence this afternoon?'

'Ms Chalmers, please call me Jo, he has already departed to see his father, apparently, there have been some complications, oh nothing serious,' she added as she heard Brenda's intake of breath to ask the question, 'he apparently has cracked the plaster, we do not know how, so Larry decided to go earlier than later, he hoped you would understand?'

'Of course, I do I will ring him later, thank you for the call.'

'I also have to advise you that a Mr. John Marshall will be round at four, he is the Jeweller, and also an appraiser that Larry has organised to check over the jewellery for you. Also, that the opening night is cocktail wear, I hope you can find something suitable? Do you need assistance, I can offer a few places?'

'Thank you for the offer Jo, but Mrs McGill has already beaten you too it, although I may take you up on your offer on my daughter's behalf, can you give me your contacts, then I will pass them on if that is all right with you?'

'Perfectly fine with me, I will look forward to her call, and will help where ever I can!'

The call disconnected, Brenda went into the bedroom, wondering which of the two cocktail dresses she had picked up from Clarissa's she should wear, settling on the blue, as the Iris Pendant and earrings would look lovely with it.

She had gathered all the jewellery found and placed it on the big kitchen table when John Marshall rang at four. He arrived with an assistant, Brenda liking the strong handshake of both young men.

They moved into the kitchen, seeing the array of jewels, looked at her with several questions waiting to be asked at once.

As they set out their equipment, Brenda told the tale of the finding of the will, adding that parts of the legacy were still being discovered, passing a hand over the table. Telling both men of the treasure hunt of all kinds that she had been on since becoming the heir of the fortunes. Knowing that discretion would be at the heart of their work, could tell them most of the tale, finally asking them to check everything, photograph and copy for the records, with one for herself others to be passed to Hugh and Michael for the insurance companies, then if they would, clean the items to allow them to be used.

John nodded absently, only half listening to Brenda, Larry had already told him the tale, advising his utmost discretion would be required. Telling Luke, his assistant to set up the cameras and the cleaning system, they would be there for a while.

Brenda left them, advising that she would be in the office, pointing out the door, and to just whistle if they needed her, asking if they wanted a tea or coffee before they began, both declined with a smile, very eager to start.

They had been working steadily for nearly an hour when Kate returned from her errands. Going into the kitchen to watch and help if she was needed. John smiling at her with thanks, this was a bigger job than they had expected. Not that he was complaining, there were some wonderful pieces in the collection. Kate pointed out the pieces she had selected, asking if he could give her more details of them so she would know what she was wearing. During the work, John gave a little more information on himself, telling her he had just taken over from his father, it was a family business going back generations, *"The Jewellery Shop"* had a long history of supplying jewels and specials pieces to the nobility and royalty, he said quietly. Kate then asked if discretion in knowing about what he was cataloguing and for whom it was being done would be required. He nodded his head, saying Mr. Morecombe and Sir James had already requested this.

Kate saying, she knew that her mum would be needing some more pieces, possibly some pearl studs to go with the necklace in front of him, pointing out her strand and the studs she had found to go with it, along with the pearl and diamond drops that were in the box. He agreed that the earrings that had been in the box with the strands were too flashy for day wear, and the pearls that Brenda had been wearing while similar were not in the same shade or size, he was sure they had some back at the shop that would work wonderfully with both necklaces for day wear. Luke added that yes there was that new antique jewellery shipment that had arrived that morning, he was sure there would be some that would be perfect!

'Thank you both,' Kate smiled, 'I might pop around tomorrow, if that will be ok and look. Then I can buy them as a present not only for myself but for mum as well!'

Happy to have a visit from her, John gave her his card, asking if it would be possible for them to take the bigger pieces to the shop, they just did not have the facilities with them to clean or repair them if needed properly.

Brenda hearing Kates voice, and the question John had asked came out to see how they were going.

'I assure you, that I will take great care with the valuables, Brenda.' John advised. Brenda had no hesitation, she knew Larry would put her in touch with only the best.

Relieved, John and Luke put the larger pieces back in their boxes, wrapping them separately, putting them into the strongbox on wheels that looked like an ordinary suitcase. Packed up the equipment, leaving after giving Brenda a list of what they had taken, and the appraised and cleaned jewellery, glittering on the table.

David arrived on the heels of John and Luke's departure, being dazzled by the array that was on the kitchen table. If he thought they were stunning in their dirty state, they were blinding now.

'We will need a couple of Jewellery Boxes, to put them in, I forgot to ask if they could supply any,' Brenda was saying to Kate.

'I will pick up a couple tomorrow mum. I will go around and check on the cleaning and valuing, then drop the details around to Hugh for you. They were going to make multiple copies for you, weren't they?'

'Yes, I did ask them too; one for their files, I don't think we need to go to anyone else the care they took over this,' and she spread her hand over the glittering mass, 'proves they love what they do; I am all for giving new hands at the wheel a go. Yes, a copy to Hugh, and you can give him Michaels copy as well, then one for us to load onto our files here. Here you go son, I think you had better wear this to tone it down a bit, looks too new to me now.'

David took the signet ring from his mother clearly now without the grime of ages you could see the coat of arms, the small diamonds tastefully inserted sparkled in the lights. Dinner and the evening was taken up with talk about his apartment and the treasures of all kinds, people and property they were finding around them all.

Chapter 71

LARRY RANG EARLY THE next morning to update Brenda on the situation with his father. It seemed he had gotten angry at the new nurse, not the one hired, but a temporary one for the day, would not give him his glass of wine with dinner. So, he had gotten up to get it himself, fallen over, cracking the plaster cast. He was fine but Larry was bringing him up to town, to stay at his club, easier to arrange help for him there. Brenda asking why could he not stay at his place? He chuckled, you have to see if first then you will know. Curios as he would not say more, she told him she liked John Marshall, and that he had to take some of the pieces with him.

'Thought he might have to love, they are might hefty items you realise; especially the Order, all of them will need careful handling.'

She agreed and listened as he told her how John Marshall Senior, had run the quiet business, very well on word of mouth alone. Discretion was his middle name, now the son had taken over, as his father had from his, he did not expect that aspect would change. John was as closed mouthed as his father, just the same brilliant jeweller. The call closed with her passing on love to his father, and both love and patience to him, looking forward to seeing him the following evening.

Brenda went to check on the progress in the gardens. Norman was very pleased and asked if she knew if Ben and Matt were going to be around the following day, as Fred needed to talk to them about the water and electricity connections to the fountains.

'Fountains, Norman, fountains as in plural? I know there is one out in the garden but where else?'

'Why yes, my dear, we have to reconnect the one in the conservatory, then the main one in the garden.' He pointed to an elegant round pond with fountain at the confluence of the paths, one from the conservatory, and the one from the fire escape joining, to lead out towards the commons gate.

'Norman, I did not realise that there were fountains in the conservatory, they were very well hidden by all that jungle. Where is the other one, it will be soothing to have the sound of water trickling in the background?'

'Ah my dear, that is the beauty of these things, there are those that you should see,' he pointed again to the main one in the centre of the path, 'then one's you should only really hear.' They had moved back into the conservatory, he pointed to the centre flower bed, with the now exposed fountain, it was a miniature version of the big one outside.

'Well, I will go and ring them now, to make sure they do come tomorrow. I want to hear the soothing sounds of tinkling water from those fountains again. Are you and the crew packing up for the day?'

'Yes, my dear, we have done all we can, at the moment. I don't want to do much planting if you will be having a lot of people walking around. I will be bringing some colour in pots from Kew, taking them back after the party, but then come autumn we will be back in force, to replant this wonderful place as it should be, adding to the plants we rescued from the jungle it once was. I would appreciate if Ben and Matt can be here tomorrow, for a catch up and work on the fountains?'

'Of course, oh by the way Norman, are you busy on Sunday by any chance. Hangover permitting of course?'

'Sunday, my dear Sundays are the one day of the week I keep for myself, although it depends on the occasion in the offing?'

'Well, I want to thank the main contributors to the wonderful transformation to my home. Oh, I know the Garden Party will be grand, but there will be a lot of people here, I want to thank the main ones personally. Yourself, with the Haddon's, Dan, Marcus, Peter, I will be also inviting Sir James, Linda and Shane, Larry of course and my two trouble makers, would you be interested in a little ramble in the country, with lunch provided, and of course some vintage wine?'

'Some of your wine, my dear how could I refuse, I might see if I can hitch a ride with Sir James, that would be fun we can discuss the merits of your wine cellar on the journey!'

He went off with his team, a smile on his face, leaving Brenda wondering if she had done Sir James a favour or not. Moving into her study she rang both Ben and Matt, asking them to come over in the morning, advised them Norman had requested their presence to pre-warn them. She then rang Glen, asking how Iris and Edward were doing, then asking if he and Julie could organise the family on Sunday, to a private lunch and country ramble, it was to say a personal thank you from her, for all the hard work that had been done. He was flattered saying it was not necessary, but it could be a fun day and relaxing. He rang off saying he would see her on Friday with the marquee, and more photos of the twins.

She then rang Dan, Marcus, Stan and Peter with the same invitation, all of them thanking her for the invites, and all saying it was not necessary with the invite to the Garden Party, but it would be fun, count them in.

The final call was to Linda.

'Hi there stranger, how are you?' Linda's cheery voice came down the line.

'Sorry I have been so distant, but I have been working my butt off, I hope that you appreciated the lengths I am going to for you?'

Linda laughed, 'and enjoying every minute of it I am sure. What's up?'

'Well first I take it you have heard you might be getting a new neighbour?'

'Oh yes, the son of quite a wealthy woman we hear. One who does not like publicity!'

'I don't think I will have any choice in the matter soon, are you going to this opening tomorrow? Larry invited me too!'

'Finally, about time you two came out in the open, yes, we will be there, it should be a good night. What are you wearing?'

'I thought the blue cocktail dress, we bought at Clarissa's, I could wear some of the Iris Jewels I have found, they will look good but still not be to gaudy, what do you think?

'Good choice, it will look spectacular but is simple and elegant. What else is up, you didn't just call to discuss dresses!'

Brenda extended the invitation to lunch and a ramble in the country on the Sunday, wondering if she could check if Sir James would be available, promising her there would be some wine from her cellar, adding the information that Norman would we looking for a lift also. As she held while Linda checked, Brenda was pleased to read the email confirmations of the Sunday Ramble from Michael and Hugh. Linda returning saying they would all love to accept the invitations, it had been an age since they had been out in the country.

Happy with the arrangements all falling into place, she then rang the events and catering company, to finalise the set up not only for the Garden Party, but also for the Sunday Ramble.

She told the children about the Sunday Ramble and lunch over dinner that evening. Both of them asking if Larry was invited as well, saying yes, she had told him about it that morning in their phone call, besides he was the only one of them that had a car. Not giving much away, but happy with their ready eagerness to get out of the city, especially after what would be a hectic day on Saturday.

Thursday arrived with not only Ben and Matt, but Glen as well.

'This is a lovely surprise,' Brenda said, greeting the three men, and the familiar box of goodies.

'Could not visit, without bringing morning tea Brenda, mum would not let us out the door!'

She led them down into the kitchen, all of them eager to see the room in action, so to speak, asking if she had any problems.

'No problems at all, how could I have in this wonderful place! I wasn't expecting you till tomorrow Glen, to what do I owe the pleasure of your company?'

'I am here because I was asked,' he got no further.

'By me, hope you don't mind mum?' David said coming into the kitchen greeting the three men around the table. 'Forgot to tell you last night, I also forgot to ask if you were free this morning. These two,' gesturing to Matt and Ben, 'are coming over once they check with Norman.'

'Free for what love, I don't have anything particularly urgent, what did you have in mind?'

'Well I thought I would show you around my new space!'

'You got it, oh David that is wonderful. But how did you get it so quickly, don't you have to wait for a cool off period or some such thing?'

'Well normally yes,' he said, 'but you forget the power of money, and the fact that this place has been empty for a long time. When Hugh offered just below the asking price (which was a low price to begin with and a bargain), for immediate occupation while all the paper work goes through, they jumped at the offer. So, I have the keys, and want to show it off like right now!'

'Show off what, oh good morning all!' Kate said coming into the kitchen; she was dressed down today, no meetings. She had been looking forward to spending some time in the house, not expecting a kitchen full of people so early in the morning. David jangled a set of keys at her.

'Oh, Dave, you got it, yeah good for you. So, can I come and take a look around as well?'

Once Norman and the Kew team arrived, they left them with Ben and Matt, Norman giving the rest a cheery wave as he pulled both men into the conservatory. Glen set out with Brenda, Kate and David to view his new abode. Glen had driven into town, offering to drive them over, as he would need some of the things in the back of the truck to check the state of the new space. On arrival, Brenda could immediately see what had attracted David to the spot, apart from the very large space, it was on the water. She had never been to Shane and Linda's place in daylight, so did not realise the nearness of the river to the warehouses. The space was big, she realised that David had bought the whole building, which was across the access to the dock, to Linda and Shane's home. Now she could see that their warehouse had been split into two. The one next to them had a second floor judging by the staircase that was featured and clearly seen through the large picture windows. Shane and Linda's of course just used the ground floor, enjoying the vaulted ceilings and openness.

Opening the very undersized door into the cavernous space, David was doing a hop skip and jump in his excitement, it was truly his space, oh boy was he going to have fun here. He took everyone over to the only flat space in the entire place; the shelf that a kitchen sink had been put into, on the only wall in the entire building. Brenda turned on the spot, enjoying the space, seeing the beams that cut across going from one side of the room to the other, large oak beams and uprights that must have been cut from an impressively large tree, which had supported the building through ages. The only wall in the place was the one with the sink bench, looking massive as it went from floor to the bottom of a beam about half way down the room, she moved over to where David was spreading out the plans he had drawn up with Shane and Peter's help, in regards to utilities and permits.

'I have checked, I can use some of this space as an office, there was already planning permission in place from the previous owner, he just never had a chance to work out the where and how; I have, with Shane's help. What do you think Glen is this doable?'

The plans, even though he admitted had been a rush job, nevertheless showed a style and precision that was clear to understand. The office, comprised of a small reception, with a cavity door giving access from the home, then a room with drawing and draught boards, and a small meeting room this faced the car park. There was a separate door leading down the side of the office to give access into the home on the water side, the laundry and a powder room making up the other wall, cavity doors helping save space on both rooms. The water views were for the living accommodation, including use of the beams that were sticking out from ground floor and above them turning them into a patio and deck above it. There were three bedrooms on the plan, all across the back of the building, two on the ground floor with their own compact shower rooms; underneath the master with its own bathroom and walk-in wardrobe, being on a mezzanine the oak beams already there being reinforced with a steel structure forming the rooms. This master was linked by a spiral staircase to the ground floor, which then had open plan living, dining room and kitchen, the space was still massive.

'Of course, I want to incorporate some of Mum's techniques to sound proof this place, and future proof it. Using your techniques Glen, and some of Marcus triple glazed windows inside and out. Matt and Ben are coming over later to see how they can help, I would like Matt to install the same sort of system he did for you mum at the Guest House, not as grand or complicated but efficient as befits a new architectural office. Just a thought perhaps we can tie both places in one unit, then Mum and Kate will have access here as well?'

'It will also come in handy when you lock yourself out you mean!' Kate said looking at the plans, Brenda smiling as she had just had the same thought, nodding her head.

They all walked around the space, Glen taking notes on a pad, telling David he would have to check with Dan in regards to additional lengths of steel required, but he liked what he saw on the initial plan he had. He had been gone for thirty minutes or so when Ben and Matt arrived, they also thought David's plans were great, asking if they could crash at his place sometimes.

Brenda left the three boys and Kate discussing various aspects of the new construction, all putting in what to her ears were very good ideas. Matt taking her out to the cab she had called, telling her to enter "Fountain" on her Iris phone when she got back. Also, advising her that Norman and the gang had left with them once they had completed their tasks, asking Matt to tell her they would be back around ten the following morning to help finalise the setting up for the Garden Party.

Chapter 72

SHE PUT HER BAG in the office, taking her cup of tea walked into the now beautiful in its starkness conservatory, it would look even lovelier once all of her plants were back in place, but the ferns and greenery that Norman had used to set the stage for the weekend gave it a sense of peace from the chaos it was only a month ago.

Dutifully she entered the word "Fountain" on her Iris phone, the sound of tinkling water filled the air; she moved to the outer doors watching the water cascading over the outside fountain. Moving back into the conservatory to see the miniature version giving the same restful sound. Looking at the instructions that had appeared on her phone, switched the outside fountain to 'off' leaving the conservatory one tinkling inside, the sound was very soothing and appropriate, sighing as yet another original feature was restored to its former glory.

She was dressed and waiting for Larry to pick her up, the children had not come home, probably still at the warehouse, or had gone out to dinner. They would get home when they did, she would not be there. Larry called a hello down the stairs, as he let himself into the house.

'Hey this is a very easy system to use, I like this. Are you ready love?'

Brenda came up the staircase, with her jacket over her arm. Larry stood with his mouth open, this woman never ceased to amaze him. This time the dress just skimmed the knee, with a deep V neck, similar to the evening dress, it tucked under her breasts and flowed from there a soft shimmering blue. The Iris Pendant and ear rings the right compliment to the softness of the dress, her hair in the soft chignon that went so well with the outfit. Her shoes a quirky accessory, being made up of a patchwork design of lace and leather, gave her a heel that brought her to his height, he enjoyed the fact that he did not have to bend to give her a hello kiss.

'You take my breath away; do you know that?' he whispered in her ear making goose bumps appear on her skin.

'You make me weak at the knees looking so handsome in your Tux!' She whispered back, watching the effect of her closeness in the deepening colour in his eyes. 'Shall we?' she said, walking towards the door, enjoying the effect she had on this man. He hurried after her, as she chuckled, helping her put on the jacket, as they went out to the waiting cab.

'That was very wicked of you, you know,' he said as they sat close in the taxi.

'I know but I just could not resist, as you knew what you were doing to me as well!'

They both looked at each other and smiled. Larry taking Brenda's hand, kissing both the back and then the palm, sending shivers up her spine. She looked resolutely forward, asking what she should expect and do that evening, as she had no reference to draw upon. Larry looked forward as well, a crooked smile on his lips, giving instructions on his best practice at these things. Saying they were really small fry in the company that would be there, as the play was a work by a 'famous Hollywood actor', the 'A List' celebrities were sure to be there, and would be what the paparazzi would be watching for. He just wanted to see the play he insisted, Brenda chuckled at his remark; seriously he continued, just smile nicely, nod occasionally and keep moving, is the best advice.

Simple to say, quite hard to do, Brenda realised, as they arrived in a bunch of people, and the 'stars' ahead of them were enjoying their five minutes of fame. Larry pulled her close, her arm through his, they manoeuvred their way through the throng. Making it inside the theatre heard their names being called. Shane and Linda were over in the corner with a group of people, some of whom Brenda recognised from Sir James dinner, they were soon surrounded and welcomed, not having to wait long before they were ushered into the theatre.

It was a good play, although Brenda did not know whether it was a real-life portrayal, or the writers very vivid imagination at work, coming to the conclusion it was a bit of both; still it was the company she was in that made the evening magical. Enjoying the glass of wine at interval, trying not to notice the glances when she took off the jacket, also the mixed looks that Larry was receiving because it was obvious to everyone she was with him; especially when she draped her jacket over his arm, as she and Linda moved their way through the crowd to the Ladies.

'*Ah, and so it begins,*' Brenda thought as she moved through the crowd, hearing the odd snippet of "who is she?' and 'love the dress!', of the other whispers going around the room.

'Don't think about it Brenda, they are only curious, will be more so next time you are out with Larry!' Linda said reading her mind.

'I think I feel sorry for Larry, he will have to meet these people more than I will. Just imagine the grilling he is going to get from all those disappointed Ladies!'

'Only at first,' Linda said, 'you realise that you will be bumping into most of these people all through the season. So, enjoy the anonymity while it lasts, which will not be long!' Linda laughed at that point, taking in the look on Brenda's face nodded her head at her.

They moved back into the theatre, both of the ladies enjoying quietly the stir caused by their joint walk across the room; Linda in her favourite vivid green, complimenting and contrasting to Brenda's blue. Brenda a little embarrassed at the attention, was very pleased when they went in for the second and final act.

When the play finished, they went for coffee, Sir James begging off as he had an early meeting the next morning. Once they were seated with coffee ordered, Shane leaned across saying he was going to watch over David when he moved in, that he was very pleased he had been able to buy the warehouse.

'Then that could be this weekend, as he already has the keys!' Brenda said.

'I knew he wanted space, it will be nice to know the vandals will have to find someplace else, but how so quick?'

Larry then told the tale of how once the offer had been given and accepted so quickly with all the conditions that Hugh had placed upon it. That once the transfer of half the money had been made, they had arrived at the offices with keys and eager to sign the papers, for the remainder of the funds. They must have thought all their Christmases had come at once. Shane laughed, saying he would go over when he saw movement the following day, as he would be working from home, and welcome David to the area.

Larry continued with a laugh, 'Oh he will be there I am sure of it, but only later in the day, as Brenda will need his help with the setting up of the Garden party!'

'If he remembers I need his help,' Brenda put in.

Taking her hand Larry nodded, 'as much as he would like to be in his new place, he has two main problems, I think you will agree Shane, one is plumbing the second electrics!'

Shane nodded, 'ah yes, that will put a hold on everything.'

Larry continued, 'he has to have certain facilities in place to get a certificate of occupancy, you know all about those Brenda. Second is a bed, it will take a few days after the certificate to organise that, in the few days I have known David, I realise he does like his creature comforts.'

Brenda laughed with the rest of them, 'although he did send his swag over before he came, he could quite easily take that and sleep rough!' Linda and Shane both looked at her 'sleep rough, swag?' they asked.

She explained the theory of sleeping out under the stars in a swag or reinforced sleeping back, to keep out the elements and also the insects, as you put it on the ground, it was a very small tent really. As he would be sleeping in a room not the outdoors, he wold be fine, except the bathroom, that would be the main problem.

They laughed at her explanation, nodding their heads, Shane added, 'well the utilities will take a few days to connect once a bathroom has been installed, but I will look out for him tomorrow.' They said their goodnights, moving in opposite directions.

Larry putting his arm around Brenda to hold her close, moved down the street to the entrance to a Mews, very like Sir James's. Down the cobbled way, leading them to a house in the corner, it had a garage on the ground level, steps up to a small porch and front door. Moving inside they passed an office on one side and bedroom on the other, Brenda could see more doorways further back. Up the stairs they went, Brenda taking off her shoes to lessen the noise on the wooden treads, Larry turning her to kiss her he could not resist as she was the right height on the step above him. Continuing up, into the open plan and spacious kitchen living room level. Offering her a night cap, Brenda asked for a scotch and ice, as she explored a little, he nodded moving off to make one for both of them.

She moved around the area, with Larry watching her acquaint herself with his home. She liked the masculine feel of the place; it was a comforting feeling, especially when he put on some music to make the mood complete.

'I found something the other day,' she said turning back to him after studying a watercolour in the corner of the room, 'in amongst some more paper work, in the desks, and I want you to have this as a gift!'

He nodded, watching her move over to her evening bag, on the dining table, she took out a small blue box, walking over to him a quirky smile on her face, which was hard to read.

'You know I would have been very lost in the last few weeks if you had not been in my life; you have been my anchor in many ways. Well I found this, I hope you will accept this as a gift from the past, from someone who also had an anchor in her life?'

He opened the box, seeing the heavy gold signet ring, with the anchor and sapphires sparkling after the clean John had given it, looking at Brenda with a question.

'Please accept this, I also want to say I like having you in my life,' she put her finger on his lips to continue, 'let me finish please,' he nodded and kissed the finger, 'as we discussed before, I, we, both have been alone for a long time, we both like our space; so, let us just keep things as they are for the time being, can we; shall we continue as we are?'

He looked at the ring in his hand, then looked at Brenda, the honesty and trust she was placing in him filled him with pride and purpose, to be the anchor she needed, for as long as he lived, was not a daunting prospect to him. He slipped the ring on to his finger, it fit perfectly.

'I like this, I also accept it for what it stands, what it means between us. I love you, but I agree we have both been alone for a while, let us just see what develops, I do not want to lose you either!'

Diana Krall, was playing on the radio, 'then dance with me,' she said as she slipped on her shoes, pulling him into her arms, they moved in time with the music. Another shock for Larry, Brenda could dance, actually properly dance, he was amazed at yet another facet of this wonderful woman. He laughed out loud when she looked at him, knowing what he was thinking.

'Arthur Murray six lessons, thought I would try it out, I kept going I like the feeling of floating, that is what I get when I dance!', she said to his amusement.

'*Oh yes*!' he thought, '*thank you, thank you*', he enjoyed the feel of her in his arms, how she was so pliable and light on her feet. The music finished on its own, she had asked where he slept, if the guest bedrooms were downstairs; he took her hand to complete the tour of his home. Climbing the stairs to the Master Bedroom that was the complete top floor of the house.

She turned at the top of the stairs, 'now I know why your father never stays here. Even without a broken leg, this house would irritate the hell out of his conservative thinking the kitchen should be on the ground floor!'

Larry laughed, flicked on the light at the top of the stairs, Brenda walked into the space, turning to see everything. Skylights, many of them on both sides of the vaulted roof, would give light to the area even on dull days. A very large cast iron claw-foot bath was in the centre of the space set aside for the bathroom, the toilet and bidet behind a frosted screen divide. The shower ran the whole side of the wall, a floor to ceiling glass screen divided the bathroom from the bedroom itself, turning slightly then surveyed the rest of the room, seeing the large king sized bed that was set on a raised platform under a large dormer skylight.

Brenda smiled turning to Larry, 'Definitely no monk, I think I am going to enjoy this!'

All Larry could do was to laugh and pull her to him.

He was admiring his ring in the sunlight, that was streaming through the windows, he could not help wondering about the other anchor, if they had appreciated as he did the depth of regard it took to be given something like this. Brenda curled into his side, stirred like a cat, sleepily greeting him, before getting up moving across the space to the bathroom.

What was it about this woman that in a month he knew that he wanted to spend the rest of his life with her. He didn't even care if they never had anything more of an intimate relationship, than what had happened, he would still be at her side. Of course, he chuckled, he would miss that aspect very much; they fit each other, he never knew what she was going to do next. He was solid reliable Larry, he was also wondering about this lunch on Sunday; she had not said anything apart from it would be fun with the children, and would require the four-wheel drive. Watching her try and work out the controls for the shower, rose and said a very wet good morning to her that they both enjoyed.

Brenda made it back to the house just as Glen and Dan were walking up the steps; she greeted the two men with a hug apiece, inviting them in, taking the morning tea box from Glen.

'Julie asked me to ask, if she can bring anything to this lunch Brenda?'

'No Glen, this is a day off for her and Gabby, so thank her for the offer, I just want you and your families company, yours too Dan. I have the directions printed out for you both, to give to everyone. Gabby and Charlie will be ok with the twins there will be enough willing arms to give them both a break if needed. Is Rebecca coming with you or hitching a ride with Ben or Matt they were included in the invitation as well?'

'Oh, I passed it on and I will make sure they remember, Becca will have them organised; Gabby and Charlie are coming in their own car, cars will be ok or do we need a four-wheel drive?'

'Cars will be just fine, this visit!' She said cryptically, then led them out into the conservatory, and then out to the sounds of industry in the garden.

David and Kate were helping Norman and his crew with the biggest marquee Brenda had ever seen. Quickly Glen and Dan ran to give a hand to the unfolding and placing of the canvas. It took a couple of hours, but once completed the marquee looked wonderful, an extra room over the garden, looking as though it belonged.

Dan pointing out the rings and brackets on the outside roofline, 'someone has used them before for this sort of thing, you can hold up a lot of things with those attachments!'

Brenda laughed, with Kate's help organised a break using the morning tea from Julie, while waiting the delivery of the tables and chairs. When they arrived putting them throughout the garden and conservatory, setting up trestles in one of the alcoves as a makeshift buffet. Checking the raised platform in the other alcove was ready for the string quartet, by the instruments in their cases she could see leaning against the baby grand piano, they had already been around to check the sound system.

David and Kate had been following Brenda around on her fact-finding tour, when they saw the piano, both of them looked at her, 'well you can have your pool table, but I have always wanted a piano, I needed something in keeping, an upright would not look the part, it will fit in the dining room, once today is over, I also intend to learn to play, what do you think?'

David sat down, lifting the lid on the keys, running his fingers up and down in a scale, then morphing into a very popular song, the sound of the piano filling the whole place, Brenda very pleased with the acoustics.

Glen and Dan walked into the area, drawn by the music, 'Man of hidden talents that son of yours Brenda, 'Glen said, Dan nodding in agreement, laughing when Kate sat beside him, they then played a very fast and professional Chopsticks.

Norman also came wandering in looking for where the music was coming from, watched the two people play together, laughing at each other's mistakes when made. Everyone laughing when Kate suddenly jumped up, grabbing a vase from the many on the side table waiting to be used, putting it gently on the piano, 'for tips' she said at his quizzical gaze, he then nodded straight faced at her wisdom, only to ruin the effect by laughing at the expressions on the people around them.

Glen turned to Brenda motioning her out of the crowd that was gathering around the pianists. 'Matt will be around later Brenda, he needs to do the final set up for the electrics, now that the marquee is up. We are done, so we are off, see you at two tomorrow!'

'That will be wonderful Glen, thank you and Dan; I don't think we would have the marquee up without both of your expert assistance. I think Norman and his team, if they can tear themselves away are just putting the finishing touches to the plants, this space looks wonderful, don't you agree?'

'That it does lass, it could not be more different from a month ago. I love the space now, even with the giant tent over it, you won't have to worry about any unseasonable showers with that over the top of you!'

'Seeing it spans the entire garden, horizontal rain is the only thing you will have to worry about!'. Dan put in, 'see you tomorrow Brenda, we are all looking forward to the afternoon!'. With a cheery wave both men left, after saying goodbye to Kate and David, who were still at the piano. Dan cheekily putting twenty pence in the vase on the piano, setting everyone off into more laughter.

Matt duly arrived with his team, to connect all the hidden and visible speakers throughout the house and grounds; Kate going to give him a hand. While David slipped out to meet Rebecca and Mia, who he had invited to his warehouse to get some premature decorating advice.

He arrived back with them, just after Norman and the Kew team had left, for what turned out to be a very happy evening, Kate ordering Pizzas for everyone, Matt staying after his team had left, they all saying they were looking forward to the following afternoon.

Larry rang to say that his sons and partners had arrived, they also looking forward to meeting her. Brenda telling him to come over to the house in the morning, she would provide lunch, so she could meet them, and his father before everyone else arrived. Great idea he said, hoping she was ok, ringing off with a laugh and see you in the morning.

The highlight of the evening was David playing the piano, to check the sound system, with the rest of the group going to all points of the conservatory, garden and house checking the quality of sound. A lot of laughter could be heard, both real and ghostly, the smell of gardenia wafting around raised everyone's spirits, knowing that this was what Iris had wanted; the house to be used again to have life and laughter in it again.

Chapter 73

B RENDA WAS AWAKE EARLY, to meet the first guest of Iris
House. The renowned actor arrived without fanfare, as
was the function of the house. He had requested a three-bedroomed
place, Brenda allocated him apartment number two; he was, as
she had been advised by his assistant, expecting a visit from his
two children. Also, making sure that the fridge and pantry had
been stocked with all the items on the lists, fresh fruit, no alcohol
with the accessories that had been forwarded from the PA, added
to the rooms, as requested. He was surprised at the high level of
appointments in the apartment, pleasantly so, asking questions as
Brenda showed him around.

'There is no room service here, myself and family, are here to
help, but this is your space. If you want a take away, I have canvassed
the best restaurants in the area and they will deliver for you, just add
it to the Iris House account that is set up, no need for you to give
your name, my name is sufficient and the apartment number. The
fridge and pantry is already stocked with your grocery items as per
your information.'

Brenda handed him the Iris Phone that was set up for apartment
two, showing him the function of how it operated everything from
lights, TV, door locks. He nodded understanding as she ran through
the functions. 'You can also use this as your phone for local calls,
within reason of course, while you are in the UK, may help to make
your phone bill a little smaller!'

He visibly relaxed, succumbing to the wonderful private feel of
the place, making a mental note to thank his PA when he got back

to the States, he had been dubious to begin with, but now he was here, he was very sure this was the place he needed.

Brenda invited him to join in the festivities that afternoon, explaining they were celebrating the opening of Iris House, as he was the first guest, he was welcome and his family as well.

'There will be other children here, if you want to mingle, you would be welcome!' Taking him out to the fire escape to show him the lift, and the conservatory and gardens, he showing surprise at the marquee and space.

'Thank you for the invitation, I am expecting the children this afternoon, and a couple of friends of mine who are also working on the same project, but staying in hotels they will be very interested in this place. You are in apartment one, right?'

'Yes,' Brenda confirmed, 'this building is not only my work place, but also my home. I hope you understand what I mean by that, and treat my home as you would this apartment as your own. I will leave you to settle in Mr. Jones, please if you need anything, or assistance in any way, a text message on the Iris Phone, or just come down and knock on the door. If I am not available, my daughter, Kate or son David, who I will introduce to you, will be available to help at any time.'

Brenda used the lift to go down to the basement, advising Kate that the first guest of Iris House was impressed.

A cheeky message on their phones at eleven, alerted Brenda, Kate and David that Larry with his father, Andrew with a glowing Beth and Ewon, had arrived. Norman in his wheelchair being fussed over by Ewon, the old man not very happy about his restrictions or the coddling. Ewon was the first to greet Brenda with an outstretched hand and cheerful smile on his face. She liked what she saw, he had the same blue eyes as his father, but she realised that he probably took after his mother in the rest of his facial features. Kissing him on the cheek saying welcome, he moved out of the way, turning to see his grandfather trying to propel himself into the room, towards them.

'Grandfather, you should have waited, I would have helped you in!' he said, with a glaring look at the gentleman in question.

'*He is worried about him*', that was Brenda's thought, as she turned to regard the gentleman in question, trying to propel himself with difficulty over the thick carpet, but not giving in. She regarded Norman with interest, seeing Larry, as he would look in his later years, as both men were definitely cut from the same cloth, she liked what she saw.

Mr. Norman Lawrence Morecombe, did not like being an invalid, that was very clear; David moved over to him with Ewon, introducing himself, helping to manoeuvre his chair through to the dining room, and onto the easier flooring. Larry following on the heels of the wheelchair, bringing his eldest son and clone with him. Ushering a glowing Beth into the room, that a burst of sunshine brightened sending rainbows throughout; making introductions all around, Brenda going over to Norman and kneeling down to say hello.

He chuckled as she gave him a kiss on the cheek and hug, 'Patience sir, we will have you out of that chair and dancing again in no time!' she said rising taking the hand he gave her, feeling the strength in the grasp. Larry moving over to them, after introducing his children to hers, giving her a hug and kiss hello.

'Would you like the grand tour?' Brenda asked.

Norman had the same quirky smile as Larry, jumped in, 'that is what we are here for, not just to meet you and your children, but to sticky beak. But how am I supposed to get around in this thing?'

David coming over to them, looked at his mum 'Let me assist sir, we have a few things that may help, that have been incorporated into the refurbishment.' Ewon smiled at him the concern in his eyes showing through, even though he was just about out of patience with him.

Kate took Beth's hand to point out the improvements that had been made asking if she had been in this part of town before. Larry then brought Andrew up to introduce him to Brenda, as the rest of the party moved out onto the landing to survey the scene of the Garden Party.

Andrew could not miss the rapport between this lady and his father, having been introduced to others in his life, this one was different, he could sense that it was deeper than his father had let on. They caught up with the others and enjoyed the tour of the revamped building; Norman laughing when he saw the lift arrangement, happy to see ramps in place where necessary, liking the detailed thought, that had gone into the refurbishment.

Lunch was a happy affair, even more so when Andrew announced that he and Beth were engaged, the wedding to be at the Registry Office the following month. Cheers went around, Brenda hugging the couple wishing them all the happiness, asking to let her know if she could help. Norman saying about time, how long have you known the girl!

Larry smiled at Brenda, hearing her comment asking if she could help, knowing he would not be alone in the organisation of the event, even after consultation had been made with Beth's family, could look forward to it being very well done indeed.

Brenda and Kate excused themselves after lunch; leaving their guests in Larry and David's hands, to move them out into the conservatory to check on how the caterers were doing. Jeans and T-Shirts definitely the wrong attire for the first ever Iris House Garden Party.

The sun was shining as Kate and Brenda came up to welcome the first guests to the Garden Party. David joining them in his tan slacks and open necked shirt, commenting on how nice they both looked in their summer floral dresses and matching summer hats. Laughing when Brenda produced a straw boater for him to wear, to get into the mood.

Sir James, Linda and Shane were the first arrivals, with Dennis and Lulu close behind, being welcomed and sent through to the conservatory where Larry and his family were helping the catering staff organise drinks for everyone.

'Don't let this one get away, my boy!' Norman told his son, later in the afternoon; they were sitting in prime position watching the people move around. Both Larry and Norman watching Brenda move easily amongst the throng, being the hostess they expected.

'I do not intend to father! But, she will make up her own mind, which she will have a lot on it in the very near future. I am going to be patient, be there for her in any way I can!'

'Good, as this one is definitely worth waiting and fighting for. Just you make sure she knows you are waiting. I don't just want her joining our family because of her wine cellar either, mind you I still want to see it for myself!'

Larry laughed, saying he would remind David of the fact when he could find him.

Brenda meandered amongst the workmen, who had wrought a miracle on the house, talking to them and their families, expressing her gratitude at the commitment they had given. Seeing the pride shine in them, as they were praised for a job well done in front of their families. Throughout the afternoon, she singled out the people she wanted, finding Marcus and Brent in deep discussion, gave them both an envelope each, telling them to give their workers their Christmas bonus, either a very late one, or early whichever they chose, as a thank you from her and Pickworths.

They were both stunned, saying it was not necessary, with a whiff of gardenia around realised that they could not refuse, thanked her anyway on behalf of their teams. Adding that all of them had enjoyed working on such a beautiful and unique house.

She found Glen, Julie, Dan and his wife Helen, listening to the music enjoying the happy atmosphere and sounds of the afternoon.

'What is this?' Glen said, he and Julie looking into the envelope together seeing the individual ones inside. Dan looking in his and then handing it to Helen for her to look also.

'That is my thank you to all of your workers, for the long hours and weekends that I took them away from their families;

'Aw Lass, that is not necessary, you know that. We all did what we did because it was the right thing to do!'

'The work that has come to us because of what has been done here,' Dan interjected, 'is worth more than anything else. Glen is right Brenda love, you don't need to do more!'

'Ah but I do, as it is Iris's idea not mine, she wanted to thank the men and women who helped in the transformation of this once ugly duckling into the beautiful place it is today.' Just then a slight breeze wafted around them, the smell of gardenia was unmistakable; Glen and Dan looked at each other, realising they could not argue, shrugged their shoulders. Julie and Helen saying that they loved Brenda's delightful perfume.

'See you cannot fight it. By the way there is also something in there for you two as well! I think both of your wives deserve a holiday, don't you?'

Julie laughed, echoed by Helen, 'that will be the day Brenda. Do you realise that our phone has not stopped ringing since our men started this job of yours? There is more work than we can really handle, I am sure Helen will agree that Dan is the same!' Helen nodded her head in agreement.

'I am glad that everything is starting on an upswing for all of you, I don't really know the situation that well, but everyone deserves a holiday?' Brenda turned to Helen, 'I am sure Greg is fully capable of running the steel works, just waiting for an opportunity I would say. As for you Julie and Glen, what did you raise such big strapping boys in the industry for, if not to help and eventually take over, as they are most capable of doing, to give you a break?'

Julie laughed, looking at her husband, eyebrow raised in query, as though to say, well why did we; seeing him looking over at Ben and Matt who were surrounded by some very pretty young women, as they had Iris and Edward in their arms. Gabby and Charlie relaxing at a table close by, watching the new uncle's antics with smiles on their faces.

'Well,' said Julie, 'what did we raise them for?' Helen looked at Dan, hands on her hips, 'don't you look away either, you know what Brenda said about Greg is true, he is more than capable, especially with the team you have in the office; they are quite capable of looking after things for a couple of weeks!'

'Thank you very much Brenda, we will not get a moments peace from now on! Ok, ok we give in; let us just get the jobs sorted then we can see about the possibility of getting away for a week, possibly!'

Glen said, Dan nodding in agreement. Julie jumped up, grabbing Helen's hand, asking Brenda if Kate would be willing to see what she could do for them, she fancied a cruise, as then Glen could not get side tracked in work. Glen started to say something, but Julie just looked at him, he stopped looked at Dan and shrugged his shoulders. Helen was caught up in Julie's enthusiasm, seeing Kate in the distance hauled her off leaving the men still unsure of what had just happened. Brenda gave both of them a hug, saying enjoy the day, they laughed hugging her back, moving off after their ladies.

Brenda sat down beside Gabby and Charlie, who had rescued the babies from the doting uncles, putting an envelope on the table in front of them. Taking both the babies, one on each shoulder, 'my turn,' she said smiling at the puzzled expressions on their faces.

'You both have some reading to do, you won't need these two as distractions!'

'Reading, what do you mean, Brenda?'

'Just read the information, Charles Waines Glass Inc. needs some signatures, with some bonuses for your workers, Charlie. Don't look too smug Mrs. Waines, your business information is in their as well. I know of at least three very interested groups that want at least two possibly three stained glass windows each, from you at my prices not yours. So, you had both better read the information carefully. I will go and find Larry, you may need him to explain a section or two, shall I?'

'Brenda just what are you up to?' Gabby asked to Brenda's retreating back.

She turned back to them, a serene expression on her face, 'Oh I see Ben and Matt, ok I will send them over to you as you are quiet here. There is something for both of them in that envelope as well!'

The young men arrived at the table, were handed their envelopes by a still confused Charlie, 'we don't know, we have one from Brenda as well!' Was all the explanation he could give.

Larry watched as Brenda a baby on each shoulder moved with grace over to where he stood with his father. Norman chuckled as he watched the loving expression pass across his son's face, instinctively he knew Brenda would eventually become part of his family.

'What are you up to Brenda?' was what Larry asked.

She deposited a sleeping baby in each of Norman's arms, he stiffened at first then relaxed, enjoying the sensation of each tiny form snuggling down in his lap.

'Meet your son's godchildren Norman, Iris and Edward, meet your surrogate grandfather!' She smiled at the look on Norman's face, 'I think you had better wheel your father over to Gabby and Charlie; oh, I see Ben and Matt are also there. I just gave them the envelopes with their business setup information inside, they might have a few questions, that I cannot answer!'

Larry just laughed at her ingenious expression, shaking his head giving her a quick hug, taking his father's chair, 'you might be needed in this dad,' he said smoothly moving them over to the confused group, explaining to his father what Brenda had done for them.

Chapter 74

T HE GENTLE MUSIC FROM the quartet, the sunshine and
fragrant breeze were the perfect backdrop as the afternoon
moved on; occasionally interspersed by the sounds of children's
laughter, both real and ghostly.

Brenda found Stan with Nona and Poppa sitting at a table in
the gardens, enjoying the music and the ambiance, watching the
children running around, she greeted them with a hug apiece, saying
didn't they look fine, in their spring best.

'I have something for you all; I hope you will accept my thanks
for the wonderful efforts you have made in the last four weeks. It
is amazing Stan, look at what we achieved, since you came into
my life!'

Stan smiled wondering what this gracious lady was going to do
next. His business had gone through the roof, he was worried that
they may not be able to cope with the extra work, but he had to
agree with Brenda the house was sparkling, and the best in the street!

'It was our pleasure Brenda, Nona and Poppa were just saying
how the house was so happy and alive; just the way it should be.'

'I hope you don't mind, but I have been thinking about Poppa,
and realised that you have probably been so busy, that a holiday has
been the last thing on all your minds. I realise you will be the last
person to take any time off, but I hope you will accept this from me
for them. There is also an envelope for you as well, I hope it helps,
perhaps it will come in handy over the next few weeks, to alleviate
your stress, as I know you are going to get even busier. Oh, and

instruction for the lunch tomorrow is in there as well, I am sure Dennis will remind you to pick him up!'

She handed Stan another one of the envelopes, as the headwaiter came up to her with a question, with a kiss on the cheek for the three of them, moved off to check on what he asked.

Stan watched her go, thinking she belonged in this space, then he looked into the envelope finding a travel wallet with two first class tickets, plus accommodation paid for, with spending money for Nona and Poppa, back to the old country for two weeks. A note stuck on the inside of the wallet read, *"A Tonic for Poppa's Health,'* and underneath it, *'To Restore Nona's Nerves!'*. He laughed, showing them to Nona and Poppa, explaining what they were, Nona just shook her head, Poppa smiling as they both watched Brenda move away.

Then he pulled out the envelope amongst the others, that had his name on it, opening it to see the cheque and a short letter.

> *'Stan, I cannot thank you enough for the help and friendship I have received from you and your family. I realise that the influx of work from the contacts made from that help will have stretched you a little. Please accept this gift, in the spirit it is given (Iris insists) hopefully it will help.*
>
> *If you need my assistance in any way, for you or any of your family, you only have to ask.*
>
> *With love, Brenda'*

The cheque was for fifty thousand pounds, he had to check it twice, wondering how she knew he was having cash flow problems; shaking his head, he put it back in the envelope to answer the questions his parents were asking him.

Brenda was smiling, after answering the caterer's query she toured the grounds, chatting to people, making sure everyone was having a good time, encouraging them to explore if they wanted.

Brenda came back to find Gabby on her own with one screaming baby in her arms, the other about to explode in the pram. She took Iris from her as one of the catering staff arrived with bottles they had warmed. Sitting with Iris next to her, soothing and comforting as she took a bottle, Gabby picking up Edward to feed him. It was suddenly peaceful the only sounds were the noises from two very hungry babies. Brenda could hear the questions running around Gabby's mind, she turned to look at her.

'I know, you have a million questions, but do not know where to start, right?'

Gabby just nodded, 'well to answer a couple, let me begin by saying I think it is about time that your father (although I love the man) realised that the sons and daughters that he and Julie have raised, have a right to their own talents, and lives of their own. Still able to assist him, but need to be out forging your own businesses. I have just given you all a push in the right direction, so Glen will shout at me, not at you lot, you also do not have to broach the question with him, as I have now done that for you. Now I want to be quite clear if you need any help or assistance, in any way shape or form, I would be very hurt if you did not ask me first! Hugh Pemberton and his excellent staff, Larry and myself will be available at any time to help if you get into strife, or have any confusion on how to proceed. I am sure Larry said much the same?'

'He did Brenda, I realise that arguing with you will be futile, I feel that I should, but you have just done what I have wanted Charlie to do for a couple of years, which he would not do, as he felt he would have been disloyal to Dad, through the tough times. You have not just given us all a push, it was a mighty leap off a cliff. I also realise that you have organised this for these two mainly,' she nodded at Edward and Iris, now contented babies asleep in their arms, 'as much for our benefit!'

Brenda nodded, putting Iris on her shoulder as she started to squirm, 'yes, I am hoping that what I have done will give her a better existence than her namesake. Oh, don't get me wrong, Iris senior had a wonderful life within the constraints of her era, without the freedoms we as women have today. Hopefully Iris Junior will be able to achieve so much more in her future!' A loud burp from the small bundle under discussion was heard, both women looking at each other, laughing as it was as though she was agreeing with them.

Brenda looked around at the suddenly empty area, Gabby saying she had heard there was something going on out on the commons. Norman wheeled himself over asking where everyone had gone? He had not seen is son or grandchildren for quite some time.

Stan arrived to argue with Brenda, but realised that would do no good, so offered to help push Norman out through to the commons to see what all the commotion was about. Being joined as they walked through to the gate, by everyone to see what was going on, all who passed her thanking Brenda for the lovely day.

It was soon clear to all, once they passed through the gate what was afoot. David had organised with Norman, for a cricket pitch to be mowed into the commons just outside the gate. David had organised everyone into teams, with Shane being the umpire, the cricket match was in full swing, with anyone who wanted joining in, the rest being spectators, cheering and clapping every ball.

The match finished with the gong announcing the food was ready, happy people flooded back into the house, to give the caterers a headache for a while until everyone had a full plate and a place to sit.

David kept his promise once everyone had eaten, he and Dennis took Sir James, Larry and his father, Hugh, Michael with Norman Greenwell bringing up the rear, expounding the delights and treats in store for the gentlemen in the "Wine Cellar"

The string quartet back in their places, after lunch, started to play some lovely tunes, keeping the atmosphere light and happy. Brenda was sitting with Glen and Dan, Julie and Helen, watching the people around them, she found her fingers taping in time to the waltz that was being played, suddenly Larry was beside her.

'Father has been dutifully delivered to the wine cellar, and I have left him in David's capable hands, now please dance with me?'

Brenda smiled, happily taking his hand, was led out into the space in front of the musicians, moving gracefully to the music, the first to dance in the house for a very long time. Everyone watching the handsome couple as they moved in unison around the small dance space. They could feel the happy atmosphere, realising this was supposed to be, laughter, music and dancing which had been missing for so long. Larry looked into Brenda's happy face, her clear blue eyes smiling at him, the smell of gardenia surrounding them, happy with the sense of peace and rightness that was filling the house. Nodding at Glen and Julie, Dan and Helen, when they joined them in the waltz, others joining in, moving tables and chairs out of the way to expand the dance floor.

People were leaving, the sunny afternoon had become very cloudy, and a typical spring shower was imminent. Matt had typed 'Gardenia' into Kate's Iris phone, bringing on the lights around the garden and conservatory turning the areas into enchanted places, becoming a haven under the marquee when the rain started to fall. Everyone as they left thanked Brenda for the invitations, telling her they had a wonderful time, voted the afternoon a stunning success, hoping to be invited back the following year if it was to become an annual event.

Larry with his family, Dennis, Lulu, Sir James, Linda, Shane, Kate and David were sitting at the last few tables left in the conservatory. The string quartet had left, the catering staff had also packed up, also leaving a few extra chairs dotted around, making sure the place was neat and tidy before they departed.

Everyone was chatting about the afternoon, Brenda going around topping up everyone's glasses, making sure all was ok, to celebrate the success of the afternoon. David and Shane were sitting at the baby grand tinkering away, when she heard her name called from the garden door into the conservatory.

'Mr. Jones, you decided to come down after all. Have you enjoyed yourself?'

'I have, thank you for the invitation. Can I introduce my children Marie, Scott this is our hostess Ms. Chalmers?'

The children about eight and ten years old both said a shy hello, thanking Brenda for a wonderful afternoon, and food, they had fun.

Brenda smiled at both of them, realising she had seen them running around with the other children at the cricket match, also playing hide and seek at one time too.

Mr. Jones turned, Brenda realising he was not alone, 'Can I also introduce you to a couple of friends of mine, there were in town this afternoon, a break in their part of the filming schedules. I took it upon myself to invite them, I hope you don't mind?'

'Of course not, I am glad they could relax and enjoy the afternoon as well. That is what this place is all about.'

Brenda turned to look at the two gentlemen walking towards them, after Mr. Jones had signalled them to come in. Slowly taking in the wonderful surroundings, very large smiles on the well-known faces, one of them especially known to her.

'Oh, but Ms. Chalmers and I have met before!' Everyone turned and looked at Brenda then at Adam Bennet, as he took her hand raising it to his lips in a formal kiss.

She looked at him and smiled, as he kept a hold of her hand, squeezing it gently. He was still as handsome as ever, but did not have that tortured look, the green eyes twinkled at her, clear of the grief and agony that had blinded him when they first met.

Everyone realised who the three men were, they could not fail to recognise the world-famous actors, but they all just greeted them as they would anyone else. No fuss or fawning, bringing them into the group offering drinks and seats to join in.

Brenda found her voice, as Larry raised an eyebrow, looking at the hand still held by Mr. Bennet. 'Fleetingly, I hope that you have recovered Mr. Bennet?' as she disengaged her hand motioning again at the spare chairs still around.

'Thank you I have. I have to thank this lady for some very sage advice, helping me over a very black patch I went through a while back. Her words to me have come to my aid many times since that day. I have always wanted to thank you, and now have the opportunity to do so; thank you!' bowing in his seat to her.

'Typical,' Dennis said, 'always helping others, even when they don't want to be helped I bet!'

Adam laughed, as did everyone, 'yes at the time of our meeting I did indeed want to strangle her, but reflecting on what she said, realised that the madwoman, 'and he smiled at Brenda who just nodded, 'was right. Of course, by the time I realised that she was right, that I should just get on with life, she had vanished, I was left wondering if she had been real!'

'Oh, she is real all right,' Dennis interjected, to laughter all around.

'Anyway,' Adam continued, 'I always hoped that when I came back to London I would be able to thank her for her sage words, and now I can, and have!'

Brenda took the thanks with a nod, then to move the conversation away from her, asked what brought him to London, asking where he was staying. He laughed saying at the Savoy, he could not stay at the house across the commons this visit, due to the owners and friends being in residence. He hoped that next time he could put his name down on the waiting list for one of her apartments, as he was very impressed with the one Mr. Jones was in.

She nodded taking him over to where Linda and Sir James were sitting, getting him a chair so he could chat and put his case forward to be added to the Iris House Guest list. Leaving everyone chatting away, moved down to the kitchen with Kate, Linda and Lulu to see what they could rustle up out of the left-over's for supper.

As Brenda moved back into the conservatory, many hands helped put out the spread on the trestle tables, she looked at the happy people chatting companionably. The smell of gardenia wafted around them all; the house was at peace. Knowing it would be hearing the sound of laughter and music, a new era had begun, and would continue for a very long time.

Chapter 75

Post Script

S UNDAY MORNING, IT WAS going to be a glorious day, the rain from the evening before had given the world a sparkle. Larry arrived at ten, picking up Brenda, Kate and a hung-over David.

'Told you not to try and out drink Sir James and my father last night son, never mind Norman Greenwell, but you and the others would not be told!'

'I know, I know and I did stop. God, what did we get through! Oh, it is ok mum, we only drank a couple of bottles of Chateau Iris, it was the Australian wines I had bought they sampled, and the quantity in which they imbibed that did the damage. Oh, my head, did you say you had coffee, anyone got an aspirin?'

Kate who had climbed into the back of the car with him, handed over an insulated cup and two tablets, thanking her profusely, settling into the seat with eyes closed.

The drive was pleasant, Brenda had only told Larry they were heading to Broadmeadows, he raised an eyebrow, but said nothing more. Watching the mischievous smile appear on her face, knowing that she was up to something. The brief case, lidded cardboard box, and box of wine, she had put in the back of the Range Rover puzzling him, it was not the picnic basket he was expecting.

As they approached the entrance to Broadmeadows, Larry realised that there had been work done, shooting a quick glance at Brenda, who just smiled and nodded, motioning him through.

The gates no longer were covered in foliage, the Iris Crest could clearly be seen in the steel gates as they were creeper free, but just propped against the weed free stone pillars. Brenda had been warned that it would be unsafe to rehang them, at that time, the work could not be completed in time for the weekend.

Larry also found he did not have to dodge the fallen debris or oak trees, even the potholes had been repaired, it was an easy and pleasant drive up to the remains of the house.

Turning into the area before the steps, he saw that a marquee had been set up. He carefully parked turned to look at Brenda, sitting serene beside him, but she would not look at him, or answer the myriad of questions his look was asking.

A catering company van could be seen, with waiters moving inside the marquee setting up lunch. Brenda picked up the box of wine moving into the marquee to make sure everything was ready, leaving Larry, Kate and a still sleepy David struggling out of the car.

'What are you up to mum, and where are we?' Kate asked as Brenda stopped them from going into the marquee, but turned them towards the steps and ruin of the building behind them.

'I have a hunch love, you should know this place is owned by the Lucas Estate!' Watching the dawning comprehension cross her clever daughters face, then David catching on, straightening up looking around with interest. She had the set of keys from the safe in her hands, and another set she had found tucked away in the back, a much older looking set. Larry looked at her again!

'Please be patient I am not going to say anything until everyone is here. I think we should wait a little before we explore, I intend to start over that way!'

She pointed out the now cleared path that had originally been made by the fallen oak tree, towards the rear of the ruins. The huge trunk of the fallen tree, lined one side of the path, a proper access path from where the cars were parked had been marked and lightly gravelled.

Before they could move a convoy of cars appeared over the rise in the driveway, to park alongside the Range Rover. They all seemed to arrive at once, which Brenda liked, the three cars of the Haddon Family, with Dennis who had cadged a lift, Stan and his family declining at the last minute, Poppa not quite up to the drive; Dennis advised. Dan with his family, then Linda, Shane, Sir James a short break with Michael and Hugh arriving together last of all.

Larry looked at her again; a dawning thought crossing his face, she looked at him, at the expression of wonder, 'not again' was all he could say.

'Not again what mum, and exactly where are we if this is the Lucas Estate?' David asked as everyone arrived around them.

Noting the slowness of some of the group, realising the party had gone on into the night, not only for David but for others too. She just gave David a hug and smiled, as Dan and Glen came up to Brenda, looking around at the ruins that were around them; looking at each other smiled, turned to her 'not again!' they said together, Larry laughed, nodding at the smile that was all Brenda gave them.

She moved everyone into the marquee, all being surprised as Brenda had organised a sit-down Sunday Dinner, not quite up to Julie's standard perhaps, but still very welcome. As the meal progressed she could hear the undercurrent of questions as to where they were, and what was going on.

Michael, of course, knew exactly where they were, he had visited the pile of rocks to ascertain exactly what state the estate was in, but he was puzzled as to why Brenda had brought them out to see it.

After the meal was finished, the caterers had left, saying they would be back the following day to take everything down and away; Brenda stood tapping her glass to get everyone's attention, it was given immediately.

'Ladies and gentlemen; Friends, family old and new, please raise your glasses for a toast to inheritance. I welcome you to 'Broadmeadows'; everyone dutifully raised the toast as requested still very puzzled.

'I am sorry to be so mysterious, but I wanted to thank you all, friends old and new in a special way, this just felt like the right thing to do.'

'To answer the questions that are going around, this estate was once a very beautiful place. The lands extend as far as the eye can see, and then some; it is still a profitable area, and the royalties that come from the industries of all kinds on and around it are ongoing and very good. This once grand place was the family seat of the Lucas Family; to those who do not know yet, that was Iris's family. Her father, Grandfather, and so on to past generations were all Lords of Broadmeadows, all of them took the name Lord Lucas."

Dawning comprehension could be seen across the room, although no one spoke.

'In fact, when Iris died, she died as the last in her line, she died as Lady Iris Lucas!'

Understanding rippled across the room, the fact that they knew she was Iris's Heir, then that made her!

'That is right Glen, the Lady B on my hard hat is actually correct. I took over the mantle of Lady Lucas, when it was confirmed that I was not only her heir, but also her fathers as well. The confirmation of the title is happening probably in a couple of months' time, I plan on throwing one hell of a party and all are invited!'

Questions came from everywhere, Glen jumping up to give her a hug, with Julie after, Dan moderating his back breaking hugs, for Helen to move him aside to bestow one as well, everyone wanted to congratulate her.

Michael and Hugh sat looking in wonder at this woman, wondering where she was going with this, they had enjoyed the meal, especially the wine, but they were curious. Brenda let them talk a little while longer, waiting for the one question she knew would be asked.

Ben was the one who stood and asked, 'Congratulations Lady Lucas,' he said with a little bow and smile, 'but why the trek out to the country, and why here?'

'I am so glad you asked that Ben, as we now get to the ramble part to work off some of the alcohol and lunch; come on everyone!'

She led them out and through the now cleared gap she had seen from the Range Rover, on her first visit which seemed an age before. Passing the oak tree resting to one side, urging both Dan and Glen to move on they could check it out later, saying to them it and the others found, might come in handy. The thought of reusing not only that tree but all the downed ones on the estate, had occurred when she was making her plans. The Arborist team she had hired to clear the debris, had been told to not cut them up, just move to the side until a more detailed plan had been developed. This massive tree had given a very level, clear walking track; Brenda making sure Shane had the assistance he needed to be with them, the twins snug in wraps on Gabby and Charlie's chests.

As they moved closer to the structure, Brenda gave a sigh, this was no Summer House, seen close up it was a huge conservatory, twice as big as the one at Steel Street. As they got closer to the doors, the reason for the brooms, spades and clippers she had given to David, Kate, Ben and Matt to bring along was clear.

Norman moving up beside her exclaiming, 'Oh my dear, once again you astound me, another treasure you have found. I take it you want to get inside?'

Brenda nodded at that moment unable to speak. Norman took a few moments to direct the young people in what to do, to clear the debris and clip the foliage from in front of the double doors, to allow access but not too much damage.

Brenda finding her voice, 'Norman please don't remove too much. We need to leave the place still overgrown and unloved for a few months more. Trust me please?'

He nodded, not really understanding, but stopping David and Ben from taking all the foliage from both doors, only on one, which would still be enough for Shane to get through.

Brenda moved up to the door, from the oldest keychain selected a filigree key that matched her own at Iris House. She sprayed the lock with WD40, waiting a few moments looking around the space, seeing plants inside the area that were running riot. Putting the key in the lock flipped it with a clunk slowly pulling the door open. It took the combined efforts of David, Ben and Matt to move it, but open it did.

Unfortunately, time had not been kind to the glass in this conservatory, not many panes remained, debris and organic refuse littered what was once a beautiful place. Plants were everywhere growing in profusion, spilling over planters, and pots that lined the room from the doors. Norman was ecstatic, telling everyone not to touch anything, while trying to see everything at once.

'What are we looking for?' Shane said wheeling into the structure with Larry's help, noting he could move easily there was a lot of space; it was the debris of ages on the floor that hindered him.

'A trap door, possibly two or more?' Brenda said, they all looked at her, as though she was mad. Larry, Michael and Hugh all started to laugh, Dennis taking it up a moment later, as he realised what she was getting at.

'You cannot be serious love,' Larry said moving to her side, putting an arm around her shoulders, 'you are serious. You think they removed everything out of the house, but not that far!'

'What Larry is saying,' she turned to the rest of the confused faces around her. 'I have finally caught up reading a few of the journals and papers; I have found a few more,' she said turning to Michael and Hugh. 'They were not Iris's Journals, a couple dated back to 1800's and beyond in the safe. This was the way the Lords and Ladies of Broadmeadows recorded their lives, Iris just continued in the family tradition. They were prolific in recording everything, the minutiae of what they did day by day. The main contributors that I found fascinating were Lords who lived in this house, when it was a prosperous estate. The one that described when the then Lord Lucas had acquired the steel works,' nodding at Dan, 'late in his life. His son was enthusiastic in the use of this new building material passing that enthusiasm onto his son as well. He persuaded his father and grandfather as the Manor House was experiencing a few foundation problems, to refurbish Broadmeadows, to rebuild it in steel to show what it could be used for; the first test and blue print was this conservatory, then I believe Steel Street and the building of Iris House. They started to pack up the manor house, it took a long time to achieve, moving goods and chattel's around to the houses they owned. There are dedicated lists of everything; they gutted the house ready for its facelift and rebuilding.'

She paused looking around at her enraptured audience as she continued, 'there was a problem, the son died in an accident, the grandson in the war, leaving the old man bereft, moving to the house in London, with the dream of rebuilding becoming a distant memory, Iris was the only child remaining. Then the fire and bomb hitting the shell of the building during the Second World War, left it in this state. For whatever reason, Iris's grandfather had started to split the London house into flats before he died, possibly to give Iris an income after he had gone, we will never know, I could not find out the reason in any of the journals, there are a few missing from that period. I firmly believe that they moved the fixtures, fittings and furniture not far, as least the excess not moved to the other houses. This structure was purposely built, I also believe it goes down and out, mirroring the Workshop and Conservatory at the house in London. Being built as prototypes to this building to prove to the old man, that it could be done. Look at how level the area is around here, compared to the rest of the space!'

They all looked around them at this, seeing the reality in her words; Ben, Matt, Rebecca, David and Kate had been looking around the floor, moving further into the structure, listening while Brenda told the tale. Using the brooms and spades to move the debris of ages aside; Rebecca and Kate shouted, 'there is something here!'

Everyone moved to where they stood, half way up the structure, a centre six -sided planter was incongruous in its placing and design in the centre of the space. Norman doing a quick two step while saying 'Curious, very curious?'

'Over here too, it's the same!' Ben and David shouted.

Both sides were swept clean, slowly a rectangle shape could be seen in the floor. David bending down, discovering a sliding plate covered the keyhole, keeping the dirt out of the workings. Brenda gave him the can of WD40, happily spraying a good amount into the keyhole, going over to discover the same system in the floor on Kate's side and repeating the process.

Everyone had smiles on their faces, David and Kate's even more so, as once again their mother had added up the details when no one else had bothered, finding they hoped something wonderful, they had no doubt after the last couple of weeks, that what was below their feet, whether treasures or empty would be a wonderful find.

Michael and Hugh moved over to her, as they waited for the oil to work, 'what do you intend to do if we do find the treasures of Broadmeadows in this place Brenda?'

It was a question, Michael felt he had to ask, more than Hugh, although both of them knowing a little about the new Lady Lucas, had an inkling as to what she would reply, they were not disappointed.

Brenda turned to them both, but realised everyone was listening for her reply, smiling at them all, 'I intend to rebuild gentlemen!' it was what they expected. Glen and Dan looked at each other, realising that Brenda would need their services again.

'I have already applied to the English Heritage commission, to check with them whether the estate is classified in any way. I am still waiting to find out from them, but as the main manor house, and all other buildings on the property are in ruins, I have been verbally informed that they may be on the lowest level, if listed at all. So, I am going to rebuild everything, if I can, I have the original plans and drawings, so we will rebuild with a nod to the past, but looking to the future. This will be a monument to what we can achieve with the modern techniques we have today, using steel for the main structural element but adding in the oak, marble and stone to rebuild the manor house looking as it did when originally built. Utilizing all the energy saving techniques to make it an efficient and energy saving construction, so it is a comfortable place to live in now and the future!'

She bent down then and put the key from the old key ring into the lock, Larry bending to help her turn the still stiff mechanism, a satisfying clunk rewarded their efforts, giving the key to Kate telling her to try on her side.

Willing hands bent to pull up the trap doors, which fitted into slots on the flat side of the planter, the design of which then made sense, a hinge system holding it securely. The opening of the door, was linked to a pulley system, as they pulled up the trap door, a ramp was lowered to the floor. Shane looked at her with wonder in his eyes.

'I don't think they had wheelchair access in mind Shane,' Brenda said to his startled look, 'but they would have had to wheel boxes down, so it makes sense!' They moved over to the other side to open that up, this time a spiral staircase appeared, the top riser lifting up as the door slotted into the frame mimicking the other side. Dan just grinned at her, itching to see how it all worked, Brenda held everyone back.

Turning to Matt asking, 'you did bring the generators like I asked?'

He nodded, now understanding the strange request, but as he and the rest of his family had found out, when Brenda asked for something, however strange, you did it, as there was usually a very good reason for the request. Grabbing Ben, they ran back to his jeep, driving it back up the track and reversing it to the doors. Larry, Dennis, David, Glen and Dan all helping them to unload the two small generators.

'How long have you known about this Brenda,' Sir James asked as he came over to her side, taking her hand to steady her, shock was still on her face. Thankfully they had to wait for the generators and had not rushed headlong down the stairs, as it gave time for the air to freshen, they could smell the stale air coming out from the trap doors.

'A week Sir James, when Larry brought me here the first time, all I could see were ruins at first. Then I realised, as I read the journals and papers, that there had to be so much more to the story. When I opened the desk in my bedroom, realised that it was one that had been packed from here and sent to London. In it was the most magnificent journal, I have it with me in the back of Larry's car.' Michael and Hugh both started to speak,' but I have copied all of the originals and have been using the copies I made when I was doing my research; never fear my friends I have taken precautions, but I thought you might like to see the original!'

They smiled, looking at each other, wondering just what they were in for, laughing when they both realised that they were looking forward to whatever came from their association with this woman.

'The drawings, and some of them are in watercolour; depict exactly how the many rooms looked. How they were furnished and what they were used for; detailed diagrams and architect's drawings, everything you would need to know to rebuild. Then when I glimpsed this place through the trees as we were driving out, knew that it had been built for a purpose, I just did not realise it was as big as it is, built to prove to the Lord Lucas at that time, that his son and grandson knew what they were doing.

Larry and David came in carrying one of the generators, Ben and Matt went over to Kates side, Glen, Dan, Dennis, carrying in a light stand each, everyone watching them go down the stairs and ramp to start them up and give light. Brenda was next down moving cautiously down the ramp while quite steep Shane could manoeuvre with care. They all moved down into a warehouse that had not been disturbed in decades, wonder shone in everyone's faces. As she turned on the spot, Brenda could see it stretched away on all sides, they had come down in the middle of the space. Ben and Matt handed out torches, at Brenda's look, Matt shrugged, 'well when you asked for the generators, thought torches might come in handy as well!' She hugged him, unwilling in that moment to move further in, but realising after a waft of gardenia floated around them how silly she was being.

'People please do not move a thing, until we can confirm exactly what is here with the lists Brenda has. Look but do not, please do not touch!' Michael beseeched everyone, he was awestruck, this woman put two and two together and came up with six every time, but her intuition was spot on. He had to believe her now, as he and everyone could see the stacks of furniture, chest and boxes that were on shelves throughout the immediate area; never mind the areas that were further out in darkness. Everyone had broken into various groups, to explore, but Brenda had remained at the bottom of the ramp with Julie and Helen astonishment on both faces.

Michael had moved over with Hugh, towards where the Manor house would have been, as they got closer to what must have been the limit of the space, a structure appeared in their torch light. He gave a gasp, shouting for Brenda to see what he had found, everyone came running, as the excitement in his voice was an unusual thing for him.

The mass of torches showed a massive safe, built in steel looming out of the darkness, it seemed to take up most of the wall in front of them. The door itself was huge, but had a normal sized keyhole, again covered with a sliding shutter. She put a very large key from the key ring into the keyhole, the clunk of the lock opening, brought a gasp from everyone. Dan, Glen, Ben and Matt putting their considerable strength to the lifting of the door lever, with Larry David and Dennis then helping to open the huge door.

Brenda was the first to move, but only getting a couple of steps inside the door, everyone else holding back, but they could all glimpse the riches inside. Shelves lined the four walls with a space for the door, also free standing metal racks running down the inside, it was remarkably clean and fairly dust free. She could just make out in her torch light on the shelf in front of her, familiar jewellery boxes that when she lifted the lid on one, had a ruby and diamond tiara snuggled inside, she could see the spaces for the necklace, earrings and bracelet, if they had not been in her safe in Iris House, with a few more boxes on the shelves either side. What else there was Brenda could not say, as Michael after he had seen the stack of paintings in one of the rows between the shelves, decided enough had been done. He and Larry hauled her out of the safe, closing the door with help, Larry taking the key from her and securely locking it.

Brenda looked at the faces of the friends around her, she could do nothing, but experts would have to be called to check everything, that would take a while of course, as she was going to have to build the house before any of the goods could be moved, but they had been safe for a long time, a few more months would make no difference.

Ben came up to them as she moved everyone back to the ramp and steps, saying they had found another door on the other side of the massive safe that would probably be access to the Manor house if it were still standing of course. Everyone shaking their heads at the last comment, watching as the trap doors were lowered back into place, and locked, carefully putting some debris back over them to hide the access into the area, moving everyone back to the marquee for a celebratory drink.

'I have some news that came in yesterday my dear,' Hugh was shocked at Brenda's discovery, but oh he was enjoying himself, he knew that there was more to come. He moved Brenda slightly away from the group, as he spoke, Brenda signalling to Larry, Kate and David to go on ahead.

'Our agent we sent to South Africa, just got back and what he found was really interesting. The assets of the Boerchermeir Group are quite extensive; you are the sole heir of the whole thing. Apart from the quite modern village and living quarters the workers that look to the group are housed in, the gold mine gives quite a good return for the workers and owner,' he nodded at her. Brenda was not sure of her feelings at that time, too many shocks, she just looked at him, a gold mine, wow. Then he stopped her, everyone had moved into the marquee, quietly saying as she realised he had not finished, 'of course not quite as good as the diamond mine just up the road!'

Brenda gasped, then laughed, looking a question at Hugh who just nodded his head and laughed with her. This was too much, much too much, oh what she could achieve, what she could accomplish.

They moved into the marquee, everyone was standing around chatting excitedly. David and Kate handing her and Hugh their own glass of champagne.

Larry stood.

'Friends and Family, please raise your glasses, let us welcome the true essence of a Lady into our midst; to Lady Brenda Lucas, may you continue to spread your common sense and good will to everyone, thank you for being here!'

Brenda could only smile as "Here, here" and toast of Lady Lucas rang around the space, and the wonderful fragrance of Gardenia was around; she could hear a ghostly voice.

'Welcome, Sister of my Heart, you will achieve great things!'

As to the rebuilding, checking of the Legacy, well that is another story entirely!

THE END (I THINK)

Table of Characters of The Iris Clan:-

Iris Fitzgibbon Boerchermier – (Deceased) Iris House Tenant
Lord Norman Lucas – (Deceased) Father / Grandfather et al. – Lucas Line.

Brenda Chalmers
David and Kate Chalmers – nee Wilmott.

Dennis Brookes – friend and confidant

Linda McGill – CEO Pickworths – Brenda's Employer
Shane McGill – husband/ architect / paraplegic car accident.

Sir James Pickworth – owner of Pickworths – Linda's Grandfather.
Giles – Sir James - Major Domo

Stan, Nona and Poppa – Ace Cleaning Team

Glen Haddon – Master Builder.
Julie Haddon – wife
Benjamin and Matthew – (twins) plumber and electrician
Rebecca – Interior Designer.
Charles and Gabrielle Waines – (Gabby) Glen/Julie's eldest daughter
Twins-Iris Brenda and Edward Lawrence
Rob 2IC at Waines Glassworks

John Sark – Glen's Forman, Fred and Jack

Patrick Greenhill – Painter
Nigel Hawthorn – Master Carpenter
Stewart Saunders - Locksmith

Dan and Helen Jones – Jones Steelworks
Greg Baines
Peter Mason – Architect / Structural Engineer
Beverly Mason – Dan / Helen's daughter.

Marcus Cannington – Glass
Brent Winegood – Winegood and Tate Lift Specialists.
Norman Greenwell –Marquis of Trent- Kew Gardens
Tristan, Mary and Stan

Original Building Team:
Mia Farrington-Smythe – Interior Designer.
William (Bill) Gardiner – builder
John Hemsworth – Architect.

Legal Teams:
Lawrence Morecombe QC
Andrew and Beth
Ewon.
Secretary – Jo Seymour
Norman Lawrence Morecombe (QC retired) Larry's father
Hugh Pemberton QC
Phyllis -wife
Michael Dranish Fawkes QC - Fawkes Inc.
Lucas Estate

John Marshall – The Jewellery Shop.
Luke - assistant